THE FORBIDDEN SPELL

"But how are you going to explain our absence if we leave now?" Joram asked.

"I don't plan to explain it," Camber said. "As far as the guards are concerned, you'll still be here."

Joram froze. "Sir, if you have in mind what I think you do—"

"Hear me," Camber interrupted. "There are times when such things cannot be avoided. We've gone too far to stop now. No matter what the risk, I'll have to use black magic. Shape-changing is the only way. You and Rhys must have other bodies— or you will never return alive . . ."

Other books in the DERYNI CYCLE
by Katherine Kurtz:

Volume I: DERYNI RISING
Volume II: DERYNI CHECKMATE
Volume III: HIGH DERYNI

Published by Ballantine Books

CAMBER OF CULDI

Volume IV in the Chronicles of the Deryni

Katherine Kurtz

BALLANTINE BOOKS • NEW YORK

Library of Congress Catalog Card Number: 76-6977

ISBN 0-345-24590-3-195

Manufactured in the United States of America

First Edition: July, 1976

Cover art by Ted Coconis

CONTENTS

Now, these are the Names of the Eleven Kingdoms,
   sung rightly well of old:
Howicce, and Llannedd, and fierce Connait;
mountainous Meara, the Land Beyond the River;
and Kheldour, the windswept;
and pastoral Eastmarch;
Tolan, and Torenth, and myth-ridden Mooryn;
and lost Caeriesse, which sank beneath the sea;
and far-reaching Gwynedd, seat of the Haldane Kings.

—LAY OF THE LORD LLEWELLYN,
    Troubadour to the High King
    of Mooryn

PROLOGUE

*Now go, write it before them on a tablet,
and inscribe it in a book, that it may be
for the time to come for ever and ever.*
—Isaiah 30:8

Saint Camber.
Camber of Culdi.
Noble-born Deryni earl.
Gifted scholar and legalist.
Patron of Deryni Magic.
Defensor Hominum.
Camber.

By the reign of Kelson I, he had been a legend
for more than two hundred years, in turn respected,
venerated, and feared.

But who was the man, Camber of Culdi? What was
the man before he became the saint—and the demon?

Was he, as later legends insist, the sole perpetrator
of the atrocities and terrors associated with the Deryni
Interregnum? The apotheosis of Evil Incarnate? Or
was there another side to this man who became a
legend in his own lifetime, saint after his death, and
curse word for generations to come?

Just who *was* Camber of Culdi?

The scant Deryni sources which survived by the
reign of Kelson tell us that Camber MacRorie, more
than any other single man, was responsible for breaking the hold of the ninth-century Festillic dynasty
he and his children who discovered, during those cha-

otic times, that the awesome Deryni powers and abilities could sometimes be bestowed upon certain, select humans. The old House of Haldane was restored to the Throne of Gwynedd in 904, and for more than a decade humans and Deryni lived in comparative harmony.

Less than a year after his death, Camber was canonized for his daring contributions. This we also know is true. To humans and Deryni alike, he became Saint Camber, Patron of Deryni Magic, and *Defensor Hominum*—Defender of Humankind. For a time, a grateful people could not find high-enough praise for the man who had delivered them from the hated Festillic yoke. Churches and monastic schools were named for him in the decade after his death. The mental techniques perfected by Camber and the Healer Rhys Thuryn were taught in Deryni institutions of learning throughout the Eleven Kingdoms. His family and followers continued to assist the restored Haldane king and consolidate the new regime, and eventually founded the Camberian Council, a form of which still existed by the time of King Kelson.

But human gratitude is short and selective, and the gratitude of kings more capricious still. It was difficult to put aside completely the reminders of Deryni dominance, especially when many Deryni still occupied positions of authority and prominence. It seemed almost disloyal to the memory of those humans who had suffered so under Festillic rule to ignore the injustices which had marked the eighty-plus years of the reigns just past. A bitter people soon forgot that salvation, as well as slavery, had come from the powerful hands of the Deryni; and the result was a rising tide of anti-Deryni feeling, culminating, on King Cinhil's death in 917, in a purge which annihilated fully two-thirds of the Deryni population of Gwynedd.

Thousands perished by the sword, in fire, at the end of a rope—brutal sacrifices in retribution for the evils done or imagined done under the Festils. Those few who survived were forced to go into hiding, eking out an uncertain existence in fearful exile, denying their once-proud heritage and awesome powers. Only a privileged few found refuge and still retained their identities, and even these were forced to live out their lives in semi-confinement, begging the tenuous and sometimes careless protection of the few human lords who remembered how it had really been. As late as the Gwynedd-Torenth War of 1121, to be a known Deryni was neither an easy nor an easily admitted thing.

Needless to say, Camber's sainthood was one of the first casualties of the persecutions. In 917, the Bishops' Council of Ramos, acting on the demands of King Cinhil's son and heir, Alroy, repudiated Camber's sainthood and forbade even the mention of his name. The Church Militant, spurred by the backlash of quasi-religious movements such as the Willimites, proclaimed anathema all use of magic, for whatever purpose; declared Deryni sorcery to be among the chiefest of her heresies; barred men of Deryni descent from any and all participation in the hierarchy of the Church. On the secular side, Deryni were forbidden to own property except under the most stringent of supervision; were denied the right to hold public office or appointment; could not marry or inherit without the leave of their liege lord. The policies set forth in the decade which followed were to persist, almost without change, for nearly two centuries.

But even repudiated saints were human once—or Deryni, in the case of Camber. Written records may be lost or destroyed, and oral traditions garbled in the telling, and the passage of years may leave a larger-than-life composite of fact and myth and outright lie. Yet there is a truth about Camber of Culdi; and the man is far more and far less than his many legends.

Camber's world was, in many respects, a land less graceful and less refined than the world of Kelson Haldane and Alaric Morgan; but it was a study in contrasts and, perhaps, contradictions. It was a land two centuries closer to the ancient gods and their arcane traditions, and yet the awesome powers of the Deryni were more a science and less of magic than they had become by the reign of Kelson.

It was a time when some few, gifted Deryni had

learned to heal most physical injuries, and were learning about the causes of disease—knowledge lost for many, many years in the dark times following the persecutions; when Transfer Portals, though still costly in terms of time and strength and power to establish and operate, were used as an ecclesiastical communication network over most of the Eleven Kingdoms; when Mind-Seeing was an openly acknowledged practice among many Deryni.

It was but a century since Pargan Howiccan, the great Deryni lyric poet, had set the known world afire with his epic sagas of the old gods; but half a century since the death of the Lord Llewellyn, the greatest bard and troubadour the world had ever seen. Castles and palaces and churches soared, using building techniques which would not be rediscovered until late in Kelson's reign. Ecclesiastical scholarship flourished at half a dozen growing universities and cathedral schools, learning becoming available to laymen as well as religious. Yet, it was the twilight of the Deryni Festillic dynasty, though none knew it yet.

Into this world had come, fifty-seven years before, the Lord Camber MacRorie, third son of the Sixth Earl of Culdi and later the Seventh Earl. A brilliant scholar and legalist, as tradition tells, a devoted husband and father, which legends generally do not mention, he was the loyal servant of two Festillic kings—though not the new-crowned Imre. For Camber had seen the trends developing under the young king's father, Blaine, and knew he could not serve the king Imre was to become.

Retiring to his castle at Tor Caerrorie, near the Valoret capital, Camber settled in to resume his studies, to become reacquainted with his children and grandchildren, and to watch further developments of the new reign. He was disapproving, but not surprised, when the vain young Imre issued his first great tariff act, shortly after his accession:

We, Imre, son of Blaine, son of the House of Festil, by the Grace of God King of Gwynedd and Lord of Meara and Mooryn, do command

*that, no later than Mid-Summer next, all male
subjects of Our Realm, who shall have attained
the age of fourteen years, shall pay into Our
Royal Treasury at Valoret the money-worth of
one-sixth of all their possessions and land holdings, the monies thus raised to be used in the
erection of Our New Capital at Nyford. There
shall be no exceptions to this tariff, whether high-
born or freedman, clergy or layman, save as the
Crown may deign to grant.*

*We further decree that those men having a
worth below a minimum to be determined by
Our Financial Advisors, shall have the option of
indenturing themselves and all their dependents
to the Crown for a period not to exceed one year,
in lieu of payment in silver, their services to be
used in the construction of Our City of Nyford.
Default, whether in coinage or in service, shall be
punishable by forfeiture of all property, impris-
onment for a term to be determined by a Court
of Crown Commissioners to be created for that
purpose, and may, in duly designated cases, be
construed as treason, punishable by death.*

*Wherefore do We appoint to Our Royal Com-
mission Our Well-Beloved Ministers: Lord Jo-
werth Leslie, the Honourable the Earl of Grand-
Tullie, Lord Coel Howell, Lord Torcuill de la
Marche, . . .*

PATENT ROLLS, 2 Imre I

The MacRorie lands were extensive and rich, and
Camber was able to pay the tax for himself and his
tenants; but many were not so fortunate. Nor would
the Great Tariff, as it came to be called, be the last
rash measure promulgated by Imre. Unrest which had
been low-pitched and mostly token became more blatant. Semi-terrorist groups began to arise, whose sole
purpose was to harass Imre's escheators and to punish
Deryni who used their status and powers to excuse
unlawful indulgences. Camber sat secure in his manor
house at Caerrorie and watched, not yet tempted to

consider open resistance, but aware of the rise of anti-Deryni feeling.

Camber MacRorie. Seventh Earl of Culdi. Gifted scholar and legalist. Retired civil servant. Sometime practitioner of Deryni magic.

In 903, he had not yet earned the title of Saint.

CHAPTER ONE

*In the multitude of people is the king's
honour; but in the want of the people is
the destruction of the prince.*
　　　　　　　　　　—Proverbs 14:28

Though it was but late September, a wintry wind howled and battered at the ramparts of Tor Caerrorie, rattling the narrow, glazed windows in their frames and snapping to tatters the *gules/azure* MacRorie standard atop the tower keep.

Inside, the only daughter of the Earl of Culdi sat huddled over the manorial accounts beside a crackling hearth, wrapped in a fur-lined mantle against the chill of the deserted great hall, a brindle wolfhound asleep at her feet. Torches guttered on the wall behind her, though it was not yet mid-afternoon, besmirching the stone walls with soot. Smoke mingled with the scent of mutton roasting in the nearby kitchens, and a rushlight cast a yellow glow across the table where she worked. It was with some relief that she finally marked the last entry with her cipher and laid down her quill. Umphred, her father's bailiff, heard her sigh and came to collect the rolls with a bow.

"That completes the accounts for last quarter, mistress. Is all in order?"

Evaine MacRorie, chatelaine of Tor Caerrorie since her mother's death seven years before, favored Umphred with a gentle smile. The wolfhound raised his great head to look at the bailiff, then went back to sleep.

"You knew it would be," Evaine smiled. She touched the old man's hand in affection as he curled the membranes into their storage tubes and gathered them into his arms. "Would you please ask one of the squires to saddle a horse and come to me?" she added. "I have a letter to go to Cathan in Valoret."

As Umphred bowed and turned to go, Evaine pushed a strand of flaxen hair from her forehead, then began nibbling at an inkstain on her thumb as she glanced at the letter on the table. She wondered what Cathan would say when he got the letter. For that matter, she wondered how her other brother, Joram, would react when the news reached him.

Actually, Cathan's reaction was not difficult to predict. He would be shocked, dismayed, outraged, in turn; but then the double bond of friendship to his king and duty to his father's people would move him to plead the king's mercy, to urge the tempering of royal wrath with princely pardon. Though the Mac-Rories themselves were not implicated in what had happened, the incident *had* taken place on Camber's hereditary lands. She wondered whether Imre would be in one of his difficult moods.

Joram, on the other hand, was not so bound by the cautious duty which ruled his elder brother. An avowed priest of the militant Order of Saint Michael, Joram was apt to explode in one of the grandiloquent tirades for which the Michaelines were so justly famous, when he heard the news. However, it was not the possibility of Joram's eloquent and caustic rhetoric which made Evaine apprehensive; it was the fact that the priests of Saint Michael were just as likely to follow verbal pyrotechnics with physical action, if prudence did not take the upper hand. The Michaelines were a fighting as well as a teaching order. More than once, their intervention in secular affairs had touched off incidents best forgotten by their more contemplative brethren.

She consoled herself with the probability that Joram would not receive the news until he got home for Michaelmas two days hence, then stood and stretched and fished for a missing slipper in the rushes with one stockinged toe, bidding the hound remain in the hall.

Perhaps, by Michaelmas, the situation would have resolved itself—though Evaine doubted it. But whatever the outcome, the MacRories' Michaelmas would
be a bit more sober than usual this year. Joram would
be home, of course, bringing her beloved Rhys with
him; but Cathan and his wife and sons must remain in
Valoret with the Court. The young king was demanding, and no more than on the time and attention of his
favorites, like Cathan. Evaine remembered the long
months her father had spent at Court, when he had
been in the old king's service.

A squire came and bent his knee to her, and she
bantered with him briefly before handing over the missive he was to deliver to her brother. Then she pulled
her mantle close and crossed the rush-strewn hall, to
make her way up the narrow, newel staircase to her
father's study. She and Camber had been translating
the classic sagas of Pargan Howiccan, the Deryni lyric
poet, and this afternoon Camber had promised to go
over a particularly difficult passage with her. She mar-
velled again at the many facets of the man who was
her father, fond memories accompanying her up the
spiral stair.

Camber's secular successes had never been quite
anticipated, nor were they by design. In his youth, he
had been preparing for the clergy and had earned im-
pressive academic credentials at the new university in
Grecotha, under some of the greatest minds of the
century. There would have been no limit to his rise in
the Church.

But when plague took two elder brothers and left
him heir to the MacRorie lands and name—and he
not yet under his final vows—he had found himself
quite rudely plucked from the religious life by his father and thrust into the secular world—and found he
liked it. Further honing of his abilities as an educated
layman, and an earl's son at that, had been accomplished, earning him wide academic notoriety long
before he was first called to the Court at Valoret.
When the old king's father, Festil III, had sought the
most brilliant men in the land to advise him, Camber

had had little competition. The next quarter-century was spent mostly in the royal service.

But that was past. Now in his late fifties, Camber had retired three years ago, on the death of King Blaine, to his beloved Caerrorie, birthplace of himself and his five children. It was not the principal seat of the Culdi earls; that was reserved to the great fortress tower of Cor Culdi, on the Kierney border, which Camber still visited several times a year to preside over the feudal court. But here, near to the capital and his children's active lives, he was free at last to resume the academic pursuits which he had abandoned for the Court so many years before—this time in the company of a fair, witty, and insatiably curious daughter whose depths he had but lately begun to discover.

If confronted, he would have vigorously denied that he favored any one of his children above the others, for he loved all of them fiercely; but Evaine unquestionably occupied a special place in his life and his heart—Evaine, youngest of his living children and the last to remain at home. Evaine accepted this facet of her father as she accepted all the others, without consciously stopping to analyze it—and without needing to.

She reached her father's door and knocked lightly before slipping the latch and going inside.

Camber was seated behind a curved hunt table, the leather surface littered with rolls of parchment and ink-stained quills and other accoutrements of the academic mind. Her cousin, James Drummond, was with him, and both of them stopped speaking as she entered the room.

Cousin James looked decidedly angry, though he tried to conceal it. Camber's face was inscrutable.

"I beg your pardon, Father. I didn't know Jamie was with you. I can come back later."

"There's no need, child." Camber stood, both hands resting lightly on the table. "James was just leaving, weren't you, James?"

James, a blurred, darker copy of the silver-blond man behind the table, hitched at his belt in annoyance and controlled a scowl. "Very well, sir, but I'm still not satisfied with your analysis. I'd like to return tomorrow and discuss it further, if you don't mind."

"Certainly I don't mind, James," the older man said easily. "I am always willing to listen to well-reasoned arguments different from my own. In fact, stay and share Michaelmas with us, if you can. Cathan won't be here, but Joram is coming, and Rhys. We'd love to have you join us."

Disarmed by Camber's reply, James murmured his thanks and something about having things to do, then bowed stiffly and made his exit.

With raised eyebrows, Evaine turned to face her father, leaning thoughtfully against the closed door.

"Goodness, what was that about? Or shouldn't I ask?"

Camber crossed to the stone fireplace—a rare luxury in so small a room—and pulled two chairs closer, gesturing for her to sit. "A slight difference of opinion, that's all. James looks to me for guidance, now that his father is dead. I fear he didn't get the answer he wanted to hear."

He yanked on a bell cord, then busied himself with poking at the fire until a liveried servant appeared at the door with refreshment. Evaine watched curiously as her father took the tray and bade the servant go. Then, cupping a goblet of mulled wine between her palms, she gazed across at him. Despite the fire and the tapestried walls, it was chill in the old room.

"You're very quiet this afternoon, Father. What is it? Did Jamie tell you about the murder in the village last night?"

Camber tensed for just an instant, then relaxed. He did not look up. "You know about that?"

She spoke carefully. "When a Deryni is killed, practically under one's window, one learns of it. They say that the king's men have taken fifty human hostages, and that the king intends to invoke the Law of Festil if the murderer is not found."

Camber drank deeply of his wine and stared into the fire. "A barbarous custom—to hold an entire village to blame for the death of one man—even if the man *was* a Deryni."

"Aye. Maybe it was a necessary barbarism in the early days," Evaine mused. "How else for a conquering race, few in numbers, to secure its hold over the conquered? But you know how much Rannulf was disliked, even among our own people. Why, I remember that Cathan practically had to evict him bodily from Caerrorie one day, when you were still at Court. If gentle Cathan would do that, I can imagine how boorish the man must have been."

"If we execute every boor in Gwynedd, I think there will be few folk left." Camber smiled wryly. "However you feel about Rannulf as a person, he did not deserve death—and certainly not the sort of death he met." He paused. "I assume, since you know of the incident, that you also know the details of the murder?"

"Only that it was not a pretty sight."

"And it was *not* the work of our peasants, though the king's agents would have it so," Camber retorted. He stood and leaned his arm against the mantelpiece, his thumb tracing the wood graining on the goblet in his hand. "Rannulf was hanged, drawn, and quartered, Evaine, in as professional a manner as I have ever seen. The peasants of this village aren't capable of such finesse. Besides, the king's Truth-Readers have already probed the hostages and learned nothing. Some of the villagers think—mind you, they *think*—that it may have been the work of the Willimites. But no one really knows, or can supply any names."

Evaine snorted derisively. "The Willimites! Yes, I suppose Rannulf *would* have been a likely target. There's been talk that a child was molested last week in one of Rannulf's villages a few miles from here. Did you know that?"

"Are you implying that Rannulf was responsible?"

Evaine arched an eyebrow at him. "The villagers think so. And it's well known that Rannulf kept a catamite at his castle in Eastmarch. He was nearly excommunicated last year, until he bought off his local bishop. The Willimites may have decided that the time had come to take matters into their own hands. Saint

Willim *was* a martyr from Deryni ill-use, you know."

"You hardly need remind me of my history, daughter," Camber smiled. "You've been talking to Joram again, haven't you?"

"May I not speak with my own brother?"

"Nay, don't ruffle your feathers, child." Camber chuckled. "I shouldn't want to be accused of fostering ill-will between brother and sister. Only, be a little prudent with Joram. He's young yet, and a bit impulsive sometimes. If he and his Michaelines aren't careful, they're liable to have young Imre breathing down their necks with an inquisition, Deryni or not."

"I know Joram's weaknesses, Father—just as I know yours."

She glanced at him coyly and caught his indulgent expression, then smiled and stood, relieved by the chance to change the subject.

"May we translate now, Father? I've prepared the next two cantos."

"Have you, now?" he asked. "Very well, bring the manuscript."

With a pleased sigh, Evaine darted to the table and began searching among the rolls. She located the scroll she was looking for, but before she could turn away her eye was caught by a small, pale golden stone lying beside one of the inkwells. She picked it up.

"What is this?"

"What?"

"This curious golden stone. Is it a gem?"

Camber smiled and shook his head. "Not really. The mountain folk in Kierney call it *shiral*. It comes out of the river that way, already polished. Bring it here and I'll show you something peculiar about it."

Evaine returned to her chair and sat, settling the forgotten scroll in her lap as she held the stone to the firelight. It glittered, slightly translucent, strangely compelling. She passed it to her father without a word as he set aside his wine goblet.

"Now," said Camber, gesturing expansively with the stone in his hand, "you're familiar with the spell Rhys uses to extend perception before he heals—the one he taught you and Joram as an aid to meditation?"

Rhys's image flashed before her for just an instant and she blushed. "Of course."

"Well, on my last trip to Culdi, I found this. I happened to have it in my hand one night while I said my evening devotions, and it— Well, watch. It's easiest to show you."

Holding the object lightly in the fingers of his two hands, Camber inhaled, exhaled, his eyes narrowing slightly as he passed into the earliest stages of a Deryni trance. His breathing slowed, the handsome face relaxed—and then the stone began to glow faintly. Camber brought his eyes back to focus and extended his hands toward Evaine, still in trance, the stone still glowing.

Evaine's lips formed a silent O.

"How do you do it?" she breathed.

"I'm not exactly sure."

Camber blinked and broke the spell, and the stone-light died. He cupped it between his hands for a mere heartbeat, then held it out to her with a shake of his head.

"You try it."

"Very well."

Taking the stone in one hand, Evaine passed her other hand over it and bowed her head, mentally reciting the words which would bring Rhys's trance. The stone did nothing for several seconds as she explored its several avenues of approach; then it began to glow. With a sigh, Evaine returned to the world, held the stone closer as the light was extinguished.

"Strange. It hardly takes any effort at all, once you know what you're doing. What is it for?"

Camber shrugged. "I don't know. I haven't been able to find a single use for it yet—other than to fascinate gullible daughters, that is. You may keep it, if you like."

"May I, really?"

"Of course. But don't think it's going to help you with Pargan Howiccan. Two cantos, indeed! If you make it through more than two *pages,* I shall be very surprised. Pleased, but surprised."

"Is that a challenge, sir?" Evaine grinned delightedly, opening the scroll and leaning closer to her father. "Canto Four, being the Rise of the Lleassi and Johanan's Quest.

" '*Now, in those days, the Lords of the Dark Places were exceedingly powerful, and their sphere was the orb of the Earth.*

" '*And the Deryni Lord Johanan said unto the Servant of the High Gods, "Send me, Lord, to cast out the Lleassi. For Thou hast seen their iniquities, and their sins are great."*

" '*And the eyes of Makurias-in-Glory were inclined with favour upon the Lord Johanan, and His hands He laid upon the head of His servant in the blessing of the Lord of Hosts.*

" '*And the Lord Johanan gathered to him his hosts of liegemen, and laid siege to the Lords of the Dark Places. And great was their strength. . . .* ' "

Chapter Two

He shall go to the generation of his fathers . . .
—Psalms 49:19

Hurrying through the crowds and morning mist, Rhys Thuryn spied the old woolen merchant's house up ahead, its thatched upper story thrust rudely among the more imposing façades of stone and brick.

Despite the early hour, Fullers' Alley was alive with sound and motion, wily merchants opening their shops and market stalls, traders unloading precious silks and brocades and velvets from protesting beasts of burden, wandering peddlers hawking their wares with raucous calls. Beggars and street urchins also roamed the narrow thoroughfare—and undoubtedly cutpurses, too, Rhys thought ruefully—but they gave his Healer's green a wide berth as he passed, some of them even tugging at forelocks in respect. He supposed it *was* a bit unusual to see a Deryni in this street these days, and a Healer, at that.

But even had the denizens of Fullers' Alley not been disposed to give him way, that could not have kept Rhys from his appointment this morning. Old Daniel Draper had been one of Rhys's first patients, and a valued friend long before that. And Fullers' Alley had not always been a den of merchants and thieves. Conditions had deteriorated since the beginning of the current regime.

Rhys gained the relative shelter of one of the brick-and-timber buildings and glanced ahead to get his bearings; then he lifted the edge of his mantle to avoid a dungheap and slipped back into the street. Daniel's door was the next one down, and already Gifford, Rhys's manservant, was battering at the door with his staff, his master's medical pouch slung from his shoulder by a stout leather strap.

Rhys started to take the pouch as he reached Gifford's side, but then he stayed his hand. Neither medicines nor the special healing craft practiced by men like Rhys could cure old Dan Draper now. When a man lived to the age of eighty-three (or so Dan said), even a Deryni Healer could not hope to do more than ease that soul's passage to the next world. And Dan had been dying for a long time.

He thought about Dan as he and Gifford waited for the door to open. The old man had been a remarkable part of Rhys's growing up—a veritable treasure trove of tales about the years immediately after the change of royal house. Dan claimed to remember the early years of Festil I, who had deposed the last Haldane king. And Dan had lived through the reigns of three other Festillic monarchs—though he would not live through the fifth: the current representative of the new dynasty was a young man of twenty-two, king since the death of his father Blaine three years before, and in excellent health. No, the old man would not see a sixth Festillic king on the Throne of Gwynedd.

They were admitted by one of the maids, who burst into tears as she recognized Rhys and stepped aside to let them pass. Several more servants were huddled together in the shop itself, some of them making half-hearted attempts to perform their customary duties, but all stopped what they were doing as the Healer moved among them. Rhys tried to appear reassuring as he crossed the beaten-earth floor and mounted the stairway to the living quarters, but he knew he was not succeeding. He bounded up the stairs three at a time, reaching the upper landing only a little out of breath. He ran a hand through unruly red hair in a nervous gesture.

Rhys did not need to be shown the master's door; he had been there many times before. He eased the door open to find the room in dimness, the draperies pulled across the windows; and the air was stifling with incense and the odor of impending death. A priest he did not know was aspersing the bed with holy water and murmuring a prayer, and for a moment Rhys was afraid he had come too late. He waited by the door until the priest had finished his prayer, then moved closer to the foot of the bed.

"I'm Lord Rhys, Father," he said, his green mantle proclaiming his calling. "Is he—?"

The priest shook his head. "Not yet, my lord. He's received the last rites and is in a state of grace, but he keeps asking for you. I'm afraid he's beyond even your healing powers—with all due respect, sir."

"I'm aware of that, Father." Rhys gestured apologetically toward the door. "Do you mind leaving us for a few minutes? He said he wanted some time alone with me, before the end."

"Very well, my lord."

As the priest closed the door behind him, Rhys moved to the left of the bed and gazed down at the face of the dying man. The gray eyes stared at the ceiling—Rhys could not be certain at first glance whether they saw or not—and the man's breathing was very shallow. Rhys reached to the drapes and pushed them aside to admit light and air, then touched the gnarled wrist and found a pulse. Gently, he bent beside the old man's ear.

"It's Rhys, Dan. Can you hear me? I came as soon as I could."

The eyes flickered and the lips moved, and then the gray head turned slowly toward the young Deryni. A thin hand was feebly raised, and Rhys took it in his own with a smile.

"Are you in pain? Is there anything I can do?"

"Just don't be so impatient," the old man breathed. "I'm not ready to die yet. Overanxious priests!"

His voice was stronger than Rhys had expected, and Rhys squeezed the old hand affectionately.

"Do you mean to tell me you've let all those servants and apprentices get teary-eyed for nothing?"

The old man gave a dry chuckle and shook his head.

"No, I'm not gaming this time. The Dark Angel is nearby. I can hear the rustle of His wings sometimes. But I wanted to tell you something before I go. I couldn't let it die with me, and you—you're something special to me, Rhys. You could almost be the son I lost—or my grandson." Pause. "I wonder where he is now?"

"Your grandson? I never knew you had one."

" 'Twas safer they thought him dead, like his father. Besides, the Church has him now, if he still lives. He went when he was nineteen, right after we lost his father. It was the plague that year, you know. But you were only a lad then, if you were even born. You probably don't remember."

Rhys laughed softly. "How old do you think I am, old one?"

"Old enough to know better than to listen to the rantings of a dying old man," Dan smiled. "But you will listen, won't you, Rhys? It's important."

"You know I will."

The old man sighed deeply and let his gaze wander the room absently.

"Who am I?" he asked in a low voice.

Rhys raised a skeptical eyebrow and frowned. "Now, don't go senile on me, after all these years. Even if you *are* a cantankerous old rascal, I'm very fond of you."

Dan closed his eyes and smiled, then looked up at the ceiling again. "Rhys, what ever happened to the Haldanes, after your Deryni Festil led the coup that toppled the throne? Did you ever wonder?"

"Not really," Rhys replied. "I was taught that Ifor and all his family were executed during the revolt."

"Not precisely true. There was one survivor, one of the younger princes—he was only three or four at the time. He was smuggled out of the castle by a servant and raised as the man's own bastard son. But he was never allowed to forget his true parentage. His foster father hoped that one day he might overthrow the House of Festil and restore human rule to Gwynedd—but of course, he never did. Nor did the prince's son. That prince would be very old by now, if he were alive."

"If he were . . ." Rhys started to repeat the old man's words, then trailed to a halt, suddenly suspecting what the old man was going to say next.

Dan coughed and took a deep breath.

"Go ahead, ask. I know you won't believe me, but it's true. I was known as Prince Aidan in those days; and in the normal order of things, I probably would have been content to rule a distant barony or earldom in my royal brother's name, for there were three before me for the throne. But with the execution of all my kin, I became the sole Haldane heir." He paused. "I never had the chance even to try to win back my throne. Nor did my son: he died too young, and the time was not right. But my grandson—"

"Now, wait a minute, Dan." Rhys's brow was furrowed in disbelief. "You're telling me that you're really Prince Aidan, the rightful Haldane heir, and that your grandson is still alive?"

"His royal name is Cinhil—Prince Cinhil Donal Ifor Haldane," Dan murmured. "He would be, oh, forty or so by now—I can't remember exactly. It's been over twenty years since I last saw him. He entered a contemplative order, walled away from the world. He is safe there, the knowledge of his true identity locked deep in his earliest memories. I thought, at the time, that it was better that way." His voice trailed off, and Rhys blinked at him in amazement, his stomach doing queasy flip-flops.

"Why are you telling me this?" Rhys breathed, after nearly a full minute of silence.

"I trust you."

"But, I— Dan, I'm *Deryni*, a member of the conquering race. You can't have forgotten that. How long do you think your grandson would be permitted to live, if anyone even suspected his existence? Besides, you yourself said that it's been twenty years. He may be dead already."

Daniel tried to shrug, but the movement brought on a coughing fit which wracked the frail old body. Rhys helped him to sit, trying to ease his discomfort, then lowered him gently to the pillows when the spell had passed. Daniel swallowed noisily, gestured with a veined, translucent hand.

"You may be right. Perhaps I am the last living Haldane, and have spent my years of hoping for nought. If so, my telling you can do no harm. But if I am not the last . . ."

His voice trailed off in speculation, and Rhys shook his head again. "Too many ifs, Dan. For all I know, what you've told me could just be the demented death rattlings of a foolish old man. Besides, what could *I* do?"

Dan stared up into Rhys's face, aged gray eyes meeting young golden ones. "Am I a foolish old man, Rhys? I think you know better. Come, you're Deryni. Your race can probe men's souls. Probe mine, then, and read the truth. I am not afraid."

"I—am not accustomed to touching the minds of humans in that way." Rhys hesitated, lowering his eyes uncomfortably.

"Don't be silly. I have felt your healing touch before. If you cannot heal age, that is not your fault. But you *can* touch my mind, Rhys. You *can* read the truth of what I say."

Rhys glanced behind him at the closed door, then back at the quiet form of Daniel Draper—perhaps Prince Aidan Haldane. He looked down at the old man's hand still twined in his and touched the pulse spot, then slowly raised his eyes once more.

"You're very weak. I should not intrude so near the end. It's your priest who should be beside you now, not I."

"But I have finished with the priest, and besides, these words were not his to know," Daniel whispered. "Please, Rhys. Humor a dying man."

"The strain could kill you," Rhys insisted.

"Then I will be dead. I am dying, anyway. The truth is more important than a few minutes or a few hours more. Hurry, Rhys. There's very little time."

With a sigh, Rhys eased himself to sit on the edge of the bed beside the old man. Surrounding the hand he still held between his two hands, he gazed down into the calm gray eyes and willed the eyes to close. The sere lids fluttered and obeyed as Rhys extended his senses, secured control, and entered.

Swirling grayness engulfed him, broken intermittently by hazy snatches of color and sound—almost as though he were making his way through patchy, rolling fog. Only, this was the fog of Death, as the Darkness encroached already on parts of the old man's mind. The images were flashing past with no discernible order. He must keep moving, lest he, too, be snared by them.

There. A fleeting ghost-image of a young man—he somehow knew it was Dan's son—with a young child in his arms. Was the child Cinhil? Then that same man, older now, laid out on a bier with candles all around, his fair face mottled by the plague signs. A young, dark-haired man and an old gray one standing fearfully in the doorway, drawn by their love yet afraid to come closer. The young man bore the glossy black hair and gray eyes of the Haldanes. Then the picture was gone.

More darkness—thick, gray-black stuff which was stifling, almost impassable. But then there was more: a tension building in the shadows, a mindless fear, and sounds—the sounds of slaughter.

He was a tiny boy, cowering and sobbing beneath a shattered stair, and there were people screaming and running past him, fire licking at the castle ramparts, blazing on the thatching of the castle's outbuildings.

Soldiers seized two older boys whom he knew to be his brothers and dragged them into the already bloody courtyard, then slew them with swords which hacked and stabbed and were raised up dripping again and again. An infant sister was dashed against the stones of the courtyard paving, another tossed aloft and spitted on a laughing soldier's lance.

And then his father, tall and gray-eyed, gory in blood-soaked nightclothes, unarmed but for a bright blade in his hand, roaring defiance as he tried to cut a path to his anguished queen. The rain of arrows falling on the king and cutting him down like a trapped animal—because the butchers feared to come within reach of his blade.

And his mother's shrieks as they pinned her limbs and ripped the living child from her belly. . . .

Rhys drew back with a gasp and severed the contact, unable to endure the visions any longer. Stunned wordless by what he had seen, he forced himself to focus on his hands and was shocked to find that they were trembling.

Willing them to calm, his pounding heart to slow, he breathed deeply several times, relaxing as the world settled into its customary order. Gently, he chafed the old man's hand to bring him back to consciousness. He was hardly aware of the tears welling in his eyes.

"Dan?" he whispered. "Dan? Prince Aidan?"

The gray eyes opened weakly and the old lips parted. "You saw."

Rhys nodded slowly, his golden eyes wide with wonder and a little horror still.

"Then, you know I spoke the truth," Dan said. "Will you guard that truth, against the time when the throne may be restored to a Haldane?"

"A Deryni king is on the throne now, Dan. Would you have me betray him to restore your kin?"

"Watch and pray, Rhys. And then ask yourself if the man on the throne is worthy of the golden circlet. Ask if this is the sort of rule you wish for your children and your children's children. Then you decide. And when the time comes, and you reach the decision which I think you must, at least consider my grandson. Once I am gone, only you will know, Rhys."

"You speak treason, old friend," Rhys murmured, lowering his eyes as he remembered what he had seen. "But, *if* the time comes, I—I will consider what you have told me."

"God bless you, my son." The old man smiled. He reached up with his free hand to wipe a tear from Rhys's cheek with his thumb. "And I, who thought ever to curse the Deryni . . ." He paused, and a flicker of pain crossed his face. "Around my neck you will find a silver coin on a cord. I do not read, but I am told that it was struck at the abbey where Cinhil, my

grandson, took his vows. His name in religion is—
is—"

The old man gasped for breath, and Rhys had to
lean forward to catch his next words.

"Go on, Dan. His name?"

"His name—his name is—Benedict. Benedictus.
He . . . is . . . a Haldane . . . and . . . King."

Rhys bowed his head and closed his eyes in sorrow, automatically searching for a pulse but knowing
that this time there would be none. He slipped to his
knees and knelt there for several minutes, then shook
his head and let the old man's hand go. Folding the
wrinkled old hands on the silent breast and closing
the dulling eyes, he then crossed himself numbly and
turned away. He was nearly to the door before he remembered the coin, and he returned quickly to take
it from around the dead man's neck.

But though Rhys could read the words inscribed in
the silver, they meant nothing to him. And with a
sudden, sinking feeling, he realized that Daniel had
given him only the religious name of his grandson—
Benedictus—and not his secular one. If he ever did
want to locate the man, it was going to be very difficult.

With a troubled mind, he slipped the coin into the
pouch at his belt and moved toward the door. There
he paused to collect his wits, to resume his professional
demeanor, to steel himself for the servants and the
waiting priest. A last glance at the old man, and then
he opened the door.

"It is finished, my lord?" the priest asked.

Rhys nodded. "The end was easy. He did not suffer
much."

The priest bowed, then slipped past Rhys to begin
chanting the final prayers, the servants slowly sinking
to their knees around the doorway, some of them
weeping softly. As the words drifted out of the room,
Rhys, suddenly very tired, picked his way slowly down
the stairs to where Gifford awaited him.

Gifford stood as his master approached, clutching
Rhys's medical pouch to his chest.

"Is it over, master?"

Rhys nodded, then gestured for Gifford to open the door and proceed.

Yes, it's over, he thought to himself, as they stepped into the street again.

Or, is it only just beginning?

CHAPTER THREE

Then give place to the physician, for the
Lord hath created him: let him not go from
thee, for thou hast need of him.
                    —Ecclesiasticus 38:12

It was raining steadily by the next morning, when
Rhys Thuryn drew rein before the Abbey of Saint
Liam. Unaccompanied by any servant or attendant,
he had ridden most of the night to reach the abbey,
for the coin Daniel had given him would not let him
sleep. He dismounted and led his horse beneath the
eaves extending around the courtyard, then waited
until a young novice came to take charge of the animal. His leather cloak was nearly soaked through, his
fur leggings spattered with mud. Rain dripped from his
cap and the ends of his hair as he strode into the
shelter of the cloister walk and scanned the area.

He had been to Saint Liam's many times before, of
course—had studied here with Joram, years ago, before he had discovered his talents in the healing arts.
The memories were happy ones, of more carefree
days.

But the reason for his visit today was not mere
nostalgia. For, of the men Rhys knew he could trust,
there was but one who might know the origin of the
worn silver coin now lying in the pouch at his waist.
Joram MacRorie, Rhys's boyhood companion and
probably his closest friend, was currently a master
here at the abbey school. If Rhys's information proved
to be correct, and the man Benedict in the unknown
monastery really was the Haldane heir, then it was

also Joram who would know how best to use that knowledge for the good of all concerned.

With a sigh, Rhys swept off his sodden cap and began to make his way along the roofed cloister walk toward the Chapter House, ruffling his gloved fingers through wet, unruly hair. Joram would not be in the Chapter House at this hour, of course. Chapter would have been concluded hours ago, before most folk were even rising for the day.

But the schoolrooms and the quarters of the schoolmasters lay through the passage just ahead. If he could not himself locate Joram, there was a good chance of finding someone who did know where the young priest was.

He stood aside as a double line of schoolboys marched past with their master, solemn in their blue school cloaks with the badge of Saint Liam blazoned on the breast. Then he was moving through the passage to the central hall, into which the schoolrooms opened. Across the hall he spied a priest he knew, and he approached with a respectful bow.

"Good morning, Father Dominic. Do you know where I might find Father MacRorie?"

The old priest peered at him myopically, then beamed as recognition came. "Why, it's young Rhys Thuryn, isn't it? Were you not one of my pupils some years ago?"

Rhys smiled and bowed again. "I'm flattered that you remember after so long, Father."

The priest's rheumy eyes had flicked to the Healer's insignia on Rhys's tunic, and this time it was his turn to bow.

"How could I forget, my lord? Your sacred calling was apparent to me even in those early days." He glanced around as though to reorient himself, then turned back to Rhys with a smile. "You're looking for Father Joram, are you? As I recall, he's reading in the library this morning. It's fortunate you came when you did, however, for I believe he said he was leaving later today to go home for Michaelmas."

"Yes, I know. I'm invited to spend Michaelmas with the MacRorie household myself this year, so I thought to lure him away a few hours early and save him the ride alone."

"Well, then, don't let me keep you, lad. God go wi' ye."

"Thank you, Father."

Retracing his steps, Rhys made his way back through the covered passageway, past the Chapter House, then mounted the wide day stair toward the library. True to Father Dominic's directions, he found Joram in the third carrel chamber into which he peered.

Joram had his feet up, the manuscript in his lap tilted to catch the light which filtered through the rain-washed window above his head. He looked up with a pleased grin as Rhys entered and perched himself on the edge of the table.

"Rhys, brother! Why, you look like the proverbial drowned cat himself. What brings you here in this weather? I would have seen you at home tomorrow."

With silence for answer, Rhys reached into his pouch and produced the silver coin, gave it a perfunctory glance, dropped it into Joram's outstretched hand.

"Ever seen one of these?" he asked.

Joram bent his head and studied the object closely for several minutes.

Father Joram MacRorie was lean and fit, blond like his father, and with the uncanny ability to appear perfectly garbed and unruffled whether serving High Mass with the Archbishop or gutting out a deer after a long afternoon's chase. Just now he was clad in the simple cassock and cowled surcoat of his order, the hood pushed back casually from tonsured yellow hair. The sandalled feet had not moved from their resting place on the table edge. The slender fingers were still as they read the silver coin.

The outward aplomb of the man was not inappropriate. Ordained at age twenty by the Archbishop of Valoret himself, it had been clear from the outset that young Joram MacRorie was slated for high Church preferment. As younger son of an extremely well-connected house, such would have been his due even had he not been so brilliant a scholar or so shrewd a judge of men. He was his father's son in every way. The fact that he would probably deserve every future honor bestowed upon him spoke well of the man, was an unexpected nicety in a world characterized by nepotism and the purchase of office and political influence.

Indeed, even in the religious life it was difficult to be anything *but* political, especially if one moved in the upper circles of Deryni society. In the past century, religious establishments had gained an unenviable reputation for being corrupt, most of the corruption blamed, directly or indirectly, on the Deryni regime. Joram's Michaeline Order was thought to be spiritually and intellectually sound, with better attention than most to the Rule of their order. But they were also a militant brotherhood, whose knights had more than once taken sides in a controversy which should, by rights, have remained in secular hands. Such was the way of the Church in Gwynedd.

Nor had Joram himself been entirely able to avoid political entanglements, for all his protestations and honest calling. Sought out by his fellow priests whenever royal crisis threatened, he was not often permitted to forget that his father, Camber, had once been a high-ranking minister of the Crown. After all, it was no great secret, among those acquainted with the situation, just *why* Camber had resigned. Though the official explanation had mentioned something about Camber wishing to retire from government service "while still young enough to enjoy his academic pursuits," it was widely known that Camber had not approved of young Imre's policies as prince, while his father lived; and still less did he approve, once the young man became king. Camber MacRorie was not a man who could continue to serve a crown whose wearer he did not respect.

Adding to the complication was the fact that Joram's older brother Cathan was a friend of Imre, and had, at the new king's request, stepped in to fill the place left vacant by Camber's departure. There was no enmity between father and son: Camber well realized that a younger, more flexible man might be better able to temper the king's rash boldness with reason. In Cathan's abilities and judgment he had no doubt.

But Cathan's entry into the political arena continued the difficulties Joram faced, as the priest must constantly try to curb the natural gift for politicking which he had inherited in full measure from his father. Joram and Rhys had discussed the quandary more than once over a glass of Fianna wine, when the wind howled outside through the long Gwyneddan winter nights.

For himself, Rhys believed that a physician, like a cleric, should try to remain neutral, despite the temptation to become politically involved. Only now that neutrality was being shaken as never before, by the simple expedient of a dying man's words and the flash of a silver coin in a priest's long fingers.

"Where did you get this?" Joram asked. There was no trace of suspicion in his question—only, perhaps, a certain wistful curiosity.

"Never mind that for now," Rhys said. "What is it?"

"It's a dower coin. They were sometimes given as mementoes to the next of kin of postulants entering the old religious orders. They aren't made anymore."

"Can you tell where it's from?" Rhys tried to keep the impatience from his voice. "I mean, can you tell which monastery?"

"Hmm. I have an idea, but I fancy you want something more definite than that. Come on, we'll look it up."

Without a word, Rhys got up and followed Joram into the main portion of the library, past the reading brothers with heads bowed over parchment membranes, past the scrivener monks painstakingly copying texts in their fine majuscule hands. A very aged monk sat atop a high stool behind a reading desk, guardian of a polished oak door barred with a stout beam.

Joram murmured a few words to the monk, then bowed and raised the bar on the door and opened it. Taking a rushlight from a stand by the monk's desk, he motioned for Rhys to follow him into the next room.

It was a small, dark chamber lined with row upon row of open shelves holding rolls of parchment and a few bound volumes. The volumes were massive and ragged-looking, since they had originally been assembled from roll entries cut to fit, and they were secured to the shelves by chains which allowed them to be moved only as far as a small reading stand.

Handing the rushlight to Rhys to hold aloft, Joram roamed the row in front of them, then pulled down a dusty volume and inspected the cover. With a grunt, he replaced the book and moved farther down the row, where he removed another volume. This one he opened and began scanning, opening his hand to glance at the coin again as Rhys peered over his shoulder.

"Hmm. I suspected as much. It was struck at Saint Jarlath's, which is the mother house of the *Ordo Verbi Dei*. They're a cloistered order based at Barwicke, not far from here. Saint Jarlath himself was a sixth-century bishop of Meara—an abbot, too, if I'm not mistaken."

Rhys lowered his eyes and was silent for a moment. Then: "Barwicke—you said that's not far from here. How far?"

"Oh, a few hours' ride. Why are you so interested in Saint Jarlath's?"

"I—" Rhys paused, then went on cautiously. "An old man died yesterday, Joram. A patient of mine. His grandson may have taken vows at Saint Jarlath's about twenty years ago. It's important that I find him."

"To tell the monk his grandfather is dead?"

"Yes."

Joram replaced the volume on the shelf and turned to eye Rhys curiously.

"And then what?" Joram asked softly. "Rhys, you're not making much sense. If the man took vows at Saint Jarlath's twenty years ago, he may not even be alive by now. Even if he is, he'll be a cloistered monk. You couldn't see him. The most you could hope from him would be prayers for his kinsman's repose—which, if he's any kind of monk at all, he'll have been giving all these years, regardless of whether his grandsire was alive or dead. Did the old man leave him an inheritance or something?"

"In a way," Rhys murmured. He took the coin from Joram and glanced at it distractedly, but would not meet the priest's eyes.

Joram frowned and folded his arms across his chest.

"What do you mean, 'in a way'? If the old man left him anything, it belongs to his order now. You know that monks haven't any property of their own."

Rhys smiled in spite of himself. "Not this inheritance, my friend. This is not for monks."

"Will you stop dissembling and get to the point? You know about cloistered orders; you know about community property; and you know what would be involved to find this man after twenty years. Who *is* this monk?"

Rhys paused, then wet his lips nervously. "All that you have said is true, or would be true in ordinary circumstances," he whispered, looking up. "But this is no ordinary monk, Joram. We must find him. God help us, and him, but we must! His father is long dead, and his grandfather also, now. But his grandfather claimed to be Aidan Haldane, last living son of King Ifor. Your so-called cloistered monk may well be the rightful Haldane King of Gwynedd!"

Joram's jaw dropped, and he stared at the Healer in disbelief. "The rightful *Haldane* heir?"

At Rhys's guarded nod, Joram reached blindly for the bench he remembered being somewhere behind him, eased himself down upon it gently.

"Rhys, do you realize what you're saying?"

Rhys shifted uncomfortably. "I'm trying to avoid thinking about the political ramifications just yet, if that's what you mean. Can't we simply say that we're looking for a monk whose grandfather died? Besides, the man himself may be dead by now, for all we know."

"But, what if he's not?" Joram replied softly. "Rhys, you may not want to think about it, but I'm not sure you can afford that luxury. If what you say is true . . ."

With a defeated sigh, Rhys sank down on the bench beside the priest. "I know," he murmured, after a long silence. "But the illusion of innocence gives me a semblance of comfort. God knows, I'm not a political creature, Joram, but I . . ." He bowed his head. "I had a friend," he said. "I gave him my hand and comfort in his final hour, and he gave me his most precious possession: the identity of his only grandson. He showed me an ancient and noble heritage, and a potential for something different from what we know. And then he said, 'Ask yourself if the man on the throne is worthy of the golden circlet,' Joram. He said, 'Ask if this is the sort of rule you wish for your children and your children's children. Then you decide.'"

"And, have you decided?"

Rhys shook his head. "Not yet. I don't think I, or you, or any one man can make a decision like that alone." He looked up wistfully. "But I *have* considered what old Daniel told me, Joram. And now— well, I think we must try to find his grandson."

"To tell him his grandfather is dead?" Joram asked.

Rhys glanced quickly at his companion, fearing to find some hint of mockery in the other's expression. But there was none—only a gentle, indulgent wisp of a smile flicking across the other's mouth.

"Thank you for knowing when not to push," he said simply, his own lips curving in response. "I'm afraid I've not been honed for this sort of thing the way you Michaelines have. It may take me a while to adjust."

Joram chuckled as he stood, clasping a hand to the other's shoulder. "You're doing fine," he said, picking up the rushlight again. "For now, let's just worry about that monk that wants finding, who will doubtless wish to offer prayers for his grandfather's repose."

Within half an hour, Rhys and Joram were gone from Saint Liam's, riding pell-mell through driving rain toward the tiny village of Barwicke, where Saint Jarlath's lay. Once the full implications of Rhys's news had sunk in, Joram had moved quickly to secure fresh horses for the two of them and obtain leave to depart

early. More details of the previous day's events had
been imparted to Joram as he changed to riding attire
in his chamber—boots and cloak and sleek, fur-lined
riding leathers. Then they were mounting up on two
of the abbey's sleek, blooded horses, clattering hell-
bent out through the abbey yard.

By the time they reached Barwicke, both men were
half frozen and soaked to the skin. It was also quite
dark.

"Where is the monastery?" Rhys croaked, as the
two drew rein under a tree at the edge of the village
square.

Joram wiped silver-gilt hair out of his eyes and
turned in the saddle, standing in the stirrups to get his
bearings.

"That way, I think." He gestured north with a
wetly gloved hand. "I only hope they'll let us in this
late. We may have to pull rank on them. Come on."

With a sigh, Rhys hunched down further in the
saddle and followed the priest, trying unsuccessfully
to keep the rain from running down his neck. He was
beginning to wonder whether they would ever be dry
and warm again, and whether the whole thing was
worth it, when he saw the monastery looming ahead
in the driving rain. Thankfully, he reined in before
the monastery gate, stifling a cough as Joram reached
up and gave the gate bell a hefty yank.

When there was no response, Joram yanked the
bell again, then dismounted preparatory to pounding
on the gate with his fist. Before he had to resort to
that measure, a small shutter was opened in the gate
and an annoyed-looking face was thrust through the
opening.

"All right, all right, don't pull the building down,"
the man said, scowling against the rain. "Why don't
you go back to the village? There's lodging to be had
there for the night."

"I wish to speak to your Father Superior," Joram
said quietly. "And while you're thinking about it, my
companion and I should like some Christian charity
from the rain."

Joram's cultured tone took the man aback for a moment, but then he shook his head. "Sorry, sir. We don't open the gates after dark. Marauders and thieves, you know. Besides, you couldn't see the Reverend Father tonight, anyway. He's in bed with a bad cold. Come back in the morning."

"My good man, my name is Father Joram Mac-Rorie, of the Order of Saint Michael. My companion is the Lord Rhys Thuryn. Now, we would not have ridden all this way in this weather if it were not important. Are you going to open this gate, or must I report your rudeness to your superiors in the morning?"

The man's eyes had gotten progressively wider as Joram spoke, and abruptly he bobbed his head in a bow and closed the shutter. When the gate opened seconds later, he was still bowing nervously.

A lay brother in coarse brown robes and hood was waiting to take their horses, and another monk in deep gray nodded greeting and indicated that they should follow him. No word was spoken as they strode down the corridor with the silent monk. They passed several others, but the men seemed not even to notice them.

They were shown into a small room strewn with sweet-smelling rushes and herbs, and with a modest fire burning well back on the stone hearth. The man who had been their escort pointed out a stack of dry blankets and indicated that they should warm themselves before the fire, then withdrew behind a heavy, carved door, which closed softly behind him.

Joram immediately began stripping off sodden cap and gloves, spreading his dripping cloak on the rushes to dry.

"They'll bring us dry clothes in a few minutes," he said, unlacing his leggings and discarding those, then beginning on his tunic. "Meanwhile, we'd best get out of these wet things before we catch our deaths."

Rhys sneezed for reply, then began following Joram's example. Wrapping himself, cocoon-like, in one of the scratchy abbey blankets, he huddled shivering by the fire, damp hair beginning to steam from the heat. Beside him, Joram was typically unruffled, looking every inch the noble's son he was, even in his currently bedraggled state. *It figures,* Rhys thought, and decided that he would probably never see Joram look anything less than impeccable.

The door opened silently, and the two of them stood as two men entered the room. The first was obviously the abbot of the place, silver gleaming on hand and breast against the burgundy richness of his habit. The man's cowl was pushed back to reveal a shaven head, and he was holding a swatch of grayish linen to his nose and sniffling audibly. The monk who had escorted them to the room bore a pair of gray woolen robes across his arms. Joram crossed immediately to the abbot, blanket clutched around himself like a royal mantle, and bowed to kiss the abbot's ring.

"Thank you for seeing us, Reverend Father. I am Father MacRorie, and this is the Lord Rhys Thuryn, a Healer." Rhys bent to kiss the ring also. "We are most grateful for your hospitality."

The abbot bowed in acknowledgment. "Be at ease, Father, and please to accept the dry clothing which Brother Egbert has brought. I am Gregory of Arden, Abbot of Saint Jarlath's." He paused to sneeze, then held the handkerchief to his nose once more as Brother Egbert assisted the two visitors into their robes. When the men had been decently clad and the monk had withdrawn, Abbot Gregory moved closer to the hearth and warmed thin hands before the fire.

"I am told that you are of the Order of Saint Michael, Father," he said, his voice croaking hoarsely. "How may I assist you?"

Joram smiled disarmingly and gave the cord at his waist a final tug. "We wish to inspect the records of postulants in this order for the past few years, Father Abbot."

"Ah, is this an official inquiry of some sort, Father?"

"Oh, no. It's personal. A matter of conscience, Father Abbot."

"I see." The abbot shrugged, obviously relieved. "Well, certainly it can be arranged. But if you're looking for a particular postulant, you must surely be aware that he has likely taken his final vows by now and, hence, could not receive you."

Rhys glanced sidelong at his companion, then cleared his throat.

"Forgive me, Reverend Father, but perhaps Father Joram has not made himself clear. He makes the request in my behalf. The grandfather of the man we are looking for was in my care until his recent death, and begged me on his deathbed to find his grandson and inform him of his grandsire's demise. Surely, you would not refuse the dying wish of a man whose only fault was in wishing his holy grandson to say prayers for his soul."

The abbot raised an eyebrow, then shrugged apologetically. "Well, the news could be taken to him by his superior, I suppose. Certainly, a man is entitled to mourn his grandsire, even if the rest of the world has been renounced. What is the man's name? Perhaps I can tell you his whereabouts."

"Benedict, now. Before that—ah, it was the grandfather's wish that we not reveal his grandson's identity, Reverend Father," Joram replied. "Might we see those records now?"

"*Now,* Father?" The abbot looked at Joram a little strangely. "Can it not wait until morning?"

"The grandfather felt himself much in need of prayer, Reverend Father," Joram lied, "and we promised to find his grandson as soon as possible. Also, we would not disturb the routine of your house any more than necessary. If one of your brothers could show us to your archives and provide us with light, we would be most grateful."

"I understand, of course." The abbot shrugged and bowed, his manner declaring that he did not understand at all. "Very well. Brother Egbert will show you the pertinent records and see to your needs. Perhaps you will at least join us at Mass in the morning and then break your fast with us?"

"We would be most honored." Joram bowed. "Our thanks to you, Reverend Father."

With a last, disbelieving look at them, the abbot dabbed at his reddened nose and took his leave, disappearing down the corridor in one direction while Brother Egbert led them along another way.

Rushlights were procured and lit outside a heavy wooden door which Brother Egbert unlocked with a large iron key. In a far corner of the library, Egbert indicated a shelf of neatly rolled scrolls—the induction records of the *Ordo Verbi Dei*—then bowed silently and turned to go.

When the sound of the closing door had confirmed his departure, Joram set a rushlight on the reading desk and pulled out a scroll at random. Spreading it open on the desk, he scanned the legend at the top.

"Decimus Blainus—the tenth year of the reign of King Blaine. That's too recent. Daniel said the boy entered the order about twenty years ago?"

Rhys nodded. "He said more than twenty, but I think we'd better check five or ten years to either side of that. Dan *said* the boy was nineteen when he took his vows, and that he'd be about forty now, but Dan was eighty-three, by his reckoning. He may be hazy on the dates."

"All right. Twenty years—that would be 883, just toward the end of Festil III. We'll go back to, oh, 22 Festil III, through, uh— 3 Blaine ought to be far enough. That's ten years back and five forward. Too bad we don't know his secular name—even Draper won't help us, since ecclesiastical records, generally fail to show commoners surnames. But there can't be that many men in a fifteen-year spread who took the religious name of Benedict. See if you can locate some writing materials while I start looking."

Joram's optimism proved to be unfounded. By the time Rhys had returned with some scraps of parchment and a quill and ink, the priest had already found four Benedicts.

"And that's only through 25 Festilus III," Joram lamented, as Rhys put down the writing materials and looked over his shoulder. "Look at this. 22 Festilus III: *'Rolf the son of Carrolan was received into the* Ordo Verbi Dei *and took the name Benedictus, and was cloistered at the Priory of Saint Piran.'*

"23 Festilus III: *'Abel the son of John the Gold-*

smith was received into the Ordo Verbi Dei *on Candlemas and took the name Benedictus, and was sent forthwith to the Monastery of Saint Illtyd.'*

"25 Festilus III: *'Henricus, youngest son of the Earl of Legain—* Well, I guess we can eliminate him, at least. Definitely the wrong father for our man.

"25 Festilus III: *'Josephus the son of Master Galiardi the Merchant . . . name of Benedictus . . . sent to Saint Ultan's.'* And we've still got eleven years to go!"

Rhys sighed and sat down at the desk, dipping quill to ink. "Well, let's get on with it, then. A lot of those earlier ones will be dead by now—*he* may even be dead, for all we know. If you'll find them, I'll copy them down."

"All right," Joram sighed. "Here's one in 26 Festillus III, when you get those three. It's going to be a long night."

Three hours later, they had compiled a list of sixteen names, three of which they were able to eliminate immediately as belonging to identifiable noble houses. Unfortunately, they did not know the father's full name, and there was no reference to grandparents in the records.

So the two were left with a list of thirteen. Further winnowing with regard to age from other records cut the list to ten. But next they must search out all the death records for the ten Benedicts and discover which ones, if any, were still alive. The eastern windows of the library were graying with approaching dawn when the last scroll was replaced on its shelf and the two sat back to relax.

"Five still alive and of the right age," Joram murmured, stretching his arms over his head and indulging in a tremendous yawn. "It's a good thing we insisted on coming here tonight. Can you imagine the whole abbey breathing down our necks in the daytime, wondering what in the world we were up to?"

Rhys laid aside his quill and shook his fingers, then picked up the list. His eyes felt gravelly from lack of sleep, but the list was in his hands.

26 F III Andrew, son of James, age 45—Saint
             Piran's Priory
28 F III Nicholas, son of Royston, age 43—
             Saint Foillan's Abbey
31 F III John, son of Daniel, age 42—Saint Pi-
             ran's Priory
32 F III Robert, son of Peter, age 39—Saint Ul-
             tan's Priory
 2 Bl. Matthew, son of Carlus, age 46—
             Saint Illtyd's Monastery

He scanned the list once more, then handed it
across to Joram.

"Well, what now? I've never even heard of half
these places. Where are Saint Ultan's and Saint Foillan's?"

Joram looked at the list also, then folded it and
tucked it into his robe. "Saint Ultan's is down in
Mooryn, near the coast. Saint Foillan's is in the Lendour highlands, about three days' ride southeast of
here. I think we'd be better off to try Saint Piran's
first, though. That's only a day's ride north, and two of
our candidates are there. Also, it's too much to hope
for, but this second one at Saint Piran's, this John son
of Daniel, is an awfully close name to be associated
with the Haldane line. The name John is close to Ifor,
who would have been our Benedict's great-grandfather,
the last Haldane king. And of course, your man's name
was Daniel. He might have named his son the same."

"And if neither of the Benedicts at Saint Piran's is
the one, what then?"

"Then we'll try Saint Foillan's, and Saint Ultan's,
and even Saint Illtyd's, if we have to—though I don't
relish heading down toward Nyford with the building
going on. I hope your riding muscles are in better
shape than mine."

He rubbed his backside and gave a droll grin, and
Rhys had to chuckle. Gathering up the extra parchment they had been using as working notes, Rhys
started to wad it up, but Joram reached across and
took it from him, held each piece to the rushlight
flame, and watched it burn to ash. Rhys said nothing

during the operation, but as they rose to go he glanced across at Joram.

"You know, you just destroyed my last illusion of innocence," he said in a low voice. "We can still say, for now, that we're only interested in finding Brother Benedict. As long as no one makes any other connection, we're safe enough. But, once we find him, then what? What do you do with a lost heir except depose the current monarch and restore the old line?"

Joram had picked up the two rushlights as Rhys spoke, and now he turned to face his companion once more, his face lit eerily from below by the flickering yellow light.

"Yes, it's high treason, quite clearly. It's treason even to be searching for him—never mind whether we plan to put him on the throne or not. On the other hand, the whole thing could end very shortly. We may find that our Brother Benedict, even if he's still alive, is so entirely unsuitable for the Crown, after twenty years in seclusion, that even Imre would be preferable."

"My God, I hadn't even considered that possibility."

"Again, just a matter of perspective," Joram smiled. "Think about this, though: Even if he should be willing to forsake his vows and reclaim his birthright— which is by no means certain—that's only the beginning. A man may be born to be king, but if he hasn't also been trained to be king, chances are he'll have a rough time of it. Even we Michaelines, critical as we are of Imre and his policies, haven't yet preached his overthrow."

He glanced down at the rushlights, his lips a firm line of shadow.

"Not that we haven't considered it, I'll grant you," he added. "When Imre proclaimed the tariff for the new capital at Nyford, there was nearly a mutiny in the ranks. A military order like the Michaelines— Well, you know our reputation. But deposing an anointed king is serious business, even with due cause. Thank God, even our hotheads realized that."

Rhys stared at Joram silently for several heartbeats,

then averted his eyes. "Your Michaelines—they could make much of the information we've gathered tonight, couldn't they?"

"I suspect they could," Joram murmured, "if they had it."

Rhys looked up. "And do you intend to tell them?"

"I don't think that decision is entirely mine to make, do you?" Joram countered. "Perhaps some of your native caution has rubbed off on me, Rhys, or perhaps I'm just remembering the thin edge my order rides just now. In any event, any action we take if we *do* find Cinhil, and he *is* suitable, will involve a lot of other people. I'd like to tell Father about him first, if you have no objections."

"Camber? Aye," Rhys breathed. "If *he* thinks a Restoration is the only answer, I'd feel a lot better about the whole thing."

"Come on, then," Joram yawned. "We'd best get what sleep we can before they roust this place for morning prayers."

CHAPTER FOUR

Hear counsel and receive instruction, that
thou mayest be wise in thy latter end.
                              —Proverbs 19:20

They got little sleep in what remained of the night, though neither counted that amiss in light of the information they had gleaned. No sooner had they staggered back to the receiving room and rolled up in blankets by the fire than it was time to rise for morning devotions. Far earlier than they had hoped, in these days of slackening ecclesiastical discipline, they were roused by one of the abbey's lay brethren, who stood vigilant watch in the doorway until both men were on their feet and pulling on still-damp clothes, however groggily.

Rhys thought the brother's behavior a little odd, and said as much when they were finally left alone to finish dressing. But Joram merely laughed at that and reminded his friend that this was, after all, a monastery. The brother had obviously taken them for ordinary travellers, who had prevailed upon the abbey for shelter from the night. In the brother's estimation, if said travellers could be induced to reclaim their undoubtedly lapsed souls in exchange for the night's lodging, so much the better.

Rhys had to agree that the logic of the argument was probably sound—a warm, dry place to sleep ought surely to be worth a Mass—but unlike Joram, Rhys's brain did not tend to function at its best so early in the morning, especially after little or no sleep.

It was with some reluctance, then, that he followed
Joram into the abbey church a few minutes later, trying to assume an air of piety which he simply did not
feel at an hour he tended to regard as ungodly.

The morning was half spent before they could break
away. After Mass, the abbot had insisted upon a leisurely breaking of the night's fast with them, and had
been full of questions about the capital and what was
happening there these days. When, at last, they were
able to take their leave, it was to face a sunless,
leaden sky which promised still more rain to come.

The horses were frisky and eager to be off, their
hooves striking sparks off the cobbles of the windswept
abbey yard. But the clatter turned to splash all too
soon, as they reached the muddy road; rain was already beginning to mist again in the sharp, cold air.
Before they had ridden two miles, both men were once
more soaked to the skin.

The rain continued for most of the afternoon, though
it had subsided to a mere annoying drizzle by the time
they reached the outskirts of the MacRorie manorial
estates. As they topped the last rise before the descent
through the village, their eyes were drawn to the high
hill beyond, to jewel-like Tor Caerrorie, Camber's
seat, green-gray slate roofs glimmering in their wash
of recent rain. The two halted at the top of the rise
and glanced at one another conspiratorially, a roguish
gleam coming into Joram's priestly eye. Then they
rode laughing down the slope and into the village,
whooping like a pair of schoolboys as they splashed
along the road.

They would have thundered on through, sending
chickens and dogs and children scurrying for safety,
had they not spied a MacRorie man-at-arms standing
with two horses outside the little village church. One
of the horses evoked only passing interest, for it was
of no particular breeding or caparisoning; but the
other was a little sorrel mare which both men recognized instantly. As they drew rein, the man-at-arms
peered at them and then waved enthusiastically, his
face lighting with pleasure.

"Father Joram!"

Joram grinned as he jumped from the saddle and embraced the man warmly.

"Sam'l, old friend, how have you been? Is that my sister's horse I see?"

"Aye, Father, you know it is," the man chuckled. "Her Ladyship's just teaching the village lads their catechism. She'll be out in a minute. Can ye wait and ride back to the castle with us?"

"Just try to make me leave!" Joram said. He turned to grin at Rhys, who had dismounted in a more leisurely fashion. "Rhys, you remember Sam'l, don't you?"

"Of course. How is everything, Sam'l?" Rhys replied, shaking the older man's hand.

Sam'l bowed, pleased at the gesture, then became guarded, lowered his eyes uncomfortably. "I, ah— Ye won't have heard about the murder, or ye would not ask that question."

"Murder?"

Rhys glanced at Joram, and the priest laid his hand on the old retainer's shoulder.

"What's happened, Sam'l? Who was killed?"

Sam'l chewed his lower lip for several seconds, then raised cautious eyes to meet Joram's. " 'Twas a Deryni, Father, here in the village a few days ago. He was none such as any of us would give a care about—you knew the upstart, that Lord Rannulf—"

"A Deryni!" Joram breathed.

"Aye, and the King is invoking the Law of Festil. He's taken fifty hostages, and threatens to hang two each day until the murderer comes forth, since the Truth-Readers canna learn the names of the guilty. The killings begin tomorrow."

Rhys whistled low under his breath. "That explains a lot. It didn't seem important at the time, but I wondered why the messengers were going back and forth from Valoret yesterday. I must have passed three or four on my way to Saint Liam's."

Joram grunted. "Haven't they any clues to the real murderer, Sam'l?"

"Not yet, Father. Not any one person, at any rate. There be those who think it was the Willimites, but we have no proof. The Lord Camber has had men out asking questions for the past two days, and his own Truth-Readers among them, but—nothing. What with the general uneasiness about the tariff and all, and now this, he's worried that other Deryni may be threatened. It was he who asked me to ride along with the young mistress today. He was afraid she might be harmed."

"Sam'l, I love you dearly, but you're an alarmist," came a light, musical voice behind them. They turned to see a cloaked Evaine sweeping down the church steps, bright hair escaping from her hood.

"Father knows I can take care of myself," she continued. "Besides, who would try to harm me? I've done nothing to offend the Willimites, if they're the ones to blame. And I certainly have nothing to fear from these good people."

She gestured toward the village with a nod of her head and smiled, slipping her arm around her brother's waist in warm greeting as her eyes met Rhys's. Rhys took her hand and kissed it, trying to control the momentary confusion which a first reunion with Evaine seemed to bring lately—and was pleasantly startled when she pulled him closer and kissed him lightly on the cheek, slipping her arm around him, too. Sam'l was also feeling the charm which Evaine could exude when she chose to, and he could not seem to find his tongue.

"Very pretty, Sister dear," Joram murmured indulgently. "But you're going to have to do better than that. Is it true that Father thinks you're in danger?"

"Of course not." She touched her forehead playfully to his and made a face. "It's our loyal servants like Sam'l who were concerned about my safety. I'll be perfectly all right, really."

"Well, I want to hear more about this," Joram said. He disengaged himself from his sister's embrace and signed for Sam'l to bring her horse. "We'd better get back to the castle, if you're through here. Rhys, you can go starry-eyed later. I want to find out what really happened."

"So, that's as much as anyone knows," Camber concluded, when the story had been told around the fire that evening. "Rannulf was found at dawn by old Widow Claret, and she went into hysterics because the body was on her land. Or I should say, part of the body was on her land. The head and one quarter. The rest— Well, let us just say that several other families in the village got similarly shocking awakenings that morning. The bailiff reported it to me shortly after dawn."

Rhys and Joram nodded knowingly as Camber refilled their glasses, imagining the activity which would have been precipitated by such an event; and no word was spoken for several minutes. The last of the servants had been sent to bed an hour ago, and now only the three men and Evaine remained by the fireplace in the Great Hall.

Rhys, sitting near Evaine, sipped distractedly at the mulled wine in his cup and glanced at Joram, catching his slight nod. Gathering his resolve, he turned to address Camber.

"Sir, there is something which Joram and I think you ought to know about. It may or may not have a bearing on what we've just been discussing."

There was something in his voice which bespoke more urgency than his mere words, and all eyes turned toward Rhys. The young man bowed his head and searched for the proper way to begin, appreciating the gentle hand which Evaine laid on his. Especially, he could feel Camber's gaze upon him.

"You all know that I am a Healer, that my calling brings me into contact with many people." He cleared his throat nervously and took another swallow of wine before continuing.

"Two days ago, an old man died. He was not an important man—at least not to outward appearances. But the story he told me on his deathbed has caused me a great deal of soul-searching." He raised golden eyes to meet Camber's squarely. "Sir, he claimed to be Prince Aidan Haldane, a younger son of the last Haldane king."

No word was spoken in response, but the listeners

exchanged cautious glances, Camber shifting to Joram's face to read in his son's eyes that what Rhys said was true. Wordlessly, he signed for Rhys to continue.

Rhys lowered his gaze once more. "I did something then that I have rarely done," he said slowly. "At the old man's request—nay, almost his command—I went deeply into his mind to confirm what he had told me; and *it was so*. He *was* Prince Aidan. What is more important, he had a legitimate son, and his son had a son. The son is long dead—of plague, twenty years ago. But we have reason to believe that the grandson still lives." He looked up, directly into Camber's eyes again. "The grandson would be Prince Cinhil Donal Ifor Haldane, lawful heir to the Throne of Gwynedd."

There was silence for a dozen heartbeats, a soft sigh of wonder from Evaine, her blue eyes wide with the implications of the statement—and then all attention turned to Camber. The Deryni lord had said nothing yet: he was still weighing and evaluating, reading the thoughts in Rhys's eyes. But then he broke the spell and let his gaze pass over them all. As he scanned them, each unconsciously deferred to him, respectful yet unafraid. Even the usually ebullient Joram was silent under his father's scrutiny.

"You say you have reason to believe this grandson still lives, Rhys. Have you any idea of his whereabouts?"

Rhys shook his head. "Not exactly, sir. But we think we have the possibilities narrowed down to five. You see, he's a contemplative monk of the *Ordo Verbi Dei*—or he was some twenty years ago, when he took his vows. That's the last his grandfather heard from him. Also, we don't know Cinhil's secular name—only the religious name he took when he was ordained: Benedictus. And we don't know his father's secular name, either—only his royal one, Alroy. There are five Benedicts of the right age in the order right now. Prince Cinhil, if he's still alive, should be one of them."

"I see."

Camber sighed and leaned back in his chair, carefully setting his wineglass on the hearth beside him. "This Cinhil, or Benedict, as he is known now, is a cloistered monk, then? Assuming that you could find him, what do you propose to do with him?"

This time it was Joram's turn to answer. "We're not certain, Father. We think that we can discover which one of the five is the man we're looking for, without arousing undue suspicion in the meantime. We have even talked about what might be involved in smuggling him out of his monastery, if it comes to that. Naturally, we would have to evaluate his potential first. After that," he shrugged, "it remains to be seen."

"Well said, Joram." Camber nodded. "Your training has enabled you to talk around treason quite glibly. But, what is it that you wish me to do? To condone your search, your possible treason? I resigned from Imre's council because I do not like the man personally. And you know my feelings about the laws he has proclaimed since his accession. But I have never advocated his overthrow. Would you have me commit myself to such an endeavor, for a man I have never even met?—whom neither of you has ever met? Even your Michaelines would not be so bold, I think. Have you told your vicar general about this?"

Joram shifted in his chair and glanced at Rhys, lacing his fingers together uneasily. "No, sir, I haven't. And I—we're certainly not asking for such a commitment from you at this time. But surely you understand why we must at least investigate, why we must find out more about this Haldane heir. Then— Well, you're the one who knows best among us how the present regime is functioning or not functioning. We were hoping you might lend us your wise counsel in deciding what must be done next."

"*My* wise counsel, not that of the Michaelines?" Camber asked gently.

"Father, I know you don't approve of—"

"Nay, my approval or disapproval has nothing to do with it, Son," Camber interjected. "I shan't try to make you choose between your family and your order. In truth, if this endeavor should go the way you obviously

wish it to, I would be the first to suggest that you seek
their assistance. A Restoration needs zealous soldiers,
and the Michaelines are of the finest. You could not
succeed without them, were your Cinhil the Lord God
Himself—which I fancy he is not."

Joram nodded cautiously, taken aback by his father's unaccustomed support of the Michaelines, however qualified.

"But, back to your missing Haldane," Camber
continued. "Suppose he's an imbecile? Or suppose he
doesn't want to be king?—which is likely, if he has
any sense at all. Suppose he holds his religious vows
stronger than a mere accident of birth? Or suppose
that he *knows* who he is, and wants no part of his
royal heritage? Did it occur to either of you that he
may have entered holy orders for that very reason, to
seal himself off forever from the temptation to bring
about his own destruction? I hardly need remind you
that the Church frowns upon suicide."

"You're assuming that we would fail," Joram said,
resentment edging his voice.

"No, I'm simply asking you to weigh as many of the
possibilities as you can. This is not a game, or an
academic exercise. Once you commit yourselves, there
will be lives in jeopardy—and not only your own."

Joram exchanged an imploring glance with Rhys, and
the Healer sat forward in his chair. "Sir," said Rhys,
"we've considered most of what you've said, believe
me. But for our own integrity, we must at least talk to
the man. If he is who his grandfather said he is, and
if he has any potential at all, then we'll decide what
to do next. But we'll need your help, once we reach
that stage." He glanced down at his feet as he continued. "We can find Cinhil, we can read him, we can
know his soul better than it would be possible for almost any other man. But we're not sure we're competent—at least I don't think that *I* am—to make the
final evaluation, that final reckoning as to whether or
not the man should be king. Of course, we won't let
him know anything other than the fact that his grandfather has died, until we're sure that he won't go
screaming off to his abbot. We only want your per-

mission to seek him out at this point. Will you give us your blessing, sir?"

"Would you give this up if I said no?" Camber countered.

Both men stared at Camber long and hard; then, in unison, they shook their heads, neither needing to ask the other's feeling. Camber flicked his glance from Rhys to Joram, and then to Evaine. His daughter's face gave no clue as to her stand on the issue.

"Well, Daughter, your brother and Rhys appear intent upon making this a family endeavor," he said lightly. "Is this why you drew me into political discussion the other day, or was that mere coincidence? How far have you been drawn into this thing?"

"Why, I knew nothing of this before tonight," Evaine began defensively, then realized that her father was teasing her—and why. "But I'm glad that we did talk," she went on, looking at him sidelong, "because I think that Rhys and Joram have some very valid arguments."

"Very well," Camber smiled. "I will play Devil's advocate and you will defend. Now, what think you of our would-be King of Gwynedd?"

"I think you cannot expect me to have any opinion, since I have not met the man, Father. But I agree that Rhys and Joram must investigate further, to discover whether their Benedict *is* Cinhil Haldane."

"Why?"

"That is more difficult," Evaine conceded. "It is not so much *this* man as it is *any* Haldane claimant to the throne."

"You would overthrow the present king?"

Evaine controlled a smile. "Come, now, Father. We all know your true reasons for resigning from Imre's court. I think we must agree that there are few redeeming features about having such a man on the throne, other than the fact that there have been no real alternatives up until now.

"But, if there is the possibility of a legitimate heir, a logical successor, a chance for the restoration of an old and noble line which ruled Gwynedd successfully and well for several centuries . . . After all, it was not for ill governing that the Haldanes were over-thrown, however much our Deryni-written histories would like to justify the coup. To my mind, the Festillic line, in their greed, have broken trust beyond repair. If a better claimant has come to light, he should be considered."

Camber had listened to his daughter's speech with a slight smile on his face, hands folded before him, forefingers tapping lightly against pursed lips. As she finished, he gave a wan chuckle and glanced at Rhys and Joram.

"You see what happens when you educate a daughter? Your words come back to haunt you. Joram, never educate your daughters."

"I hardly think it likely that the opportunity will arise," Joram grinned.

"No, I suppose not. Rhys, you mind what I say, at any rate."

Rhys could not resist a sidelong glance at Evaine. "I suspect that my lady wife will have something to say about that, sir."

"Hmm, I dare say. Evaine, answer me this. If their Benedict *is* Cinhil Haldane, do you propose to place an untried, uneducated—"

Joram cleared his throat insistently. "Sir, I suspect he's very well educated. The *O.V.D.* places great emphasis on scholarly pursuits."

Camber raised a hand in resignation. "Granted. But he's not been educated for kingship, and there's a difference. Don't interrupt. Evaine, do you propose to place such a man on the Throne of Gwynedd?"

"Did a royal education help Imre?" she countered. "And, given his background and the record of his past actions, can we not anticipate the kind of king he will continue to be? On the other hand, our Cinhil may have the potential to be a very good king. And if he has the potential, never mind the actual knowledge of kingship; he can be taught, can't he? And what better teacher than you, who have served under two kings and had enough sense to resign when you could not serve the third?"

"Touché!" Camber exclaimed, emphasizing both

syllables and slapping his hand against his thigh in de-light. "Rhys, did I not tell you she was a paragon of logic? And now she's trapped me in my own argu-ments. But I suppose that I have only myself to blame. Tell me, Daughter, do I understand rightly that you would be in favor of a coup, if this Cinhil proves him-self worthy of rule?"

"Do we really have a choice?" she retorted. "Even so, we cannot do it without your counsel and assist-ance."

"We?" He gave a slight smile. "Very well. But there are conditions."

"That is understood." Joram nodded, relieved.

"In that case, I shall make you the following pledge: Joram, Rhys, *if* we can find this Haldane heir; and *if* he's not an imbecile or worse; and *if* he agrees to let us work with him; and *if* we adjudge him to be more worthy than the present man who occupies the Throne of Gwynedd—then *perhaps* we can begin to think of ways in which such a change might be accomplished. But you must, as you promised, keep me apprised of your progress at all times. You should also keep in mind that your brother Cathan is under constant scru-tiny, and may eventually be endangered by anything we do. So you must not go beyond a mere search un-less all of us agree that such action would be best for Gwynedd."

Joram and Rhys exchanged glances, and then Joram turned back to his father. "Your terms are more than reasonable, sir. And we had already agreed be-tween us that Cathan would be safest if he knows nothing of this for now. If you have no objections, we thought to ride to Saint Piran's Priory later this week. Two of our candidates are there, and perhaps we can eliminate one or both of them at the outset."

"You'll not reveal anything at this time?" Camber queried.

"No, sir. We'll only deliver the news to the proper one that his grandfather is dead and asked to be re-membered in his prayers. Does this meet with your approval?"

"I have no objections. When will you be back?"

"Within three days, if all goes well. It's a day's ride each way, and—"

There was a great baying and barking in the yard outside, and then a muffled pounding at the outer gate. Shortly, the inner door swung open to reveal one of the household servants, with another man behind him, the wolfhounds rubbing happily against his legs.

"My lord, it's young Jamie Drummond to see you," the servant said, barring the way with an arm across the doorway.

"Jamie, lad, come in and join us," Camber said, standing and extending an arm toward the newcomer. "Pull up a chair and share a glass of wine. I thought you'd forgotten your promise to toast Michaelmas with us."

"I hadn't forgotten," he said, striding across to kneel and kiss Camber's hand formally, the dogs at his heels. "I was attending to a matter of some urgency. I've brought news from the capital, from your son."

He pulled out a sealed packet and handed it over to the older man, then hooked a stool with his toe and pulled it closer to the fire, nodding greeting to the others. "You'd best read it," he said, as Camber stared at him curiously. "Cathan sent me with all haste."

Without further delay, Camber broke the seal and scanned the contents of the letter. His face was grim and solemn as he passed the parchment to Joram.

"Cathan has been unable to stay the execution of the first two hostages tomorrow," he said, snapping his fingers for the dogs to lie down. "He will continue to press Imre for a reprieve, but he does not hold out much hope. Coel Howell, the kinsman of Cathan's wife, is urging reprisals against the Willimites, and is convinced that Rannulf's murderers were part of a Willimite plot. He will not hear of a reprieve, nor will he permit Imre to consider it."

"Father, couldn't *you* plead the peasants' cause to Imre?" Evaine whispered.

Camber shook his head wearily. "Nay, child. If Cathan, whom Imre loves, cannot persuade the king's favor, what chance have I, who rejected Imre when he gained his crown? No, it must be Cathan's work, if our peasants are to be saved."

He glanced at all of them, then crossed his arms carefully and stared at one slippered toe protruding beneath his robe.

"But this is not totally unexpected news, I fear: Cathan also wishes us a joyful Michaelmas and drinks to our health. I think it only fitting that we should drink to his."

With that, he reached slowly to his goblet and raised it in the air, nodding as his children stood and did the same. The toast was drunk in silence—a silence which persisted for several thoughtful minutes until conversation once more resumed, this time on more neutral topics.

Chapter Five

*Now the king sat in the winterhouse in the
ninth month . . .*

—Jeremiah 36:22

But neither neutrality nor sobriety were common at
Court in Valoret, and certainly not on the night of
Michaelmas. The young King Imre had done his reluctant duty by his people by day, had attended Mass
and held formal Court and shown himself at the Lan-
tern Gate, as was customary at that season.

But the night belonged to Imre and his courtiers
and friends. No solemnities at the Court of Valoret
after the sun had set. Feasting past, the king had retired to change to even more resplendent garb for the
dancing and revelling to come. Even now, the royal
musicians were tuning shaum and sackbutt and tam-
bour, trilling snatches of jaunty airs and stately pavanes
in the music gallery. Imre's favorites strutted peacock-
proud in the now-cleared feasting hall where their
master loved to entertain, exchanging small talk and
gossip and awaiting the return of their gay young liege
lord. Amid that gaiety, the dour Cathan seemed
doubly out of place.

Cathan MacRorie was well known at Court. Son of
the famous Earl of Culdi and heir one day to all the
MacRorie lands and titles, Cathan was a member of
Imre's council and a royal commissioner for the Tariff
Court as well. He was also, as his father before him,
a trusted personal friend of the king. Tonight, standing
with one of Imre's young officers toward the left of the

50

Great Hall, many saw his father Camber in him, though the famous gilt features were distorted a bit in the great man's eldest son.

He was not so tall as Camber, and a little darker of hair and eye and skin than his illustrious sire, yet he was still unmistakably a MacRorie; and it was to Cathan that many now looked as a voice of reason to the headstrong young king. Even the privileged Deryni did not always approve of Imre's excesses and his occasional fits of cruel humor. That Cathan alone had sometimes managed to temper the king's wrath remained a source of constant wonderment. Whether he could be as successful tonight remained to be seen.

Cathan glanced toward the doors through which Imre would shortly emerge, then returned his attention to his companion, Guaire of Arliss.

D'Arliss was one of Cathan's closest friends at Court, aide to the notorious Earl Maldred, who would be in charge of executing the fifty hostages, beginning tomorrow. Just now, Guaire was ticking off on his fingers the many virtues of his present employer, Maldred, compared to his previous master, Earl Santare. The latter gentle was glaring at both of them from across the hall, and obviously mouthing insulting comments to one of the junior officers at his side. So far, Coel Howell had not yet made an appearance, for which Cathan was distinctly grateful. His unctuous brother-in-law would be certain to be in league with Maldred and Santare when he did arrive.

"So, though I'll give you that Maldred may be cruel, too," Guaire was saying, "he does reward faithful service, and a man can keep his personal integrity. Tanadas knows, I like a tumble in the hay with a wench as well as the next man—but with a *wench,* mind you! Do you think that's asking too much?"

Cathan shook his head slightly and controlled a smile. "No, but apparently Santare does, or he wouldn't have dismissed you. Besides, it's Maldred I'm concerned about tonight. Do you think he personally supports the king's policy on this matter?"

"Maldred supports the king, whatever his policies."

Guaire frowned. "I don't think you have much of a chance, Cathan."

"It's the hostages who don't have a chance. And it's not as if they've even done something wrong. They just happen to live in the wrong village. The Truth-Readers know that they're innocent."

Guaire snorted derisively. "You don't have to convince me. I'm on your side. But you know the answer to that argument as well as I—probably better. What does a Deryni king care for the lives of a few dozen peasants, when a fellow Deryni has been killed? Especially when the peasants are human, and the Deryni was of the nobility."

"He was a rotten man, Guaire, and you know it."

"Granted, he was a rotten man. But he was still Deryni, and of the nobility, and his murderer has not come forth or been found. Imre is simply following the law set down by his grandfather. Fifty human hostages against the life of one Deryni—it's about even, as far as Imre is concerned. Back in the days of the original coup, it was the price one had to pay for conquest. Today— Well, apparently it's the price Imre feels he has to pay to hold the conquest for his descendants." Guaire snickered, a lewd glint in his eyes. "At least, that's the theory. He's not likely to *have* any descendants, at *his* rate."

Cathan looked at Guaire sharply and was about to probe further on the meaning of that last comment, when the trumpeters raised their instruments and blew a preliminary fanfare. From the opposite end of the hall, a double line of guardsmen in formal brown and gold cleared a swath through the center of the room and took up their stations behind the twin thrones. Then the trumpets were raised once more, the golden notes reverberating across the hall as the door fanned apart to disclose the king: Imre of Festil, by the Grace of God King of Gwynedd and Lord of Mooryn and Meara. At his side stood his sister, Ariella, six years his senior and yet unwed.

The two posed in the doorway for effect until the fanfare had died away, light glowing around their

heads in arcane splendor, as High Deryni were wont
to appear on formal occasions. Then, with a nod of
acknowledgment, they began to pass slowly toward
the thrones at the opposite end of the hall, courtiers
and their ladies bending like wheat in the breeze of
the royal couple's passage. Whatever might be their
other faults, no one could say that the scions of the
Deryni House of Festil did not know how to maxi-
mize an entrance.

Imre himself was a striking young man, for all that
he was of small stature and relatively few years.
Shorter by half a head than most of the men in the
room, yet he still cut a regal figure as he and his
sister traversed the hall. On his head was a tall crown
of gold filigree set with rubies, cunningly wrought to
add unobtrusive inches to his height and blazing in the
glow of his nimbus of power. His hair was of a deep
chestnut hue, cropped shoulder length, surrounding
lively brown eyes which bulged slightly in a pleasant,
albeit somewhat vacant, face. A short, skin-tight tunic
of brown velvet revealed every line of the hard, young
body and emphasized a pair of well-turned legs en-
cased in brown silken hose; he wore leather dancing
slippers on his feet. A gold-and-amber cloak lined
with red fox brushed the floor behind him as he
mounted the two steps of the dais, and bright gems
winked on slender fingers and at throat and ears.

On his arm walked his sister, Ariella, every inch
his match and more in beauty and sheer visual splendor. Gowned in dark brown velvet stamped with gold,
the perfection of her form was captured in a supple
flow of color from neck to wrist to slippered toe, save
where the neckline made a plunging V to caress the
curve of her breasts. A tawny jewel lay a-tremble in
the hollow of the cleft; a tumble of chestnut curls
cascaded negligently over one shoulder where they had
escaped from beneath her coronet and veil.

Her quick hazel eyes missed nothing as she and her
royal brother took their places on the two thrones
atop the dais. With a smile, she leaned back in her
chair to bask in the admiration of the Court, then

reached to touch Imre's arm in a gesture which Cathan somehow found disquieting.

"My gentle friends." It was Imre who spoke, his young tenor carrying to the furthest recesses of the smoky, torchlit hall. "My sister and I bid you welcome, and pray that you will long remember this Michaelmas festivity.

"But you have not come to listen to your king speak, rather to make merry with him. Therefore, we give you leave to enjoy yourselves—in fact, we command you to enjoy yourselves." There was a murmur of polite laughter.

"My Lord Music Master." He stood and held out his hand to his sister, who rose and placed her hand on his. "We shall lead the Bren Tigan."

A murmur of approval sounded as the royal couple descended the dais and took their positions in the center of the cleared floor, bowing first to one another and then to the spectators as the musicians droned the opening bars. Then, as the strains of the old Deryni melody floated through the hall, Imre and his sister trod the opening pattern of the ancient dance, moving alone for the first few measures. Only when they had completed the first set of figures did other couples begin to join them in the dance.

Cathan watched moodily for several minutes, then turned to take a goblet of wine from a servant and exchange greetings with another of the king's courtiers. When he returned his attention to the floor, Guaire had disappeared to dance with a lady he had been eying all evening, and Imre was nowhere to be seen.

Cathan sipped at his wine as the music shifted to a gavotta cadence, and slowly eased himself to a relatively quiet corner where he could observe without being disturbed—or so he thought. He was leaning against one of the main support pillars, nursing his wine and his conscience, when he felt a light touch on his shoulder. He turned to find the Princess Ariella standing beside him, a coy smile on her face and a filled goblet in her hand. Quickly, he collected himself and made a courtly bow.

"Your Highness honors me with her presence," he murmured.

Ariella smiled and extended her hand to be kissed. Her Deryni nimbus had been put aside with her coronet, which now rested on her empty throne. The chestnut hair nearly glowed of its own accord, though. Ariella of Festil did not need Deryni sorcery to make her alluring.

"Why so glum, Cathan?" she purred, clinging to his hand just an instant longer than necessary, once the salute had been performed. "I thought to claim you as a dancing partner, and instead find you moping in the shadows. Where is your charming lady? Not ill, I trust?"

Her eyes danced teasingly above smiling lips, and Cathan felt his gaze being drawn almost unwittingly toward the deep cleft of her breasts. He swallowed uneasily, knowing full well where the conversation might lead if he were not careful. He had no particular desire to bed Imre's sister as ransom for the imprisoned peasants—though he knew that he would, if there were no other way.

"My lady sends her regrets, Your Highness," he said carefully. "She had not seen her parents since the birth of our second son, so she has gone to visit them in Carbury. I should likely be there myself, were it not for the current crisis."

"Crisis?" Ariella repeated brightly. "I was not aware of any crisis."

Cathan found himself becoming annoyed at her coy façade; he lowered his eyes to disguise his true emotion. "Your Highness will surely have heard of the fifty hostages taken at Caerrorie. Your royal brother means to have them slain."

"Hostages? Oh, yes, I remember. The ones who were taken for the murder of Lord Rannulf. How does that concern you?"

Cathan blinked rapidly, unable to believe she could be so ill-informed, then realized she was toying with him. "Your Highness cannot have forgotten that Caerrorie is my father's estate," he said coolly. "The hostages are my father's tenants—and mine. I must find a way to spare them."

Ariella raised one eyebrow and touched his arm lightly. "Why, then, find the murderer, Cathan. You know the law. If the people of the village will not come forth and name his killer, then the village is amerced for the value of the man. In this case, considering that Rannulf was both Deryni and of the nobility, I think that fifty lives is quite a reasonable fine, don't you?"

"I—" Cathan lowered his eyes, controlling the urge to twist the stem of his goblet out of all recognition. "I must contradict Your Highness. The villagers have been Truth-Read. His Grace *knows* they were not responsible for Rannulf's death. We're almost certain it was the Willimites."

"Then, bring us some Willimites." The princess smiled sweetly. "Surely you cannot expect my brother to release his hostages without some retribution. The law is the law."

"Yes, the law *is* the law," Imre's clear tenor echoed, as he glided in to slip his arm through his sister's. "Maldred, I thought you said he'd given up this insane idea of saving peasants."

Maldred, a tall, florid man with the beginnings of a paunch, bowed unctuously. "Indeed, he gave me the impression he had, Sire."

Imre humphed, then turned back to Cathan. "Why are you being so stubborn, my friend? It's not as if they're Deryni—they're peasants. You're making an issue out of nothing."

"Sire, I beseech you," Cathan said dully. "If you do this, the weight of it will be upon your conscience. Amerce the villagers in coin, if you must. My father will be willing to pay. But do not take out your wrath in innocent human lives. The peasants of Caerrorie did not slay Rannulf. You know that."

Imre looked around at his growing following of courtiers in wry amusement, though it was apparent that he was beginning to be a little annoyed. "Cathan, you're making me out to be a bully," he said under his breath. "You know I don't like that."

"Please, Sire," Cathan repeated, dropping to his knees and lifting one empty hand in entreaty. "For the sake of our friendship, have mercy. Will you condone the taking of innocent human lives?"

"Oh, come now, get up from there! Ariella, why is he doing this to me?"

Ariella started to shrug, then looked at Cathan carefully as he got to his feet, her mouth curving in a strange smile. "I have a thought, Brother. Why don't you give him what he wants? Give him one of those lives he finds so precious. For the sake of your friendship."

Cathan's head snapped around to stare at her aghast, and the room suddenly became silent. Imre glared at her owl-eyed, then glanced at Cathan uncomfortably. His annoyance had changed to uncertainty.

"One life?"

Ariella nodded. "If Cathan is indeed your friend, dear brother, you could hardly refuse him this. Forty-nine peasants are enough for the life of Rannulf. He *was* a dreadful bore."

"One life . . ." Imre repeated, savoring the sound of the words on his tongue and wetting his lips beneath the tiny smudge of mustache.

He looked at Maldred and Santare, at the courtiers watching expectantly, at the growing horror on Cathan's face as he realized that the king was considering the suggestion seriously—then folded his arms across his chest with a sly grin.

"It *would* be novel."

"And merciful," Ariella crooned, clinging to his arm and gazing up at him adoringly.

Imre glanced sidelong at her, his mouth curling in a pleased expression, then returned his gaze to Cathan. The royal lips parted.

"Very well. Done. One life. Granted." He glanced at Maldred and gave a curt nod. "Maldred, take Lord Cathan to the keep and let him choose a prisoner."

"Yes, Sire."

"And it's not to be by lot or anything, either, Maldred," Ariella added, smiling sweetly as Cathan stared at her in astonishment. "Our Lord Cathan has been granted the power of life and death—if only over a single person. If he's to save a life, he should experience the exquisite torture of having to choose which one it is."

As Maldred bowed, Cathan fidgeted in disbelief and started to turn to Imre.

"Did you have something to say, Cathan?" Ariella snapped, before he could speak.

"Your Highness, I—"

"Before you speak, let me remind you that His Grace can retract the boon," Ariella warned, hazel eyes flashing. "It can be all fifty dead, you know— or more, if you press the issue. Now, do you still have something to say?"

Cathan swallowed heavily and bowed his head. "No, Your Highness. I—thank you, Sire." He bowed. "If Your Highnesses will excuse me, I—will attend to your command."

"You are excused, of course," Areilla purred. "And, Cathan . . ." He stopped, but did not turn to face her. "You *will* be riding to the hunt with us in the morning, won't you?" she continued. "You promised."

Cathan turned beseechingly. "Aye, I did promise, Your Highness. But if I might prevail upon you to relieve me of—"

"Nonsense. If you stay home, you'll simply brood about those peasants and become even duller than you've been these past few days. Imre, make him keep his promise. You know it will be good for him."

Imre glanced at his sister, then at Cathan. "She's right, you know. You *have* been almost boorish lately." He touched Cathan's shoulder in a comradely gesture. "Come, Cathan. You mustn't take things so seriously. After a week or so in the country, you'll forget all about this peasant thing."

Cathan knew the tone of Imre's voice, and knew better than to argue—especially when Ariella was nearby. With a defeated sigh, he nodded in acquiescence and bowed once more, then turned to follow Maldred from the hall. Just now, he had more important things on his mind than royal hunting expeditions.

Unexpectedly, victory of a sort had been won—but it was dark, indeed. For out of fifty prisoners, he must choose one to live. Life for one; death for forty-nine. He shuddered at the power he now held in his choosing.

Ten minutes later, he was standing with Maldred before a heavy door, watching numbly as a guard raised the iron bar and swung the door back on groaning hinges. Maldred bowed, and gestured toward the open doorway with a lazy wave of his hand.

"When you've made up your mind, come to the door and call," Maldred said, not bothering to disguise a yawn. "I'll await you here. I find prisons quite depressing."

Cathan nodded, not daring to trust himself to speak, then slipped past Maldred and onto the landing. A torch blazed in a cresset on the wall to his left, and a long flight of stone steps descended into murky darkness before him. Shielding his eyes against the glare, he took the torch and began descending the staircase. The brand gave off a greasy smoke that made his nose itch and his eyes water.

Eight steps. The steps turned. Then a narrower progression down eight more steps, another turn, and he was at the bottom. A corridor stretched off into a brighter area, and there were roughly forged iron bars along one side of the passage. On the other side of the bars was a series of interconnected cells, each with eight or ten human forms lying huddled together in the straw for warmth.

A few of the forms stirred as he began moving down the corridor, and shortly there were soft murmurs. "Lord Cathan, it's Lord Cathan!" The prisoners roused themselves and shuffled to the bars to peer at him. He noticed with a shock that there were at least five women among the prisoners, and several young males who were scarcely more than children.

"Lord Cathan?"

A familiar voice called from the end of the row of cells, and he approached to find old Edulf the Ostler clutching at the bars in amazement. Edulf had been one of his first riding instructors when he was a boy, the keeper of his father's stables for as long as he could remember. He found his vision blurring, and he had to look down. He knew it was not caused by the smoke from the torch.

"Lord Cathan?" the old familiar voice called again.

"Yes, Edulf, it's Cathan," he said.

He looked up at the old man, then let himself scan the others briefly. He found that he could not meet their eyes, and focused instead on their feet.

"I've come from the king," he finally said. It was all he could do to keep his voice from choking, but he managed to control it. "I—I've tried, from the instant I knew, to gain your release, but I'm afraid the news I bring is not good. The—executions will proceed to-morrow, as planned—with one exception."

He took a deep breath and dared to look up at them again, forcing himself to search their eyes. "I can save one of you. Only one."

There was silence as the words sank in, and then a few gasps, a muffled sob from one of the women. Old Edulf shuffled his feet in the straw and glanced at the others, then looked back at Cathan carefully.

"Ye—ye can only save *one*, lad?"

Cathan nodded miserably. "My Michaelmas 'gift' from Imre. Whom I choose shall live; the others die. I—don't know how to make a choice."

A murmuring broke out among the prisoners, and then dead silence as all eyes turned to him. Faced with the anguished knowledge that only one of them could live, and that the choosing lay in the gift of this one man, whom many of them had known from boy-hood, they looked instinctively to him, blindly trusting, each of them, that he would be the one Cathan would save. The thought that all forty-nine others would die was pushed to the recesses, as something which could not be comprehended. The MacRories had always taken care of them in the past. Surely this was all some kind of terrible jest. And yet, they could not conceive of Lord Cathan being the perpetrator of so grim a charade. Dazedly, they watched as Cathan turned away to jam his torch into an empty cresset and bury his face in his hands.

Cathan was no less affected. How could he choose? How dared he be the arbiter of life and death, and for his own people—some of them folk he had grown up with? Justice called for a cool, analytical, unemotional evaluation of the prisoners, with life given to the one best suited for survival and positive contributions for the future.

But there were women, and young men scarcely into manhood. His chivalry cried out for the weak, the helpless. How could he possibly decide?

He raised his head and inhaled deeply, forcing himself to hold the breath for a moment and then exhale slowly, the while reciting the words of the Deryni charm which would mask his fatigue. He must have a clear head to make so grave a decision. Another deep breath, and he felt his pulse steadying, the flat taste in his mouth receding.

Squaring his shoulders, he turned slowly to face his people.

Edulf was standing, hopefully, near the bars of his cell, two older men behind him, a young woman and two boys to their right. He recognized one of the boys as a herdsman from the village, and reasoned that the other was probably his brother, the girl possibly a sister or cousin. He did not know the two with Edulf.

"Edulf?" he said softly.

"Aye, m'lord." The old voice was low, scared.

"Much as I regret it, only one of these fine people will be able to leave with me tonight." He swallowed to regain his composure. "And since I shall not have the opportunity to meet the others again, would you be so kind as to introduce the rest to me? I'm sure you know them all."

The old man blinked. "Aye, m'lord. Ye mean— ye want to meet each one by name, sir?"

Cathan nodded.

Edulf shuffled his feet uncomfortably and looked at the floor, then turned slightly toward the two men standing behind him. "Well, sir, if that's what ye want. These are the Sellar brothers, Wat and Tim."

Cathan bowed acknowledgment and the brothers tugged their forelocks in embarrassment.

"An' this is Mary Weaver, an' her brother Will an' a cousin, Tom . . ."

The introductions went on, Cathan often recognizing a name, or a face, or remembering that he had heard of this man or that as being particularly skilled at his trade, or a troublemaker, or reliable.

He saw a young couple whose wedding he remembered Joram celebrating a year or so ago, the girl big with child, huddling in the protective circle of her husband's arm; another, older man whose house Cathan had always seen teeming with happy, laughing children—children who would now have no father, unless Cathan intervened. A young man whose name Cathan recognized as having been one of Evaine's brightest pupils in the village school—he was perhaps thirteen by now, and an apprentice carpenter by trade; another boy, the son of the manor bailiff, whom Camber had been thinking of sending off to Saint Liam's for proper schooling as a clerk, so quick was the boy's wit, and he but eleven, at that.

And the list went on, each human soul unique in its own way, each properly entitled to life in its fullest; each, save one, condemned to die—and he must decide.

When the last one had been presented, Cathan scanned them all again, his eyes touching briefly on Edulf, the pregnant girl and her husband, the young apprentice. Then he turned away and bowed his head. When he moved again, it was to walk briskly to the stone steps and vault up them two at a time. There was a grillework in the door at eye level, and it opened as he reached the landing.

"Made up your mind, Cathan?" Maldred's cruel voice said.

Cathan leaned a forearm against the door and peered at the vague outline of Maldred's head on the other side of the grille.

"Maldred, you've got a pregnant woman down there."

"That's right," the voice responded. "Do you want her or the child?"

"Her or—" Cathan cut off his retort in midsentence. "You mean that if I choose her, I could have only her? Not the child as well?"

"His Grace said one, not two, Cathan," the voice replied. "And you'd better make up your mind before he changes his. The guards will be here any minute to take the first two out."

Any minute! Cathan glanced at Maldred's shadow, then at the floor, as he tried to calm his thoughts.

"Then, by the same token," Cathan continued, "if the woman should have her child before her turn comes for execution, you'd have to let another one go, wouldn't you? I mean, a living child would make the number fifty instead of forty-nine. He'd have to release another one besides the one I take tonight, wouldn't he?"

There was an appreciative chortle from behind the grille. "That's what I admire about you, Cathan. Always thinking. As a matter of fact, I suppose he might let another one go, if that were the case. Of course, that assumes that the woman survives that long, and isn't chosen before her time comes to deliver."

Cathan glanced down the steps again, his lip between his teeth, then stood clear of the door.

"All right, then, I'm ready to make my choice. Come down and let's get on with it."

The door opened, and Maldred and two guards came through and followed Cathan down the dark stairs as two more guards closed the door behind them. They reached the bottom of the stairs and Maldred swept his gaze over the prisoners.

"Well, which one is it to be, Cathan? I haven't all night."

Cathan gestured for one of the guards to open the bars, then stepped through the opening to stand among his people. As he did, several went to their knees, and one of the women began sobbing softly. His hand brushed her bent head as he passed, and then he was moving among them, touching a hand here, a face there, this time extending his Deryni senses to the fullest, delving deep into the emotion filling the room, searching for the best of them to save.

There—he had caught it!—the spark for which he searched. Now, to localize. It was coming from the right, from one of three young—

He heard the sound of the door being opened at the top of the stairs, and he froze.

"They're coming to take the first two," Maldred said behind him. "You'd best make up your mind."

He could hear footsteps descending the stair, the measured tread of well-trained soldiers coming to do their duty, however grim, and he cast a last, lingering look across the people gathered around him. Some of the younger men—boys, really—were trying to hold back sniffles, and two of the women were weeping openly. As the footsteps reached the bottom of the stairs, Cathan took two quick steps across the straw and held out his hand.

"Revan, come with me," he said, mentally flinching a little as the boy looked up at him in blank amazement.

It was the carpenter's apprentice, who walked with a slight limp, and from whom Cathan had read the thoughts worthy of salvation.

"M—me, m'lord?"

The boy's eyes were wide, frightened, awed, and he stood frozen there, unable to reach out his hand to Cathan's. The footsteps were approaching the cell now, the door being swung back to admit three of the soldiers, who were heading in his direction.

"Take my hand, Revan," Cathan commanded, his eyes boring into the boy's. "Come out of this place of death, and live."

The guards took one of the women out of the cell, and she began moaning softly as the shackles were fastened to her wrists. As the guards re-entered the cell, the boy slowly reached out his hand. It touched Cathan's just as the guards were about to take him, and they hesitated but a moment before fastening, instead, on Revan's young companion, the bailiff's son, who wailed as they carried him, kicking and crying, from the cell and shackled him as well. His cries sent the trembling Revan sobbing to his knees at Cathan's feet, his hand still linked with the young lord's.

Maldred observed the scene with amused distaste.

"Well, if that's your choice, let's get him out of here," the Earl finally said, motioning out of the cell as the guards took the two prisoners back up the stairs.

As Maldred withdrew, taking the torch from the wall cresset, Cathan drew the boy to his feet and hugged him close for a moment, letting the boy's tears relieve his anguish, then brushed the boy's head with his palm, forcing calm into the boy's mind. After a moment, the sobbing stopped and Revan stood on his own. With a weary sigh, Cathan put his arm around the boy's shoulder and guided him out of the cell. When the guard had locked the bars, Cathan turned to look at them once more.

"Good night, my friends," he said quietly. "I dare not hope that I shall see you again in this world." He lowered his eyes. "I pray that the next will give you more justice. My prayers will go with you."

As he turned to go, there was a faint rustling in the cells, and then all within were on their knees.

"God go wi' ye, young master," Edulf called gently.

"Keep the lad well," another called.

"We thank ye."

CHAPTER SIX

O that my head were waters, and mine eyes a
fountain, that I might weep day and night for
the slain . . .

— Jeremiah 9:1

Later, Cathan was unable to remember leaving the
keep. Somehow, he got the boy home safely and had
him fed and put to bed by the servants. He remembered the hour he had spent writing to his father
about the night's failure (for so he viewed it), which
missive was dispatched straightaway by messenger
when Cathan had signed and sealed it.

But of the rest of that evening's aftermath, he remembered not a thing, from the time he put his head
down on his arms at the desk, intending only to rest
his eyes for a moment, until he felt a hand on his
shoulder, shaking him to wakefulness, and heard the
voice of his steward, Master Wulpher, quietly inform-
ing him that it was near dawn and his bath drawn.

Cramped muscles protesting, he allowed himself to
be led into his chamber to bathe and don fresh clothes,
fidgeting in irritation as his body servant tried to shave
him. But he could not stomach the morning ale which
Wulpher brought him. The mere thought made him
queasy. After giving Wulpher instructions to cover his
absence with the royal hunt, he looked in once more
on the sleeping Revan before making his reluctant
way down to the courtyard where Crinan, his squire,
waited with the horses.

Half an hour later, he was elbowing his way through

66

the throng gathered in the yard of the Chapel Royal, his head—though not his heart—much cleared by his ride. Cathan looked neither left nor right as he crossed the yard toward the chapel, hunching down in the fur collar of his cloak and hoping to avoid conversation about the night before.

But anonymity was not to be his that morning. Confrontation in the form of his wife's kinsman, Coel Howell, was looming unavoidably in his path. Coel had apparently been watching from the instant Cathan and Crinan rode into the yard. The older man's thin lips contorted in a smug, strained little smile as he nodded greeting to his brother-by-marriage.

"Good morning." He moved closer so that there was no way Cathan could gracefully avoid him. "Did you sleep well last night, brother mine? You look a little tired."

Cathan bristled mentally, but managed to keep any outward sign of his anger from showing.

"Well enough, thank you. And you?"

"I generally have little trouble sleeping," Coel drawled, watching hawklike for any sign of weakness or regret. "But then, I have no reason to be anxious." He toyed idly with his riding crop, glancing up at the watery sun, then returned his attention to Cathan. "I hear that you have a new page," was his next remark.

"A new page?"

"Yes, recruited from among your peasants."

Cathan felt his jaw muscles tighten, and wondered how the man had known. Maldred must have told the entire Court, after he and Cathan left the keep.

"That's true," he finally said. "I bring several to Tal Traeth for training each year. Why do you ask?"

Coel shrugged. "No special reason. I was just curious, I suppose. Surely you will have guessed that you were a topic of merry conversation after Maldred returned last night?"

"How fortunate that I could provide such amusement for His Grace's Court, even in my absence," Cathan said, in as droll a tone as he could manage.

"Now, if you'll excuse me, I have things to attend to, as I am sure you must."

He started to push past Coel and flee into the chapel, but Coel put a gloved hand on his shoulder and restrained him.

"His Grace is in very good spirits this morning, Cathan," he said pointedly. "He has asked me to ride at his side in the hunt today."

"Should I offer my congratulations?"

"That is your concern. However, if you were to say or do something which distressed him, so that he became irritable and nasty, as is sometimes his wont, I would not look upon it as a kindness. In fact, I would be greatly annoyed, kinsman or not."

"You need not worry on my account," Cathan said evenly. "I have no intention of speaking with His Grace unless he himself requests it. Now, if you will permit me to pass, I should like to pray in private before Mass. Innocent peasant folk are to die today."

"Innocent?" Coel arched a skeptical eyebrow as Cathan pressed past him. "Why, Cathan, I'm surprised. I shouldn't think that peasants ever qualify as innocent. But then, you MacRories always were an odd lot."

When Mass was over and Cathan had received the Sacrament, he was able to make his way back to his horse and mount up without having to converse with anyone. Mercifully, Crinan had made a place for them near the rear of the procession of huntsmen, away from anyone to whom his master might have felt obliged to speak. It was an awkward moment when the Princess Ariella rode past with several of her ladies and blew him a lighthearted kiss from the tips of her gloved fingers; but she did not stop, for which Cathan gave great thanks. He was not certain he could have faced her just then.

It was well that Crinan had made such provisions; for as they rode out the city gates a little while later, the huntsmen winding their hunting horns and whipping the hounds into order, two bodies were swinging from gibbets a little way above the wall, one of them, by size, hardly more than a child.

Cathan's vision swam at that, and for a long time he rode in total silence, head bowed, one arm clutched lightly across his aching, throbbing chest. He tried not to think about the identities of the two victims, much less of the others who would join them over the next twenty-four days. But try as he might, he could not resolve the guilt he was feeling, the sorrow which ate like a canker at his heart and mind. He could have saved them, if he had tried harder—surely he could have.

He could find no comfort, nor would he for a long time.

Most of October passed, and with it the executions of the hostages. True to his word, Imre did not relent in the slayings; nor, on the other hand, did he threaten any further reprisals against the village whose people had failed to come forth with the killers of his vassal, Lord Rannulf. The peasants mourned their dead, but at least there were no more deaths.

But besides the kinfolk of the people who died, it was probably Cathan who suffered most from the tragedy—Cathan who, for twenty-five days, anguished anew with each rising of the sun, each dawn portending the deaths of two more of his people; each of whom, but for his choice, might have lived if he had chosen that one instead of the boy Revan.

Somehow he retained his sanity, possibly because of the special tenacity which has always been a characteristic of the Deryni race. Through the enforced merriment of the hunt with King and Court, he tried hard—and successfully—to mask the loathing he found himself feeling for Imre's stubbornness, so unlike the Imre he had known and loved in times past.

The hunting expedition lasted not one week or even two, but nearly three, in the end. And by the time the royal party returned to Valoret, it was all Cathan could do to contain his rage and frustration at not being able to get through to Imre and make him stop the slayings.

Imre was likewise provoked at Cathan's dogged obstinacy, and began snubbing him at Court. Cathan, not trusting himself to remain in the capital with the recalcitrant king, betook himself and the boy Revan to Saint Liam's and the comfort of his priest-brother. There he went into retreat for the duration of the appointed days, sinking into ever deeper depression with each new sunrise.

Toward the last, he took to staying more and more in the room they had assigned him, speaking little, eating hardly at all, unable even to look at Revan, whose salvation had been bought at the cost of the other lives. When, on the final day, he received word of the last death—the pregnant girl, her child born dead the week before, on the day her husband died— Cathan could no longer contain his grief. Joram's frantic message brought both Camber and Rhys hurrying to the retreat at Saint Liam's; and it took many hours of talk and prayer and gentle reasoning before Cathan began to come out of his depression. Even then, Rhys's healing gifts had to be applied more than once, before the old Cathan began to re-emerge.

A week later, on All Souls' Eve, Cathan kept vigil alone in the cold abbey church, all through the long and lonely night. He never spoke of the preceding month again, nor would he discuss what must have gone through his mind during his private vigil. But after Mass the following morning, he and Camber and Joram and Rhys set out at last for the MacRorie manse at Caerrorie. It was a very quiet homecoming.

Understandably, then, it was some time before Rhys and Joram were able to resume their search for the Haldane heir. During the executions, they had felt their places to be with Camber and his people; and Cathan's breakdown had delayed them further. Thus it was not until the Feast of Saint Illtyd, in the first week of November, that they found themselves at last on the road to Saint Piran's.

Anticipation was high as they covered the few remaining miles.

The first snow was on the ground. It had fallen during the night while they slept, covering the ground with a fluffy blanket of white which dazzled the eye and made the horizon blend in with the blank, featureless sky. The damp air chilled them to the bone, and the horses frisked and pranced at the new sensation, frost coating the tiny whiskers on their muzzles and making them snort in annoyance. The two riders sat straight in the saddle, watching the road for hidden potholes and other hazards; they were the first to come this way this morning. The horses' hooves broke the virgin snow in a spray of fine, feathery wake.

"Are we nearly there?" Rhys asked, after they had ridden in silence for nearly an hour.

Joram blew on a gloved hand and held it to his face to warm it. "It's just ahead. Those are some of the outbuildings off to the left. Actually, we could have made it last night, but it would have been late. We stand a much better chance of getting what we want by showing up at a decent hour."

They topped a rise, then drew rein to gaze down into a wide valley. Less snow was on the ground here, and the outbuildings of the monastic compound could be seen spread across the whole valley floor. At the other end of the valley, the priory proper stood atop a slight promontory, a gilded cross glinting from the church tower. In between, the neatly ordered fields were spread in early-morning tranquillity, the high-piled haystacks and barns covered lightly with the season's first snow. To the right, brothers in heavy brown habits and tabard-aprons were turning the cows out to pasture, the morning milking done. A thin curl of smoke drifted from the top of the refectory hall, adjacent to the main monastic buildings.

"They must have hundreds of hides of land here," Rhys remarked, as they made their way toward the main gate. "I thought that the *Ordo Verbi Dei* was fairly small."

Joram nodded. "There are some younger sons of a

cadet branch of the royal family in holy orders, though
—the current royal family, that is. I think the gift of
land dates from the time of Festil I."

Their reception was far different from the last time
they had ridden together through monastic gates. The
gate warder, a layman in gray working tunic, bowed
from the waist and swept off his cap, clutching it to
his chest as they passed. No sooner had they reined in
than their horses' bridles were taken by a pair of
black-robed novices. The novices bowed respectfully
as the two men dismounted, though they appeared to
regard the Michaeline badge on Joram's mantle with
some trepidation.

A gray-clad lay brother hurried across the courtyard
to meet them, bowing nervous greeting first to his
fellow religious, then to the Healer's green.

"Good morning, Father, my lord. God's blessings
be upon you. My name is Brother Cieran. How may
I serve you?"

Joram returned the man's bow politely, maintaining
a cool and slightly aloof air. "Good morning, Brother.
I am Lord Joram MacRorie, of the Order of Saint
Michael. This is Lord Rhys Thuryn. We should like to
speak with your prior."

"Certainly, noble sirs." The man bowed again. "If
you will come this way, please, I shall ask His Ex-
cellency to attend you."

As the man turned away, Joram cast a sidelong
glance of reassurance at Rhys, then fell into step behind Brother Cieran.

They were led across the courtyard and through a
long passageway, then along one side of a cloister garden, snow-dotted now, and into a rather large presence
chamber. There they were left to wait, surrounded by
four wainscotted walls and an assortment of religious
paintings—no chairs or benches—until an elderly
man in a white habit entered from the opposite end
of the room. He had pure white hair and rather
startled-looking brown eyes, and wore a plain silver
cross on a braided leather thong around his neck.

"I am Father Stephen, Prior of Saint Piran's," he

said, bowing slightly. "How may I serve you, Father, my lord?"

Very soon, the two were being shown by Brother Cieran into a small, close room with a wooden bench along the wall opposite the door. There was an opening at about waist level, no more than a handspan in diameter, filled in with a grille made of tightly woven rushes or strips of bark—Joram could not be certain in the dim light.

Brother Cieran indicated that they should be seated, then bowed and gently closed the door behind him.

Air and some light came through a tiny skylight in the ceiling, but otherwise the room was very gloomy. A brighter light came from beyond the grille, but the light source was apparently the open doorway of a room similiar to the one they now occupied. A shadow momentarily blocked the light as someone entered, and then the door closed. They could hear someone breathing noisily through his nose—a someone who then drew near the grille and sat.

There was a short silence, during which no one said anything. Abruptly, Joram sat down to the left of the grille, motioning Rhys to sit opposite him.

"Brother Benedict?"

The man cleared his throat. "I am Brother Benedict. You must forgive me, but I am ill-accustomed to speaking anymore."

"I understand," Joram replied, glancing at Rhys and steeling himself before continuing. "Ah, Brother Benedict, our mission is a rather delicate one. I am a priest of Saint Michael, and my companion is a Healer. Recently we had occasion to attend upon a dying man who claimed to have a grandson called Benedict in your order. Could you be that man?"

They heard a gasp on the other side, a pause, and then, in a low voice: "What was his name, Father?"

"Ah, we would really prefer to have you tell us, Brother Benedict," Joram replied. "I can tell you that he lived in Valoret."

A low-breathed sigh followed, and the man cleared

his throat. "Praise be to God, my grandfather lives in Rengarth, and always has. He is a poor cobbler, and would have no business in the capital that I know of. His name is Dunstan."

Dunstan. Not Aidan, or even Dan. This, at least, was not their lost Benedict. Joram sighed, glanced a Rhys, who had lowered his forehead weakly against his hand.

"Dunstan," Joram repeated. "No, this was not the name of the man we attended. Perhaps the other Brother Benedict is the man we seek. Would you ask him to come to us, Brother?"

"Of course, Father."

"And may your grandfather Dunstan live many happy years to come."

"Thank you, Father."

There was the shuffling sound of the other rising, the glint of light as the door was opened, then silence on the far side of the grille.

Joram glanced at Rhys, who was raising his head and looking very frayed around the edges.

"What's the matter? Too much pressure?" Joram murmured, with a slight smile.

Rhys sighed and shook his head, worrying his lower lip with his teeth. "I don't think I'm cut out for a life of intrigue, Joram. I was a simple Healer before you came along. I moved openly, in high circles. This stealth—"

The light on the other side of the grille was blocked again as someone entered, and Rhys broke off quickly.

Whoever had entered walked with a pronounced limp, dragging one foot behind him. He was shaken with a coughing fit before he could cross to the other side; and when the coughing finally stopped, the effort of lowering himself to the bench was almost a physical thing. Rhys reached out a mental probe to read the man's soundness, but recoiled almost instantly. If this was their Benedict, their quest would end very shortly; even in finding him, they would soon lose: the man's lungs were nearly eaten away by disease.

Rhys swallowed with difficulty, then signalled Joram to go ahead.

"Good morning, Brother Benedict," Joram said easily. "We thank you for coming to us."

"I try to be compliant," the man murmured. "It would do little good to complain at this late date. If I could but fly— But, no matter, I'll elude them yet. There is more than one way to breach these walls."

Rhys glanced sharply at Joram. "You wish to leave, Brother?"

The man coughed again. "It matters little anymore. If, twenty years ago, my enemies had been less cruel . . . Still, there are worse ways to be locked away. How may I assist you, my sons? You did not come to hear my problems."

Joram glanced at Rhys, certain that the same questions were probably going through the Healer's mind. What had happened to this man twenty years ago? He knew what the man was implying: unprincipled men had been known to place their enemies into enforced monastic seclusion before. And twenty years ago . . . But if this was their Benedict, a diseased and dying man . . .

"Ah, I am a priest of the Order of Saint Michael, Brother Benedict. My colleague is a Healer. Recently we had occasion to attend upon the death of an old man who may have been your grandfather."

A sharp intake of breath was audible on the other side, which brought on another coughing fit. When it had ceased, there was a long silence, and then: "May he rot in Hell!"

"I beg your pardon?" Rhys stammered.

"I said, may he rot in Hell, that miserable man! He and his friends were the ones who put me here, who stole my youth, my dreams—"

"A moment!" Joram interjected. "What was his name?"

"His name?" the monk repeated. "His name was one hated by me, though it was the same as that of my blessed father. His name was James."

James. Not Daniel. *Praised be,* Joram thought, *that this bitter man is not the prince we have come to seek.*

It meant that their search must continue to the remaining three Benedicts, but at least there was still hope.

He stood easily, beckoning Rhys to do the same, suspecting that the other was as eager as himself to move on, now that this possibility had proven false. He cleared his throat to gain the attention of the man on the other side of the grille.

"We thank you for your trouble, Brother Benedict. However, the man we attended was apparently not the man of whom you speak. I—cannot, in conscience, wish you the vengeance you seek, but I shall pray that your escape will be quick and merciful."

The man cleared his throat again, his tone almost meek. "You—you won't tell the Father Prior what I said, will you, Father? I— Forgive me. Perhaps this is why we are allowed so few visitors, why enclosure is so strictly enforced. I thought I had mastered my hatred, but with death approaching— Forgive me."

"Of course," Joram replied.

They took their leave of him then, and were soon emerging into the main courtyard once again, beckoning to the novices for their horses to be brought. Brother Cieran, who had greeted them before, accompanied them now, and ran an approving hand along the neck of Rhys's horse as the Healer mounted up.

"A beautiful animal, m'lord. Before my profession, I too owned horses such as these." He shrugged. "But that is past. I hope that you were not too disappointed. I gather that you did not find the man you are seeking."

Rhys shook his head. "That second Benedict to whom we spoke—has he seen a Healer recently?"

Cieran gave a deep sigh. "I fear not, noble lord. He does not wish it."

"He has only a little time left," Rhys replied. "Does he know how little?"

"I think he does, nor does he care," Cieran said. "He has been a bitter man from the first time I met him, and that is ten years ago and more. He is entitled to his own kind of peace, I think. All of us enter these walls for different reasons."

"Even against your will?" Joram asked quietly.

"Oh, did he say that? I'm afraid his mind has slipped in the past few years. He's mentioned that several times, but of course it couldn't be true. No one is here who does not wish to be."

"Of course not," Joram said, keeping all hint of sarcasm out of his voice. "Thank you for your help, Brother Cieran. God keep you well."

"And you, my lords," Cieran replied, lifting his hand in blessing.

He watched wistfully as the two rode out the priory gates and back up the road they had come. In the distance, another storm was brewing.

CHAPTER SEVEN

*The skill of the physician shall lift up
his head: and in the sight of great men he
shall be in admiration.*
                              —Ecclesiasticus 38:3

It was a few days before the search could be resumed; and this time it was not Joram who rode at Rhys Thuryn's side, but Camber himself, disguised as a Gabrilite monk.

Joram had wanted to accompany them, had begged his father to delay until he could secure leave from his duties at Saint Liam's. But they could not wait, and dared not permit Joram to arouse suspicion by an unsanctioned absence. Time was of the essence now, the need for action intensified by a series of new scandals perpetrated by the brash young king.

After the first snows at Nyford, where Imre's new capital was under construction, more than one hundred serfs and indentured workers had died of exposure because Imre had failed to provide adequate winter clothing and shelter. Another thirty-two perished when an earthwork collapsed for want of sufficient shoring. At Rhemuth, the old Gwyneddan capital, two score and ten peasants were bound over to serfdom and a half-dozen lesser nobles hanged for refusing either to pay the building tariff or submit to voluntary servitude. At Marywell in the north, a royal garrison ran amuck one night and destroyed most of the town without being punished, though the Archbishop of Valoret himself appealed to Imre to avenge the innocents who had perished there.

Camber had all but flown into a rage as the news of Imre's actions assumed greater proportions, for such wanton disregard by a king for his subjects' welfare was inexcusable. Before a week had passed, he and a nervous Rhys Thuryn were making their ascent into the Lendour highlands toward Saint Foillan's Abbey. They had been travelling for nearly three days, on a road which daily became more devoid of fellow travellers, before they began the final, snow-swept approach.

Now, riding alone between the vast, terraced fields of the abbey's holdings, they could see coils of smoke rising from the abbatial kitchens, the only signs of life against the frozen landscape. The great granaries were sealed tight against the winter blizzards, the last crops harvested weeks before. Even the enormous dairy herds, which roamed the mountainsides in milder seasons, were nowhere to be seen.

The two riders huddled in fur-lined clothes, their horses blanketed and hooded against the icy, needling wind, as they waited for admittance outside the abbey precincts.

"Who seeks entrance at the gate of Saint Foillan's?" an ancient voice cried from a window high in the stone gatehouse.

The wind whipped his words away, and Camber edged his horse a few paces closer to the wall.

"Pray, open your gate to a pair of fair-frozen travellers," Camber shouted. "I come from the Archbishop. I'm Brother Kyriell, and this is Lord Rhys Thuryn. We have been riding long to reach you."

"You're a monk?" A hooded head was poked through the window and appeared to stare down at them, but the expression was lost in the shadows.

"Yes, of the Order of Saint Gabriel. Lord Rhys is a Healer. May we be admitted, please? We have business with your abbot."

No answer came, but the head withdrew, the window closed, and shortly a postern door opened in the main gate. Camber dismounted and led his horse through, followed by Rhys, and a monk closed the door behind them before taking their horses. Another monk bowed wordlessly and indicated that they should follow him across the snow-covered Great Court.

The stone towers and walls of the abbey church loomed gray and forbidding against the snow, but they were dwarfed and completely overshadowed by the sheer rock face of the neighboring mountain, which formed the abbey's north and eastern limits. That slope was wind-scoured and bare of snow. Near the monastic church itself was an artificial façade on the mountainside, with a large, timbered door set into its face. The horses were led through that door just before Camber and Rhys and their escort reached the shelter of the abbot's gate. *It must be a stable,* Camber mused. *If so, it is probably where Saint Foillan's dairy herds go during the winter.*

Five minutes later, Camber and Rhys were sharing a bench before a roaring fire in the abbot's parlor, each with a tankard of mulled cider in his hands and a cushion beneath his feet. The abbot had not yet made an appearance, but their monk-escort was bustling around the room, lighting candles in sconces and generally tidying up.

Camber cast a sidelong glance at Rhys as though to suggest keeping an eye open, then loosened the collar of his fur-lined mantle and let it slip back from his shoulders. Rhys, too, was beginning to warm up, and as he stood to move farther from the fire, a door opened into the room and the abbot entered. Immediately, Camber was on his feet as well, setting down his tankard on the bench as he rose.

"Good morrow, Father Abbot," he said, moving to kiss the cleric's ring. "I am Brother Kyriell, in the service of His Grace, the Archbishop. This is my colleague, Lord Rhys, a Healer."

Rhys set down his tankard and came to kiss the ring. The abbot, when the duties had been done, raised a bony hand and shook his head.

"Nay, Brother Kyriell, my lord, stand not on ceremony. You have ridden far, and in hostile weather, and Brother Jubal tells me that your coming is not by chance. How may I assist you?"

He gestured for the monk to move his chair before the fire, then signed for the two to resume their seats as he took his. When they were settled and the abbot held a tankard of cider in his hand, Camber folded his hands before him and cleared his throat.

"Father Abbot, this is a matter of some delicacy, especially in light of your hospitality." He glanced at his tankard. "But we have come to speak with one of your claustral brothers. It is rather important."

The Abbot studied both of them over the rim of his tankard, then warmed his hands on its sides. "So one might gather," he finally replied, his eyes sweeping their snow-bedraggled condition. "Might one ask why, however? My compliance with your request would involve a considerable relaxing of our Rule. If I am to do that for you, or for, His Grace, the Archbishop, I should like to know why."

Camber inclined his head in agreement. "A few months ago, an old man died. He had been under the care of Lord Rhys, and on his deathbed asked Rhys to inform his grandson of his death. Unfortunately, he could only tell us that his grandson was a monk of your order, and that his name in religion was Benedictus. Rhys asked my help in locating this monk, and our search has led us here."

"I see." The abbot glanced down at his cider. "This grandfather—was he an important man?"

"Only to me—and to his grandson," Rhys answered. "He was in a greatly agitated state about his past life, and hoped that his grandson might be induced to pray for his soul. I promised that I would try to find his grandson—and so I believe I have. Might we speak with him, Father Abbot?"

"This is highly irregular—" the abbot began.

"We can appreciate your position, Father Abbot," Camber said. "But surely it could do no great harm. The old man felt he had much to atone for, and that his grandson's prayers might substantially ease his way to Heaven, if only the grandson knew. I have spoken with His Grace, the Archbishop, in the matter, and while it is not his general practice to interfere in the local governance of the establishments under his jurisdiction, he did indicate that he felt this a reasonable relaxation of your Rule. We would require but a few minutes."

"Hmm," the abbot grunted.

It was obvious that Camber's invocation of the archbishop's name carried considerable weight with him, and also that he resented that invocation.

"What was the grandson's name again?" he asked grudgingly.

"We know him only as Brother Benedict, Father Abbot."

The abbot rose and began pacing the chamber, hands clasped in the sleeves of his white robe. His thin face mirrored his annoyance.

"You place me in an awkward position, Brother. You must understand that Brother Benedict has taken a vow of silence. He has not spoken, other than in his Divine Office and to me, his Confessor, in more than twelve years. His vocation is certain. He is a most holy man. I do not know if he will wish to see anyone from the outside world."

Camber stood in the abbot's path, and the abbot stopped his pacing. "I am a monk, Father Abbot. Lord Rhys is a Healer, which is also a divine calling. Though we live and work in the world, I think our vocations as certain and as holy as any cloistered priest's, if in different ways. If your Brother Benedict is as upright and holy a man as you say, I think his compassion for his grandsire will compel him to see us. But, let us not take such a decision upon ourselves. Brother Benedict is the one who should decide."

The abbot searched Camber's face carefully, looking for he knew not what; then he switched his gaze to Rhys.

"And you, my lord—do you concur with Brother Kyriell's estimation of Brother Benedict, whom you have never seen? Do you deem yourself worthy to speak with so holy a man?"

Rhys bowed his head, guilt at their charade playing at the corners of his mind, then looked the abbot in the eye. They had played no sham. All that they had said so far was true, even if it was not *all* the truth. Why should he be ashamed?

"Who among us is truly worthy of anything, Father Abbot?" he said softly. "Do we not say in the liturgy, *'Domini, non sum dignus'*—'Lord, I am not worthy'? But in the next breath we add, 'Speak but the word and my soul shall be healed.' As a Healer, I daily feel His healing power working through me, and I know it is a gift of God. If Brother Benedict will see us, I shall strive to continue to be worthy, in my own way."

The abbot smiled wanly and bowed. *"Touché,* my lord. Your training as a Healer has not overshadowed your theology." He became sober again. "Very well, I shall ask Brother Benedict if he wishes to see you. I cannot promise anything, but I will ask."

With that, the abbot walked slowly out of the room.

Ten minutes later, after being led through the abbot's hall and cloister yard, Camber and Rhys were shown into a small, wainscotted chamber with a brass grillework in the wall at one end. The room was warm enough, opening off an annex of the abbot's hall, but it was very dim. A single candle in a sconce beside the door was the only illumination except for a faint light coming through the grillework from the other side. A padded kneeler lay against the wall beneath the grille, just wide enough for two people.

Camber stood easily in the center of the chamber, inspecting it carefully as the outer door was closed behind them. Rhys regarded the grille suspiciously.

"Apparently he's agreed," the Healer murmured.

"Aye. Now pray God he may be the right one," Camber replied. He moved closer to Rhys and laid his hand on the other's arm, his voice dropping to an almost inaudible whisper. "Stay close, my friend. I have a strange premonition, and I'm not certain I like it."

Rhys nodded agreement, knowing that the closeness of which Camber spoke was not physical proximity; then he knelt beside the grille as a rustle of movement on the other side caught his attention. Camber immediately eased down beside him, his hand resting lightly on the other's arm as he signed for Rhys to speak.

"Brother Benedict?" Rhys murmured.

The rustling ceased. Rhys could sense the new-comer's face behind the grille and caught a whiff of his breath, clean and fresh. It was impossible to see anything.

"Brother Benedict?" Rhys repeated softly.

There was a slight sound from the other side—not quite a cough.

"I am Brother Benedict," a low voice said. "How may I serve you?"

Healer and pseudo-monk exchanged tense glances, each abundantly aware of the anxiety in the other. Camber leaned closer to the grille.

"We beg your pardon for this intrusion, Brother Benedict, but we hope you may be the man we seek. My name is Brother Kyriell. The man with me is Lord Rhys Thuryn, a Healer. We believe he may have attended your grandfather in his last hours."

A gasp of surprise. "My grandfather? Dear Jesus and all the Saints, I thought him dead these ten or fifteen years!"

"Dead?" Camber said. "I'm afraid I don't understand. What was your grandfather's name?"

"His name? Why, it was Daniel. I tried to reach him some ten years ago, before I took my solemn vows. When I did not hear, I assumed— But you said —forgive me, you said that Lord Rhys attended him in his last hours. Then, he *is* dead—now."

"I fear that he is," Camber answered lamely. "He—" His voice failed him momentarily, so overcome was he by the growing knowledge of the man's true identity, and Rhys's grip on his arm was like a vise as he leaned closer to the grille.

"Brother Benedict, this is Lord Rhys. You said your grandfather's name was Daniel. What was his last name? If you are the man I seek, I have a message for you from him, but I must be sure. Tell me what you remember of your grandfather."

A pause. Total silence from the other side. Then, quietly: "His full name was Daniel Draper, and he was a merchant in woolen cloth when I left him to join the order. My father, Royston, had died in the plague the year before . . ."

At the mention of the name, Rhys had a flash of the same picture he had seen in Daniel's mind: of the father, Royston, laid out for burial, old Daniel and the boy Cinhil looking on fearfully. He suddenly knew what the man on the other side of the grille would look like, grown to middle age: the glossy black hair, silvered at the temples with the passing years; the clear, gray Haldane eyes, sage and serene in the lean, handsome face; the slender hands, smooth through years of prayer, but strong, capable of whatever the man should will . . .

He shared the image with Camber and felt the older man wince with the intensity. But in that instant he was aware of another impression coming from Camber himself: the knowledge that Cinhil—no, Benedict, for now, for it was safer that way—was not alone!

No malice was inherent in that realization; Benedict himself had probably requested a witness. In fact, it was the abbot who stood so quietly beside the door on the other side. But now they would have to be very careful what they said to their quarry. And how were they to find out more about him, without arousing suspicion?

". . . but I prattle on in a most unseemly fashion," Benedict was saying. "You must pardon me, my lords, but my heart is so overjoyed at learning that my dear grandsire lived these many years, that I find myself quite addled. Pray, tell me, did his later years go well with him? Did he die a good death?"

"He was a good man," Rhys said gently, raising an eyebrow to Camber as though to ask what next. "I was privileged to attend him from the time I first began to practice my healing craft. He asked on his deathbed that I find you and entreat you to pray for his soul."

"Oh, that poor, gentle soul," the other breathed. "Your pardon, my lord, but I must pray a moment."

There was a rustle of movement on the other side, and Rhys looked at Camber.

What now? He spoke mind to mind.

I'm not certain. We must find out more, but we dare not arouse the abbot's suspicion.

That won't be easy. He—

I have an idea, Camber's thought broke in. *Rhys, could you make him ill?*

What?!

No, listen to me. Use your healing powers to simulate illness. Make him pass out or something. That may enable us to get inside and see him face-to-face. I doubt they have a Healer of their own.

But, to—to use my powers to harm instead of heal . . .

Not to harm. To help, in the long run. There would be no lasting effect unless you make it so. Rhys, we must get closer to him. We must find out whether it's worth the risk to get him out of here!

"I beg your pardon, my lords," the Haldane's voice broke in. "I was momentarily overcome, and . . ."

Do it! Camber urged. *He's disoriented, confused. You can easily bring on a fainting spell. Do it!*

". . . you will forgive me. What was it you wished to tell me about my grandfather?"

Camber cleared his throat, nodding to Rhys, who began: "I wonder if there might be anything of which you know that could account for your grandfather's fear of the afterlife, Brother Benedict? Daniel felt that he had sinned terribly. I spoke with his confessor, and the good father assured me that he had made a proper contrition, but . . ."

Rhys steeled himself and calmed his mind, letting Camber's words run over his head unheard, willing himself to the state of tranquillity which was necessary to reach out and tamper with another's body. Closing his eyes, he blocked out all input from the external world, mentally articulating the words which would bring him into his full healing trance.

He felt the tingle of heightened awareness in his fingertips, in his lips, behind his eyes; he sensed the nearness of the man Benedict on the other side of the grille, listening carefully to what Camber was saying, though Rhys himself heard not a word. Gently, he brought his right hand up to the brass of the grillework, rested his fingertips against the metal, warm to the touch.

Slitting his eyes open, bringing them close to the grille, he could see the outline of Benedict's head against it, see the skin of his face pressed against the metal as he leaned close to hear the words which Camber spoke but Rhys did not hear. He marshalled his strength for a leap across the short space separating him from the man on the other side, letting his hand go flat against the grille, only millimeters of brass separating hand from other's head.

Then he was extending himself across the greater void of mind to mind, slipping undetected through the other's consciousness, which was so intent on words, mere words, while the real meaning wrapped itself around his mind. Then Rhys was in the other's mind, questing gently for the proper spots to touch, probing relentlessly, but undetected, for the contact which would bring temporary oblivion.

He found it. He steadied his healing hold around the cause of consciousness, exerted pressure, and felt the other's growing dizziness, the buzz of blurred responsiveness as Camber's words ceased to make sense. Then the other was slumping against the wall, sliding to the floor unconscious, and another was rushing to his side, amazement and fear radiating from him.

Rhys gave a final touch to the other's mind, to be certain that consciousness would be gone a sufficient length of time, then withdrew abruptly. He found that he was drenched with sweat, his left hand gripped tightly on Camber's arm, the older man staring at him with respect and a little discomfort. He let go of Camber's arm, reverting to spoken speech with a tremulous voice.

"What's happened?"

"He's fainted," Camber murmured, a faint smile playing across his lips. "Brother Benedict!" he called. "Brother Benedict, are you all right?"

"He's passed out. I think he's ill," came the voice of the abbot from the other side. "Brother Paul, Brother Phineas, attend us!"

A sound of running feet.

"Benedict, speak to us! Phineas, send for the infirmarian. He's had a shock and passed out. Benedict, are you all right?"

Rhys tried to peer through the grille, but Camber merely continued to kneel, his head cocked slightly as he listened.

Offer to help, he mouthed silently.

Rhys pressed closer to the grille.

"Father Abbot, is there anything I can do to help? It's Lord Rhys."

Again they were ignored. There was the sound of more running feet, a low murmur of voices, and then a new voice saying, "I don't understand why he doesn't come around, Father Abbot. If he's just fainted, he should have come around by now."

"He's been bled too much, if you ask me," another voice said. "I told him that twice in the same month was too much."

"Perhaps it isn't just a fainting spell," said a third. "Maybe it's the plague!"

"The plague?" someone whispered. "Heaven preserve us!"

"Nonsense. Do you want to start a panic?" It was the voice of the abbot. "Lord Rhys, are you still there?"

"Yes, Father Abbot. I heard what happened. Is there anything I can do to help?"

He looked at Camber, and Camber nodded in hopeful anticipation.

"I'm not certain, my lord. Brother Benedict seems to have fainted, and our infirmarian is unable to revive him. Would you be willing to see him?"

"Please, Father Abbot, I would be most honored to lend whatever assistance I can. I feel somewhat responsible." Camber rolled his eyes, smothering a chuckle, and Rhys flashed him a nervous glance. "I had no idea he would become so overwrought at the news of his grandfather's death," he added hastily.

"You are not to blame, my lord. Brother Phineas, please bring Lord Rhys inside. The rest of you, help me to take Brother Benedict to his cell."

As sounds faded from the adjoining room, Camber stood stiffly and gave a great sigh.

"How long?" he whispered.

"Perhaps fifteen or twenty minutes." Rhys hauled himself to his feet while trying to peer again through the brass grille. "I had a devil of a time putting him out, though. I should try to read him properly before I bring him around. It may be our only chance."

"At least we'll get a look at the inside of the compound," Camber agreed. "If we—"

He broke off and coughed just before the door opened, and was straightening his robe as Brother Phineas peered into the chamber.

"Lord Rhys?"

"May I bring Brother Kyriell with me? We've worked together before."

"Well—"

"Please, Brother. I *am* a monk," Camber reminded him. "Come, there isn't time to waste."

That night, in their room at a distant inn, Camber and Rhys sat on either side of a small table, a lighted candle between them, their hands linked loosely to either side. On arriving, they had eaten a hasty meal in the common room downstairs, again thawing out from their wintry ride, then had hied themselves to their chamber. The past half-hour had been spent in deep trance, as Rhys imparted to Camber the little he had learned in his brief exploration of Cinhil's mind; the impressions were more easily conveyed from mind to mind than in spoken words.

Cinhil. Now they were free to voice the name.

Camber was the first to stir, and he sat back in his chair with a sigh as he broke off contact, shaking his fingertips to restore the circulation. Rhys's eyelids fluttered, and then he too was taking one deep breath, two, three, clearing away the residual effects of the trance from his mind. Camber suppressed a yawn as he poured mulled ale for the two of them.

"Your reading was only superficial, of course— and had to be, under the circumstances. But offhand, I will have to say that I'm impressed."

Rhys rubbed his eyes and forced them to focus on the older man. "Aye. He's brilliant, if undeveloped. But—" He sighed, a weary, frustrated sound. "Damn it, why does the man have to have a true vocation for the priesthood? That's going to complicate things."

"The man must be true to himself, else he would not be a true Haldane," Camber smiléd. "Cinhil is a priest, he feels that he was called to be that, and he is a good one. He could be no other, given his present circumstances."

"Joram would understand that; I don't," Rhys said testily. "The question is, will he forsake that vocation for a crown? I think it's clear that, with proper training, he has the *ability* to rule. But *will* he? Which will come first for him? The duty of his birth, or the duty of his vows? He's going to have to make one hell of a choice. For that matter, can we even afford to let him make that choice?"

"To forsake his vows and wear the Crown." Camber sighed. "To take a wife, produce heirs, re-establish a dynasty—things which, for most men, would be a joyous task. But it will never be so for Cinhil. He *is* a priest forever, I fear. And though we may force him to put aside his monkish robes, and walk the world again, and take a wife, and wear the crown of his ancestors—and we *must* do that, I know that now—I suspect he will nevermore be a truly happy man. We dare not even let him make the decision for himself, if there is any chance he will refuse us. Cinhil Haldane must be King."

"Aye . . ."

Rhys rested his elbows on the table and let his hands support his head, strangely melancholy.

Camber was silent for a long time. Then: "You're not certain, are you?"

Rhys shook his head wearily. "We know so little about him, Camber. What if we're wrong?"

"That's supposed to be *my* line." Camber chuckled. "You and Joram are the ones who were going to be the crusaders against tyranny, and oust the evil king, and restore the true heir."

Rhys smiled despite his fatigue, but his expression

was solemn as he looked again at Camber. "I know. And you're right, of course. Cinhil has too much potential for us not to attempt a Restoration. But the price . . ."

"It will be high for all of us," Camber nodded. "The peasants' deaths will not be the last we shall have to pay. And Cinhil— Even if we bring him out of Saint Foillan's, there's still the matter of convincing him that he and only he can make the coup successful. I hesitate even to contemplate what that will cost the inner man."

Rhys could only nod agreement as he readied himself for bed. But sleep did not come easily that night, for all his bone-weariness and mental fog from the day's exertions. Long after Camber's deep breathing told him that the other slept, Rhys lay staring at the dark ceiling of the chamber, listening to the night sounds of the inn, the winter wind whistling outside the shutters.

He kept thinking of the parts of Cinhil which he had not been able to read, which lay behind close-guarded shields that he had not expected to find in a human, and which he had not dared to probe, for fear of discovery.

He wondered how much Cinhil really knew of his true identity. And he wondered if the thought had ever crossed Cinhil's mind that he might one day be called upon to assume his Haldane heritage and the Crown of Gwynedd.

CHAPTER EIGHT

*Wrath is cruel, and anger is outrageous;
but who is able to stand before envy?*
                                    —Proverbs 27:4

In the practice yard of the royal armory at Valoret, Imre of Festil was hacking at a pell with a blunted blade, under the sharp-eyed scrutiny of a master of arms. A score of his retainers watched from the perimeter of the yard and occasionally shouted out words of encouragement and advice. But all other arms play had ceased when the king took the field. The caprice of Imre's favor being what it was of late, few men were anxious to risk a misunderstanding of their intent.

Imre was exceedingly nervous of unsheathed steel in his presence, even when it was borne by men known to be loyal to the Crown. Some few men he permitted this liberty—Armagh and Selkirk, his chief weapons masters, and a handful of others. But to raise steel against the king at any time could be construed as treason, if the king chose to view it that way—even if the alleged traitor believed himself to have acted in sport. Would-be sparring partners risked contending with the king's bodyguards, two of whom were lounging even now, with deceptive casualness, near the entrance to the armory proper, within easy hearing of the royal voice. It made the session less than relaxed.

Imre's own martial abilities were not outstanding, which partly accounted for his attitude. His slight sta-

ture and indulgent upbringing had not been conducive
to the molding of a master swordsman, nor was this
really in Imre's area of interest. He was judged by his
fighting masters to be merely competent with broad-
sword and shield, and they had long ago despaired of
teaching him to wield a greatsword or couch a lance
with any degree of proficiency. However, this did not
mean that the king's skill should be taken lightly. His
apparent level of competence was often deceiving.
More than one adversary had made a mistake, only
to have Imre's blade slip suddenly home beneath a
careless guard. Though his bodyguards were always
nearby, it was clear—to those who knew—that Imre
did not always have to rely on others' steel to save
him from would-be assassins.

Indeed, Imre's favored weapon was not the sword
at all, but the more subtle dagger. At this deadly game,
even his instructors had to concede that the king had
few peers. Armagh, the master now scrutinizing Imre's
swordwork with the pells, bore a long, raised scar
across one forearm to this day—lasting reminder of a
practice bout in which he had allowed himself to become careless.

Imre, his pell work completed, turned and saluted
the instructor in question, then strode into the center
of the yard and began readjusting a vambrace that had
begun to slip.

Master Selkirk, who had been arming on the side-
lines, took this as his signal and moved onto the field,
ponderous in heavy padding, mail, and great barrel
helm. Bending knee before the king, he offered up
his blunted sword, hilt first, as was customary when
requesting permission to cross blades with the Crown.

Imre laughed inside his helmet and touched Selkirk's
helm lightly with his own sword in acceptance, then
saluted his retainers with a flourish as they burst into
scattered applause. Soon he and Selkirk were circling
warily, each looking for the best opening blow. The
retainers resumed their low conversation as Selkirk
and the king began sparring.

Cathan MacRorie was among the circle of intimates
waiting upon the king this morning. Indeed, it was

Cathan's first appearance at an inner Court function in many a week. Though he had dutifully appeared at Court each day since his return after the executions, he had not been summoned to the royal presence until this very day. In fact, Imre had made pointed detours to avoid any encounter with his former favorite.

But today had been different. Cathan had presented himself at the Chapel Royal for the morning devotions of the Court as usual, fully expecting to be royally snubbed as he had been for the past three weeks. But instead, when the king had emerged from his session with his confessor, he had headed straight for Cathan and embraced him warmly, declaring his unhappiness at having shunned his friend for these many weeks. He had realized, he said, that Cathan's behavior regarding the executed hostages was out of filial duty to his father, and not out of defiance of his king and friend. And he, Imre, had been wrong to exclude his good and faithful Cathan from his presence for doing only what he ought, as a dutiful son. Could Cathan ever forgive him?

Cathan could. Much taken aback, and flattered by the king's public show of reconciliation, Cathan was only too willing to renew the royal friendship: despite Imre's faults, Cathan was still devoted to the king. The invitation to watch Imre at the armoury was further proof that all was forgiven.

Now Cathan stood in the place of honor beside Imre's squire, the king's tankard and towel in his hands. He smiled and nodded approval as Imre completed a particularly difficult combination move against Selkirk and glanced in his direction. Behind him, Jamie Drummond and Guaire of Arliss applauded politely, their faces betraying none of the misgivings they felt about the entire morning's events. Cathan, in his happiness, had already decided to ignore the glares which were coming this way from the other side of the yard.

The source of the majority of these glares was Coel Howell, standing sullenly beside the two warrior-earls, Maldred and Santare. It was Coel who had supplanted Cathan with Imre during the past few weeks, and who now faced possible exclusion if Cathan should be restored to the royal favor.

After a few minutes, Coel called his squire and began pulling on gauntlets, coif, and helm. He made an inaudible remark which set his companions to sniggering as they glanced in Cathan's direction. The sparring slowed to a halt as Coel took up sword and shield and strode onto the field.

"Sire, I mean no offense to Master Selkirk, but 'tis apparent that he is weary today, and cannot give Your Grace the challenge you desire. I am hardly a match for Your Highness, but I would be honored to provide you more energetic sport."

"Aye, friend Coel," the king grinned, dismissing Selkirk with a wave of his sword. "Come and have to!"

Coel bowed in formal request to approach with steel, and then the two began to spar.

Cathan's mouth tightened as he watched, not certain what to make of his kinsman's move. Coel was more than ten years the king's senior, and outweighed Imre by a considerable amount—a fact which made for a distinct advantage against the small and lightweight king.

Imre was fast—there was no doubt about that. And his form was basically sound: the finest swordsmen in the land had been his mentors at one time or another. In fact, Cathan had never seen him in better form than he was today. But Coel was the better swordsman, though he rarely made a public spectacle of this talent. And he was pulling his blows whenever he could get away with it.

Cathan's lips compressed in a hard, tight line as he realized what Coel was doing.

It was a typical Coel maneuver. By slowing his speed just a fraction, by deliberately misjudging openings, responding to feints, he could make Imre appear to be the master, pandering to the royal ego, which so needed bolstering. Cathan watched as Imre slipped and recovered on the beaten earth, backed off to straighten his helm with a gauntleted sword hand, and resumed his stance. As the fighters closed once

again, Cathan saw that Coel was playing with his op-
ponent, maneuvering him around so that the sun
shone in his eyes and made his blows even less sure.
Cathan frowned, for he did not recognize this as part
of Coel's apparent plan.

But it was part and parcel of a larger plan.

A seemingly chance parry raised a little to the right
brought a flash of sunlight lancing into Coel's helm—
not Imre's—reflecting blindingly off a leaded window
behind the king. Coel missed his step and faltered,
dropping his shield just a fraction, and Imre used the
opening to advantage. His blunted sword came swooping from behind his head in a solid blow to the
side of Coel's helm, connecting with a sound which
echoed across the yard and made Coel stagger.

Playing the game to its proper conclusion—for,
with proper weapons, he would have been dead—
Coel reeled and let fall his sword, then toppled slowly
and noisily to the ground. Imre's courtiers applauded
politely as the king doffed his helmet and extended a
hand to help Coel up.

"Well fought!" the king laughed, clenching the older
man's wrist in his fist as Coel scrambled to his feet.
"I'll swear, you nearly had me there. Bad luck for the
sun to flash in your eyes that way!"

"Nay, 'twas your skill, Sire," Coel replied, smiling
as he gave his shield to a waiting squire. "I fought
well enough today, but you are improving. The best
man won—that is all." He pulled off his helm and
gauntlets, as well, and gave them to a waiting page.

Imre grinned delightedly, raising a hand to summon
Cathan. As Cathan approached, he forced himself to
ignore the indulgent look which Coel was giving him
behind the king's back. Imre took the towel and
mopped it across his sweat-begrimed face. Then, handing it to Coel to use, he took up the tankard and
raised it to Cathan.

"To your most excellent kinsman," he said, tipping
back his head to drink thirstily. What was left was
passed to Coel, who tossed off the remainder with
casual ease.

Then the king was turning to go, his hand outstretched to bid Coel attend him. He did not see the expression on Coel's face as he handed Cathan the empty tankard and dropped the soiled towel across his arm, or hear the laughter of Coel's friends as Cathan's face went crimson at the affront.

Cathan watched until the two had disappeared from view, then shoved the towel into the tankard in hurt disgust and gave it to Imre's page, stalking off in the opposite direction to nurse his pride. Apparently Coel had made greater inroads with Imre than he had dreamed. Nor had the king totally forgiven him.

Later, in the royal bath, Imre lounged tranquilly in a steaming pool sunk several feet into the bathhouse floor. The water was scented with fine herbs and spices, the steam rising from the surface and swirling lazily in the cold air above. Imre lay back in the pool with his head resting on the edge, eyes closed, the rest of his body totally submerged.

Coel had doffed his armor and washed perfunctorily before dismissing the bath attendants, and now he brought a fresh towel from a cupboard on the other side of the room, dropped to his haunches beside the dozing king. His face betrayed no emotion, but the tension showed in his voice.

"Are you comfortable, Sire?"

Imre opened one languid eye and peered at Coel. "What is it? You've been bustling around like a hen who's lost her chicks."

Coel pulled a stool closer to the pool and sat on it, cradling Imre's towel in his lap. "Sire, this may be none of my business—and if that is the case, you have only to say it and I shall withdraw the question —but I wonder whether, as it appears, you intend to take Cathan back into your confidence."

"You think I shouldn't?"

Coel raised an elegant eyebrow. "Well, perhaps I oughtn't to say this of my own kinsman, but I'm not at all certain he's stable anymore, Sire. He's changed since he came back after the executions last month. He's grown moody, a bit secretive. And then, there's the talk about him and Rannulf."

"What talk?" came the bored query.

"Well, that he may know more than he's indicated about Rannulf's murder—that he may know who did it."

"What?" Imre sat bolt upright in his bath, then immediately hunched back down into the warm water. "Who told you that? That's preposterous."

Coel assumed an injured expression. "Is it, Sire? Cathan has never liked Rannulf. He disapproved of his life-style, his methods of handling the peasants of his demesne. I understand he even threw Rannulf off his father's manor once, during your Lord Father's reign, while Camber was here in the capital."

Imre thrust out his lower lip in a petulant expression. "That doesn't mean he murdered Rannulf."

"I didn't say he did, Sire," Coel rejoined quickly. "I simply said that there's been talk that he knows who did, and that he may be protecting the real murderers. We're fairly certain that it was the Willimites who actually did it."

"Then, Cathan knows the Willimites? He knows who they are?"

Coel shrugged. "I cannot say, Sire. I merely relate what I have heard. However, until you are convinced of Cathan's innocence in this matter, I should keep my counsel to myself, if I were you. You know how Cathan's father feels about you. And his brother, Joram, is a priest of Saint Michael, which order is also not your friend. If those elements were to come together to oppose you . . ."

He let his voice trail off suggestively, and Imre's eyes narrowed. It was obvious to Coel that Imre had taken the bait, and that his mind was churning in exactly the direction Coel intended. Abruptly, Imre sat up in his pool, then lurched to his feet.

"Mind you, I'm not saying I believe what you say," the king told him, wrapping the towel around himself and stepping from the bath, "but one can't be too careful. Send my dressers in, and then bring Earl Maldred to my study. If there *is* anything amiss, I want to know about it, and I don't want to arouse Cathan's suspicions. Hurry, it's cold standing here."

It was later that same afternoon when Joram and Rhys arrived in Valoret, heading immediately for Cathan's town house of Tal Traeth. Since Camber and Rhys had made their visit to Saint Foillan's and gained confirmation of Prince Cinhil's presence there, Camber had spent the past two weeks exploring possible approaches to the situation with Joram and Rhys and Evaine, making preliminary plans. In a strained meeting with Joram's Vicar General Cullen at Cheltham, the Michaelines had been tentatively committed to the endeavor; Camber and Cullen were even now mapping out the Michaeline strategy in the overall plan.

It now fell to Joram and Rhys to determine Cathan's circumstances, and to decide how much, if anything, he might or must be told in advance of their move, now planned for the week before Christmas. If Cathan was still reliable, after the traumas of the months before, there was a chance he could be of great help to them. But if they had any doubts, they would simply have to work around him, trusting that events would permit them to pull him to a place of safety after Cinhil was in their hands. For now, their greatest strength lay in surprise, in not allowing any hint of their plans to reach the royal ears. There was no room for error, for they would have no second chance. If Cinhil died without issue, there would never be another Haldane heir.

They were met in the loggia by Wulpher, the steward, who informed them that Lord Cathan would join them presently in the solar. The November day was brisk, and the solar chill; but the sunshine was warm on the roof beyond. There it was that Cathan found them a few minutes later, leather riding cloaks thrown back on their shoulders.

They turned and smiled as Cathan stepped onto the roof.

As on the last time they had seen him, when he rode out of Caerrorie a month before, Cathan was pale and drawn-looking, though his cheeks were flushed as though from recent exertion. A child's ball was clutched in one hand, and he glanced at it and shrugged apologetically.

"I've been playing with the children in the garden," he said uneasily. "I'm afraid I'd been neglecting them."

"It's a good day for such things," Joram smiled. "How are my two hellion nephews?"

"They're well." Cathan returned the smile automatically, then tossed the ball into a corner and gestured nervously for them to be seated. He pulled a wooden stool closer to their bench and straddled it, a shadow of pain flitting across his face as he added, "Revan's been playing with them, too. He's very good with young children, you know."

As he glanced at the floor to compose himself, Joram and Rhys exchanged worried glances.

"Don't you think it might be better if you sent Revan back to Father?" Joram asked softly. "If every sight or thought of him reminds you of the pain . . ."

"No," Cathan whispered. "Revan stays with me. He is the one good thing to survive those awful weeks, and I need to be reminded of that—that something good did come of it. Otherwise, I think I should go mad."

"But—"

"The subject is closed!"

He pivoted on his stool to turn his back to them, fighting for control, then slowly returned to face them once more, his eyes not meeting theirs.

"But you didn't come to hear me speak of that. What brings you to Valoret this close to Yuletide? I wasn't expecting to see you until I got to Caerrorie for Christmas."

"Ah, I had some business to attend to for the order," Joram lied easily, "and thought I would pay a visit to our future brother-in-law here." He gestured toward Rhys. "So we decided to see how you were doing. How are things at Court?"

Cathan glanced up, panic-stricken for just an instant, then concentrated on his hands, folded between his knees. "Strained, unpredictable, exasperating, fragile."

"If you would rather not talk about it . . ."

"No, I suppose I should. Actually, it has been fairly constant up until today—constantly dismal, that is. Imre has been ignoring me, acting as though I wasn't even there. Then this morning, before chapel, he came out of Confession and embraced me like a brother. He said that he had been wrong to be angry with me, that I had only been doing my filial duty by pleading for the villagers. I thought he had forgiven me. He even invited me to watch his weapons play in the armory yard."

"Isn't that what you wanted, to be forgiven?" Joram asked carefully.

Cathan sighed. "I don't know. I suppose so. But once we got there, everything started going wrong again. Coel started to play up to Imre, as he always does, and then let him win in a practice bout—though you know what a poor swordsman Imre is, compared with Coel. But Coel managed to make it look like an honest defeat—or at least, he convinced Imre. When Imre left, it was Coel who was asked to attend him in the bath—not I. And Coel left me holding Imre's empty tankard and dirty towel, with the Court snickering behind my back."

"Isn't that getting rather blatant, even for Coel?" Rhys finally said.

Cathan raised his hands in a helpless gesture, then slumped back on his stool. "What am I to do, Rhys? I'm beginning to think he actually *hates* me. It's gone far beyond mere rivalry. God knows, we were never what you would call friends, even before I married his sister, Elinor, but lately . . ." He sighed. "I keep telling myself that if he's Elinor's brother, there must be something good to the man. But if he cares for her—and I sometimes even wonder about that—his fondness certainly doesn't extend to the rest of her family. He's ambitious, Joram. He wants to rule. And if he can't rule, he at least wants to be the power behind the throne. Do you know that he's even brought Elinor's half sister to Court? I wouldn't be surprised if he tried to get Imre to marry her."

"Is that likely?" Joram asked.

"Who knows? She's beautiful, well connected, God knows! Imre will probably never even notice how deeply she's in thrall to her brother." He smiled sardonically. "On the other hand, Princess Ariella has hated Melissa Howell from the moment she set eyes on her. Too much competition. I'm sure she realizes that Imre will have to marry eventually—if only for dynastic reasons—but in the meantime, *she* wants to be the one to influence him. In fact, that could be part of what turned Imre against me. I—ah—haven't been terribly receptive to Her Highness's advances."

"I had heard Court gossip to that effect." Rhys grinned wickedly. "A very vindictive lady. Serves you right for being a happily married man!"

"Which reminds me, how is Elinor?" Joram asked. "After our sister, I'll swear your Elinor is the fairest damsel in the kingdom—enough to make a man consider forsaking his vows, I'll warrant. Is she well?"

Pleased at the compliment despite his depression, Cathan managed a smile. "Aye, she's well enough, though she doesn't deserve the black moods I've been showing her lately. I wish I could shake this—this notion of impending doom, but— Damn it, Joram, what am I going to do? This constant tension, the indecision—it's ripping me apart!"

"I know," Joram replied with a sigh.

He gazed off at the city lying spread against the horizon, inclining his head slightly at Rhys's silent query. When he finally spoke, his voice was very low.

"Cathan, do you remember, when you were ill, how we talked about Imre?"

"Yes."

"How do you feel about the situation now, after the past month, after today?"

"I—"

Cathan lowered his eyes, and the words came slowly, haltingly, each word dragged from deep within him, his voice recalling prior pain. He did not seem to notice when Rhys's hand crept to rest lightly on his wrist—ostensibly to gauge his pulse, should Cathan ask, but also better to read his overall condition, both mental and physical. Or if he noticed it, he did not show it. His voice was scarcely more than a whisper.

"I—don't know anymore. Before, there would have been no doubt. I loved him like a brother, as I love either of you. We were very close. When he did— what he did—last month, it nearly killed me, Joram —both to see what he caused to happen to those people, and to see what his act did to us. But you don't desert your brother just because he's made a mistake, do you?—even if it's a terrible one." He looked up defiantly, first at one of them, then the other. "I still love him, Joram. God help me, but I do. The past month—even today's humiliation—they don't change that. I suppose I—I'll just have to learn to live with the situation."

Joram sighed, the sound telling Rhys all he needed to know of Joram's assessment, and the physician let his hand fall away. They could expect no help from Cathan. Rhys rose as Joram also stood.

"I'm sorry, Cathan," Joram murmured, clasping his brother's shoulders in sympathy. "But at least you seem to be looking at the situation realistically. I don't have to tell you to be wary of the caprices of kings."

Cathan shook his head, and Joram nodded.

"Aye. Well, I wish we could stay longer, but Rhys has patients to see, and I have a lot to accomplish before I head back to Saint Liam's. Take care."

Cathan stood, feeling suddenly alien and alone. "When will I see you again?"

"For Christmas, I suspect. Imre *will* let you come home, won't he?"

"I suppose so, once he's opened the Yule Court. He likes to have everyone at the formal ceremonies, but after that I have no particular reason to stay. Elinor and the boys will be there, at any rate."

He clasped the hands that were offered and exchanged good-byes, then raised hesitant fingers in farewell as the two, suddenly strangers to him now, made their way back into the solar and out the door. He sat alone on the roof for a long time, until the chiller wind of approaching evening reminded him that it was time to go inside.

The two who descended the stairs at Tal Traeth had planned their next move even before letting themselves out through the courtyard gate. They had discussed with Camber the possibility that Cathan would be incapable of assisting them, so confirmation of that eventuality did not delay their plans. Making arrangements to meet at Rhys's house by dusk, they mounted up and went their separate ways. They did not notice the men-at-arms who watched from across the square, nor were they aware that they were followed, each by a single rider.

The man following Joram had a short ride, for the priest went only as far as the parish church of Saint John's, not far from Fullers' Alley and the former abode of a deceased textile merchant—though the man could not know of the latter. There he watched the priest dismount and enter the parish house, emerging nearly an hour later with a new briskness to his stride.

Joram saw the guardsman across the way, fiddling with a harness buckle and checking his horse's hooves, but he did not make a connection: he had not seen the man across the square from Cathan's. Nor did he note that the man followed, at a discreet distance, all the way back to Rhys's house. It simply had not occurred to him that he might be watched so soon.

The other man had a more difficult time of it. He was able to follow Rhys to the castle without mishap, and observed the Healer enter the royal archives there. But from his hastily gained vantage point outside the window, he could not see what his subject did with the several bound volumes which he pulled from the shelves after the attendant had left the room. Mentally, he marked the places of the volumes on the shelves and, when Rhys returned them and left a while later, he went into the room and took the books down again to flip through their pages, another guardsman being sent to follow the subject from the archives.

But the volumes were very old, and the man's limited schooling did not enable him to read them. Furrowing his brow in annoyance, he returned the books to their places and left to report to his master. He found his colleague already there, and the master waiting.

The priest had gone to Saint John's Church in the textile district, the first man reported, where he had entered the parish house and then left a short while later. He had then been followed to the house of one Lord Rhys Thuryn, a Healer. No, he had no idea what the priest had been doing at Saint John's. There had been no one with him, so he had not dared linger to investigate, for fear of losing his quarry.

The second man told his story, then, and added that he had discovered his subject to be that same Rhys Thuryn to whose house his colleague had trailed the priest; he had asked the attendant in the archives. Yes, he could identify the volumes which the young lord had consulted. No, he had no idea what the man had been looking for. A second pair of men were now guarding the house where the two were holed up. Did his lordship wish the two brought in?

His lordship did not.

Turning the information over in his mind, Coel Howell considered what his agents had told him, then gestured for one of them to bring his cloak. This was working out just fine. He had no idea what Rhys Thuryn and Joram MacRorie were up to; but it certainly looked suspicious, and it might well fit in with what he was already planning. He picked up his riding gloves and began pulling them on.

"Bors, I want you to go back to Saint John's and find out what your man wanted there. From your description and the fact that he ended up at Rhys Thuryn's he *has* to be Lord Cathan's brother, Father Joram—a Michaeline, I might add, so be careful."

"Aye, m'lord. I'll see to it right away."

"Do that. It would be interesting to learn whether Father Joram also asked to see written records at Saint John's. Fulk?"

The second agent, who was adjusting his master's cloak around his shoulders, inclined his head as he closed the clasp.

"Aye, m'lord?"

"I want you to come with me and show me the books that Thuryn took off the shelves. I want to know what they were looking for."

And in another part of the city, unaware that their afternoon's actions were even then being pondered and analyzed, Rhys and Joram were spreading the results of their labors upon a small table in Rhys's chamber, the room warded against hostile influence, the high windows sealed from light.

Rhys unrolled his discovery, a painting of a man crowned with gold, a coat of arms embroidered on the arras behind him. The man was slender and dark, black hair and beard and mustache silvered with middle age, gray eyes direct, clear, but unable to foresee the fate which had awaited him but a few years after he sat for the portrait. The shield on the arras showed the royal arms of the Haldanes of Gwynedd: *gules, a lion rampant guardant or*. The name inscribed at the bottom of the painting read: *Iforus, Rex Gwyneddis*.

"The blood does run true," Rhys whispered, holding the painting closer to the light and appraising it with a critical eye. "Camber will be pleased. Put a beard and mustache on our Cinhil, grow out his tonsure, take him out of that monk's robe, and it could almost be the same man. It's amazing that no one has ever noticed the resemblance before."

"Not really," Joram replied. "Who would make the connection? Everyone thinks all the Haldanes died in the coup, and most of the people who could remember what Ifor looked like, first-hand, are long dead. Besides, who looks closely beyond a monk's habit and tonsure, or would have reason to?"

"You're right. I hadn't thought of that."

"You're not a priest." Joram grinned. "Are there any other paintings?"

"A few. I tried to take the one least likely to be missed. How did *you* do?"

"Pretty well."

Joram pulled a packet of parchment from his cas-

sock and began unfolding it into two separate pieces.
He spread the first one on the table.

"Here we are: the third entry for December 28,
Anno Domini 843, being 5 Festilus II, under baptisms.
*'On the Feast of the Holy Innocents was baptized
one Royston John, son of Daniel the Draper and Avis
his wife.'* Which makes our prince's father legitimately
born.

"And here"—he spread the other page—"under
baptisms for the 27th of April, Anno Domini 860,
being 10 Festilus III, the Feast of Saint Maccul: *'Father Edward did baptize one Nicholas Gabriel, son of
Royston the Draper and Nellwyn his wife, who died in
his birth.'*

"And with those, our prince is legitimate, his descent
unbroken, and we have written proof to show to Father
and my vicar general. I wanted to pull the pages reg-
istering the marriages of both sets of parents as well,
but one of them must have taken place in another
parish—at least it wasn't in Saint John's records—
and the other spread onto a second page. These are
sufficient, though. And I doubt they'll be missed, unless someone is looking for a specific entry that got
pulled with these."

"That should do it, then." Rhys nodded, stifling a
yawn as he scanned the two pages and handed them
back to Joram. "By the way, I've left word for Gifford to wake us just after Lauds, so we can be away
by first light. Wat will have the horses saddled and
ready."

Joram, with the contented smile of a man with a
job well done, nodded and indulged in a luxurious
stretch, then refolded the two pages and slipped them
into the medical pouch which Rhys brought, next to
the rolled portrait. Unless total disaster befell them,
the documents would be safe there, for the medical
pouch of a Healer was nearly as sacrosanct as a priest's
person, and arcanely guarded as well.

As Joram spread his hands to neutralize the wards
and Rhys leaned to blow out the candle on the

table, however, they could not know that their abode was being watched. Nor would they guess that they would be followed the next morning when they rode out of Valoret.

CHAPTER NINE

When he speaketh fair, believe him not:
for there are seven abominations in his
heart.
— Proverbs 26:25

True to their plan, Joram and Rhys were among the first travellers to ride out of Valoret when the Watch opened the city gates the next morning.

There was not yet any snow on the ground. Valoret, lying in the lowlands at the foot of the Lendour range, was usually among the last to feel the brunt of winter. But a heavy frost had silvered everything during the night, banishing the previous day's warmth with portents of colder weather to come. That, plus the copious amounts of rain they had already had in the weeks before, had left the road muddy, slick, and sometimes partially submerged. Hidden holes and stones were a constant hazard to the horses, and once, after a particularly nasty near-spill, Rhys even had to dismount to check his horse's legs for injuries. The animal had been favoring one foot for several minutes.

It was after this stop, when he and Joram were starting off again, that Joram first noticed the three men following them. They had been aware, for several hours, that there were other travellers on the road behind them. That was to be expected, for this was a major track into the Lendours. The men wore livery; they were probably in the service of one of the local barons. It was probably coincidence—and the basic paranoia of the two conspirators, now that incriminating evidence was secreted in their belongings.

But when the three men dropped back after the stop, Joram's suspicions were kindled. There was no benign reason for anyone to be following them; and for whatever reason, the men represented a potential threat to their mission. Joram had gotten a good look at the men when they had come their closest, and one of them was familiar from somewhere. When the connection came, the priest swore softly under his breath, drew his horse alongside Rhys's with an annoyed tug on the reins.

"We are being followed!" he said in a low voice. "One of those men was outside Saint John's yesterday when I left. He probably picked us up at Cathan's."

"At Cathan's?" Rhys forced himself to keep his eyes straight ahead, resisting the impulse to look over his shoulder. "My God, do you suppose I was followed, too? What if they've found out we took the pages?"

Joram shook his head. "I don't think they have. And if they have, they can't have discovered why yet. Imre's not that astute."

"Don't underestimate him," Rhys said doubtfully.

He took several deep breaths to steady himself, swallowed with a throat that was suddenly dry. Joram controlled a smile.

"Relax, Rhys. If they'd wanted to take us, they could have done it last night at your house, or this morning when we left, or just now when we stopped and they almost caught up with us."

"Then why are they following us?"

Joram shrugged. "To find out where we're going, I suppose. Imre may be keeping track of everyone who contacts Cathan these days. Or he may be watching Michaelines this week, and it's just coincidence. We have to assume that someone is asking questions at Saint John's and the archives, too, though. I wonder . . ."

"You wonder what?"

"I wonder if we should force their hands, let them know that we know they're following us, and confront them." He glanced sidelong at Rhys, noting the other's growing discomfort. "Or, we could try to lose them."

"And risk confirming that we have something to hide?" Rhys retorted, almost without thinking. "Innocent people don't generally have any reason to suspect that someone is following them."

Joram laughed out loud. "Very good. You're learning." He glanced over his shoulder, but their pursuers were out of sight behind a bend.

Rhys breathed a mental sigh of relief. "Then, we're not going to do anything?"

"Just ride on to Caerrorie, as we'd planned," Joram said. He touched spurs to his horse and speeded up the pace, then laughed again as the mud flew up behind them. "And if they want to sit and watch Caerrorie all through Yuletide, they're certainly welcome. They'll do it in the snow, though, if I'm any judge." He glanced at the sky. "I'll bet one of them will be riding back to report to Imre as soon as we've arrived."

Joram was not far wrong in his last surmise, though it was to Coel Howell, not Imre, that the man reported.

The man arrived at noon the next day to relate that Joram and Rhys were apparently planning to stay at Caerrorie for some time. Questioning of the peasants in the adjoining village had revealed that it was the custom of Clan MacRorie to spend most of the Yule season at the castle, though Father Joram would probably split his time between his family and his duties at Saint Liam's. Lord Cathan and his family were expected to arrive within the week.

Coel received the news with thoughtful interest, adding it to the rest of the storehouse of knowledge he was accumulating about the MacRories and their associates. He had not yet been able to ascertain what part Joram and Rhys had in all of this. In attempting to oust his rival, Cathan, he had not dared to hope that Cathan's own kin might supply corroborative evidence for his ruin; nor was this in any way certain even now.

But he did know that Joram MacRorie had appar-

ently taken several pages from the parish register at
Saint John's—perhaps as many as four or five—
though it was possible that some of the missing pages
had been removed before Joram came. The priest at
Saint John's had been able to recall which volumes
Father Joram had asked to see, and had, for a price,
been quite cooperative about furnishing an index by
which the missing pages might be reconstructed. Coel
had several clerks working on that already.

He further suspected that more pages would be
found missing from the volumes which Rhys Thuryn
had inspected in the archives—and more of his men
were checking on that. So far, however, Coel could
see no real connection with Cathan—not that that
meant there *was* none, or that he could not make it
appear that there was.

Thanking the messenger for the information, Coel
gave orders for him to continue the surveillance at
Caerrorie, then dismissed the man and returned to
his immediate plans.

Tonight, if all went well, he would set into motion
the wheels which would destroy his rival once and for
all. As for the information on Joram and Rhys, it was
not necessary for his other plan at all—though it
might be added fule for the fire by morning. He would
see how Imre reacted after tonight. That would tell
him a great deal about what he would do next. . . .

Early evening found Coel hunched over a pint of
good dark ale with Earl Maldred, whose men had been
assisting in the investigation.

The inn where they had met was not far from
Cathan's Tal Traeth, which was ostensibly why Coel
had asked Maldred to join him here this evening—
to discuss what he had learned of Cathan's alleged actions so far, and to inspect the area for themselves.
Maldred, who did not often have the opportunity to
indulge in personal investigations anymore, had leaped
at the chance to get involved again. For the past hour,
he and Coel had been trading tales of their younger
days. Maldred even had stories told him by his grand-

father, who had fought at the side of the first Festillic king some eighty years before.

Coel drained off the rest of his ale with a hearty swallow as the Watch cried the second hour of the night, then slapped the tabletop lightly and pushed back his chair.

"We'd best take our positions, my lord," he said, standing and tugging his swordbelt in place. "My informant said that a man came shortly after Curfew last night. If he comes again, we ought to be there."

Maldred grunted and tossed off the rest of his tankard as well, then wiped his beard across his sleeve and lurched to his feet. With Maldred's height and build, it would have been foolish to think that Maldred was drunk, or even a touch fuddled. An old military man like himself would have learned to hold his drink long ago in order to have reached his present station. Nonetheless, Coel suspected that the ale had taken the edge off Maldred's alertness—and that was precisely what Coel intended. Controlling a self-indulgent smile, he led the way out of the inn.

It was dark and cold outside—it would likely snow before midnight—and the grooms waiting beside the horses were huddled around a torch stuck in the ground, hunched down in their warm winter cloaks. They snapped to attention as Maldred approached and gave them some low-voiced orders, then melted into the black beyond the circle of torchlight.

Maldred took up the torch and strode back to Coel, his manner quite matter-of-fact.

"I've sent Carle and Joseph around the side to join your men. Where do we go from here?"

"This way," Coel murmured, leading down a dark, narrow side street.

Coel's shadow was harsh before him as he walked; Maldred's footsteps echoed close behind. A few turns, and they were moving along an ever darker alleyway, the glow of other torches at the far end making a beckoning haven a few hundred yards away. Senses attuned, Coel forced himself to move briskly, confidently, with Maldred unsuspecting at his heels—for who would attack two armed men?

The slightest scuff of boot on gritted stone, and it was begun!

As the torch fell from Maldred's fingers, Coel whirled, cloak swirling to conceal the dagger he now clutched in his hand, the blade tucked close along his forearm. Maldred made no outcry—could make none. His assailant was a dark shadow close against his back, sinewy arms pinioning struggles as Maldred clawed frantically, futilely, at the fine cord biting into his neck.

But Maldred's silent struggle was for naught, and quickly finished. In seconds, the assassin was lowering his lifeless body to the ground, knotting the cord, which had disappeared into a thin, bloody crease in his victim's neck.

Coel reached to his belt with his empty hand and withdrew a small, weighty pouch, which he tossed to the ground with a golden clink as he stepped closer to the torch guttering on the ground.

"Let's be quick about it," he whispered, drawing his sword and laying it quietly beside the torch. "Finish up and get out of here. I haven't got all night."

Quickly, stealthily, the assassin glided to the pouch and stooped to pick it up, never seeing or even sensing the dagger which spun from Coel's hand to bury itself in his heart.

As the man toppled soundlessly to the ground, Coel darted forward and seized the pouch, jamming it into his tunic and withdrawing instead a piece of parchment, burned across the top, a pendant seal attached below. This he placed very near the torch beside the slain assassin. Then he drew the assassin's dagger and laid the blade against his own thigh, steeling himself before plunging it deep into the muscles of his left leg. As the pain swept over him, he screamed.

To the Watch's credit, they were not long in coming. But they were too late to save the illustrious Earl Maldred from the assassin's garotte, or to get any information out of the assassin himself. They found Lord Coel half fainting in a pool of his own blood, trying to beat out the smouldering edges of a piece of parchment which was signed and sealed with an all-too-familiar name.

Lord Coel, as they stanched his wound, was able to tell them how he and Maldred had been beset while they walked through the alley, and that the assailant had tried to burn the piece of parchment as he died. But Coel urged them not to let news of Maldred's death or the parchment become known until he had a chance to tell the king in the morning. And then he passed out.

The Watch, well-trained men that they were, obeyed his orders without question, conveying him swiftly to his working quarters at the castle, where his own body squire tended to his wound and bandaged him. It was not too serious a wound, the squire assured them— not even serious enough to warrant a Healer's efforts —though his lordship had lost a great deal of blood, and would surely be walking with the aid of a stick for a week or so.

Shooing them all out of his master's chamber, the squire gave orders for the two bodies to be held at a nearby abbey, then assured the men that Lord Coel would give further orders when he awoke in the morning. Coel, when he was certain he was alone, opened his eyes and glanced around the room triumphantly, then closed them and promptly went to sleep.

It was still very early the next morning, when Coel made his way, with the help of a staff and leaning on the arm of a servant, to the entrance to Imre's suite. He was dressed soberly but tastefully in gray velvet lined with fur, his thigh heavily bandaged under its thick woolen hose. One of the watchmen who had shared the previous night's misadventure was hovering anxiously at his elbow, clutching the piece of parchment which Coel had rescued from the torch.

A guard challenged them at the door, but there was something about Coel this morning which forbade resistance.

"I must speak with His Grace," Coel said.

"His Grace is still abed, my lord. I shouldn't disturb him, if I were you."

"I'll be the judge of that," Coel said, and with a weary sigh reached past the guard and opened the door.

The guard stood aside in confusion, not daring to stop him, and Coel and the watchman passed into the room. Imre's sleeping chamber lay beyond another door on the other side of the room, and one of the king's body servants ran to announce him as Coel limped across the polished floor.

"Sire, Lord Coel is here to see you."

"What?"

A rustling of bedclothes and muffled protests sounded from within the room, emphatic but unintelligible, and then: "Coel? What's he doing here at this hour?"

Coel stepped into the doorway and addressed the closed curtains of the royal bed. "A thousand pardons, Sire, but it was unavoidable."

He hobbled into the room, his staff echoing hollowly on the lozenged tiles.

Abruptly, the royal head was thrust through an opening in the bed curtains, the brown hair disheveled.

"Coel, what the devil?"

As Imre's eyes took in the staff, the limp, the bandaged thigh, then flicked beyond to the watchman standing guard at the door, Coel bowed deeply from the waist, spreading his empty hands in an apologetic gesture.

"I fear I suffered a mishap during the night, Sire. Fortunately, I was not badly injured. The wound appears far more serious than it actually is."

"But what happened?" Imre nearly shouted. He threw back the curtains of his bed and started to leap out, then thought better of it as he realized how cold it was, and pulled the bedclothes around himself instead. "By God, Coel, don't just stand there. Bring a stool and tell me what happened. You mustn't fatigue your leg."

Coel did as he was bidden, settling painfully with

his leg outstretched before him, cradling his staff against his knee.

"We were beset by an assassin, Sire," he said, letting a hint of real pain touch his voice. "Earl Maldred is dead. I'm sorry."

"Maldred dead!" Imre drew the bedclothes more closely around himself and huddled down, stunned at the news. "How?"

"Garrotted," Coel said in a low voice. "We were cutting through an alley, and the man came at him from behind, got him before I could even turn around. I drew my sword, but the man was fast—cursed fast. He got me in the leg with his dagger before I could more than clear the scabbard. When he tried to rob my money pouch, I stopped him with my throwing knife. I'm afraid I killed him."

"You're afraid—" Imre was at once delighted and horrified. "Well, my God, Coel, he was trying to *kill* you!"

Coel lowered his eyes. "True, Sire. But now we can never be absolutely certain who hired him to make the attempt."

"What?" Imre scrambled to the edge of the bed and leaned toward Coel eagerly, the long hair falling in his eyes. He pushed it behind his ears with an impatient gesture, clutching the bedclothes around himself with his other hand. "You mean, you think he was a hired assassin? Do you have any idea who hired him?"

"Unfortunately, I do," Coel murmured.

He gestured to the watchman, who approached and bowed, keeping his eyes averted. Imre stared at him, then at Coel, sensing that he was about to learn more than he had bargained for.

"Watchman, please tell the King's Grace what you saw."

The man swallowed and nodded his head. "An' it please Your Grace, I was the Watch of the Guard in the sou'western sector of the city last night. It was nearly Curfew, and I and my partner was walking our rounds, when we hears this scream from one of the alleys. We runs toward the scream as fast as we can and finds His Lordship wounded, with the two bodies beside him. He was trying to stop this from burning in the torchfire."

The man held out the piece of parchment, and Coel took it from him and extended it toward Imre. The king started to reach for it, then withdrew his hand and sat up straighter, a sudden foreboding flashing across his mind.

"What is it?" the king asked.

Coel swallowed. "Your Grace will not be pleased to see this, but justice must be done. I myself do not even remember doing what the watchman just described."

"What is it?" Imre repeated, his voice edged with impatience and a little apprehension.

Coel signalled the watchman to leave, then moved his stool closer to the royal bedside. "Apparently the assassin was trying to destroy this as he died, to keep it from being discovered. I can only conclude that he was trying to protect whomever had hired him to attempt the assassination. He nearly succeeded."

"Who do you think it was?" Imre asked, his eyes wide.

"You won't like it, Sire."

"Damn you, Coel, I already don't like it!" Imre shouted, slamming his fist into the bed beside him. "Who was it?"

Coel held the parchment down where Imre could read it.

"Cathan MacRorie," he said in a low voice.

There was no mistaking the signature or the seal.

CHAPTER TEN

Wine is a mocker, strong drink is raging:
and whosoever is deceived thereby is not wise.
                                        —Proverbs 20:1

"Cathan!" Imre whispered, after he had resumed breathing. "But, that's not possible. There must be some mistake. He would never . . ."

Coel nodded slowly, closed his eyes as though unwilling to believe it himself. "I know, Sire. Now you will understand my reluctance to tell you. In light of the rumors concerning Cathan and the Willimites—Well, the apparent connection is rather incriminating."

"A connection . . ." Imre repeated, lying back on the pillows and staring up at the canopy for a long moment. "How—how do you see this connection?"

Coel cleared his throat uncomfortably. "Well, it was Maldred who was responsible for the execution of Cathan's villagers. If Cathan *is* in league with the Willimites, as they say, then Maldred would have been an extremely likely next target."

"But, Maldred was acting on *my* orders. *I* ordered the executions," Imre said plaintively. "If Cathan wanted revenge for the villagers, he should have struck at m— Oh, my God!"

He broke off suddenly, realizing what he had almost said, then brought a clenched fist to his mouth in horror, turned his face to the wall. For a full minute he remained that way, Coel longing to know what he was thinking but not daring to attempt to touch the royal mind.

Finally, Imre turned his face upward again, studying the ceiling of the canopy with eyes that were cold and dry. His voice, when he spoke, was a deadly monotone.

"Bring me my robe."

Coel, not daring to disobey, did as he was bidden, holding the fur-lined robe until Imre climbed mechanically out of the bed, shrugged bare shoulders into it, and knotted the cord around his waist. The king strode to the fireplace and stood there staring into the flames for a long time, the firelight reflecting redly off his tousled hair. Then he turned his face slightly toward Coel. The older man had not moved from his place near the curtained bed.

"If Cathan has done this thing, he will be punished. Do you understand?"

Coel nodded, not trusting himself to speak.

"But I will not have any official action taken against him. Is that also understood?"

Coel looked across at Imre carefully, trying to discern the reason behind the statement. "No official action, Sire?"

"None," Imre replied. He turned back to the fire. "If Cathan is guilty of the crimes which you have suggested, he is clearly a traitor and shall meet a traitor's fate. But I will not have him come to public trial, do you understand that? Cathan MacRorie will never bow before the headsman's ax."

"Then, how—?"

"That is not your concern!" Imre snapped. "I shall deal with this myself. Where is the parchment?"

Coel glanced at the writing in his hand, then brought it to Imre. Without the batting of a royal eye, Imre consigned it to the flames, watching until there was nothing left but ash. He poked the ash to powder with a piece of kindling, then threw that into the fire.

"That no longer exists," Imre whispered, as the flames leaped up again. "Who else knew of it?"

"Only the watchman and his fellow, Sire. I was

apparently clearheaded enough to order them to keep it secret."

"Very well. You will obliterate their memories of it. Use whatever means you must, though I would have you spare their lives, if at all possible. It was not their fault they saw what they ought not."

"I shall execute your orders myself, Sire," Coel replied with a slight bow, glad that Imre could not see his face.

"And you are to mention this to no one."

"My lips are sealed, Sire."

"You may go."

"Your Grace," Coel murmured, bowing against his staff and turning to leave.

"And one last thing," the king's voice added, when Coel had nearly reached the door.

"My Liege?"

"I wish you to send a messenger requesting Cathan's presence here in my chambers before the feast tonight."

Coel turned as fast as his wounded leg would permit. *"Here,* Sire?"

"You have heard my command. Now, go!" Imre choked.

As Coel slipped through the doorway and closed the door behind him, he could hear faint sobs coming from within.

The summons was relayed to Cathan. Obedient to the king's command, he presented himself at the castle at the appointed time, garbed in the prescribed tunic, robe, and cloak of winter white.

It was dark outside already, and had been snowing steadily since mid-afternoon. Looking up at the bleak façade of the castle keep, Cathan found himself wishing he were somewhere else—anywhere but here. He could not explain the feeling; he had never felt it about Imre before. He put it from his mind as the door was opened and he climbed from his litter.

He was given admittance by an under-steward, who took his outer cloak and cap without ceremony and then entrusted him to a young page bearing a torch.

The page lighted him through a series of narrow passageways and vaulted chambers, finally leading him up the steep, spiral staircase to the royal apartments. The lad's knock brought one of Imre's own white-liveried squires to the door, and the young man bowed correct welcome before ushering Cathan into an austere presence chamber. There was no word of explanation.

As soon as Cathan was alone, he turned to survey the room. He had been here many times before, but that had always been in summertime, at the intimate little supper gatherings Imre loved—his closest friends and advisors, and perhaps a few musicians or bards. But Cathan had never been here alone before, and never in winter. The room—floored, walled, and ceiled in white marble and alabaster—was cold and drafty, despite the fire burning on the hearth—and it was darker than he remembered it, though there were lighted candle sconces spaced around the walls. He supposed it seemed so because the room was empty.

He started toward the fire, but then his eye was caught by a door standing slightly ajar, a gleam of brighter light streaming from within the adjoining room. Drawn by the light, he wandered over to it and peered in.

It was a tiny, private chantry, hardly more than a closet, also totally lined in white marble and ablaze with candles. Even the kneeling cushion before the tiny altar was covered in pale, silvery damask. The place reminded Cathan of nothing so much as a tomb. Now, why had he thought that? he wondered, as he folded his arms across his chest against the chill. In summer, this chamber had always been a cool refuge from the noonday heat, banked with flowers and rush-lights, the scent of sweet spices and rosemary mingling on the air. How else should it be in winter, except cold and bleak, especially when its master—

No, he would not dwell on that. He knew what made the room so bleak, what laid the weight of winter on his soul. Imre would come—else, why had he called him here? But it would never be the way it was in the old days, before the murder of a corrupt and debauched Deryni had rent their friendship for the sake of human lives. Accept it, Cathan: the world is not what it was.

He bowed his head and breathed a silent prayer at that, then crossed himself and turned to go back to the fire in the presence chambers but was startled to discover Imre standing beside the closed outer door, leaning against it with his hands behind him. Cathan froze and stared. He had not heard the king enter.

"So solemn for Yule Court?" Imre said, slowly crossing the distance separating them.

He was garbed from chin to toes in a sweep of ice-white velvet, furred at hem and sleeves and throat with bands of white fox. A belt of gem-set silver plaques bound the fullness of the robe into deep folds which scarcely stirred as he walked. A heavy silver chain encircled his neck and hung almost to his waist. His head was bare, the chestnut hair spread shining and loose on his shoulders. His face was still, guarded, as he gazed across at Cathan.

Cathan dropped to his knees and kissed the hand which was extended. "Pardon, Sire. I was not certain of the reception I should receive."

"Have you any reason to be fearful?" Imre inquired, clasping his hands behind him once more and moving to the chantry doorway.

Cathan blinked and scrambled to his feet, to stand awkwardly a few feet behind his king.

"I know of no reason, Sire. If I have offended in some way of which I am not aware, I pray you to tell me how, so that I may make amends. Surely the King knows me to be his good and faithful servant. At one time, he did me the honor to call me friend."

Imre glanced at the floor at that, then leaned his hands along either side of the chantry doorjamb with a sigh. A sheathed, silver-chased dagger was thrust through the back of his belt; it had not been apparent before beneath the wide, fur-lined sleeves. He did not turn his head as he spoke again.

"Aye, you are that, Cathan," he said quietly. "You

must forgive me if I am but poor company tonight. I have just learned of the death of a friend."

Cathan controlled the urge to breathe a sigh of relief. Perhaps he was not the source of Imre's moodiness after all.

"I'm sorry, Sire."

"Don't you even want to know who it was?" Imre said, half turning to gauge Cathan's reaction. "It was Earl Maldred."

Cathan's lips made a silent O of surprise.

"He was struck down by a hired assassin," Imre added, watching Cathan's face change to an expression of shock. "Garrotted. In fact, I thought you might be praying for him when I came in—but of course, you couldn't have known."

"No, I . . ."

Cathan turned his face away and tried to compose himself, aware of Imre's eyes on him, searching out his reaction.

Maldred dead! And struck down by a hired assassin! But there must be more to it than that. There was a tension in Imre, an anticipation. Imre was waiting for him to say something. But what? That he was sorry? He dared not lie. He had never lied to Imre— never, in all their years.

"If you mourn, then I am sorry," Cathan said carefully.

"You're sorry because I mourn—but not because Maldred is dead." Imre laughed bitterly. "Well, I suppose that's sufficient. I know you had no great love for him. He killed your peasants, after all. By your reckoning, he deserved his fate."

"I—"

Cathan glanced at the floor in confusion, not understanding the direction the conversation was taking— then fearing that he did.

"Sire, if you suggest that I would have wished this upon Earl Maldred, I beg you to put it from your mind. Perhaps Maldred did carry out his orders with more zeal than was necessary. In fact, I am almost certain he did," he added, almost under his breath. "But I cannot fault him for doing his duty."

"But you fault *me,* don't you?" Imre snapped, whirling on Cathan to look him in the eye. "*I* gave the orders for the executions, Cathan. I am the king. The law is the law. Do you dare rebuke me for carrying out that law?"

"Sire, I never said—"

"Of course, you never said!" Imre shouted. "Even *you* would not have dared to presume upon our friendship to that extent. But you thought it, didn't you? Ah, Cathan, I had thought to be better served than this from *you,* of all people!"

Cathan shook his head in disbelief, no longer certain he was following Imre's logic. Or that there *was* logic. "I never blamed you personally, Sire. I swear it! If there was bitterness in my heart, it was for your office, your crown, not the man who must stand and sometimes bend under the weight of it."

As he raised his gaze to meet Imre's, there were tears in his eyes. Imre saw and looked away, into the chantry, his arms clasped tightly against his chest.

"You never, in thought or deed, held me to blame for the deaths of those peasants?"

Cathan dropped to both knees, lifting his hands in supplication. "As God is my witness, I swear it, Imre," he whispered.

A long silence followed, broken only by the sounds of their breathing, and then Imre reached slowly to the chantry door and pulled it closed. He stood in the presence chamber with his back to Cathan for a long time, hands resting loosely on the latch, then turned and leaned against the door once more.

"Well, perhaps the Willimites killed Maldred, then," he said calmly. "That's who they say killed Rannulf, you know. Get up, get up."

Cathan obeyed, standing awkwardly before the now subdued Imre, but the king would not look him in the eye. He seemed as ill at ease as Cathan felt, and Cathan had the feeling that he should say something—anything—but the words would not come. Silently, he watched as Imre wandered idly over to one of the candle sconces and gazed up at the candle flames, touched his finger to a rivulet of hot wax. What could he say? What could Imre say?

"There are other rumors afoot about Rannulf's murder, Cathan. Did you know that?"

"Other—rumors, Sire?" Cathan said, swallowing uneasily.

"There are those who would like to implicate you in some way."

"Me?"

"Yes. Preposterous, isn't it?" Imre said. The lips were smiling as Imre turned, but the eyes were cold as flint. "They postulate that the reason you were so distressed at the executions is that you could have saved those people, that you were a Willimite sympathizer, and countenanced Rannulf's murder. That's specious, of course, but you and he did have words more than once, didn't you?"

"Sire, he was a cruel, sadistic man," Cathan said defensively. "Deryni or no, I did not permit him on our lands, nor did my father. Everyone knew that. I did not countenance his murder—but I cannot, in conscience, say that I was sorry to hear of it."

"Even when you learned that he died a common traitor's death? He was noble, Cathan, *noble.*"

"His murderers apparently thought he deserved it," Cathan said enigmatically.

Imre started at that, turning his head away and closing his eyes in pain, though Cathan could not see that.

"*Noble* traitors face the headsman's ax or the sword, not the gibbet and knives, the horrible agonies which Rannulf suffered."

"And nobility is not necessarily a thing conferred by birth, Sire," Cathan said softly. "If a man be without it, all the laurels and diadems and crowns in the world cannot make him so."

"No," Imre breathed. "Nor can the meanest death take it away."

He stared down at his hands, turning them front and back dazedly, as though he did not really see them, then schooled his face to a gentler mien.

"But, we digress," he said, turning to walk slowly

toward Cathan, his hand outstretched. "And the hour of Court draws near. Come, my friend. We must seem to be merry, though in our hearts we mourn."

He reached out as though to embrace Cathan, his lips smiling even as his heart twisted itself in his breast. But as his arm encircled Cathan's shoulder, and Cathan smiled with relief, Imre's other hand was moving to the hilt of the dagger he wore in the hollow of his back. A deft shift of weight, a flick of the wrist, and it was done, the dagger driving upward beneath the ribs, piercing arteries and nerves and pounding heart in one fatal stab.

Cathan died as he collapsed in Imre's arms, his handsome face guileless, astonished, as innocent as a child's.

Imre, when he saw what he had done, sank slowly to the floor with the dead Cathan in his arms; cradled his beloved friend wordlessly, mindlessly, Cathan's blood clotting on the bold robe of winter white and silver which he wore.

It was thus that Coel Howell found them a quarter-hour later, after repeated inquiries of Imre's squires had revealed only that the king was still alone with Lord Cathan and did not wish to be disturbed.

Coel accepted that excuse at first, toying with the head of his staff in annoyance as the minutes dragged on. Finally, when he could stand it no longer, he limped to the door and knocked—then knocked again, louder. When there was no response, he eased the door open a crack and peered in, froze, then slipped inside and closed the door securely behind him, his breath catching in his throat.

Imre, his back to the door, was slouched motionless over a still, white-garbed form, a dark smear of blood staining the tiled floor beside him. The king did not move as Coel made his way haltingly across the polished marble, and for just an instant Coel wondered if all the blood was Cathan's.

"Sire? Your Grace, are you all right?"

Imre still did not respond, though by now Coel could see that he was breathing. The king held Cathan's lifeless body loosely in his arms, the tawny head laid close against his chest, Cathan's dark hair tumbling down to hide his face. There was blood on Imre's hands and on a silver-chased dagger lying by his knee.

Carefully, Coel knelt beside the pair, wincing as he eased his bandaged leg.

"Your Grace, are you injured? What happened?"

Imre flinched at the voice, but he did not look up.

"I killed him, Coel. I had to," he whispered, so softly that Coel missed the first few words. "What you said, it was true. He lied to me, but—but— Oh, God, what am I going to do? I've killed him!"

He raised a tear-streaked face to stare miserably at Coel, his eyes puffy and red from weeping. Then he looked down at Cathan and slowly relaxed his grip, let the body sag from his arms to lie across his lap. The face was startled still, even in death, the eyes half open and staring. Imre shuddered as he saw them, but when Coel tried to reach across and close them, Imre struck his hand away and closed the eyes himself. Then he eased the body to the floor, shaking his head as though on the verge of tears again, stifling a sob.

Coel swallowed nervously and wiped damp palms against his thighs, acutely aware that he must end this scene before Imre broke down completely. He had not expected this. He had caught Imre's meaning clearly enough this morning—that Cathan would not die by the headsman's ax or other public execution—but he had not anticipated that Imre would do the deed himself. A calculated accident, perhaps, or even an assassination—but not this bloodying of the royal hands.

Still, he must not falter now. Imre believed himself to have been betrayed by Cathan; and he must continue to believe that, if Cathan's death were to do Coel any good. He must plant the seeds of confirmation now, while Imre was still vulnerable. Besides, with the investigation proceeding on the activities of Joram MacRorie and Rhys Thuryn, perhaps soon he would not have to manufacture evidence.

"Come away, Sire," he said gently. "There is nothing you can do. The past is past forever. You did as you must do."

Imre sniffed noisily several times, shook his head from side to side. "He lied to me, Coel," he whispered. "I gave him trust and love, and he returned betrayal."

"Yet, even in that, you showed your love through mercy, Sire. Not every king would let a traitor die so well."

"Not precisely traitor," Imre breathed. "No, this was private treachery we settled. I could not let him face the ax for that."

"Then, best to die the way he did, before ought else could be discovered, Sire," Coel murmured, casting the new seed and hoping it would grow.

There was a short pause, and then Imre looked up at Coel in dull dismay.

"What?"

"I am sorry, Sire. There are indications that he may have been involved in something more. Pray, do not trouble yourself with it now. The man is dead."

"What else?" Imre insisted. "I want to know."

"I don't know myself, exactly," Coel said, feigning reluctance. "Something involving his family, his brother Joram and a Healer named Rhys Thuryn, probably his father as well. I have no certain proof as yet, only suspicions. But all of them bear watching. Shall I see to it?"

The king blinked and swallowed hard, his eyes glazed with his grief, then nodded once, curtly. He raised his arm as though to wipe his sleeve across his face, but there was blood on his hand and spattered down the fur cuff, as well as the great stain across his chest where he had held the dying Cathan close. He froze, as though seeing the blood for the first time, then looked up at Coel with eyes that were suddenly frightened, like a small, lost boy's.

"My God, he's dead. What will his father say?"

"What does it matter?" Coel replied archly. "Though you choose to view him otherwise, Camber MacRorie is a subject like any other. You need not justify your actions to him. Besides, he himself is suspect."

"But—"

"So far as the outside world need know, Cathan MacRorie simply collapsed and died while speaking with his king before the opening of the Yule Court," Coel said sternly, his eyes catching and holding Imre's. "You are the king. Who will dare to gainsay you?"

"But, the wound—"

"If you do not acknowledge its existence, then it does not exist," Coel said firmly. "Come, Sire." He held out his hand. "The Court is waiting, and you must change your clothes. While you do that, I will make arrangements for the body to be returned to Caerrorie."

Dazedly but compliantly, Imre gazed down once more at the still form of Cathan and touched his shoulder a final time in farewell. Then he sighed deeply and climbed to his feet.

But he did not take the hand which Coel offered, nor would he meet the older man's eyes. And when Coel left the king in the hands of his dressers to wash and change, the nobleman was both thoughtful and uneasy. Coel's words, as he penned his orders to the guards, were studied, cautious.

Half an hour later, armed with the orders he had written, Coel knocked on the door to Imre's inner chambers and then opened it, not waiting for the servants to admit him.

A crash of breaking glass rang out in the next room, followed by the emergence of a red-faced squire who was trying to mop a purple stain off his white winter livery. Almost immediately, Imre could be heard calling for more wine. By the sound, he had already had more than was wise.

"My Liege," Coel called, stepping cautiously into the sleeping room, "it's getting very late."

With a clatter of wooden rings, the curtain of a dressing alcove was pulled back to reveal a flushed and wild-eyed Imre clutching at the fabric with one bejewelled hand, a silver goblet in the other. Hair awry, he was wearing a court tunic of scarlet velvet, almost indecently short, which was richly encrusted across the front and at throat and wrists with threads of gold bullion.

. Two body servants, clad in white velvet and fur as Imre had been earlier, were looking very uncomfortable, one of them holding Imre's crown in nervous, gloved fingers, the other clutching an ivory comb. Beyond them, in the next room, Coel could see the ruin of what had been Imre's dressing chamber, chests of clothes dumped in disarray, a mound of crimson-stained white velvet lying in a heap in the middle of the floor. It took little imagination to picture the royal mayhem which must have taken place once Imre was alone with his servants and had a copious amount of wine in his otherwise empty stomach.

The servant with the comb shifted uneasily and started to bring it toward his master's head, then thought better of it and glanced warily at Coel.

"His Grace has decided to wear scarlet tonight, my lord," he announced, his tone clearly indicating his disapproval and that he hoped for the older man's support.

"Whatever His Grace wishes," Coel replied. He sketched a short bow in Imre's direction and tucked the parchment he was holding into his tunic. "Sire, your appearance will dazzle all the Court. However, if you will permit, I would be honored to assist you to finish dressing, so that these gentle lads can be about their other duties."

Imre looked at him closely, swaying slightly on his feet, then stifled a slight, uncontrollable giggle. "Of course, my dear man. Send the louts away."

Snatching the comb, he made an energetic attempt to tame his hair, nearly sloshing wine down the front of his new tunic with the vigor of his attack; then he stood meekly as Coel rescued the goblet and set it on a side table.

Coel ushered the servants to the door of the dressing chamber and gestured toward the bloodstained robe, mouthing the order to burn it, then closed the door behind them and returned to where Imre was cheerfully tangling his hair worse than it had been before.

With a bow and a smile, Coel prised the comb out of Imre's hand and began working the tangles out of the long chestnut locks. When he had finished, he turned away to pick up the crown which the squires had left, and returned his attention just in time to keep Imre from draining the goblet again.

Luckily, Imre was still at the pliable stage, so he did not resist when Coel took the cup from him. But God knew, the king had had enough to drink for a while. Whether Imre came out of the Great Hall under his own power was his own business; and if he had to be carried out, that would not be the first time. But he must at least be able to maneuver his way into the hall, or the Princess Ariella would be even more furious than she was certain to be at their late arrival. Coel put the cup out of reach and hoped that Imre would not make a scene. Imre, drunk, could be a very difficult young man.

But Imre did not resist. He let himself be drawn up to attention, and the crown put on his head, then stood still while Coel fastened the short, ermine-lined mantle over one shoulder, the fur contrasting vividly against the blood red of tunic, hose, and shoes. Only when they were heading for the door, Imre leaning heavily on his arm, did Coel remember the orders stuck inside his tunic. Abruptly, he turned the king around and marched him back to a writing desk, pulling the parchment out.

"Just one last thing, Sire," he said, spreading the parchment on the writing table, "and then we'll go into the hall and get you some more wine."

As he dipped a quill in ink and extended it to Imre, the king's eyes grew cold, like agate, and Coel suddenly realized that much, if not all, of the drunkenness was a façade.

"The orders concerning Camber?" Imre asked, enunciating each syllable with great care.

Coel nodded, an instant of uncertainty racing through his mind, though no trace of it showed on his face.

Imre studied him for a long moment, then snatched

the pen from him and scrawled his name at the bottom of the page. Half in apprehension and half in amazement, Coel watched as Imre thrust the quill back into its holder, ruining the point in the process, and turned away. Imre had not even read the orders, had not glanced at the contents.

"Do you not wish to read it first, Sire?"

"No."

Imre took a few steps away and bowed his head, and Coel looked down at the page, at the drying ink, at the words he himself had inscribed—innocuous, this time, at least—then decided to risk further inquiry.

"I could have written anything, you know, Sire. It could be death warrants for all of them."

"Not even *you* would dare that," Imre replied in a low voice, not looking back at him. "I have signed it; most men would take that as a sign of trust. Do you question the judgment of your king?"

Coel contained a smile, then picked up the parchment and inspected the signature—dry now—before creasing the orders sharply. "Certainly not, Sire. Do you wish to seal it, or shall I?"

"The seal is in the box," Imre said softly. "Once, it was *his* province. Now it is yours, to tell of his foul murder."

"His sad demise, Sire," Coel corrected, in a similar tone but with growing confidence. "Unfortunate" —he paused for emphasis, plucking the seal from its box—"but necessary."

"Necessary," Imre repeated in a strained whisper.

He did not hear the wax as it hissed and spat, falling on the parchment and receiving the imprint of the royal seal. And shortly after that, they were striding down the corridor toward the Great Hall, Imre with a cup in his hand once more—Coel had not dared to refuse it to him—and the orders on their way to the guards who would escort Cathan's body home to Camber.

The feast that night went even more badly than Coel had feared, given Imre's initial state of inebriation.

Ariella, predictably annoyed at her brother's failure to appear at the appointed hour, had waited a reasonable amount of time, the guests milling restlessly in the hall, then had made her own entrance and ordered the company seated—though even she did not dare to begin the feast without Imre. But the musicians played and the wine flowed freely, and the conversation sparkled at the Yule Court of Imre of Festil, as did his guests.

Seated at the high table beside her brother's empty chair, Ariella laughed and drank and flirted with the great lords and gentlemen seated near her, her vivid beauty glowing from its setting of velvet and satin and snow-white fur. Diamonds blazed at throat and wrists and around the hem of her gown; more trembled seductively on her forehead beneath the silky fur hood which confined her hair and framed her face like some strange winter flower.

All the company was garbed in white tonight, out of deference to Imre's wishes for a true winter court, and thus it was with a breath of surprise that the assembled gentles greeted the appearance of their monarch in the doorway of the Great Hall, clothed from head to toe in scarlet, except for the lining of the mantle he wore. From his demeanor and the cup in his hand, it was simple to deduce what had delayed the King's Grace—or so they thought.

Without pausing for ceremony, Imre wove his way down the hall, Coel limping in a little embarrassment at his right elbow. The surprised guests knocked over benches and stools to get to their feet and bow as he passed, though Imre would not have known the difference if they had not moved. Ariella, better accustomed than most to her brother's idiosyncrasies when he had been drinking, picked up a new goblet of wine as he approached and offered it to him with a curtsey as she reached the dais and staggered to his seat.

"You're drunk and you're late," she whispered, *sotto voce,* as he took the cup and drained it to the dregs. "Where on earth have you been?"

"In Hell, madame, in Hell."

Imre burped, then waved the Court to their seats and bade the musicians play.

As music and conversation resumed, Coel slipped to his accustomed seat near the high table and sat, watching apprehensively, as Imre drank a second goblet, ignored Ariella's further attempts to question him, then paused while a page refilled his cup and drained that, too. The stewards had not even been able to get the first course served before the king lurched to his feet, his face flushed from the wine, the cup unsteady in his hand.

"Why do you laugh and sport among yourselves?" he shouted.

The room was quickly hushed, and the musicians broke off with a few discordant notes.

"Why do you make merry?" the king repeated, indignation coarsening his voice, his eyes glittering dangerously. "You, Selkirk, why such merriment on this night, of all nights?"

The weapons master, seated at a table partway down the hall with a number of his fellows, jumped hastily to his feet and bowed, his face as white as the tunic he wore.

"By your leave, Your Grace, but you did command it."

"I?" Imre paused to take a deep draught from his goblet. "*I* did command it," he repeated incredulously, as though he had never heard of anything so preposterous. "Damn you, Selkirk, do you not know that a man is dead?"

He hurled the goblet toward the shrinking weapons master, where it narrowly missed a page's ducking head, then swept his arm across the table, sending silver ewers and platters crashing to the floor.

"Damn you, get out! All of you, get out!"

He picked up another ewer—this one of glass— and dashed it to the floor with an oath, then lurched backward and overturned his chair as he stumbled from the hall.

His sister, stunned and outraged at his actions, murmured instructions to the head steward to clear the hall, then followed in the direction Imre had gone. A wide-eyed guard pointed out the chamber into which the king had disappeared, but all of Ariella's cajoling and pleading could not induce him to come out. Finally, in a fit of temper herself, Ariella stalked back to the hall to see that her orders had been obeyed, before retiring to her chambers to sleep.

Imre also slept, after a time, sprawled facedown on the floor of his refuge chamber, a cup of wine staining the carpet beside his head. But guilt and an urgent bladder awakened him before many hours had passed, and it was with extreme care that he staggered, still quite drunk, into the room's garderobe to relieve himself. His head was reeling from the wine, and he poured himself another cup with shaking hands before venturing to the chamber door and raising the bar.

Outside, the torches in the cressets were nearly burned down, the corridors silent. A lone guard snapped to attention and gave a royal salute as the king made his way down the narrow passage, fending himself off from the walls with his empty hand. Faintly, from the direction he had come, Imre could hear the sounds of servants clearing away the disaster in the Great Hall, and abruptly the reason for his drinking came back to him.

With that, he was taken by a fit of shaking, and it was all he could do to bring the cup to his lips and drink again. Then he was climbing the winding stairs toward his chambers, halting to rest halfway up, then turning and descending again, shuffling uncertainly down another passageway to another winding stair.

He would go to Ariella. She would understand—though he thought he remembered her shouting at him through the door as he fell asleep earlier. She would know what to do. She who had soothed his childhood hurts and held him close against the terrors of the dark—she would find the words to comfort him now. She would not fail him, though Cathan and all others did.

Within minutes, he was standing hesitantly outside

her chambers, swaying uncertainly on his feet, staring into the depths of his nearly empty cup. Abruptly, he drained off the contents and then knocked thunderously on the door.

"Ar—Ari?" he called, his voice cracking on the first attempt. "Ari, open the door—please?"

"Who—who is it?" came a timorous voice on the other side of the door. One of the servants, no doubt.

"I want to see Ari. It's me, Imre."

There was a gasp, an unintelligible command from farther away, and then the door was open and a maid was making a deep curtsey. Ignoring her, Imre stumbled past and headed for the doorway of the inner chamber. Candles were being lit by another servant within, and as he entered he was aware of the shadowy form of his sister pulling on a robe over her sleeping shift near the great, curtained and canopied bed. The glare of the candles hurt his eyes, and he could not seem to see her clearly.

"My cup is empty, Ari," he whispered plaintively, turning the cup upside down and giving it a shake to demonstrate that it was indeed so.

His sister's voice came from the shadows, soothing, reassuring. "Maris, pour some wine for His Grace and then leave us."

The girl by the candles came to him then, dipping in a quick curtsey before filling his cup. But when she started to go, he caught her sleeve and held her fast while he drained the cup and extended it again. With a glance at her mistress, the girl filled the cup a second time, then left the flagon on a table and went out. Imre began to drink again, but something blocked his light and he looked up. His sister was standing between him and the candles, her reddish hair tumbling down around her shoulders. He could not see her face, but the flames touched her hair with fire.

"Ari?" he said in a small voice.

A slim white hand was extended toward him, resting on his where he held the cup.

"Don't you think you've had enough for one night?"

"Never enough to wash *this* away," he mumbled,

starting to raise the cup again and frowning as she did not release his hand.

"You don't understand, Ari. He's dead. I killed him."

The hand on his did not move.

"Who is dead, Imre? Whom did you kill?"

His hand jerked spasmodically at that, and he lost his grip on the cup; he would have dropped it had she not caught it. His sob stuck in his throat and shook his body as he buried his face in his hands.

"Cathan. I've killed Cathan. He was a traitor, and I had to do it, but— Oh, God, Ari, I've killed him. And I—loved—him."

Ariella closed her eyes briefly, remembering the solemn, determined Deryni lord, whose price she and Imre had never found, and slowly raised Imre's cup to her lips and drank deeply in ironic salute. Then she let the empty cup fall to the carpet beside her and took her brother in her arms as she had done when they were children.

"It will be all right, Imre," she murmured, as he clung to her shoulders and the tears stung his eyes. "You are the king, and must do what you must do. But you are also a man, and a man may mourn a friend."

With that, Imre's grief came pouring over him and he sank, sobbing, to his knees, to bury his face against her waist. So he remained for a long time, sobbing bitterly. She stroked his hair, rubbed the tension from his shoulders, and brushed the top of his head with her lips. At length the anguish faded, to be replaced by a growing tingling in every part of his body—and in hers. And as he raised his tear-streaked face and read the passion in her eyes, he was suddenly aware of the soft promise of her body locked in the circle of his arms.

In one dazzling flash of revelation, he knew that both of them had been moving toward this moment for a long time.

As he struggled to his feet, her mouth sought his, as hungry as his own need. He was aware of her pressing hard against him as they clung to one another, the exquisite softness as his lips moved down her throat, as he crushed his face against her flawless breasts.

Then they were being drawn, one by the other, toward the shadowed recesses of the great, curtained bed, and his blood was roaring in his head, and he lost himself in the urgency of sweet oblivion.

CHAPTER ELEVEN

The just shall be in everlasting remembrance.
                                    —Psalms 112:6

It was a stunned and hushed contingent which met the royal escort that next day bore Cathan MacRorie home.

The cortege from Valoret arrived amid light snow-fall near noon, bearing Cathan's body on a two-horse litter, the horses plumed and caparisoned in black, the body covered with a velvet pall, snow-frosted. The king's men, a score of them, carried their spears reversed in their stirrups. A pair of monks walked to either side of the bier, swinging censers and chanting prayers for the soul of the departed. After the royal escort, another litter bore the dead man's widow and children, young Revan following behind on horseback with Wulpher and a handful of the loyal Tal Traeth servants. None of them were misled by the royal pageantry, for they had seen the blood-stained body before it was washed and dressed and laid out in state for the short journey home. They knew the king's hypocrisy for what it was, though even they did not dream of the extent.

Word had flown from the capital as only news of tragedy can fly, reaching Tor Caerrorie in the small hours of the night. The man who brought the news was Crinan, Cathan's devoted body squire. He had been at Tal Traeth when the soldiers brought his master home; he had watched, mindless in his grief, as the king's lieutenant barked orders for the preparation of

the body; and he had bristled with pride as old Wulpher, the steward, pushed the man aside and himself
performed this last service for their slain young lord.

Torn at first between his wish to stay at his master's
side and the necessity to warn the rest of the family of
what had happened, Crinan held his peace until the
king's men had bedded down in the Great Hall for
the night—for they would be accompanying the body
to Caerrorie the next morning. Then, spurred by the
fear that the king might make retribution against all
the MacRories, Crinan left his grieving vigil and took
horse for Caerrorie. Three hours later, he was pounding up the approach to the outer gate.

The sound of his horse's hooves shattered the night
silence of the castle and set the hounds to baying, and
soon the entire household was awake and shivering in
the cold, ill-lit Great Hall.

At first Crinan could not tell them—he was physically unable, after his long and breathless ride in the
cold and snow. But he was sure that Camber knew
before he spoke, in that uncanny way which only
Deryni seemed to have. Camber had received his
words with wooden silence, had turned his face away
for a mere instant before tonelessly asking Sam'l to
ride on to Saint Liam's and pass the word to Joram.
Rhys Thuryn was already in the house, had been
working late on documents in the MacRorie library,
and he, too, came into the Great Hall at the commo-
tion, to hear the news in shock and hold the weeping
Evaine close in helpless comfort. After a few more
low-voiced commands to the servants regarding necessary preparations for the morrow, Camber had requested them all to return to their respective chambers
to try to rest. There was little further sleep for anyone
at Caerrorie that night.

Next morning, under a cold, sapphire sky, Camber's
household gathered in Caerrorie's village church to
pray for the soul of Cathan MacRorie and wait for his
body to come home. Joram arrived before dawn, and
young James Drummond an hour later. Evaine and
Rhys knelt together at Camber's side, with Crinan

and Sam'l and a dozen of the closest household servants, as Joram led the prayers for the dead.

Outside, the people of the village gathered, and Camber permitted as many of them to enter the church as could be accommodated, the rest of them kneeling quietly in the outer yard. When, at last, word came that the cortege was approaching, the villagers still outside went and lined the road in silence, each one making a deep obeisance as the bier passed.

The king's lieutenant was visibly annoyed at this sign of devotion—which, to his mind, should have been reserved for their sovereign—but he dared do nothing. For there was a grim, proud man waiting on the steps of the church to receive his son—a High Deryni Lord capable of unspeakable vengeance if he chose to wreak it. The lieutenant was Deryni himself, and not unskilled in the use of his powers, but he did not relish an arcane confrontation with Camber of Culdi. The lieutenant ordered his men to stand quiet, and silently prayed that the Earl of Culdi would not defy the king's commands.

The lieutenant's fears were unjustified. He should have known that violence was not Camber's way, even in extreme grief. Camber stood straight and calm—deadly calm—as the cortege drew to a halt, fixing the soldiers coldly with his gaze as Joram, Rhys, and the faithful Crinin and Sam'l removed the bier from the horse-litter and bore it into the church. He embraced Elinor and his grandsons before sending them inside. Then Camber stood watch until Wulpher and Revan and the other servants from Cathan's household were permitted to come forward, to kneel weeping at his feet until he raised them up and, with low and gentle voice, bade them also go inside.

Slowly and deliberately, he himself followed them and closed the doors, making it clear to the most hardened of them that the king's men were not welcome in this hour of grief. The lieutenant wisely chose not to challenge that statement, but bade his aide command the men to stand at ease. Inside, Joram MacRorie began the Requiem Mass for his slain brother. . . .

When the Mass had ended, Camber remained kneeling for a long time beside the body of his son, pondering his next move. Burial would not be until that evening, for the grave was not ready, so most of the villagers had gone into the courtyard after Mass, leaving only members of the immediate family and household to keep silent vigil.

But the guards were still outside, and Camber wondered about that, wondered why they were staying, what orders they had received besides the command to escort Cathan's body home. Though the king's lieutenant had said nothing to him—indeed, he had not given the man a chance—Camber considered whether their mission might entail more than they had done thus far. (Or was this his own guilt projecting suspicion?) What if they were holding arrest warrants for the entire family, and awaited only the conclusion of the burial rite tonight to serve those warrants? There had been some reason for Cathan's murder. Suppose Imre had somehow gotten wind of their quest for Prince Cinhil?

He let his eyes search those remaining: Rhys at his side; Evaine, comforting the grieving Elinor; James Drummond, kneeling sullen and alone far to the right of the nave; the family servants of his and Cathan's households. Sam'l had taken the children back to the castle minutes before—no need for them to stay in the church for the rest of the afternoon, grief-strained and frightened. What he now planned would be difficult, but it must be done.

With a slight sigh, Camber crossed himself and got to his feet, shaking his head when Rhys looked up and made as though to accompany him. Moving alone toward the back of the church, he stopped beside one of the young pages still kneeling there and spoke with him quietly for some minutes, the boy nodding vigorously from time to time. Then Camber was tousling the boy's head in affection, a slight smile crossing his face as he turned and moved back up the aisle. Just before Camber reached his former place by Rhys, the page glanced around nonchalantly, got to his feet, and slipped away through a side door.

Now, what was all of that about? Rhys wondered, and started to ask as Camber knelt beside him once more.

But the proud old Deryni shook his head and held a finger to his lips, his head bowed as though in prayer once more. Puzzled, Rhys watched as Camber reached out and caught the edge of the pall shrouding Cathan's body, to bring the silk-fringed velvet gently to his lips.

It was not the pall which Imre had sent, Rhys knew. That had been removed as soon as the body was safely inside the church and the doors closed, to be replaced by another one bearing the MacRorie arms, Cathan's label of cadency stitched to it lovingly in the pre-dawn hours by his sister Evaine.

Rhys watched with compassion as Camber let the velvet fall, sharing the older man's grief as few men could. As he laid his hand on Camber's arm in a spontaneous gesture of comfort, Camber looked up, his gray eyes sage, serene beyond all expectation.

"Gentle Rhys, dear to me as any son," he murmured. "Will you come with me and help me?"

Rhys nodded, not trusting himself to speak, and Camber smiled fleetingly, covering Rhys's hand briefly with his own as the two of them stood. Walking quietly behind the altar rail and out of the sanctuary, they went to the sacristy chamber, where Joram had retired after Mass. Joram was kneeling at a *prie-dieu*, devoid of vestments save for the black stole over his cassock, head cradled in his arms. He looked up as his father and Rhys came into the room, hastily wiping a sleeve across his eyes. The pale hair was dishevelled, and he smoothed it in an automatic gesture.

"Is anything wrong?"

"Nothing else," Camber said gently. He closed the door behind him and leaned against it, warding the chamber from interference with a casual wave of his hand.

"We have to talk, Joram," he said then. "Imre's guards are still outside, and they don't appear to be leaving. Did you tell Cathan what we have been trying to do?"

"No, sir, we decided against it." Joram removed his stole, touched it to his lips, and paused before putting it away in the vestment press. "My God, you don't suppose Imre suspects, do you? He couldn't! There's no way he could know!"

Camber raised an eyebrow. "You were followed from Valoret two days ago, weren't you? He obviously suspects something, though I agree that it seems unlikely he could have put all the pieces together so soon. But he apparently thought that Cathan was involved in something treasonous. Or what happened—wouldn't have happened." He glanced at the floor. "At any rate, and for whatever reason, Imre is taking a hard look at us. I'm not sure we can stand the scrutiny."

Joram sat carefully on the edge of the vestment press. "Are you saying we should give it up?"

"Good God, no! I'm asking you to ride with Rhys to Saint Foillan's *now, today!* If we don't get Cinhil out now, we may not get another chance."

"Now?" Joram whirled on Rhys. "Did you know about this?"

As surprised as Joram, Rhys shook his head. "Sir, I mean no disrespect, but what makes you think we have the chance now? You yourself said that Imre's soldiers are still outside. We can't even use the Transfer Portal in the castle. It's three weeks before we're expected in Dhassa." Dhassa was the free, holy city in the Lendour Mountains—a place where Imre's power could not touch them.

"You'll have to ride the entire way, then," Camber said. "There's an underground passage leading out of this very room; Joram knows where it is. I've already sent a page to secure horses and the other things you'll need. He'll be waiting at the edge of the north woods within the hour."

"You've obviously thought this out," Joram said slowly. "But how are you going to explain our absence, if we leave now?"

"I don't plan to explain it," Camber said, folding his arms across his chest and studying the floor. "As far as the guards are concerned, you'll still be here."

"We'll still— But—" Rhys broke off uncertainly and glanced at Joram, who had frozen at his father's words and now drew himself up stiffly.

"Joram, what is it?" Rhys whispered.

Ignoring Rhys, Joram stared steadily at his father. "Sir, if you have in mind what I think you do—"

"Hear me," Camber interrupted.

His voice was low, but it suddenly crackled with authority. Rhys, who had been about to ask what Camber was talking about, shut his mouth in surprise. Joram was bristling with hostility, though he had not continued speaking, and Rhys could feel the tension suddenly generated between the two. Meekly, he backed off a pace, wanting no part of the clash of wills which he sensed was about to unfold.

"Father—" Joram began again.

"No. Hear me out. I understand your reluctance. But, believe me, I have pondered the moral aspects long and carefully. To be sure, there is deceit, but there are times when such things cannot be avoided."

"They *can* be avoided! Father, I don't think—"

"You don't *think?* Then, you admit that your view is only opinion!" Camber snapped. "You don't *know* that it's morally wrong." He glanced at Rhys briefly, his voice still low, controlled, coolly logical.

"Joram, if there were any other way, you know I would take it. And if you can offer me another option that will not endanger more lives than my way, I shall be delighted to concede. But if we ever hope to see our Haldane on the throne, we must act now. Imre's soldiers are without. Someone suspects something, or they would not still be here, and Cathan would not be dead. Even if Cathan was innocent of conspiracy, we most assuredly are not. We've gone too far to stop now."

Joram, his eyes blazing defiance, had stood stiffly, fists clenched at his sides, throughout Camber's argument, but now he turned his face away and let his shoulders sag. Rhys, mystified at not knowing what the two were arguing about, sensed only that Joram had lost and Camber had won. Wordlessly, he turned to Camber, watching as the older man moved slowly to the side of his son; though he did not touch him.

"I'm sorry, Joram. I understand, believe me. You know that I would never subject you to this if it were not absolutely necessary. Oh, I admit that at first I thought your plan the rash enthusiasm of youth. The arguments I gave you and Rhys nearly two months ago are still valid, logically. But that was before I met Cinhil, and before Cathan was murdered by that man who sits on the throne at Valoret. We have no option but to proceed."

There was a long silence, a period of several heartbeats in which no one moved. Then Joram bowed his head.

"*Concedo*," he murmured.

Muffling a sigh of relief, Camber turned his attention back to Rhys. Before he could speak, however, Joram pulled himself together and laid a restraining hand on his father's arm.

"Rhys, have you understood any of what we've been talking about?" the priest asked.

"Well, frankly, no. I gather that you—don't approve of something on moral grounds, but I . . ." His voice trailed off lamely, and Camber sighed again, rubbing a weary hand across his eyes.

"Rhys, we're talking about shape-changing. Do you know what that is?"

Rhys's lips made an awed O and he blinked in astonishment. "Well, I've read a little about it, of course, but I thought it was only theory. And the sources that say anything about it at all, claim that it's—bl—"

"Black magic," Camber said softly, speaking the words which Rhys only mouthed in awful fascination. The older man cleared his throat, searching for the right words. "Actually, it's considered to be a gray area—a shade more dark than light, perhaps, because it *is* deception; and deception is rarely used except for personal gain. At the risk of sounding hypocritical, I'll maintain that this is a fair example of the end justifying the means. The escape of innocents from danger not of their own doing is a generally accepted defense by all but the most rigid purists."

Joram raised an eyebrow at that and folded his arms across his chest. "I suppose that will suffice for a logical argument for now, though we hardly qualify as innocents."

"But Imre doesn't *know* that yet—he only suspects."

Rhys, nagged by the suspicion that he had just missed something crucial, cleared his throat uneasily. "Just what is it you plan to do, sir?"

"Um, sorry. I assumed you realized. I intend to place your shapes on two of the servants whose presence won't be missed. I'll use Crinan for you, Rhys, and Master Wulpher, the steward, for Joram. Both of them have been loyal retainers of the family from early boyhood, and I know they can be trusted. Also, they're somewhat used to magic, after having been around us for these many years."

"They're not used to *this* kind of magic," Joram said sullenly. "And another thing: I was to read the final rites for burial tonight. Wulpher is not a priest."

"No, but he's a well-read, God-fearing man who loved Cathan very much, and we can give him the knowledge he needs to get by. I know you would rather be the one to do this last thing for your brother, but it's more important that you and Rhys be on your way. You've already performed the essential rites. Besides, there will be other priests here."

"But—"

"I know, son," Camber said gently. And with a sigh, he placed a hand on the shoulder of each man.

"Rhys, would you please find Crinan and Wulpher and bring them here? Don't tell them why I want to see them, just ask them to accompany you. But give me a few minutes with Joram first, will you?"

"Yes, sir." Rhys spoke with difficulty.

Still stunned by what he had heard, and sensing how Joram must be churning inside, judging from his outward lack of composure, Rhys slipped from the sacristy and, outside, leaned his forehead against the door, hands on the latch. He took several deep breaths to calm his racing heart, but his mind refused to approach the topic of shape-changing, ancient fears nibbling around the edges of his soul without discipline until he, at length, applied one of his own charms for calmness and willed his thoughts to order. He felt tranquillity wash over him like a gentle wave. Only then was he able to approach the forbidden area with any degree of rationality.

Shape-changing. . . . He remembered a passing mention of it in an old volume of conjury, of how the conjuror superimposed the image of one person over that of another. The book had mentioned penta-grams and blood circles, and charges to keep evil in-fluences out of the spell, but had not gone into any specifics as to how it was actually done. Another source—now he found himself able to scan his mem-ories like a written index, ferreting out the information he needed—another source had mentioned animal sacrifices and the assistance of demons. He counted that as spurious. Still another text had insisted that shape-changing was not possible at all—though that was obviously false in light of what Camber had just said. Searching through his memory, Rhys found that he could not pin down a single fact about shape-changing. He concluded that he was probably about to learn far more about it than he really wanted to know.

With a sigh, he raised his head and went back into the church. Enough time had passed that Camber and Joram should have resolved any remaining differences. He found the servants easily enough, and managed to get them to the sacristy door without too many ques-tions. He paused only long enough to knock lightly be-fore opening the door and ushering them inside.

The room was aglow with candles, several dozen of them placed about the perimeter and dispelling all sense of gloom or prescience of what was to come. Camber was standing motionless before the vesting altar in one corner of the room, the candles turning his hair to ruddy gold. Joram had his back to them, leaning with both hands on the lid of the vestment press. His shoulders tensed as he heard the door open, but he did not move. As the door closed and the wards were re-established, Camber turned and came to greet the servants.

"Thank you for coming, my friends," he said, extending his hand to each of them in turn.

Crinan clasped the hand nervously, eyes downcast, but Wulpher took it and, kneeling, kissed it, tears welling in his eyes.

"Forgive me for bringing the young master back to you thus, m'lord," the old man croaked, his voice husky with grief. "I promised I would look after him for ye, and I—"

"You are not to blame, old friend," Camber said, tenderly raising the old man up. "I know how you loved my son. Your devotion shall not go unrewarded."

Wulpher could not speak, but nodded gratefully. Crinan, too, swallowed hard and bowed his head.

"But, I did not ask you here for further grieving," Camber said then, glancing at Rhys and signalling with his eyes that he should go to Joram. "I wished to ask if you would be willing to undertake a great risk for the sake of your master's memory. I cannot tell you in detail why I ask what I do, but it would be a final service which you could render. Will you do this for him?"

As the two nodded, eyes wide and awed, Rhys moved silently behind them to touch Joram's arm. The priest nodded, then turned to face them. His expression was calm, composed, his hair silver-pale in the candlelight. His eyes, like Rhys's and the two servants', turned toward his father.

"Very well," Camber said lightly. "It is necessary, I cannot tell you why, for Father Joram and Lord Rhys to leave here now, before the burial tonight and without being seen. This, in itself, presents no problem. Horses and supplies are being prepared even now. However, their presence will be expected at the burial tonight, as well as to be seen casually here on the grounds for the rest of the afternoon, so that the king's soldiers do not become suspicious. Your assistance will give us the time we need."

The two servants looked at one another, then back at Camber. Crinan wet his lips apprehensively.

"You need someone to play their parts, m'lord?"

"Yes."

Crinan looked at Joram and Rhys, at Wulpher, at himself, then back at Camber.

"Begging your pardon, m'lord, but I don't think we look very much like Father Joram and Lord Rhys. Oh, I could maybe pass for Lord Rhys in the dark, but—"

Wulpher, too, had finally found his tongue, and could not contain his skepticism any longer.

"That's right, m'lord. We don't look anything like the young lords."

"I can make you look like them, if you will permit it," Camber said.

His tone was such that both men froze, suddenly suspecting what he was talking about. Wulpher gulped, and when he spoke, his voice was very small.

"By—magic, m'lord?"

Camber nodded, and Crinan, too, swallowed nervously.

"Isn't that—dangerous, sir?"

"Not to you. A little to me, to Joram and Rhys. You would remember nothing of it, once the shape-changing was past. I would restore you to your own forms this evening, after the household has retired for the night."

Crinan coughed nervously, trying to formulate his question. "Ah, what if something goes wrong, sir?"

"With the spell?"

"No, I mean, suppose we're recognized by the king's men?"

Camber smiled, relieved. "You will not be recognized by anyone—not even my daughter, unless I tell her. To all outward appearances, all voice and movement, you will *be* Joram and Rhys. But I would rather not go into details which might alarm you needlessly. Trust that I will not allow you to come to harm, and that I can do what I say. Will you permit this?"

There was a long silence as each man thought about it, and then Wulpher dropped to his knees and bowed his head with a sob.

"I am your man, my lord, and the Lord Cathan's, as I have been since I swore you fealty many years ago. If I can perform this last service for the young master, then I will do it."

"Thank you, Wulpher," Camber murmured, clapping the man on the shoulder and looking across at Crinan. "And you, Crinan? I would not rush your decision, but we haven't much time."

Crinan bowed his head. "This—task that the young lords will undertake— They do not ride to slay the king?"

"They seek no vengeance, Crinan. They ride not to Valoret or to Imre."

"Very well, then, sir. I am also your man. What must we do?"

With a slight smile, Camber offered his hand, then signalled Wulpher to rise.

"Wulpher, I'll ask you to wait outside with Joram for a few minutes. Rhys, please exchange clothes with Crinan."

As the four moved to do Camber's bidding, the Deryni went back to the vesting altar and took up a single candle, staring into its flame for a long time to prepare himself for what was to come. When he was ready, he turned to inspect the room. Rhys was helping a fumbling Crinan with the clasp of the physician's mantle around his shoulders, the physician now wearing the simple riding garb of Cathan's former squire.

"The green of the Healer becomes you, Crinan," Camber said, walking leisurely to stand before Crinan and trying to put the young man at ease.

Crinan swallowed awkwardly, then squared his shoulders and stood a little taller as Camber put the candle in his hands.

Four more candles were placed on the floor, forming a five-foot square inside of which Camber bade Crinan stand. Another candle was procured for Rhys, this one unlighted; and then the two Deryni, Healer and Sage, joined Crinan within the square, Rhys standing to Crinan's right and Camber facing them. Casually, Camber laid his hands on Crinan's where they held the first candle. Crinan flinched.

"Be not afraid," Camber smiled, his voice already lulling his subject to obey. "Thou hast but to gaze

into the flame and let thy thoughts go slack. Relax
and watch the flame, which blocks out thine awareness of ought else within these walls. I shall not leave
thee; thou art safe with me."

Unable to resist, the squire did as he was bidden,
staring deeply into the candle flame as Camber's voice
soothed and silenced. After only seconds, Crinan
swayed slightly, his head drooping lower toward the
flame. Abruptly, Camber tightened his grasp on the
man's hands and extended control. Crinan's eyes
closed as though in sleep.

"Good," Camber breathed, releasing the hands and
looking across at Rhys. "Now, stand while I set the
wards"—he gestured toward the candles of the square,
and a circle of silver light flared around them—"and
we begin."

He lowered his head and murmured a short passage which Rhys could not catch, before blowing out
Crinan's candle with a scarce-breathed "Amen." Then
he held his left hand beside Rhys's darkened candle,
fingers spread slightly. His eyes met Rhys's, calm,
serene.

"Match hand and mind with mine, my friend, and
let your candle flare when we are one."

With a solemn nod, Rhys touched his fingertips to
Camber's, stilling his thoughts that the other might
come in. His eyes slitted shut, the better to exclude
the outer world, and then he was aware of Camber's
palm pressed firmly against his own. In total calm and
all control, he bade the light flare in his other hand,
and felt the still, almost musical resonance he had
come to cherish, as his thoughts meshed with those of
the Master.

Then he was seeing through Camber's eyes, noting
the candle burning steadily in his own left hand, his
right pressed palm to palm with Camber's. He watched
Camber's other hand rise slowly to rest on Crinan's
forehead.

The Master's eyes closed, and there was only the
crystal stillness, the peace, the all-pervading oneness
of the bond they shared. Camber's voice was like the
whisper of leaves rustling in a summer breeze, which

no mere mortal may command; and Rhys knew that what Camber bade would be.

"Behold the light in thy mind's eye," the Master said to him. "It is the essence of thine outward form upon the earth. Extend it now, and let it flow around the man here standing. His visage shall be thine until the need is past, as like to thee as any man may see."

And as he spoke, Rhys felt a soothing lethargy coursing through his limbs, a pulling of energy which tingled on his skin and centered in the hand that held the flame, which now ached to leap the void to Crinan's hands. None saw the mist which gathered round, or watched the fire flare from hand to hand. But suddenly Rhys knew the deed was done, the spell complete.

He staggered as the bond dissolved away, and looked to see his candle dark, the one in Crinan's hands ablaze with light. And as his gaze swept upward to the face, he gasped to see his own. His hands dropped to his sides in wonder; the candle fell forgotten to the floor.

"My God!" was all Rhys could manage to whisper.

Camber smiled distractedly and sighed, the silvery eyes veiled now, shrouded with fatigue. "And no demons or other evil that I could detect," he quipped. "Joram will be pleased."

He passed his hands above the wards and murmured words, and the silver circle died. Then he bent to douse the candle in Crinan's hand, touched the squire lightly on the forehead. Rhys could only stand and watch, speechless with awe, as Crinan's eyelids fluttered wide.

"Crinan, attend us. Look at me."

Crinan did so, his face—or rather, Rhys's face—bewildered. "Did it w—work?" He faltered as he realized the voice was not his own.

Smiling reassurance, Camber took his arm and led him to the vestment press and showed him a small mirror. Crinan gasped and ran his hands over his face; and even the gesture was Rhys's. Rhys shook his head disbelievingly as Camber laid a hand on Crinan's shoulder and calmed him once more.

"Crinan, I'll ask you to assume your role now, and to go outside with Rhys. Then, when you're ready, you're to go back into the church as Rhys, and meditate. I'll join you directly. If anyone tries to make conversation, which I doubt, just do what you think Rhys would do. You'll be guided when there's need."

"I will, sir." The voice was crisp, professional— and Rhys's.

Rhys was still shaking his head as he opened the door and let his double go through.

Joram and Wulpher were directly outside, Wulpher already in a light trance from Joram's ministrations, so the steward did not see the two Rhyses who emerged from the sacristy. But Joram did, and he froze in amazement as the first one, wearing Rhys's clothes, nodded acknowledgment and then went past to wait, hand on the outer door latch; a second Rhys stood hard against the wall.

Joram looked at the second one then, and realized that this must be the real one. But Rhys only shook his head and put a finger to his lips in silence as his double opened the door and went back inside the church.

Rhys himself was still a little dazzled at what had just occurred, though he had been privy to every part of the operation. He watched silently as Joram and the entranced Wulpher disappeared behind the sacristy door, but he did not care to envision what was about to occur. Not that he felt guilty, in any wise, about the deed just done: they had done no wrong. But there was something vaguely disquieting about the whole thing, if only because of the shock of meeting his twin when he knew he had been an only child.

Instead, he went to the spy hole in the door to the church and watched his double kneel by Cathan's bier, saw Evaine touch one hand in compassion before returning to her own devotions. He was still watching a few minutes later when the sacristy door opened and Camber and Joram emerged, neither giving him a second glance as they passed on into the church and knelt together beside the other Rhys. A second Joram stayed in the doorway of the sacristy, and he beckoned to Rhys to join him as the physician turned to stare.

"I'd rather not talk about this until we're well away from here, if you don't mind," Joram murmured, standing aside so that Rhys could enter. "Come, the passageway is open."

An hour later, they were on their way to Saint Foillan's.

Chapter Twelve

For by wise counsel thou shalt make thy war.
—Proverbs 24:6

The burial that evening took its sad course. The words were said, the earth scattered, the gravesite blessed by old Father Jonas, the parish priest, as well as Wulpher/Joram and the two monks who had come with the soldiers from Valoret. Snow had begun falling gently as the grave was closed, softening the harsh outlines of earth and stone and frost-burned sod piled grim in the dancing torchlight. The final psalms floated clear and lonely on the crystalline air. The incense swirled and made a small child sneeze.

After, the folk of the village escorted their beloved lord and his family back to the castle—for Camber had had his son buried in the village churchyard, close by the people he had loved—not in the vaults beneath the keep. The walk was ghostly silent, made more so by the muffling snow which drifted down and glittered in the torchlight, making torches sputter and snap. Only the metallic clink of the soldiers' harness punctuated the slow procession back. Other than that, stunned silence prevailed—a reluctance to speak of the unspeakable, the incomprehensible.

The king's soldiers displayed an unexpected sympathy throughout. Despite their orders to keep Camber and his family under watch, they had also been instructed to interfere as little as possible with the baring of MacRorie grief. And so they merely followed along at the end of the procession, their lieutenant requesting—and receiving—permission from Camber himself to camp that night in the castle yard.

Camber gave his unbidden guests good night and retired to his chambers, the ensorcelled Crinan and Wulpher taking Rhys's and Joram's rooms until Camber should determine that it was safe to release them. Presently, Evaine came to his study, and father and daughter communed as only two Deryni might. When they had finished, they stepped into a corner of the room which glittered with hidden power. Camber wove the magic of a spell, and they were no longer in Caerrorie.

"Where are we?" Evaine whispered, as her eyes adjusted to the near-darkness and she pressed a little closer to her father's side.

Wainscotted walls and ceiling surrounded them at arm's reach all around, covering solid rock such as lay beneath their feet. The walls glowed faintly—arcane wards to keep one's power in, not out. Camber reached out tentatively to explore the fastness of the warding spell, then sighed and withdrew, pressing his daughter's shoulder with his encircling arm.

"Someone will be along directly to let us out," he said in a low voice. "This is the Michaeline Commanderie at Cheltham."

"Will the Vicar General come to meet us?"

"I suspect so, though I doubt he'll be pleased to see us—especially when he hears the news we bring."

Evaine scanned the walls around them—it was getting more difficult to breathe—and acknowledged that it was one of the most secure confinements that she had ever experienced. Even without the wards, this Portal chamber would have been impervious to invasion, for no Deryni could reach through so much solid rock and loose the bolts which held the rock door closed. If no one chose to give admittance, a would-be intruder had but two choices: to stay and slowly suffocate, for there was no ventilation, or to quit the place entirely and go back the way he had come.

That could be a problem, if one had been forced to destroy the Portal used to get here, she realized, as her eyes continued to sweep the panelled walls. If one had no place to go back to, and knew no other portal place, he could die here.

The closeness of the air and walls was growing more oppressive, when there was a scraping of stone against stone before them, and a vibration as the outer rock was unsealed. Then the wall swung back to reveal cold steel thrust into the opening before them—swords held by faceless men in cloaks of midnight blue, their identity obscured by the glare of blazing torches.

Evaine raised her hand to shield against the unaccustomed brightness, trying to see beyond to the shadow forms who stood without. Camber merely stood and closed his eyes, willing them to adjust to the light, but not moving his hands.

There was a brief silence, and then: "It's Lord Camber," a low voice said.

The swords were lowered and the torches withdrawn a space.

As the glare receded, Camber opened his eyes again and stepped forward, his hand on Evaine's elbow. Outside the Transfer Portal, a tall, blue-cassocked man with steel-gray hair was waiting, while three blue-mantled knights of the Michaeline Order sheathed their swords and moved into the background with their torches. Their leader, Alister Cullen, bowed stiffly as Camber saw and recognized him—for he was still wary of the turn of events which had made Camber MacRorie ally instead of adversary, however much he loved and trusted the great man's son. Camber returned the bow, himself a little ill at ease, and gestured toward Evaine.

"My daughter, Evaine, of whom I've spoken," he said, by way of introduction.

Cullen nodded in her direction, as Evaine returned a slight curtsey; then he directed his attention back to Camber, eyes glittering like sea ice, heavy brows nearly meeting on his forehead.

"We had not expected you tonight, Lord Camber. Is something wrong?"

"I'm afraid there's been a change of plans," Camber said. "May I speak freely?" He gestured toward the three Michaelines and raised an eyebrow.

Cullen's mouth set in a firm line. "I will stand pledge for their loyalty. What is it?"

"Joram and Rhys will be at the haven with the prince within four days, if all goes well."

"Four days!" Cullen exclaimed, his composure rattled. "But, we had agreed—it was to be the week before Christmas!"

"I know. We will simply have to adjust somehow. My son Cathan is dead. We buried him but a few hours ago."

Cullen's jaw dropped in shock, and then he closed his eyes and shook his head, crossing himself with a hand which was suddenly a century older than it had been three heartbeats before. The three behind him likewise signed themselves and bowed their heads.

Cullen, when he looked up, was visibly shaken. He yearned to reach out to the shining man and comfort him, to try to ease the pent-up grief; but his hands remained slack at his sides. He could not do that yet. Pride forbade. Through Joram, he had known Camber's resistance to his order for far too long to trust fully so soon. And so he folded his hands together awkwardly and searched for words, sighing at the inadequacy of whatever he might say.

"I'm sorry," he finally murmured. "Joram spoke of his older brother quite fondly, and I always felt I knew him myself, though we never met. How did it happen?"

"We don't know for certain," Camber said quietly. Evaine bit her lip and clasped her father's arm more tightly, blinking back the tears. "The guards who brought his body back to Caerrorie said that he simply collapsed and died with Imre, before the Yule Court last night. The truth is that there was a wound in his chest, however—of a sword thrust or a dagger. He must have died instantly."

A strained silence followed. Then: "Do the guards know who did it?"

"If they know, they will not say," Camber answered. "I believe Imre suspects us of something, though, else the soldiers would not still be in my castle yard. To-morrow, I will have to make some excuse that Joram and Rhys left before dawn, to go into retreat or on some other errand. We've not been formally forbidden to leave the castle, so perhaps the ruse will work. Actually, they left for Saint Foillan's just after mid-day, though the soldiers don't know that. With luck, they should reach the abbey two nights from now."

Cullen's quick mind caught the glossing over of time, the half-omission, and he looked steadily across at Camber.

"You say the guards don't know?"

"I—ah—covered their absence by placing a shape-changing spell on two of the servants," Camber said reluctantly. "I'll restore them when I return."

Cullen's face hardened at the mention of the spell, though he had, in a way, been prepared for such a revelation. Nonetheless, his hand twitched as if longing to move in some protective counter-spell, though he knew that was superstitious nonsense.

"Though I cannot condone your action, I can see the necessity for it," he permitted himself to say. "But, ignore that for the moment. We must make our own preparations. How many people do you intend to bring to the haven?"

"We'll be ten in all: eight family and two servants —the ones I shape-changed; if Imre finds out what I've done, it might not be safe for them to remain be-hind."

"I see," Cullen nodded. "When may we expect you?"

"We'll try to stay at least the four days it will take Joram and Rhys to get Cinhil to safety. If Imre doesn't move against us before then, there should be no diffi-culty. If he does—well, we'll have a problem. If we must escape through our own Portal, and I see no reasonable alternative if we're discovered, we run the risk of Imre placing troops before every known Portal in the kingdom to try to catch us. If he goes that far, I doubt that Joram and the others could reach safety without being captured. We'll just have to do our best to stall."

Cullen nodded thoughtfully. "We can probably cut our safety margin to three days, if necessary. Imre can't close off all the Portals that quickly, even if that occurs to him: we may be giving him credit for more astuteness than he possesses. And there's no way for him to guess that Dhassa is our target. A calculated risk, but it may be our only chance."

Camber controlled a smile, admiring the logic of the man. "How are your preparations? Can your people be ready?"

Cullen turned to the three behind him, his clasped hands behind his back. "You've been listening, Jeb," he said to the tallest of the men. "We're talking about a three-week compression of our timetable. Can you gather the order in three days?"

Jeb, Lord Jebediah of Alcara, Grand Master of the order's military arm, stepped forward with the easy assurance of a trained warrior. "It will require judicious planning to keep down suspicion at the increased Portal activity, Father. But, yes, I think we can do it."

"How many men?" Camber asked.

"Two hundred knights, my lord, carefully dispersed to places of safety until we have need of them." He smiled. "Your own son's prowess with weapons will tell you of their training."

Camber returned the smile, and Cullen nodded. "Nathan?"

The second man, a scar sleek and white along his chin, stepped forward and bowed.

"Provisioning will be finished within a day, Father General. The grain ship arrived this afternoon. We should have it unloaded and transferred to our hidden storerooms by nightfall tomorrow. Everything else is in readiness."

"And the non-combatants?" Cullen asked the third man.

Jasper Miller laid a hand on the Michaeline emblem on his mantle and bowed. "Three days hence, even the king himself will find no servant of Saint Michael upon the land. Until the true king comes again, the Michaelines shall cease to exist."

"You risk much for an untried prince, sir," Camber breathed, marvelling at the man's faith.

"Better the untried prince of a once-noble house than the usurping son of regicides who now sits on our throne!" the man retorted. "The Haldanes were ever friends to our order, and to the people of Gwynedd."

"God grant that they always will be," Camber replied. "And pray that this Haldane comes. It will be two days at best before Joram and Rhys even reach his side, and longer before we see his face. Suppose he is unwilling to take up his crown?"

"He will not fail us," Cullen said. "He *must* not. But in the meantime, our energies were best spent ensuring him a safe haven when he comes. And at Caerrorie—is there ought we can do to ease your work there?"

Camber shook his head. "We'll begin tomorrow to bring through the few things we will need, in small lots. Evaine will help me," he added, laying his hand over his daughter's, who had been watching and listening all the while.

"Very well," Cullen said.

He stroked his chin in a thoughtful gesture, then looked up at Camber with a slightly sheepish expression which seemed doubly out of place on his dour, craggy face.

"Ah, knowing how I feel about the darker aspects of our abilities, you will probably think me addled to ask this, but might I suggest that you leave the shape-changes on the two servants for a few days—since the deed is already done," he added defensively. "It would help to alleviate needless suspicion, and perhaps gain us a little more time."

Camber raised an eyebrow and smiled in spite of himself. "I had not considered it, and might not have mentioned it if I had, but yes, it could be done, provided Crinan and Wulpher are willing—and I see no reason to suspect that they would not be."

Cullen looked very uncomfortable, and cleared his throat uneasily. "Yes, well—ah—good. It should ease matters a little. Are there—ah—any Deryni in the guard contingent?"

"The lieutenant is Deryni. There may be others. I've not spoken with anyone else, however."

"Hmm, well. I don't suppose I need remind you to be careful."

Camber controlled the urge to smile again—he had the distinct feeling that he had taken the measure of the gruff old vicar general, and found himself liking the man—then held out his hand.

"We'd best get back before we're missed. Will you pray for us, Father?"

Cullen, taken by surprise at the request, automatically put his hand in Camber's and clasped it in farewell. "If you truly wish it, my lord," he said, as he realized what he had done. "Though, frankly, I had not thought to hear such a plea from your lips."

"Because of our past differences? I think we both, perhaps, misread the other badly. God keep you, Father."

And as Camber, with his daughter, turned and stepped back across the Portal threshold, he heard Cullen murmur, "And you, my son."

Then they were back in his study at Caerrorie, and the newly widowed Elinor was rushing toward him to fling herself into his arms.

"Thank God, you've returned," she whispered, hugging him close for comfort. "The king's lieutenant wants to see you. I've been stalling him for nearly five minutes."

"Did he say why he wants to see me?" Camber asked, stepping from the Portal and beginning to strip off his outer garments.

"It's snowing harder. He wants to move his men into the hall. I have the distinct impression that they plan to stay longer than just overnight."

"That's splendid," Camber answered, his tone indicating that he did not think it splendid at all. "Where will I find this lieutenant?"

Five minutes later, he was entering the Great Hall, where the lieutenant was waiting, having paused to don a nightrobe and to clear his mind of his recent activities. (After all, the man was a Deryni.)

The lieutenant was pacing the floor before the hearth, rustling the sweet rushes and disturbing the sleep of the hounds sprawled by the fire. Several of his men were gathered silently at the other end of the hall, muffled in great cloaks. Camber took in the scene at a glance as he emerged from the stairwell, then crossed to the hearth. The dogs raised their heads to greet him, but he stilled their motion with a firm hand signal.

"I'm sorry you had to wait, Lieutenant," he said quietly, drawing his robe around him against the cold. "It is my custom to meditate before retiring, especially in times of stress. I'm afraid I have trained my daughters too well that I am not to be disturbed."

"I understand, my Lord Earl." The lieutenant bowed. "I came to ask whether I might move my men into the hall for the night. It's beginning to snow harder. I think we're in for a storm."

"Certainly, sir, though I hope you will not overstay your welcome," Camber said softly. "I'm afraid I haven't the means to house an entire garrison indefinitely."

"Well, I hardly think a score of men constitutes a garrison, my lord—" the man started to protest.

"No, but it is a reasonable substitute at a time like this. And I did not hear you clarify my 'indefinitely,' either. Just how long do you intend to stay?"

The lieutenant looked down in embarrassment. "I'm sorry, my lord. I dislike being here at such a time just as much as you dislike having me here. But I am commanded to remain until I receive further orders. You are acquainted with soldiers, sir, though you were not one yourself. I'm sure you will understand—"

"I understand your orders, sir. I am not that far removed from military matters after twenty-five years at Court. What I do not understand is the reason for those orders. Am I and my household under arrest?"

"Of course, not," the lieutenant said uncomfortably. "We were sent to escort your son's body home in honor, and, I assume, to render you that same honor until it has been determined just what really happened to your son."

"Then, you acknowledge that he did not merely collapse and die, as your instructions first gave you to say?"

"I—er—I am not permitted to discuss that, my lord. I'm sorry."

His voice trailed off, very uncomfortably, and Camber smiled, with a gentle, resigned lifting of one corner of his mouth.

"I suspected as much. You are not to blame," he said. "Please feel free to billet your men here in the hall, by all means. I will have the steward see to building up the fire."

As the man bowed thanks, Camber turned and made his way down the hall, nodding civilly to the soldiers as he passed. One of them, who stood apart and made an especially respectful bow, seemed strangely familiar. When Camber had instructed the steward about the fire, he paused thoughtfully in the shadows at the end of the hall, studying the young man's back. Almost immediately, the man turned and peered in his direction, then glanced casually at his fellows and began to walk slowly toward him. Camber retreated farther into the shadows, to an alcove hidden from the rest of the hall, and waited. The man joined him almost immediately.

"Do I know you, sir?" Camber said, his eyes searching the young man's face.

"Guaire of Arliss, Lord Camber," the young man murmured, going down on one knee. "Your son and I were friends at Court. You probably don't remember me."

"But I do!" Camber replied, taking Guaire's hand and raising him to his feet. "Cathan spoke of you often, and affectionately. But"—he glanced toward the hall—"what brings you here with the likes of them? I thought you were aide to one of the military earls?"

"I was. To Earl Maldred," Guaire nodded. "Only he's dead, killed by an assassin three days ago. That's part of what I came to tell you about. There's something—"

He broke off as Camber glanced beyond him and held a finger to his lips, then led him into a small storage room near the kitchens, away from the growing noise of the hall as the king's men made their camp.

"Are you Der— No, I can see that you are not of us," Camber murmured, taking Guaire urgently by the shoulders. "Young friend, we daren't take much more time. Did you ever link minds with Cathan? Were you and he that close?"

Wordlessly, Guaire nodded, his brown eyes wide.

"Would you be willing to share that bond with me, Guaire?" Camber continued. "I would not ask it if I did not feel it needful."

As Guaire nodded a second time, Camber moved his hands to either side of Guaire's head and closed his own eyes, thumbs resting lightly on the other's temples.

"Then, do it now. Open your mind to me without delay. For Cathan's sake, I beg it."

There was a breathless pause, a lengthening time of stillness, and then Camber was opening his eyes and pulling the younger man into close embrace, staring sightlessly over the other's shoulder as he analyzed what he had seen. Then he put Guaire at arm's length and looked into his eyes. If he had lost a son, he had gained a worthy friend—though one more human, he could never hope to find.

And now he knew, too, that he was doing what had to be done. There was no proof yet that the king had killed; but there was little doubt in Guaire's own mind that Imre was, in some way, responsible—or that Cathan's own kinsman, Coel Howell, had had a heavy hand in what happened at Valoret.

Camber smiled and clasped Guaire's shoulders reassuringly, then glanced out of the storage room to see if the way was clear.

"You'd best get back. I'll wait until you've gone."

"Aye, sir. I'll bring you word when other orders arrive. They'll not take you by surprise."

"God bless you, son," Camber murmured, as the young man slipped back into the passageway and out of sight.

Camber waited for several minutes, composing himself to traverse the hall again, to be certain he would give no inkling of what he had just learned. Then he left the tiny chamber and made his way back through the hall, nodding distractedly to the men as they stood at his passage, some of them saluting him courteously. The dogs stirred as he came near the fireplace, but he stayed them with his hand as he continued on. He did not see Guaire in the hall, but a very young soldier stood and bowed as he approached the foot of the newel staircase.

"Thank you for allowing us inside, m'lord," the young man said, tugging at his forelock. " 'Tis no fit night for man nor beast to be outside."

Camber glanced up at the high windows, saw them rattling under the attack of the storm, and nodded acknowledgment as he stepped past the man. And as he made his way up the stairs to his chambers, he thought about his son and son-to-be, riding the road to a distant abbey in the storm; and of the other son, whom he would never see again except in dreams, who slept outside beneath the storm's reach, in the growing cold of an early grave.

He did not sleep until very late.

CHAPTER THIRTEEN

For your hands are defiled with blood.
—Isaiah 59:3

The next two days were spent, for the most part, in uneasy seclusion, awaiting further royal reaction which did not come. Receiving no new orders to the contrary, the king's men stayed on, trying to intrude as little as possible on the MacRories' grief, but they were forced by the worsening weather to remain close in the hall. Camber was a gracious host under the circumstances, going out of his way to see that the men's physical needs were provided, but relations grew strained as the days wore on. He spoke once more with Guaire, on the second day, when the waiting had grown almost intolerable, but their meeting was short, and nearly interrupted by Guaire's lieutenant. Besides, the young lord had nothing to add beyond what he had already made known to Camber. Further evidence of familiarity could only breed suspicion where there was none as yet.

The residents of Caerrorie were careful not to engender such suspicion, either. Below stairs, nothing occurred which was not in keeping with the expected behavior in a household recently bereft of its eldest son. Life went on, but in a subdued fashion. The growing tension in those who waited did not manifest itself within the sight of the royal guards.

But above stairs, where the guards were not invited, preparations continued at near-fever pitch. Camber and Evaine spent hours gathering and transporting the few belongings they deemed essential for their impending exile, and briefing the others—Elinor, James —on the method, if not the precise reason, for their escape. Wulpher/Joram and Crinan/Rhys remained in their chambers except for meals and family devotions, engaged, as Camber explained to the guard lieutenant, in prayer and meditation for the soul of their departed brother. In point of fact, both spent the greater part of their time in dreamless Deryni trance, both to keep them safely out of sight and possible discovery, and to conserve their strength. Camber's spell had never been intended to last so long, and had to be reinforced periodically.

And elsewhere, others made preparations and played their various waiting games.

In the haven, the Brothers of Saint Michael completed the last of their provisioning for the long winter exile ahead, dispersing the noncombatant brethren and arranging for the safe billeting of the militant arm of the order.

At Dhassa, four Michaeline knights set up a watch to be certain that three very important riders would reach safety without mishap.

In Valoret, a tense Deryni conspirator, unwittingly playing both sides of a desperate game, perused five reconstructed pages from a parish register and sent out his agents to learn more about the only three names on those pages which appeared to be connected: members of a family named Draper—Daniel and Royston and Nicholas. And so the time passed. . . .

But if the days were taut for MacRories and Michaelines and a wayward Deryni lord, they were as nothing beside the misery of their king and liege lord, Imre. Grief stalked the towers of the royal apartments like an uninvited specter, wept and raged and hoarded vengeful thoughts in the keep of the House of Festil.

The king, his senses no longer dulled to gray oblivion by the balm of too much wine, spent the day of Cathan's funeral thrashing in sweat-soaked delirium, the fire in his brain assuaged but little by the

tender ministrations of his sister. Sick with the after-
effects of wrung emotions, as well as the spirits he had
consumed, unable to draw the strength to quell his
pain arcanely, too proud to ask another's aid to ease
the ache which lay upon him like a stifling mantle, he
brooded in the sunless rooms and bore his suffering
with an ever-sharper temper, terrorizing the servants
until they feared to venture past the outer threshold.

Only Ariella seemed to understand, as she had always comprehended, from his youngest childhood days.
And that, too, plagued him: the dimly recalled memory of her body next to his; their passion; a quirk of
conscience urging condemnation while another, more
fleshly part of him still yearned for her again.

In the end, he succumbed—though that, too,
brought him little comfort for the rending in his soul.
For two full days he kept his morbid isolation within
his sister's chambers, seeing no one but her, taking
little food, sleeping less, and indulging in hysterical
fits of weeping rage at fate, at Maldred and Rannulf for letting themselves be slain, at Cathan for his
betrayal, at Coel for telling him about it and compelling him to act, and at God, who had somehow
conspired to make a shambles of Imre's world.

It was with full knowledge of this indulgence in
kingly self-pity that Coel Howell dared to approach
the royal apartments on the afternoon of the second
day—with that knowledge, and armed with protection
in the form of a handful of new parchment scrolls ob-
tained but lately from his scribes.

He was received in Ariella's presence chamber,
where the king sat in fur-lined robes before a roaring
fire. Imre was strained and nervous—one had only
to watch the tremor in his hands to ascertain that—
but his mental faculties had not been impaired, and
he listened to Coel's findings with great attention.
Ariella sat on a cushioned stool at his side, her hand
resting negligently on his shoulder, her darting eyes
missing no nuance. When Coel had finished, Imre
perused the scrolls superficially, then handed them to
his sister.

"Birth records of a father and son," he said, furrowing his brow. "Why the interest in them, and why now?"

Coel frowned. "I don't know, Sire. The father, Royston, has been dead for more than twenty years. But *his* father, Daniel, died only a few months ago. In fact, Rhys Thuryn was his physician—which makes me wonder why he and MacRorie stole the records. I can only surmise that it was because of something the old man said on his deathbed."

"How about the son, this Nicholas? Does he still live?" Imre asked.

"Unknown, Sire. If he *is* still alive, he did not follow the profession of his father or grandfather—at least not in this city. He seems to have disappeared shortly after his father's death. It's possible that he died of the plague as well."

Ariella coughed and turned her attention entirely on Coel. "This Daniel Draper, who died recently—who was he?"

"A merchant in woolens, Your Highness. He apparently did moderately well in his trade, paid his debts, and left his goods and business to his apprentice, one Jason Brown—which would seem to indicate that his grandson was either estranged or dead. Other than that, no one seems to know much about him. He was in his eighties, after all. Most of his contemporaries died long ago."

"His contemporaries," Imre repeated. "I wonder . . ."

"Beg pardon, Sire?"

"His contemporaries . . ." Imre said again. "If he was as old as you claim, he was probably alive in my great-great-grandfather's time. He may even have lived through the Coup."

"Do you see a connection?" Ariella asked.

"Probably not. Still—"

Imre cocked his head to one side and then rose thoughtfully to begin pacing slowly back and forth across the room. Ariella watched him curiously, a little possessively. Coel wondered what Imre was driving at.

"Alive at the time of the Coup," Imre murmured,

thinking out loud. "And Thuryn and MacRorie have stolen the birth records of his son and grandson. Coel, what does this suggest to you?—the theft of the records, I mean."

"That they . . . were trying to establish a line of legitimate descent?" Coel ventured.

"Correct." Imre nodded, picking up a stylus from the table and gesturing to make his point. "But for whom? A family of woolen merchants? We're missing something here. There's something we're overlooking. But what?"

"What about the books, Imre?" Ariella said, after a long pause, obviously thinking in tandem with her brother now. "Coel, did you not say that Thuryn had consulted certain volumes in the royal archives?"

"Yes, Highness."

"That's right." Imre stopped his pacing. "Coel, what volumes were they? From what time?"

Sensing the direction Imre's thoughts were taking, Coel consulted his notes, then looked up in fascination. "From the time of the Coup, Sire."

"And why," Imre whispered to the room at large, "why would Thuryn be interested in such books, when his accomplice has stolen records to prove the legitimate descent of a man possibly living now, unless they hoped somehow to forge a link with the past?" He whirled to point the stylus at Coel like a weapon. "What link were they trying to form? Who was this mysterious Daniel Draper *before* he became a merchant in woolen cloth?"

"I—don't know," Coel stammered, uncertainty hampering his speech.

"But one can guess," Ariella stated, her voice edged with steel. "They plot against you, Imre. They seek to establish a link with the past, with the old regime, perhaps with the Haldane line itself! It would be fascinating to learn whether any pages were removed from the volumes Thuryn used. And if there are, and they deal with the old nobility—" She bared her teeth in a predatory smile. "Then I think we have certain evidence of a MacRorie conspiracy."

Coel, thunderstruck at the turn of logic she had

taken, bowed deeply as his mind raced to catch up with all the implications. If Ariella's reasoning was sound, then Cathan MacRorie undoubtedly *had* been involved in his brother's treachery, and Coel's position was considerably reinforced. He allowed himself a slight smile as he straightened from his bow.

"I will investigate the possibility, Your Highness. In the meantime, all of the MacRories are under surveillance at Camber's seat at Caerrorie, where they gathered for Cathan's funeral. Do you wish Thuryn and Joram MacRorie brought in for interrogation?"

Ariella nodded briskly. "An excellent idea. Imre?"

But Imre had moved to stare stiffly out a window at the mention of Cathan's name, his chestnut hair silhouetted darkly against the snowfall, his hands clenched tightly at his sides. Ariella, realizing that he had resumed his previous depression, started toward him to try to comfort him, but he whirled before she could reach him, and stood glaring both at her and at Coel.

"Arrest them all," he said in a low voice.

"Thuryn and Joram *and* Camber, Sire?" Coel asked, with some surprise.

"I said *all,* Coel," the king repeated, his eyes glowing with an almost hysterical light. "You were right about Cathan." He swallowed heavily. "And doubtless you are right about the rest. I want *all* the MacRories in chains by nightfall, do you understand? *All* of them! There is not one who can be trusted!"

The royal warrant actually reached Caerrorie just past suppertime, when all of Camber's family had gathered in his study, ostensibly for evening devotions.

Guaire of Arliss was dicing with the lieutenant and two of the other officers when the courier arrived, and even as the man approached, he knew how the message must read. He controlled the urge to glance over his shoulder at the doorway to the newel-stair leading to Camber's chambers, forced himself to maintain an appropriate air of detached boredom as the lieutenant broke the seal and scanned the missive. He had already decided what he must do, if it came to this, so he was fully prepared for the lieutenant's next words.

"It's a warrant for the arrest of the entire household, to bring all the MacRories back to Valoret for questioning," he said, reaching down to gather his sword and baldric from the rushes. "Sergeant, see to the security of the hall. You men, come with me."

He gestured in Guaire's direction and slipped the baldric over his shoulder as he stood, waiting while his men armed themselves. Then he picked up the order once more and headed for Camber's stair. If he noticed that Guaire had made certain to get there before him, he gave no sign of it. Consequently, Guaire was the first to reach the door. The others stood back a few paces, all but two of them around the curve of the staircase, as Guaire, at the signal of the lieutenant, rapped gloved knuckles against the heavy oak.

"My Lord Earl?"

For a moment, the only sounds were those of the men's breathing in the close stairwell, a few furtive clinks of metal against stone, and then the door opened.

Camber stood in the doorway, his body blocking vision of the rest of the chamber. His eyes flicked over Guaire seemingly without particular recognition, then came to rest on the guard lieutenant two steps farther down the stairwell. Guaire knew that the glance had been far from inconsequential.

"May I assist you in some way, Lieutenant?"

His words were the essence of courtesy, and the lieutenant cleared his throat uneasily before extending the order he had just received.

"I have a warrant for your arrest, sir. You and your family, and especially your son Joram and the Healer they call Rhys Thuryn. By order of His Grace, King Imre of Festil."

There was a skipped heartbeat in which no one moved or breathed, and then Camber slowly reached out and took the parchment. Behind Camber, Guaire thought he detected the sound of furtive movement, but he could not be sure. The lieutenant, his Deryni senses more keen than Guaire's, evidently heard it, too, for he came up another step and laid his hand on the hilt of his sword as Camber read the missive.

"There is no provision for question, sir," the lieutenant said, as Camber reached the bottom of the sheet and took in the royal seal. "I must ask you to step outside now, and to open the door. We don't want to use force, but we will if we must."

"Yes, I'm certain you would, Lieutenant," Camber said, a little sadly, Guaire thought.   -

He started to open the door further, James appearing at his side and looking very grave, and for a moment Guaire thought he meant to surrender, after all. Then he noticed that James's sword arm was hidden behind the door, and that there were fewer people in the room behind Camber and James than there should have been.

But before that could register with the lieutenant, James was bursting past Camber and pushing the lieutenant down into the arms of his waiting men, while Camber dashed back into the room to bundle Father Joram and Lord Rhys into a corner of the room, where they promptly disappeared—all three!

Then Guaire and James were holding the stair at swords' length, keeping the lieutenant and his men at bay in the narrow stairwell while flashes of light behind them told only that something arcane was going on, which Guaire did not care to know anything more about.

He parried a sword thrust and slashed at a wrist, to send a second adversary screaming down the stairwell into the arms of his comrades with a nearly severed hand. James took another by surprise and ran him through the thigh, pushing the wounded man back so he only narrowly missed impalement on one of his own weapons.

Guaire glanced over his shoulder to see the Lady Evaine pop into existence in that same corner of the room where Camber had just disappeared, and then he was fighting for his life again, warding off a concerted rush from two of his former fellows who had somehow managed to slip past James and his adversary and both attack at once. When he had remedied that situation, and could hazard another glance behind him, he was just in time to see Camber emerge from the corner of the room and herd the Lady Elinor and her younger son into the space with Evaine. Then the women and the child were gone, and Camber was the only one in the room; and he was dashing toward them and shouting at Guaire to look out.

A stabbing pain in his side brought his attention back to the stairwell—too late to avoid the lieutenant's blade. He felt a searing wetness all down one side of his body as the lieutenant withdrew apace, his blade crimsoned with blood Guaire knew was his own.

But then sweet reprisal was upon the lieutenant in the form of Jamie's sword. The man staggered back with blood spurting from severed jugular and carotid, a scream gurgling in his throat. The damage to Guaire was already done, but even as the young lord started to crumple, he found himself being whisked into the strong arms of Camber and borne toward that same corner of the room where such strange things had been happening only seconds before.

James slammed the door and dashed to join them, but as the door gave under the fresh onslaught of men from below stairs, Guaire's world began fading to a blissful shade of gray. Just before he lost consciousness, he had a sickening, swooping sensation, as though he were falling, and a blast of pure, brilliant energy which nearly held back the darkness. For just that instant, he could have sworn that Camber glowed.

CHAPTER FOURTEEN

*Blessed shall they be that shall be in those
days,/He bringeth back His anointed.*
                                        —Psalms of Solomon 18:6

In another part of the kingdom, darkness came
early that night. The wind drove a new storm through
the mountain passes, turning the twilight to white-
shrouded blankness as two riders approached the fastness of Saint Foillan's Abbey.

They had met no one on their ride that day. The
road was little travelled once the Yuletide season had
begun, and there had already been more snow than
was normal for this time of year. Even without the impending storm, the way would have been difficult.
With the drifts growing higher by the hour, most men
would have deemed the journey impossible, and have
waited until the spring.

Joram and Rhys were counting on that, reckoning,
rightly, that even if Imre could have discovered their
intent by now, word of their flight could not have
reached Saint Foillan's before them—and might not
now until the spring thaws came.

But this knowledge did little to ease their minds
about the immediate problem. Somehow, they must
enter the abbey confines undetected, find Prince Cinhil,
and bring him out without being apprehended. Though
they had reviewed their plans and all their combined
knowledge of the place at least a dozen times in the
past two days, with a thoroughness possible only for
Deryni, they still could not know in advance what

human agents might unwittingly shatter the best laid of their plans.

It had been dark for several hours when they drew rein in the shadow of the abbey's outer wall. The moon had gone behind a heavy cloudbank, and would likely remain there for some time.

Rhys huddled closer in his fur cloak—white, to help him blend into the snowbanks—then turned in his saddle to pull the extra horse in beside him. All of the animals were hooded and blanketed in white, both for protection against the elements and for camouflage, and in the dimness he could hardly see Joram, sitting his horse not four feet away.

Joram swung down and secured his horse to a stump of winter-blasted tree, then moved to lay a hand on Rhys's bridle.

"Our timing is good so far," he whispered. "They dare not ring the abbey bells at this time of year because of snowslides, but it must be close to Compline. Remember, no more talking until we're out. Sound carries."

And that was not the *only* kind of communication they had agreed not to use, Rhys reflected, as he dismounted and began taking another fur cloak and a pair of woolen leggings from the spare horse's saddle. Even their Deryni mind-speech must be used sparingly, if at all. The *Ordo Verbi Dei* was not a Deryni order, but there might be a few individual Deryni in it. And if one of them should be in deep meditation and chance to catch a careless word . . . It was not likely, but it was possible. And far too much was at stake to risk all on a chance which could be avoided.

He moved close against the wall and watched as Joram drew out a coil of braided cord ending in a leather-padded, three-pronged throwing hook. The priest spent several seconds ordering the coil, arranging the loops to his satisfaction. Then he stepped carefully out a few paces from the wall and looked up. Rhys glanced back the way they had come and was relieved to note that he could not see the horses.

The snow was falling harder now, and the snowflakes caught and glittered in Joram's furred hood. After a studied appraisal of the wall, the priest swung the padded hook on its cord and flung it up and over. There was a muffled clunk as it hit the other side a few feet below the edge, and immediately Joram darted back to the shelter of the wall to freeze and listen, gradually raising his head only when he was certain that the slight sound had aroused no alarm. Slowly, he began pulling on the cord—then stifled an oath as the hook failed to catch, and came tumbling back, nearly on his head.

The process was repeated three more times before the hook held. But then they were very quickly up the wall and over. A narrow catwalk ran along the inner edge of the wall, and snow-caked steps led to the ground a few paces to the left. Soon they were safely on the ground and huddled in the shadows between two outbuildings, their escape cord firmly anchored to the edge of the wall and camouflaged in the shadow of a seam in the stone.

In the next twenty minutes, the two worked their way through the south applegarth and over the nearest footbridge, then past the lay brothers' range, the cellarer's yard, and under the very windows of the darkened abbot's hall; past the abbot's yard and across a final expanse of open court; and then they were crouching in the darkness of the abbey's outer porch, listening for any sound of activity within.

Through here lay the safest route to their quarry— provided, of course, that Saint Foillan's followed the traditional monastic building plan. Along the nave and up the night stair, they should reach the monks' sleeping quarters and the tiny cell where Rhys had last seen Cinhil. (The Healer did not even wish to consider what would happen if they could not reach Cinhil through the abbey proper. If they had to go through the abbot's hall and cloister yard, the way Rhys and Camber had gone to see Cinhil the first time—no, better not even to think of that for now.)

A sudden twinge of panic seized Rhys, a fear that he was a child playing at a very dangerous man's game, but he forced the feeling down and concentrated upon removing his cloak, on bundling it with Joram's and the one for Cinhil in the darkest corner of the porch.

Then he was hovering anxiously at Joram's elbow as the other slid a slender dagger from his boot top, knelt beside the entry door, and slipped the thin blade deftly between door and jamb until the latch gave with a satisfying *snick*.

Flashing a grim smile, Joram sheathed the dagger and eased the door a crack, peering into the dimness for a long time. Finally he whispered, "Clear," and glanced at his partner.

The word was more breathed than spoken, and as he edged the door open enough to slip through, he motioned Rhys into the shadows to the right of the nave. A short pause, just long enough to relatch the door, and he was kneeling behind a column with Rhys to scan the long expanse of nave, straining to pierce the gloom which the few candles only barely touched.

They watched for a long time, studying the arrangement of pillars and side chapels and occasional funeral effigies along the clerestory aisle. A processional door was given their fleeting attention, but then they cast wary eyes on the lay brothers' stair, which disappeared into the darkness to their right. There was no need to fear the door, for it was used only by day; but the stairway was an entirely different matter. If some zealous lay brother, seeking extra devotions, should slip down those stairs undetected before they could gain the relative safety of the south transept, they would surely be discovered. They must penetrate beyond the nave altar, with its revealing candles and exposed approach and its side chapels potentially housing hostile monks. And once that was accomplished, there still remained the other night stairs, which led to Cinhil's cell. Best not to think of that yet, either.

Touching a finger to his lips, Joram glided to the foot of the lay brothers' stair and peered up into the darkness, casting out with his Deryni senses for some indication of movement above. But there was none, save the slight echo of snoring. This early after Com-

pline, most of the brethren should be getting what
meager sleep the Rule allowed such an order. From
now until Matins, well after midnight, should be the
quietest time for the entire abbey.

With an inclination of his head, Joram gestured for
Rhys to follow, then began making his silent way down
the side aisle, staying close to the wall, taking advantage of every possible shadow. The first of the side
chapels lay ahead, flanking the nave altar.

The chapels on the left were empty—they could
see that already—their recesses dimly lit by Presence
lamps and the banks of vigil candles guarding the nave
altar itself. Behind the main altar, the brass interlace
of the rood screen glowed darkly in the candlelight,
mostly in shadow. Beyond that stretched the rest of
the nave, with more side chapels, and the choir looming in the transept crossing. The night stairs they were
seeking lay in the south transept itself, hard against
the west wall. So far there was no sign of movement,
but they could not count on that until they had made
certain.

They reached the side wall of the first chapel on the
right, and Joram peered gingerly around the corner
and inside.

Deserted.

The process was repeated with the second.

Again, deserted. Thus far, their luck was holding.

They crossed the second chapel, venturing as close
to the rood screen as they dared, to peer up the rest
of the nave and scan the north chapels before venturing further into the open for the breaching of the
screen itself. But the remainder of the nave appeared
to be clear, and the darkened choir showed no sign of
movement. If anyone was stirring in the cloistered
portion of the church, they could only hope that whoever it was would stay safely in the apse, far beyond
the transept and the stairs which Rhys and Joram
sought. Neither man wanted to have to desecrate a
church by harming anyone within its precincts—and
both men knew, though they had never voiced it, that
they *would* kill, if necessary, to ensure Cinhil's safe
removal from Saint Foillan's.

They crouched and listened for several minutes, finally satisfying themselves that all was still. Then Joram eased his way behind the altar to the rood screen and laid his hand on the gate latch, cursing silently under his breath as the thing resisted and he realized it was locked. He cast a tense look at Rhys, who was anxiously scanning back the way they had come; then he knelt and laid his hands on the locking mechanism and extended his senses around it. After a few seconds, which only *seemed* interminable, the latch moved in Joram's hands. But before he could begin easing the gate open, wondering whether it would squeak, he caught Rhys's frantic hand signal out of the corner of his eye and flattened himself against the back of the altar.

Now he, too, could hear the *slap-slap* of sandal-clad feet moving up the nave. The man was alone, for which Joram thanked Providence, but if he continued on his present course he would soon be abreast of Rhys's hiding place. Silently, Joram willed the man to move into one of the first side chapels—he *had* to choose one of the first side chapels, or Rhys would be discovered.

He was never precisely certain, later, whether he or Rhys had any influence over the choice made by the hapless lay brother. But for whatever reason, the monk paused only briefly to bow before the nave altar, then moved noisily into the first chapel on the right, next to the one where Rhys was hiding. After several minutes, in which there was no further sound from the chapel in question, Joram eased his way to the left of the altar and peeped around the corner.

He could not see into the chapel where the monk must be—but that was good, because it meant that the monk could not see him, either. Rhys had crept silently to the wall common to the two chapels and was peering around the edge when Joram looked out. After a moment, he withdrew and glanced at Joram, giving a slight nod of his head. If the monk's suspicions should be aroused now, at least Rhys could silence him before he could give the alarm.

With a deep breath to steady his nerves, Joram

moved back to the rood screen and turned the latch. No sound came from the metal as he eased the gate back far enough to enter. Thank God for the monks' industry; the hinges were well oiled and silent. They gained the relative shelter of the next side chapel without mishap, leaving the rood-screen gate closed but not latched as they passed into the domain of the cloistered monks.

A sound from the direction of the occupied chapel froze them in the shadows, and they watched unmoving as the monk shuffled before the nave altar to bow again. They had about decided that the man meant to pray there forever, when he bowed again and moved into a chapel on the other side of the nave. Grateful for that, at least, Joram and Rhys turned their attention to the tasks ahead. They dared not worry where the man might be when they had to come out again, or that next time there might be more than one.

They were within the cloister precincts now, and doubly damned should they be caught. Creeping past the great processional door—barred now—which led, by day, from cloister garth to church, they found their way blocked by yet another brass grillework. Joram had already dismissed it, and was moving on to try entrance through the choir, when Rhys laid his hand on the gate and felt it move under his hand. Sending the briefest and weakest of calls to Joram, he swung back the gate and slipped through. Joram, startled, doubled back and followed him through the gate to crouch silently at the foot of the night stairs. Rhys's shoulder pressed hard against his as they peered up the stairway into the darkness.

"Now?" Rhys mouthed silently.

For answer, Joram took a deep breath and nodded resolutely. Then they began making their cautious way up the stairs.

The door stood open at the top, and another, narrower stair continued upward from the landing beside the door. They listened for several minutes, but other than the sounds of sleep, they heard only the creak of the building itself as the snow settled on the leaded roof. Now they must find Cinhil and bring him safely out.

There was a single vigil light burning at the top of the stairs, but it cast only scant illumination down the long dormitory. Straining to see in the dimness, Rhys led Joram slowly past the first of the curtained sleeping cubicles, moving to the right of the chests and shelves ranged down the center of the room. Cinhil's cell was the fifth from the end—Rhys had marked it well on his last visit here—and as he paused in the curtained entryway, Joram pulled two spare white robes of the professed brothers from a stack just outside.

Stealthily they entered the cell, to stop with pounding hearts until Joram had conjured a tiny sphere of handfire. By its light, Rhys moved toward the head of the narrow pallet and leaned close enough to verify the sleeper's identity. Then they were pulling on the robes over their clothes, Joram nudging the handfire near while Rhys bent to gaze at their sleeping quarry's face. Gently, he sought to touch Cinhil's mind, hoping to ease the man from sleep to deep control without awakening him.

But the touch was not gentle enough, or Cinhil's sleep not so deep as they had thought. Cinhil's eyes popped open with a start; he was fully awake at once. And when he saw two figures bending over him, illuminated by the ghostly glow of Joram's handfire, his immediate and natural impulse was to panic.

Rhys had clamped his hand against the monk's mouth at the first sign of movement, so Cinhil could make no outcry; but now the monk was trying to twist from under his hand, legs kicking frantically underneath his thin blanket. Joram threw himself across Cinhil's body to hold him quiet, pinning arms and legs while Rhys tried to force control, but the Healer could not seem to get through. It was as though the shields which he had sensed before grew doubly strong under assault, to keep Rhys from even touching the mind behind those shields. Clearly, they would not take Cinhil this way. And if they did not subdue him in the next few seconds, his struggling would awaken his brethren all around him.

It was a time for drastic measures.

Without further waste of motion, Rhys clamped his free hand across the Prince's throat and applied carotid pressure, not relenting even when Cinhil's body arched a final time before going limp beneath his hands. There was resistance still, as Rhys extended his senses, Cinhil's shielding of memory and intellect remaining intact; but his center of consciousness, at least, was taken.

Securing control as he had on his previous visit, Rhys straightened carefully and allowed himself a scarce-breathed sigh of relief. Joram cast a nervous glance at the curtained doorway as he picked himself up.

There had been no sound outside, no indication that their scuffle with Cinhil had awakened the other monks. Nonetheless, they waited for several strained minutes to make certain. Finally, Rhys bent and pulled the unconscious Cinhil to his feet, got a shoulder under his arm. He watched anxiously as Joram let the light vanish and peered out the curtains. Miraculously, the dormitory still echoed only to the sounds of snoring men.

They slipped out the way they had come, Cinhil between them, keeping close to the shelves and chests until they reached the vigil light again. They had just stepped onto the landing when Joram froze in a listening attitude, then motioned urgently for Rhys to get their unconscious burden up the stairs toward the tower. As Rhys struggled to obey, he could hear the sounds of sandal-clad feet approaching the night stairs from below.

There must have been monks in the east end of the church all this time!

Not daring to breathe, they eased their way up the spiral staircase past the first bend, to huddle motionless as the feet ascended the night stairs. They heard no conversation, nor did they expect to, and at length the footsteps faded away into the dormitory. They waited for several minutes, in case the monks just returned had come to awaken replacements for some all-night vigil, but no further sound came from above or below the night stairs. Finally, they gathered the courage to bundle their senseless charge down the stairs and through the transept gate, to shrink breathlessly against the closed processional door and listen again for a long moment.

The next half-hour was later to be remembered only hazily by both of those conscious enough to recall it at all. They were able to make their way back through the rood screen without being detected, and actually gained the shelter of the last side chapel. But their plans were nearly foiled by the approach of another lay brother from the stairs at the west end of the nave.

Joram heard him long before he came into view, for the man coughed and wheezed asthmatically all the way down the stairs. But there was nowhere to hide. Quickly, they arranged the unconscious Cinhil on one of the *prie-dieus*, Rhys kneeling to support him while Joram hid in the shadows at the back corner.

But it was not sufficient to fool the old brother who came shuffling down the nave. One look at the pair kneeling in the side chapel was enough to convince him that something was amiss. After all, the two wore the white robes of professed monks, not the gray of the lay brethren. Not that there was anything wrong with the monks using the lay brothers' area of the church—especially in deep winter, when there was not likely to be an outsider on the premises. But the lay brother, being the friendly, talkative sort, was curious as to who the two monks might be, kneeling in what he had come to think of as *his* chapel.

And naturally, he had to ask them.

He had time only to gaze in astonishment at the fierce, redheaded stranger who looked up from beneath his cowled hood, and at Brother Benedictus, who appeared to be asleep. Then there was another brother standing behind him and taking him by the shoulders—a tall, golden man with piercing eyes which bored into his and made his head spin.

As he sank to his knees, oblivious to all around him,

his memory of the entire encounter conveniently fled. He would awaken during Matins, when the rest of the brethren joined him in the great nave, joints stiff and aching from the hours he had spent kneeling in the cold church, unable to explain what urgent need he had felt to spend his night in prayer. . . .

By the time the abbey was rousing for the Great Office of the Night, Joram and Rhys were lowering their precious burden over the wall, wrapped once again in their white fur cloaks, their quarry bundled into a similar cloak and bound hand and foot to his horse for his long, unconscious ride.

The snow fell more heavily now, erasing all sign of their passage, and they rode with their backs to the storm, Cinhil's horse between them on a double lead. They would ride thus until tomorrow night, with stops only as necessary, until they reached the relative safety of Dhassa. There, if all went well, they would make their way to the Portal held by the Bishop of Dhassa. By now, it was probably the only Portal which was not barred to them, one way or another. They should be safe in Camber's haven by this time tomorrow night.

But for now, there remained only to ride, and to try to keep the cold a thing apart, that they might eventually reach Dhassa alive and uncaptured. If the hue and cry had been raised against them in the past three days since Cathan's burial, as it well might have, they would have to be doubly careful. Capture now would be certain disaster for their new and fragile cause.

CHAPTER FIFTEEN

*I have forsaken mine house, I have left
mine heritage.*
—Jeremiah 12:7

As it happened, they were never in any real danger
on the journey to Dhassa, for news travels slowly
across winter-bound Gwynedd. But Rhys and Joram
learned a great deal about their captive in the course
of their ride.

The first few hours, and those most crucial to their
escape, were accomplished under cover of darkness
and the gradually slackening storm—that and the
snow-filtered moonlight which slowly faded as gray
dawn approached. The snow layered everything with
a drifting powder which muffled sound and concealed
their tracks; but it also concealed holes and buried
branches—hazards to the horses, who stamped and
shied at every snap of snow-laden bough. Their unconscious captive, bound hand and foot to his horse
between his two abductors, had a less than gentle ride.

They had been riding without speaking for some
time, alternating between a trot and a brisk walk,
snatching what fitful naps they could, when Rhys first
became aware that he was being watched. He had
been drifting on the edge of consciousness while the
horses walked, mentally rehearsing what they would
do and say when they reached the Dhassa gate the
next evening. To discover the gray eyes observing
him, albeit somewhat dazedly, gave him a start in that
first instant of realization.

He flashed a reassuring smile at the man, mentally chasing the cobwebs of sleep from his mind, but the gesture brought no response other than the continued fogged appraisal—and perhaps a glimmer of recognition.

Raising an eyebrow at that, Rhys glanced across at the still-dozing Joram, hunched down in the saddle and swaying easily with the motion of his mount. Though he knew that Joram needed the sleep—they had been largely without for nearly thirty-six hours now—it was important that they establish communication immediately. He suspected from Cinhil's expression that the monk remembered who he was.

"Joram, we have company again," he said in a low voice.

Joram raised his head immediately, to become instantly alert and awake as only Joram seemed to be able to do, and their captive turned his head to blink at his other escort.

"Why have you brought me out of Saint Foillan's?" he asked, without giving Joram time for amenities. "Who are you?"

The priest studied the fur-hooded face for several seconds, apparently considering how best to answer the question, then decided on the truth.

"My name is Joram MacRorie. I'm a Michaeline priest. As for why we have brought you out of Saint Foillan's, that should be abundantly clear, my lord—or should I say, Your Highness?"

The man recoiled as though struck, an instant of terror darting across his eyes before he could mask it, but both Joram and Rhys heard the scarcely whispered "No," as Cinhil lowered his head and tried to turn his face away.

The two exchanged glances, and then Joram gestured ahead to where a stand of pines afforded some protection from the wind. It was time to rest the horses anyway, and better they say what they must on solid ground, face to face, where there could be no mistaking their intent.

The horses blew and snorted gratefully as their riders reined in beneath the snow-laden trees, and

Joram, with a sigh, hitched their captive's lead over his saddle and jumped to the ground. Moving around to Cinhil's right, Joram released the thongs binding the man's foot to the off stirrup, then repeated the process on the other side. Rhys, Cinhil's other lead still in his hands, swung his right leg over his horse's neck and around the saddletree to ease cramped muscles. They had already agreed that one of them would remain mounted whenever Cinhil was on horseback, for they dared not risk an ill-considered escape.

"Come down and walk a bit, Sire," Joram said, loosing Cinhil's hands from the saddletree but not from the thongs which bound them together. "You must be stiff. I apologize for the rough treatment, but we feared you would not come with us of your own free will."

Cinhil turned his head away and shrank from the offered assistance. "Call me not Sire," he whispered. "I am sire to no man, nor ever like to be. You have mistaken me for someone else. I am a simple, cloistered monk, having quarrel with no one."

Joram shook his head slowly, understanding what the man was trying to do, but knowing that he could not permit it. He cast a resigned glance at Rhys, and knew that the Healer recognized it, too.

"You are Nicholas Gabriel Draper, known in religion as Brother Benedict," Joram said. "Your father was called Royston, and your grandfather Daniel. But both had other names, my lord, and other names have you."

"No," the monk murmured. "No other names."

"Your father's other name was Alroy, an ancient royal name; your grandfather was known as Aidan, Prince of Haldane, in the years before the Coup," Joram continued relentlessly. "And you—you are Cinhil Donal Ifor, Prince of Haldane and last of your grandfather's royal line. The time has come for you to claim your birthright, Your Highness. The time has come for you to mount the Throne of Gwynedd."

"No," the captive choked. "Say it not. I will not hear you. Such names are past, and best forgotten. I am only Benedict, a monk, a priest. I have no other birthright in this world."

Joram glanced at Rhys uneasily, trying not to show the distaste he was feeling for what he must do. They had planned the strategy for miles, on the long ride toward Saint Foillan's, crafting arguments to cover every possible contingency. But they had not reckoned on the gentleness of the man, or the childlike grief evoked by the threat of an ending to the life he had known until now. Joram steeled himself for the next words he must utter, but it was Cinhil himself who broke the silence, raising his head to stare unseeing between his horse's ears, not deigning to look at them.

"I pray you, take me back to Saint Foillan's."

"We may not, my lord," Joram said.

"Then, send me. You need not go yourselves. I will tell no one what you have done."

"We *may* not, my lord," Joram repeated. "Other lives than your own have been touched—and some ended."

"Ended? You mean that men have died on my account?"

Joram nodded, unwilling to meet the man's eyes just then, and the monk shifted his stunned gaze to the winter-bare forest beyond, as though reading a half-forgotten vision which he had tried to put aside.

"Where are you taking me?" he finally asked.

"Among friends."

"I have no friends outside the walls of my abbey. Nor are they friends who would end my life."

"One life ends, another begins, my lord," Joram said, laying a hand on the horse's bridle and gazing up unwaveringly. "You were born to other than monastic cells and hours of prayer, however comfortable you may have found that life in recent years. It is only now that you begin to enter your true destiny."

"No! It is *this* I was born for!" He struck his white-cloaked breast with his bound hands and turned frantic eyes to Rhys in appeal. "You, my lord—the story told you by my grandsire—it was a fantasy he wove. I am not what he would have you think. I am not of the stuff from which princes are made."

"You are a Haldane, my lord."

"No! The Haldanes all are dead. I was a Draper

before I took my vows—and my father before me. I
know no other names."

Joram sighed and glanced at Rhys, then shrugged
lightly. "I think it's pointless to continue for now,
don't you? He's tired and frightened. Perhaps later—"

"That will not change the truth," Cinhil interjected.

"No, but the truth may be different than you now
perceive it, my lord. You have been away from the
world for many years. Why not reserve judgment until
you have a chance to become reacquainted?"

"It is a world I have renounced. You, who claim to
be a priest, should understand that."

"All too well," Joram sighed. "However, it does not
change my present intent. Come, if I have your word
you'll not try to escape, I would be pleased to release
your bonds. You'll feel better if you get down and
walk a bit."

Cinhil stared at Joram for a long moment, as though
weighing what he had said, then lowered his eyes.

"I will not resist you."

"Your word on it?"

"My word," the captive whispered.

With a nod, Joram reached up and cut the thongs
binding Cinhil's wrists. But when he held out a hand
to assist the man from his horse, Cinhil pursed his
lips and brushed the hand aside, sliding down the
other side, past Rhys, to stagger but a half-dozen steps
before sinking to his knees in the snow.

As the man bowed his head and fought dry sobs,
Joram frowned and glanced at Rhys, then hitched his
cloak back on his shoulders and folded his arms resignedly. Both were painfully aware that the rest of the
ride to Dhassa was likely to seem even longer than
they had feared.

And indeed, the rest of the ride was accomplished,
though without further incident, in nearly total silence.
They stopped once at midday to change mounts at a
small hostelry, Rhys guarding the prince while Joram
negotiated for the horses' exchange. But Cinhil volunteered not one word of further conversation or resistance in all that time.

By that evening, they were within an hour's ride of their destination. A small, swiftly-running stream wound alongside the road they travelled, crusted with snow along the edges but not yet iced over for the winter. Men and horses were showing the effects of the journey. Rhys was especially concerned about Cinhil, for the prince was totally unaccustomed to the rigors of riding. He had nearly cried out from the pain of aching muscles when they dismounted at their last rest stop a few hours before, only pride maintaining the silence he had imposed upon himself. It had taken both of them to assist him, half fainting, back into the saddle when they were ready to ride on.

Cinhil had been looking more and more pale for the past half-hour, and Rhys knew that they would have to rest soon or risk having Cinhil pass out. There was also the very real uncertainty as to what Cinhil might do when they entered the city and tried to make their way to the bishop's palace. If he should resist, if his seeming compliance all day was but preparation for a public denunciation— Rhys preferred not even to think about that possibility.

Nor had Rhys been able to probe their royal captive's mind during the long, silent hours of riding. It was as though a sleek, rigid wall had been erected— one which Rhys felt certain he could eventually broach, given time and rest and the proper preparations, but one which he dared not even attempt without making Cinhil more alert than he already was to the potential power of the Deryni men who held him captive.

No, some more insidious method would have to be used on Cinhil—at least until they were safely among allies, where his protests would do no good. What Rhys had in mind for now would also help to numb the pain of tortured leg and thigh muscles until more thorough and lasting methods could be applied.

As though sensing Rhys's growing disquiet, if not the exact reasons or solution for it, Joram stood in his stirrups to stretch and yawn, then gestured toward the side of the road where the configuration of the stream bank allowed an approach to the swiftly running water. Dismounting, he moved to Cinhil's side to assist

him from his horse, then supported the limping prince
to a seat on a rock sheltered from the wind. Rhys,
in a more leisurely manner, got down and led the three
horses to the stream to drink, then took an empty water flask from his saddle and knelt by the water, hiding
the flask with his body as he filled it from the icy
stream.

Joram was helping to massage the knots from Cinhil's legs when Rhys returned. The prince, when he
had drunk deeply from Rhys's flask, passed it to
Joram without thinking. Before the priest could drink
in turn, Rhys reached across and took the flask with
a slight shake of his head, pouring the rest of the
contents into the snow.

"You've drugged him." Joram's words were a simple
statement of fact, only a little surprised.

Rhys nodded as Cinhil turned his head to stare.

"The water?" Cinhil whispered.

"It was necessary. A sleeping potion to calm you, to
ease your discomfort until we can rest properly."

"And to guard against my betrayal, as well," Cinhil said, a strained smile playing across his lips. A
muffled sob escaped him and he bowed his head, closing his eyes briefly. When he looked up again, he
would not meet their eyes.

"What—what will happen to me?"

"From the drug?" Rhys looked across at him steadily. "You will become very sleepy. Your perception
will be blurred. You will probably drift in and out of
consciousness. It will be better this way, believe me."

"Better for whom?" Cinhil whispered. "Did you
really fear I would betray you? I gave my word. It"
—he gestured toward the flask—"it was not necessary."

At that, Joram stood abruptly and strode back to
the horses, to kneel at the edge of the stream, his back
to Cinhil. Rhys followed, keeping a wistful eye on
Cinhil, to hunch down beside the priest. He could tell
that Joram was annoyed.

"*Was* it necessary?" Joram asked, leaning down to
scoop water from the stream and drink.

"I thought it was. Joram, I've been trying to read

him for hours, hoping something would slip. Nothing. He's like a blank wall. He has some kind of natural shield when he's under pressure, which I couldn't penetrate—at least not without letting him know what I was trying to do. I think that's why we had trouble controlling him last night. I didn't think we could afford to take chances with him in Dhassa, especially with both of us as tired as we are."

"No, I suppose not." Joram dried his hands on his cloak, then half turned toward Rhys. "He really has that kind of natural defense, eh? Do you think you'll be able to get through to him later?"

Rhys shrugged, permitting himself a slight, nervous smile. "There are ways to overcome anyone's resistance eventually, especially if one is a Healer. Besides, I'll have Camber working with me, once we reach the haven. It's a bit of a challenge, but I think we'll be able to handle it between us."

With a raise of his eyebrow, Joram stood and stretched, then glanced toward the resting Cinhil. "Did you tell him the truth about the effects of the drug?"

"Yes. We should have ample time to get him through the Portal before it wears off. And he *will* sleep, if we let him."

"Hmm. Won't he attract attention, if he's in a stupor?"

"Not as much as he would if he made a scene," Rhys replied. He put the flask back on his saddle. "If there should be any question, he's ill and we're taking him to the Bishop's Healer. That seemed like a simple enough ruse to me."

"Aye." With a resigned sigh, Joram shook his head and gave a smile. "I must be more tired than I thought. I must say, though, you've certainly caught on to the ways of conspiracy with the proper enthusiasm. And this is a man who never played the treason game before."

"I wish you wouldn't use that word."

"What, 'treason'?"

With a chuckle, Joram clapped Rhys on the shoulder and gestured toward their nodding prince. Now they must get Cinhil back on his horse and ride. On the next hour rested the fate of a kingdom.

Fortunately for the three who rode toward Dhassa at that hour, the wheels of feudal bureaucracy were grinding with their accustomed slowness, with the result that only now was the Abbot of Saint Foillan's putting the pieces together properly to explain the absence of a man known as Brother Benedictus.

As Rhys and Joram had suspected, Brother Benedict's absence was not first noted until after Matins, when it was remarked by the precentor that he had not seen Brother Benedict in choir during that Divine Office. But the precentor was a busy man, with many duties to perform, and it was not until several hours later, when Brother Benedict did not appear at Lauds or Prime, that he became truly concerned.

Fearing that Brother Benedict might have taken ill, the precentor checked with the infirmarian; but Brother Reynard had not seen the missing monk for several days. A thorough search of the rest of the abbey precincts after Terce likewise revealed no trace of the missing monk. To be sure, his bed had been slept in; but no one remembered seeing him after Compline the night before.

A pair of lay brethren went out on horseback to scout the road as far as a man might have strayed on foot—just in case Brother Benedict had, indeed, taken ill and wandered off in delirium. But the storm had done its work well. If Brother Benedict had managed to wander off and die, they would not know for sure until spring. Sadly, but with the resignation necessitated by the situation, the abbot had a Mass sung for Brother Benedict the next morning, and life went on in the abbey as usual.

So the matter might have remained indefinitely, had not the abbey's vestiarian, Brother Leviticus, chosen the next afternoon to begin his winter inventory of the abbey's clothing supply. Checking the shelves near the cell of the missing Brother Benedict, Brother Leviticus was astonished to discover that two robes could not be accounted for. Careful inquiry among the brethren who shared the area revealed that the robes had almost certainly been there two days before, but no one could explain their absence now.

Puzzled, the vestiarian reported the matter to the subprior, who told the prior, who eventually told the abbot himself, that evening after dinner. The abbot started to shrug it off, but his mind had been lingering all day on the disappearance of his friend, Benedict. Abruptly, the pieces began to fall together.

"Brother Patrick, how many robes did Brother Leviticus say were missing?"

"Why, two, Father Abbot."

The abbot picked up a quill pen and twirled it between bony fingers. "Tell me, do you remember the two men who came to see Brother Benedict a few weeks ago?"

"The Healer and the monk?" The younger man blinked. "I remember the visit, of course, Father. And the monk was in the service of the archbishop, but—"

"Aye, I remember that," the abbot snapped. "He was a Gabrilite brother—or claimed to be!"

As the prior watched owlishly, not daring to say a word, the abbot pushed back his chair and extracted a calendar roll from a shelf behind his desk. Not finding what he sought among its notations, he tossed it back on the shelf in annoyance and drummed his fingers on the desk.

"Please ask the infirmarian to attend us at once, Brother Patrick. Also Brother Paul and Brother Phineas and Brother Jubal."

"At once, Father Abbot." The prior blinked myopically and backed out the door.

For the next ten minutes, the abbot sat and chewed at a hangnail, suspicion growing in his mind that his theory would prove correct. The two men had come on the same day that Benedict had fainted and had been speaking with him when it happened. Something about an important message from Brother Benedict's dead grandfather. He himself had been standing in the background, listening.

And the one had been a Healer—what was his name? Lord Re—Ro—Rhys— Yes, that was it. And when Benedict had not responded to the ministrations of the infirmarian, they had asked this Rhys person to take a look at him, had even permitted the man to enter the cloistered area. *Why, he and the monk with him had been permitted to attend Benedict in his very cell!*

Stifling an unholy but entirely provoked oath, the abbot sat bolt upright and crumpled the letter he had just finished writing to his vicar general in Valoret. He tossed it into the fire with an angry gesture.

Benedict had not become delirious with some new illness and wandered out of the abbey to die in the snow. Indeed, he probably had not been ill at all, either two nights ago or a few weeks earlier! He had been kidnapped from right within the abbey walls— from the cloistered area itself!—and spirited away by those two—

His anger was interrupted by a timid knock on the door, and he forced himself to submerge his anger and assume the proper paternal mien.

"Come."

Brother Patrick peered in apprehensively before entering, followed by Brothers Jubal, Paul, Phineas, and Reynard. The abbot stood as each came forward to bow and kiss his ring, then waited until Brother Patrick had closed the door before sitting down again. The monks stood silently, hands folded and hidden in their voluminous sleeves, as the abbot dipped his quill to ink and drew a fresh piece of parchment in front of him.

"Brother Reynard, do you recall the date of Brother Benedict's last illness?—the day he fainted whilst speaking with the two visitors."

Brother Reynard studied his sandalled toes for a moment, then looked up. "That would have been about the Feast of Saint Margetan, Father Abbot. No, it was the day after, Saint Edmund's Eve."

"Which one, Brother Reynard?"

"Saint Edmund's Eve, the"—he consulted his cal-it."

"Saint Edmund's Eve, the"—he consulted his calendar again—"the fourteenth of November." He jotted down the date, then looked up at Brother Jubal.

"Brother Jubal, you were gate warder that week, I believe."

"Yes, Father Abbot."

"Can you recall the names of the two visitors? There was a Healer and an older man, a monk."

After considering the question for a moment, the monk raised an eyebrow. "I believe the monk's name was Brother Kyriell, Father Abbot. From the Order of Saint Gabriel."

"Ah, yes. Brother Kyriell," the abbot repeated. "Did he give any other name?"

"No, only his order," Brother Phineas volunteered. "And that he was in the service of Archbishop Anscom, of course, Father Abbot."

The abbot chewed on the tip of his quill for a moment, then shook his head. He could associate nothing more with the name, though he had the feeling he should be able to. But even the one name ought to enable the vicar general to do something—if the monk called Brother Kyriell really was in the service of the archbishop, of course.

He wrote the name down, tracing each letter carefully, then scanned the brethren once more.

"Now, the name of the Healer—Lord Rhys Something."

"Moorin, or Toorin, or something like that?" Brother Jubal interjected.

"I think it was *Thoorin*, Brother Jubal," Brother Reynard murmured, craning his neck a little as the abbot started to write it down. "I'm not sure about the spelling, but that was the sound of it. *Thoor-in*. He was a Healer, all right. I had a toothache that day, and he—"

He broke off as the abbot looked up at him sharply, then bowed his head self-consciously. After a long moment, the abbot bent his head to write again. The pen scratched briefly on the parchment, and then he dismissed all of them with a wave of his hand. As the doors closed behind them, he took out a fresh piece of parchment and began a new letter to his superior, this time making all his letters clear and round.

"*Most Reverend and Excellent Father General,*" the letter began. "*I regret to report the abduction from Saint Foillan's of one of our brethren in Christ, Brother Benedictus, two nights past. The wise of his taking is described as follows. . . .*"

"'*And so,*'" the vicar general read to his superior, the Archbishop of Valoret, five days later, "'*it appears likely that Brother Benedict was taken by the said Brother Kyriell and Lord Rhys Thuryn in the manner I have described, though for what reason I cannot discern. I am forwarding copies of all our records pertaining to Brother Benedict, in the hopes that Your Reverence will be able to make some connection which I have missed, and beg to remain Your Reverence's good and faithful servant, et cetera, et cetera.*'"

The vicar general lowered the letter and glanced up at his superior with something of a perplexed expression on his face. The archbishop, who had been sipping at an earthen goblet of goat's milk, drained the glass with a final swallow and made a face, then held out a gnarled hand for the missive. As he sat back to read, the vicar general helped himself to another slice of cheese.

It was mid-morning, and the archbishop's custom was to break his fast with his subordinates while reviewing the day's correspondence. Of course, Robert Oriss, Vicar General of the Order of Saint Jarlath, hardly qualified as a mere subordinate. Born within a week of the archbishop, he and Anscom of Trevas had been reared a scant ten miles apart, and had first met at the tender age of ten, when both boys were enrolled in the famous monastery school at Saint Neot's. Though Anscom was Deryni and Robert was not, this had not diminished the friendship which had sprung up between them. In fact, when Robert was resident in Valoret and not out inspecting the abbeys and monasteries under his care, it was his custom to meet with the archbishop at least once a week. Anscom was one of those rare men who did not forget his old friends simply because he had risen above them; and Robert, though he did not always understand everything his Deryni colleague did, greatly valued their continuing interaction.

But the good vicar general had already made his visit for this week, two days before. It was the receipt of the letter now in the archbishop's hand which had prompted his urgent message last night, and that same letter which accounted for Robert's presence here this morning. The vicar general poured more goat's milk for the archbishop—Anscom hated it, but drank it to soothe a delicate digestion—then nibbled at a piece of bread until the archbishop looked up. Anscom's seamed face was puzzled and a little sad.

"What is so special about this particular monk, Robert? Why would anyone want to abduct him?"

The vicar general shook his head. "I am at a loss to explain it, Your Grace. I've gone over his records: He's a poor draper's son, an orphan. He has taken a vow of poverty. . . . I simply don't know."

"And this abbot of yours, this Zephram of Lorda—is he trustworthy?"

The vicar general started to protest—for he believed all of his subordinates to be trustworthy—then spread his palms in a yea–nay gesture. "I have received no unfavorable reports of him, so I must assume . . ."

The archbishop grunted, and dropped the letter on the table, staring past the vicar general for several seconds.

"Did you know that Cathan MacRorie died last week?"

"The king's advisor?"

"The son of Earl Camber of Culdi," the archbishop amended. "And Camber's daughter Evaine is betrothed to Rhys Thuryn."

"Rhys Th—" The vicar general broke off and flicked a glance at the letter on the table. "The same Rhys Thuryn?"

"The same."

The vicar general let out a long sigh and sat back in his chair, all thought of breakfast forgotten. When his superior did not volunteer further comments, the vicar general pursed his lips and gazed thoughtfully across the table.

"Your Grace, you're not implying that Earl Camber had something to do with Brother Benedict's abduction, are you?"

The archbishop looked up with a start, an instant of pain darting across his usually inscrutable face. "Are you mad?" he whispered softly. "I *know* Camber. He and I studied for the priesthood together at Grecotha, before his brothers died and made him his father's heir. I married him to his wife, baptized all his children, ordained his son Joram, married Cathan and Elinor— Besides, what possible reason could he have?"

"I don't know, Your Grace. By your comment, I thought *you* might." He sighed. "This Rhys Thuryn— I've never heard of him. Is he active at Court? You seem to know him."

"I know *of* him," the archbishop replied. "He is very young for a Healer, but has an excellent reputation. He is also very close to Camber's younger son, Joram, who is a Michaeline— Hmm, I wonder."

"You think that this Joram may have been the monk?"

"I don't know," the archbishop replied, though his tone sounded doubtful. "On the other hand, Joram *is* a Michaeline, and they have long been agitators."

"Agitators, yes," Robert Oriss snorted. "But, against a fellow priest? I see no political issue in a man like Brother Benedict."

"Nor do I," the archbishop sighed, "But there *is* a political issue surrounding the MacRories. You've heard the rumors about Cathan MacRorie's death, haven't you?"

Robert had not.

"Well, there is now some talk that young Cathan did not simply die—that he was killed, some say by the king's own hand. If true, it could explain Imre's erratic behavior at his Yule Court feast. And it certainly gives Joram, or Camber, or Rhys a motive for political retaliation of some kind." He frowned. "But not against a cloistered monk. I'll confess, I haven't any answers, Robert. Have you?"

The vicar general had none.

After another silent period, the archbishop stood and slowly walked to the window, laying his hands wearily along the wide casement edging. Outside, the snow was falling.

"Leave us, please, Robert," the archbishop finally said in a low voice.

The vicar general, noting the lapse into the formal "we," stood at once and bowed, backing silently out the door and closing it behind him. The archbishop, when he had gone, returned to his chair and sat down, touched the discarded letter briefly, folded his arms on the table, and lowered his head to pray.

Though he had not indicated so to Robert Oriss, Archbishop Anscom knew who had accompanied Rhys Thuryn to Saint Foillan's, and was now implicated in an abduction. He and the "monk" had studied for the priesthood together at Grecotha and had shared a thousand moments of the joys and sorrows of the world.

For "Brother Kyriell" was the name which had been used in religion by Camber of Culdi.

CHAPTER SIXTEEN

*There is one alone, and there is not a
second; yea, he hath neither child nor
brother; yet is there no end to all his
labour; neither is his eye satisfied with
riches.*

—Ecclesiastes 4:8

Whatever Anscom's personal feelings about the
MacRories, and about Camber MacRorie in particular, the good archbishop was also a servant of the
Crown; and duty dictated that, even though the abduction of a monk was an ecclesiastical matter, it must
be reported to the king.

Anscom did delete the physical description of
Brother Kyriell; let Imre figure out who the mysterious
monk was. In the meantime, perhaps Anscom could
contact Camber and find out what was going on. For
Camber to reassume his old religious name as a subterfuge was very much out of character for the Camber
Anscom knew. Perhaps Camber was trying to tell
him something; or perhaps there was another Brother
Kyriell, and it was all coincidence—though Anscom
tended to mistrust coincidence. Whatever the explanation, Anscom wanted to know.

Accordingly, the archbishop's missive went through
regular channels; no sense in giving the king a head
start, if Camber was involved.

And so, in due course, it was delivered, not to the
king but to Earl Santare, named but the week before

to head the investigation of the apparent MacRorie conspiracy. Coel Howell had made it his practice in the past week to shadow Santare and be as helpful as possible, even to the extent of sharing with Santare some of the intelligence he had gathered on his own; and thus he was also present when the missive arrived. But even before they received the new information, their combined resources had already turned up some interesting coincidences—or were they coincidences?

They had known for some time, for example, that Daniel Draper, one of the men named in the documents stolen by Joram, had died of natural causes but a scant two months ago—and that he had been attended on his deathbed by none other than Lord Rhys Thuryn.

But further inquiry, in Thuryn's household and surrounds, had revealed that the same Rhys Thuryn, on the evening after the old man's death, had taken horse and ridden out of the city. Though his servants insisted that he had but gone to Caerrorie for Michaelmas, the brethren of Saint Liam's Monastery School— where Father Joram MacRorie was currently assigned —claimed that Thuryn and Father Joram had ridden off in great haste the same day, and in driving rain, in the direction of Saint Jarlath's Monastery.

Curious.

And as if that were not enough, the monks of Saint Jarlath's told how the two had inveigled permission, in the dead of night, to consult the abbey's induction records. The crowning touch to the entire piece of work was the statement of one Gregory of Arden, Abbot of Saint Jarlath's, who remembered the two saying that they were looking for a Brother Benedict whose grandfather had died recently in Valoret. Coel's scribes were compiling a list of Brothers Benedict in the order even now. It was just possible that they were on the verge of locating the missing Nicholas Draper.

Coel and Santare were together with a couple of Santare's aides when the archbishop's messenger arrived, and it fell to Coel to receive the letter and break the seal. His feet propped comfortably on the edge of the raised hearth, a tankard of ale at his elbow, Coel read impassively until he had come almost to the end, the silence broken only by the crackle of the fire. Then he started and sat up abruptly, swinging his feet under him in astonishment.

"S'blood! Would you look at this?" He shoved the parchment under the earl's nose. "You wanted to know what Joram MacRorie and Thuryn were doing? Well, I can tell you about Thuryn. And I'll bet that this Brother Kyriell was MacRorie! What do you want to bet that this Brother Benedict and our Nicholas Draper are one and the same person?"

Santare pulled the missive before him and scanned it briefly. When he had finished, he leaned back in his chair and hooked thumbs in his ample belt, nodding slowly.

"No wonder we couldn't find Draper. He's been holed up in a monastery all these years. They must've traced him through the records at Saint Jarlath's, the same way we were trying to trace Benedict. And yet . . ."

The earl got to his feet and began pacing, his boots stirring the rushes beneath them. Coel watched him, hawk-like, scarcely able to contain his impatience.

"You know, that's odd," Santare continued, after several circuits of the room. "According to the archbishop's report, they went to Saint Foillan's for the first time a good month ago, but they didn't do anything. It's as though they weren't sure he was the right one. The question is, the right one *what?* Why all this interest in a simple monk from a family of merchants?"

One of the aides cleared his throat hesitantly. "There—ah—*have* been the rumors of the Haldane, m'lord. You've seen the handbills that are starting to appear."

"Willimite speculation and wishful thinking!" Coel snapped. "That may be what they're trying to imply, but it simply won't work."

"But, Thuryn *did* steal the painting of Ifor Haldane,

sir," the second aide volunteered. "He must have had a reason."

"It's a fraud. It has to be!" Coel insisted. "No Haldane survived the Coup. Everyone knows that."

"But if one had, wouldn't this be a bloody good time for him to turn up?" Santare said, motioning the aides to leave them.

Coel sat back and planted a booted foot on the edge of the hearth in disgust as the door closed behind the aides. "Yes, it would," he agreed grudgingly. "But, it doesn't make sense. This whole thing doesn't make sense. What is a Haldane to the MacRories? They're Deryni, the same as you and I. Certainly, Camber has no reason to love the king, especially after the way Cathan died; but, damn it, they're *all* Deryni! He can't seriously mean to replace Imre with a human king of the old line—or worse, one who only says he's of the old line. Where's their *proof?* And where is Camber?"

"I don't know," Santare shrugged. "We've questioned the servants and peasants at Caerrorie, of course—"

"And learned nothing! Santare, I find it difficult to believe that skilled inquisitors were unable to extract even one jot of information about Camber's plans or motivations. If it were up to me—"

"If it were up to you, I have no doubt that half of Camber's servants would now be swinging at the ends of ropes, the way those peasants ended up in October —for not divulging information which they did not have," Santare said pointedly. "Don't you think that a Deryni as powerful as Camber could manage to keep his plans secure from a few human servants, if he wanted to—and be certain that no one could get that information out of them?"

"But, he's got to be somewhere!"

Further argument was curtailed by the explosive entrance of a very out-of-breath young squire in Imre's personal colors. A look of relief crossed the lad's face as he swept off his cap and bowed.

"My lords, the King's Grace commands your pres-

ence in his chambers at once. He—" The boy paused
to gulp another breath. "He is most distraught, my
lords. It would do well not to tarry."

As one, Coel and Santare bolted for the door.

"Miserable, ungrateful, misbegotten whoresons!"
Imre was screaming, as Coel and Santare were admitted to his chamber. "Lying, deceitful— Coel! Do
you know what they've done? Can you conceive—"

"What *who* has done, Your Grace?" Coel interjected,
bowing cautiously.

"The Michaelines! Filthy, two-faced, double-
crossing, treacherous—"

"Sire! What have they done?"

Imre glared at him, wild-eyed, then flung his hands
into the air and flounced into a chair. "They've disappeared—every last treasonous one of them! They
took their treasury, their altar plate—everything!
They're just—gone!"

"Gone . . ." Santare breathed.

His reaction was lost on Imre, who lurched to his
feet and immediately launched into a new stream of
invective, proclaiming fluent and obscene descriptions
of the base birth and gross physical habits of the order
in question. Santare, awed and more than a little apprehensive, tried to discern a motive, forcing himself
to begin planning for the safety of the realm.

Such action by an order as wealthy and powerful
as the Michaelines, coupled with the evidence of a
MacRorie conspiracy, pointed to only one thing: there
was a plot brewing to attempt the overthrow of Imre
and replace him with an alleged Haldane heir. And if
the Michaelines were involved, then they must be well
convinced that this heir was a true Haldane, and that
they looked for at least a reasonable chance of suc-
cess in their endeavor. Even now, the Michaeline
knights must be gathering somewhere, preparing to
make their move. By removing their noncombatant
members to places of safety, they had rendered themselves invulnerable to reprisal. Why, the Michaelines
could be anywhere!

Coel, too, was not blind to the ramifications of the Michaeline disappearance, though his thoughts, as the king raged on, were of a more personal and immediately sobering bent. He had thought himself so clever. Why, he had not been clever at all! All of his planning, his merciless engineering of Cathan's apparent betrayal, the assassination of Maldred, Cathan's own murder—all of these had been unwittingly aiding a real conspiracy. He had seen himself as architect of a new power base in Gwynedd, not dreaming of the real enormity of the greater plan. He was but a pawn in a game whose magnitude he was only now beginning to comprehend. And now he could envision himself being swept along in that game, impelled by forces which he, himself, had helped to focus. Would he eventually be a sacrifice for his own king?

"I'll show them!" Imre was shouting, as Coel's attention snapped back to the immediate crisis. "They'll be sorry they dared to defy me!"

Still cursing under his breath, Imre flung himself into the chair behind his writing desk and began scribbling furiously, muttering all the while as Coel and Santare exchanged stunned glances. At length, the king sanded the ink, sealed the foot of the page with his personal signet, and stood, flourishing it under Santare's nose with a malicious smirk contorting his face.

"You will see to the execution of these commands immediately, Santare."

"Sire?"

"Go ahead, take it!" Imre said, shaking the page impatiently. "The Michaelines dare to oppose me? They think to replace me with another king? Well, we'll see! The present king intends to make things very uncomfortable. See to it!" he barked.

Santare bowed his head, not daring to look at the page he now held in his hand.

"Aye, My Liege."

"And if, in the process, you should happen to run any stray Michaelines to ground," Imre added, "I want them brought to me immediately. Do you understand? Regardless of the hour. I want to question each one of them personally, before he's executed as a traitor!"

"Yes, Sire."

"Then get out! Both of you!"

Outside, Santare exhaled in relief—the first real breathing he had allowed himself since entering the king's presence—then unrolled the parchment, turning away pointedly when Coel made as though to read over his shoulder. The earl scanned the document slowly, meticulously, as Coel fidgeted in impatience; then he handed it over, as Coel had known he would.

Imre, by the Grace of God, etc., to all leal subjects of Our Realm, greeting.

Know that We have this day been most grievously and treacherously betrayed by members of the Order of Saint Michael, which Order We do dissolve, disband, and abolish. We declare its former brethren outlaw, its goods and lands forfeit to the Crown. We include in this ban all those bearing the name MacRorie: especially Camber, the former Earl of Culdi; Joram MacRorie, a priest of the Michaeline Order; and the Healer known as Rhys Thuryn.

To Our well-beloved Santare, Earl of Grand-Tellie, we give command to proceed to the Michaeline Commanderie at Cheltham with a royal force and take into custody all persons residing there. The establishment shall be sacked and burned, its buildings levelled, its lands sown with salt, this to be accomplished no later than the Feast of Saint Olympias, one week hence. An additional Michaeline establishment shall be dealt with in this manner each week, until the Vicar General of the Order shall present himself before Us on bended knee and surrender both his Order and all members of Clan MacRorie, severally and collectively. Reward is offered for the capture of any and all . . .

There was more, but even Coel had no stomach for it.

"Per intercessionem beati Michaëlis Archangeli, stantis a dextris altari incensi . . ."

The words of the liturgy floated fervent and a little desperate on the incense-laden air, barely audible in the listening gallery where Camber MacRorie waited. The celebrant was Cinhil Haldane, thurible in hand, a deacon following behind to lift the edge of his chasuble as he circled and censed the altar. Camber observed in silence as priest-prince and monk completed their circuit and incensed one another again, watching as the deacon put the incense aside and then poured water over Cinhil's fingertips into a small earthen bowl.

"Lavabo inter innocentes manus meas . . ."

He had not talked with Cinhil yet today—in fact, had not seen the prince since the previous afternoon, just prior to his last discussion with Alister Cullen. But he had not been heartened by their progress to date. Though Cinhil had been with them for nearly two weeks now, they still had not been able to win him to their cause.

Physically, Cinhil was docile enough. He went where he was told and did as he was bidden. He read the writings they brought him, answered dutifully when questioned on what he had read—even, on occasion, showed sparks of genuine insight into the problems of this land he was but now coming to know about. But he volunteered no word or action and did his best to show no sign of interest or caring about the position for which he was being groomed at such great cost.

It was not resistance as such. That they could have coped with, with force, if necessary. It was an almost studied apathy; an immersion, to the exclusion of nearly all outside influence, in the world he had chosen as a very young man over twenty years before. He tolerated his present situation because he must; but he would allow no inkling of human feeling for his denied birthright to intrude upon his conscience and the world in which he had lived for the past score of years. So long as they permitted him to celebrate Mass daily, he was reluctantly compliant.

Except that this morning, for the first time since his arrival, he was showing signs of human apprehension, almost despair. Camber suspected he knew the reason why.

Footsteps warned of the approach of another in the passageway behind him, and then Alister Cullen was slipping into the gallery to join him. Nodding greeting, Camber stepped aside to let the Michaeline general peer down into the chapel. Cullen's demeanor betrayed nothing.

"*Orate fratres,*" Cinhil prayed, his arms spread in desperate supplication, "*ut meum ac vestrum sacrificium acceptabile fiat apud Deum Patrem omnipotentem.*"

Camber glanced at Cullen carefully. "I assume you've told him?"

Cullen sighed and nodded once, wearily, then gestured with his chin that they should go outside. By the brighter torchlight in the outer corridor, Camber could read the concern which had not been evident in the dim listening gallery. He suspected that Cullen was suffering from more than lack of sleep.

"I spoke with him last night for a long time," Cullen said.

"I surmised as much. And?"

Cullen shook his head in frustration. "I really don't know. I think I've finally convinced him that he really will have to give up his priesthood, but he's scared witless."

"So was I . . ." Camber mused, almost without thinking. Then, realizing that Cullen might not understand, he continued. "Of course, I didn't give up mine for a crown—only for the promise of an earldom, after my older brothers died. Nor had I actually been ordained—I was only a deacon. But I recall the anguish, the soul-searching. I thought at the time that I had a real vocation as a priest."

"You would have been wasted on the Church, and you know it," Cullen growled, admiration tinging his voice despite the actual words.

"Perhaps—though I think I could have been a good priest. On the other hand, I like to think I've been privileged to do important work in the outside world. And of course, if I'd ignored my family obligations and gone your way"—he chanced a sidelong glance at Cullen and controlled the urge to smile—"there'd have been no Joram, and probably no Prince Cinhil, here and now, causing us our present dilemma. What, besides his understandable apprehension, seems to be the problem?"

"He's convinced that he has a true vocation—which he has," Cullen said brusquely. "He also feels that, even if he were to make the sacrifices we're demanding, the people wouldn't accept him. After all, why should they?"

"Ask those who have suffered at the hands of our current king, whether they be human or Deryni, and you need not ask any further. The Haldanes were never guilty of such acts. Besides, no one has seen Cinhil yet." He broke into a grin. "For that matter, he hasn't seen *himself* for a few weeks. With that beard, and with his tonsure grown out!" He permitted himself a grim chuckle. "Well, let's just say that when the barber gets through with him this morning, he's going to bear very little resemblance to the clean-shaven, ascetic Brother Benedict who came to us two weeks ago."

"Has he seen the painting yet?"

"It will be waiting for him after he's trimmed, right beside the mirror. And if that doesn't jolt him into an awareness of who and what he is, I don't know what will."

"I do." The Michaeline general extracted a much-folded piece of parchment from his cassock. "Take a look at this."

"Which is?"

"My list of candidates for future queen of Gwynedd." Cullen smiled wanly as Camber uncreased the parchment. "I know he's going to fight this, too, but we've got to get that man married. We need another heir after Cinhil, and we need one quickly."

"It still takes nine months, the last I heard," Cam-

ber murmured. He was aware of Cullen folding his
arms across his chest as he scanned the list.

"If I could get him married today, it wouldn't be
soon enough to suit me," Cullen muttered. "As it is,
I'd like to make a choice by the end of the week,
and marry them on Christmas Eve. That's a week
from today."

"I see," Camber said. "I notice that your list in-
cludes my young ward, Megan de Cameron. Do you
consider her a serious contender?"

"If you have no objections. My main concern, other
than her ability to bear children, of course, is that our
future queen be of absolutely impeccable background.
Other than Cinhil's having left the priesthood, there
must be no breath of scandal touching the marriage
and eventual heir."

"Well, you'll find none concerning Megan," Camber
said. "She's young, but I suspect that's what Cinhil
needs. Besides that, she has a strong sense of duty, no
other attachments, she's healthy—and I think she
just might like him."

"That's coincidental," Cullen rumbled. "My main
concern is finding someone who—"

"No, it's not coincidental, Alister," Camber interrupted. "Megan may be my ward, and technically I
have the right to bestow her marriage on whom I
choose, but I would never match her with someone
she couldn't care for. No more than I would force my
own daughter to marry for dynastic reasons."

"For God's sake, stop sounding like a father, Camber. I haven't even picked her yet."

"I—"

Abruptly, Camber closed his mouth and stared at
Cullen, then shook his head and began to chuckle.
After a few seconds, Cullen, too, began to smile.

"Christmas Eve . . ." Camber finally said, as the
tension dissolved away. "Do you plan to perform the
ceremony yourself?"

"Unless you have someone better in mind."

"Not intrinsically better, but better for Cinhil,"
Camber replied. "May I make the arrangements?"

"Please do."

"Thank you."

"Can you tell me whom you have in mind?"

"No. But I assure you, if I can get him to agree, you'll approve."

"Hmm. Very well." Cullen glanced at his feet, then raised his eyes to meet Camber's once more. "There's —ah—one other thing. I wasn't going to tell you yet, but I suppose you ought to know. Imre has started reprisals against the order."

Camber was instantly serious once more. "What happened?"

"The Commanderie at Cheltham," Cullen said dully. "Imre's troops occupied it two days ago. They took everything they could carry off, torched the rest. Now I understand they're pulling down the walls that are still standing and salting the fields. The rumor is that they will destroy a former Michaeline establishment every week until I surrender you and the order. Of course, that's out of the question."

Camber could only nod mutely.

"So, it seems that honor extracts a high price from all of us, eh, my friend?" Cullen finally said, recovering some of his former bravado. "But no one ever promised us it would be easy." He glanced toward the gallery and sighed. "Well, I'd best be waiting when His Highness finishes Mass. I'll send him to you when the barber and I are done with him."

"Send him to Joram, if I'm not in my chamber," Camber agreed. "Perhaps some of Joram's enthusiasm will rub off."

Cullen shrugged at that, as though to indicate his doubt that anything enthusiastic could rub off on the despondent Cinhil, then lifted a hand in farewell and headed off down the corridor.

Camber returned to the listening gallery, but Cinhil had finished his Mass and was disappearing with his monk escort through the door. With a sigh, Camber made his way down to the chapel door and slipped inside. Rhys was waiting for him, standing expectantly to one side of the altar.

"How is he this morning?" Camber asked.

Rhys shook his head gravely. "He didn't sleep last

night. His hands were shaking during Mass. I think he sensed that this might be the last time. His distress was so poignant that I could sense it in the air, like a gray pall surrounding the altar. Didn't you feel it, too?"

Camber looked at him carefully. "I was called away. When did this occur?"

"During the Consecration," Rhys said. He glanced toward the altar, then back at Camber, whose face had gone quite still. "What are you thinking, Camber?" the Healer whispered. "I can't read you at all when you do that."

"I am thinking," said Camber, slowly mounting the three low steps, "that our Cinhil Haldane may be even more remarkable than we thought."

He spread one hand above the altar and extended his senses, careful not to touch anything physically. After a moment, he turned his head slightly toward Rhys.

"Rhys, will you help me, please?"

The physician moved to Camber's left to stand expectantly, one reddish eyebrow arched in question.

"Now, lend me your strength and support while I probe this more thoroughly," Camber continued. "There is something very strange here, which I've never encountered before. If Cinhil is the cause of it, we may have some very interesting times ahead of us."

With that, he closed his eyes and laid his hands flat on the altar cloth, flinching at the initial contact. Rhys stayed at his elbow, a hand resting lightly on the other's sleeve as he poured his strength into the other's mind and shared the impressions gathered. When Camber withdrew, his brow was beaded with perspiration, his eyes slightly glazed. A trifle unsteady on his feet, he allowed Rhys to help him turn and sit on the altar step, noting with detachment that the younger man's hands were shaking, too.

It was several minutes before he dared to speak, and then his voice was tinged with a little awe.

"How much of that were you able to pick up?"

"Nearly all, though not with the same intensity second-hand, of course. What do you think?"

Camber shook his head. "I'm not sure I have it all sorted out yet. We're going to have to discuss this with the others, of course. But if we could pick up impressions like that when Cinhil isn't even in the same room, I don't wonder that you and Joram weren't able to breach his shields when you took him out of Saint Foillan's. In fact, I'm surprised that you were able to make him faint, when we first found him."

"He wasn't expecting it then," Rhys countered. "He was agitated, but not directly about himself. His shields were down."

"But his shields also went down during Mass this morning—again, an instance of great mental stress which wasn't directly threatening. He was agitated because he knows that we're going to make him give up his priesthood, sooner or later, but—" Camber shook his head again. "No. That's the wrong approach. It's his ability to maintain these shields of his *in* stress which should concern us—the power he must be able to generate without even thinking about it. My God, do you realize that if we could teach him to concentrate and direct that power, he could do anything a Deryni can do? With power like that, he could be a king for both humans *and* Deryni!"

"For Deryni? Oh, come now, he'd have to be Deryni for that," Rhys replied. "The best we can probably hope for is simple tolerance from a human king, even if he *is* powerful."

"No, wait. Of course he's not Deryni, Rhys. But he's not entirely human, either. And I mean that in the finest sense of the term. We've always maintained that there is something extra in our people which sets them apart from humans—but maybe it's not something extra, but only something *changed*. And if that's the case, maybe we could make Cinhil Deryni."

"But, that's impossible—"

"I know it's impossible to make him an actual Deryni. But perhaps we could make him a *functional* Deryni. Perhaps we could give him Deryni powers and abilities. You have to admit, if we could do it, it would make it that much easier for him to oust Imre."

Rhys thought about that for a moment, pursing his lips in concentration. "I don't think it would work, even so. We've been basing our entire strategy on human support when we actually make our move— on the fact that Cinhil, the last living representative of the line usurped by the Festillic dynasty, is human, as opposed to Imre, who is the symbol of all the Deryni atrocities."

"But don't you see, there's danger of a backlash," Camber said. "If we incite the humans to rise against the Deryni Imre, we may start a reverse persecution the likes of which we've never dreamed. There have been only a few Deryni responsible for the evil that's happened in the last eighty years. We have to be certain that our revolt is against the man Imre, and his followers—not against the Deryni race."

Rhys whistled low under his breath. "I see what you mean. If Cinhil were more than a human king, if he were also Deryni, or nearly so, he could be a ruler for both peoples. He might accomplish the overthrow of Imre and the re-establishment of the Haldane rule with a minimum of bloodshed."

Camber nodded. "Cinhil, a human king with Deryni-like powers, would unite us, instead of letting us continue to tear ourselves apart with interracial bickering, and oppression by whichever race is currently in power."

"And we thought we were talking about a simple coup," Rhys finally said, when he had digested what Camber was suggesting. "I guess things are never as simple as they seem."

"Never," Camber agreed. "And wait until I tell you what Imre's done *now*."

CHAPTER SEVENTEEN

*But he shall take a virgin of his own
  people to wife.*

—Leviticus 21:14

But Imre's latest move, at least so far as Camber
and Rhys knew, was not to have nearly the impact of
his next and far less obviously menacing one. For
Imre's men, four days after the destruction of the
Michaeline Commanderie began, chanced to capture
one Humphrey of Gallareaux, a Deryni priest of the
Michaeline persuasion.

Taken captive at Saint Neot's, while claiming sanctuary with the Gabrilite Order there, Humphrey had
been spirited away to Valoret under close guard, permitted no sleep and but little food on the grueling,
three-day ride to the capital. Imre was informed of the
prisoner's capture within half an hour of his arrival.
It was but minutes before he had taken leave of his
sister and friends and was striding into a lower room
where the Deryni captive waited.

Coel and Santare were already there, Coel paring
his nails with a jewelled dagger Imre had given him,
while Santare conversed softly with the guard captain
who had brought the prisoner in. The prisoner himself was nodding in a heavy wooden armchair, prodded
to wakefulness from time to time by one of the two
guards stationed to either side of him. He glanced
up dully as Imre entered the room, seeming about to
faint when the guards jerked him roughly to his feet.

Imre waved the others to their ease, then signalled

the guards to release the prisoner's arms. The man swayed unsteadily under the king's sharp gaze.

Humphrey of Gallareaux was an unimposing man, of the indeterminate years which are so often attributed to those in religious life. By appearance alone, he would have alerted no one to the fact that he was anything but the simple country cleric his habit proclaimed him to be. (It was *not* the Michaeline habit, Imre noted disdainfully. The man had obviously been trying to pass as an itinerant friar.)

But the real clue to his otherness was in the way the eyes, even dulled with fatigue, gazed across at Imre with a calm serenity which came only with Deryni discipline. Imre reached mentally to Truth-Read the man, and was not surprised to find that he could not. With a grim smile, he gestured for the man to be seated, then nodded curt thanks as one of the guards brought a second chair for him to sit facing the prisoner.

"Dispensing with formalities, you are Humphrey of Gallareaux, a Deryni of the Michaeline Order, despite your habit," Imre said, his eyes locking with Humphrey's in a no-nonsense stare. "I believe you know who I am."

"The King's Grace is well informed." The priest's voice was carefully neutral.

"Thank you. Do you know why you have been brought here?"

"I know only that Your Grace's soldiers broke sanctuary at Saint Neot's to take me from retreat," Humphrey replied. "And that I have not been permitted to rest in the three days since my arrest. May I ask why?"

"You may not. Tell me, is it usual for a Michaeline to go into retreat in a Gabrilite establishment?"

"Not usual, no. However, the novice master at Saint Neot's was my spiritual director before I chose my own order. I had sought out his guidance."

"I see." Imre studied the priest's face for a long moment. "And I suppose you will next tell me that you did not know that your order has been outlawed, that the rest of your brethren have gone into hiding, that

I have ordered the destruction of Michaeline establishments and the surrender of your vicar general?"

"I have been in retreat, Your Grace," Humphrey replied softly. "I can only say that I am shocked to hear Your Grace's words."

Imre flicked his glance down Humphrey's spare body, then back to the face, irritation beginning to touch the corners of his mouth.

"Are you aware that you will likely be executed as a traitor?"

Humphrey's face blanched and his hands tightened on the chair arms, but other than that he did not move. "I claim benefit of clergy," he whispered.

"Coel?" The king swung to face the older man, who had been watching and listening in silence.

Coel sauntered to Imre's side with an easy grace, folding his arms across his chest. "Archbishop Anscom claimed benefit of clergy for the Michaelines when be first learned that they had been put to the horn. Unfortunately for him, and for any Michaelines who chance to fall into our nets, Archbishop Anscom does not know that Father Humphrey is our guest. Nor is he likely to find out."

"How regrettable." Imre smiled. "For Father Humphrey, that is. Of course, if he were to give us certain information which we seek, his release might be arranged . . ."

His eyes, slipping over Humphrey's face, hardened as he saw defiance written there. In a single, abrupt movement, he was standing at Humphrey's knee, leaning both hands on the chair arms to stare into the grim brown eyes.

"Don't be a fool, Humphrey," he whispered. "I may lack the finesse of your Michaeline training, but I come from a long line of ruthless Deryni, who were not afraid to take what they wanted by brute force. I can break you if I must."

"Then, do what you must, Sire," Humphrey said in a low voice. "And I must resist you with all my might. I give you my word as holy bond that I am innocent of treason, but beyond that I may not go. My mind is mine own and God's, holding the secrets of many men, imparted to me in perfect trust. Not even my Lord King may command that of me, though it cost me my life."

"The seal of the confessional," Imre said with a sigh, straightening wearily to shake his head and lean back against the arm of his own chair. "How convenient. And how useless. Santare, ask the Healer to attend us. I want to be certain of his physical condition before I start tampering with his mind."

Mind-tampering of a sort was the concern elsewhere, as well, only there it must be coercion rather than brute force; for the mind to be influenced was that of Prince Cinhil Haldane, who must be persuaded to take up his inheritance and become his people's champion.

Some outward progress had been made. The lean, elegant man who stood so defiantly before the fireplace this Christmas Eve bore little resemblance to the frightened monk whom Joram and Rhys had whisked from Saint Foillan's but a scant three weeks before. Clad in a winter robe of claret velvet, his high, Haldane cheekbones accentuated by the trim of the neat beard and mustache, the physical resemblance to his great-grandsire was uncanny. Even Cinhil, looking at his ancestor's portrait when he must, could not control a shiver of kinship whenever his eyes met the identical gray ones of his predecessor. He avoided this whenever possible, but a life-sized copy of the original portrait now hung above the fireplace, where he could scarcely miss it. Time and again he found his eyes drawn to it when he thought he should be meditating.

But if Cinhil looked a prince, he did not yet act it. Camber, with the aid of Rhys and Joram and even Evaine, had worked with Cinhil daily, trying to coax a yielding in the royal will, hinting at the power which might be bestowed, if he would only cooperate. The prince was polite but firm.

Today, the Eve of Christmas, was doubly difficult, since each of the five of them present in the room knew what the night must bring—and Cinhil was still having none of it. He had been telling them so for the past two hours.

Camber decided that it was time to change the direction of the discussion.

"Tell me, Your Highness, does your silence mean that you condone what the king is doing?" Camber asked, when Cinhil's arguments against matrimony had at least temporarily run down.

Cinhil looked at the older man sharply and started to make an indignant retort, then remembered who he was desperately trying to be and folded his hands piously instead.

"I am a man of God," he said evenly. "I could never condone the deaths of innocent men."

"No, but you could cause them," Joram said. "By your non-action," he added, when Cinhil opened his mouth as though to protest.

Cinhil turned back toward the fireplace, hands clasped stubbornly behind his back. "I cannot be concerned with the affairs of the world. You do not understand my mission."

"No, it's *you* who don't understand," Camber corrected. "Can't you get it through your head that you're involved already with the outside world, that a great number of people are going through a lot of pain and suffering, and some of them dying, because they believe in you and your cause?"

"*My* cause?" Cinhil retorted. "Nay, 'tis *yours*. I never asked to be made king. I never wanted anything but to be left alone, to find my peace with myself."

"And can you be at peace," Evaine murmured, "when you know that you could make a great change in the world, that you could ease much suffering? And yet, you do nothing."

"What would you know of such things?" Cinhil snapped. "Am I not a man? Am I not entitled to lead my own life as I see fit?"

Camber sighed impatiently. "If you were my son, speaking that irresponsibly, I'd thrash you within an inch of your life, even at your age!"

"You wouldn't dare!" Cinhil stated, a hard edge of command biting into his words.

Camber controlled the urge to smile a little as he noted the reply. "No, you're right, I wouldn't. And part of the reason is because you're starting to sound like a prince, despite your best efforts to the contrary. Do you think that Brother Benedict would have answered me the way you did just now?"

Cinhil dropped his gaze to the floor uncomfortably, the whir of his tangled emotions almost audible, then fumbled his way awkwardly to his chair and sat. He would not look at Camber, and he was keeping his hands folded in his lap only with a visible exertion of control.

"I—I'm sorry. Please forgive me."

"Forgive you? For acting like a man for once? Certainly not. Don't you see, you *are* Prince Cinhil Haldane. That is where your destiny lies—not in the alias of your Brother Benedict. Think of that identity as a temporary refuge, which you used when it was needed, which kept you safe until it was time to answer your greater call."

"But—"

"Princes are not like ordinary men, Cinhil. They have obligations—don't you understand?—to push back and defeat the destroyers. Your royal line had a knack for it in the old days. Your great-great-grandsire, father to that same Ifor Haldane whose portrait hangs on yonder wall, was known among his people as Saint Bearand, even during his lifetime. It wasn't all for being gentle and pious, either, though he was that. He pushed the Moorish invaders back into the sea and broke the back of their naval power once and for all. Their legions have never dared to cross the great wastes or to sail the Southern Seas again. That saintly man did all of this."

Cinhil was silent for a long moment, but when he spoke his voice was edged with bitterness. "Saint Bearand. Very pretty. Of course, you're not asking me to do anything as spectacular as pushing back the Moors —no, only to forsake my priestly vows and depose a powerful Deryni king. And you'll have to admit that there's little chance of an apostate priest ever being known as Saint Cinhil."

"Is *that* your aim: sainthood?" Rhys asked quietly. "Most of us are not so proud as to think that we could ever attain that kind of perfection."

Cinhil recoiled as though struck a physical blow, myriad emotions flashing across his face in rapid succession. Then he sagged in his chair, his hands fluttering uncertainly as he searched for the proper words.

"It—it isn't like that at all. How can I make you understand what it's like to be able to live a life totally committed to God? Father Joram might, if he weren't constantly playing devil's advocate, but . . ."

As he spoke, the door opened quietly behind him and Alister Cullen appeared in the doorway, pausing unseen to listen as the prince continued.

"It's as though you're shielded in a soft, golden light, floating about a handspan off the ground, and you're safe from anything that might try to harm you, because you know that He is there, all around you," Cinhil said, wrapped up now in his own remembrance. "It's as though—you reach out with your mind and grasp a beam of sunlight, yet even as you grasp it, it's all around. You . . ."

As Cinhil spoke, his eyes took on a strange, *other* glow, and the air around him became gently suffused with light—a pale, ghostly flickering which was almost, but not quite, indiscernible in the firelight and wavering candle flames. Camber was the first to notice it, followed almost immediately by Rhys; and Camber shook his head slightly as Rhys started to make a reaction. While Cinhil rambled on dreamily, his words no longer important to Camber, the Deryni lord reached out with his own senses and poised on the brink, mentally ready to fling himself across the void to essay the opening he could sense was imminent.

Cullen must have made some indication of his presence at that instant, for Cinhil suddenly turned in his chair and saw the vicar general. He broke off his detached monologue in mid-syllable, before Camber could make the contact he had so desperately sought. As Cinhil scrambled to his feet to bow nervously to the vicar general, Camber let out a long sigh which was mentally echoed by Rhys. Joram and Evaine appeared unaware of the exchange, until Camber saw Evaine touch her brother's hand and nod.

"Father Cullen," Cinhil murmured.

Cullen returned the bow, scowling somewhat. "Your Highness." He flicked his gaze past Cinhil to Rhys. "Lady Megan is here, Rhys. I think you should see her before she's given any further information. Camber, we told her you'd sent for her. I think you ought to be the one to tell her why."

Camber got to his feet with a sigh and nodded, glancing at the wide-eyed Cinhil with an almost fatherly mien, despite the fact that there was only a dozen or so years' difference in their ages.

"Your bride has arrived, Your Highness. I'll send her in to meet you in a little while."

"My—my bride?" Cinhil croaked, his face gray against his velvet robe.

"The Lady Megan de Cameron, my ward," Camber said, studying Cinhil's reaction hopefully. "She's human like yourself—a lovely, well-bred girl. She'll make you a worthy queen and wife."

"I— My lord, I *cannot!*"

"Your Highness, you *will,*" Camber replied, his eyes flint-hard on Cinhil's face. "Evaine, will you join Rhys and me? Megan is far from home, and will appreciate another woman's reassurance." He bowed stiffly. "By your leave, Your Highness," he said, and turned and followed Cullen out the door.

When they had gone, a shaken Cinhil turned back to the circle of chairs by the fire, startled to find Joram still sitting there, unmoving, studying him with an infuriating detachment.

"You're still here," Cinhil said—then immediately felt foolish because that fact, at least, was abundantly clear.

To cover his discomfiture, he wandered to the fireplace and poked the toe of his slipper dangerously close to a smoldering coal, then ran a trembling fingertip along the wing of an ivory statue of the Archangel Michael on the mantel.

"Father Joram, is there nothing I can say which

will soften your heart?" he finally asked in a small voice.

"Yours is the heart which must be softened, Your Highness," Joram replied. "Weighed in the greater balance, one man's personal wishes have little substance. You have the wherewithal to stop the slayings, the persecutions, to restore order and peace to the people your forefathers ruled and loved. I should think the choice an easy one. How can you, who claim to know the love of God, turn your heart from His people, your people, while Imre ravishes the land and brutalizes them?"

"They're not my people," Cinhil whispered. "Not in that sense."

"Ah, but they are," Joram replied, pointing a finger at him emphatically. *"I am the good shepherd, and know my sheep, and am known of mine."*

"No!"

"I am the good shepherd, and I lay down my life for the sheep."

Cinhil cast a desperate, frantic look at the door through which Camber and Rhys and Evaine had disappeared. "I beseech you, Father Joram, spare me this. I cannot do it. You know the vows I took. You, of all people—"

"Priest or prince, sheep or people, you can stop Imre, Your Highness."

"I pray you, do not do this!"

"Think on it, Your Highness," Joram said, rising and moving toward the door. "Where, if anywhere, is the break between your duty to God and your obligations to His people, *your* people? Is there even a difference?"

"I vowed vows," Cinhil moaned.

Joram paused in the doorway to gaze compassionately at his fellow priest.

"Feed my sheep," he whispered—then slipped out and closed the door behind him.

Cinhil spent the next hour on his knees, storming the heavens relentlessly for the answer he craved so desperately, and which he feared, more and more, would not come. At length, when his supplications had left him no more comforted than when he had begun, he lurched to his feet and stumbled to a small table near the fireplace. Hands shaking, he poured a cup of wine and gulped it down.

They would send her to him soon. Only, he had no idea what he was supposed to do or say. He supposed that he was to make sure he did not find her too ugly, or stupid, or whatever it was he was supposed to use as a gauge for measuring what his future—*wife!* —the word shook him—should or should not be.

But he didn't want to see her. It was unthinkable enough that he must face her in the chapel tonight, before God and all his Deryni captors. They would force him to go through with it. His and Camber's parting words had been almost a threat.

"My lord, I cannot!"

"Your Highness, you will!"

And, he realized sickly, he would. He would have to. It was clear by now that they were determined to have their way with him, that they would settle for nothing less than a crown on his head, a wife at his side, the Deryni Imre toppled from his throne.

He trembled anew at that thought, his mind going back immediately to the very real threat of their power. They were Deryni. God knew, they would probably *make* him obey, if he continued to resist them. Even the usually patient Camber had become almost menacing today.

The idea that he did not really have control over the coming event was comforting for a moment, for it relieved him of the responsibility for making the decision himself—at least for a time. But then he was forced to recognize another, darker part of himself which he had thought buried for many, many years, and somehow that frightened him even more.

Was he afraid of the wrath of Heaven if he broke his monastic vows and left the priesthood? Or was he afraid that it would be all too easy to break them, that he was actually beginning to look forward to this new life they had been waving so tantalizingly before him for these past weeks? The remark Camber had made about him beginning to sound like a prince had hit agonizingly close to home. He *had* sounded like a prince—or what he had always imagined a prince would sound like—and, at the same time, it had been the most natural thing in the world. It terrified him in a way he had never been frightened before in his life.

And to marry! He poured another cup of wine—fortunately, the cup was small—and drained it. To take a wife he had never seen, to—he forced himself to think in the scriptural term—to "know" her, to beget heirs—

He found his hands shaking, and he could not seem to make them stop. What was he doing? This was not the sort of thing a man should have to worry about —especially not a man of forty-three who had never known a woman. Why, marriage was supposed to be a young man's game. It was madness. They were insane!

He heard a fumbling at the doorlatch, and he turned away and froze. There was a pause, and then the sound of soft footsteps entering the room. He closed his eyes. He did not want to see her. He could not bring himself to turn.

"Your Highness . . . ?"

The voice was timid, shy, and sounded very young. Cinhil's eyes flew open and his shoulders tensed, but he found himself rooted to the spot, unable to move. They had sent him a child, a mere girl! He could not marry a child!

"I—I beg your pardon, Your Highness, but they told me I should come to you. I'm Megan de Cameron. I'm to be your wife."

Cinhil bowed his head, leaning heavily against the table in front of him. The irony of her position, coupled with his own, had suddenly struck him, and he had an almost uncontrollable urge to laugh.

"Is that what they told you, child? How old are you?"

"Fif—fifteen, Highness." She paused. "I beg Your Highness's pardon, but—have I misunderstood my guardian's intent? Are we not to be married this night?"

Cinhil smiled, a bitter chuckle escaping his lips despite his best efforts. "Aye, little lass. Though 'tis dynastic considerations and none other which ordain this marriage. The lost King of Gwynedd must have a wife. You're to be the royal broodmare, don't you see?"

"No, Your Highness, I'm to be your Queen," the young voice replied, strangely mature-sounding now, in the hollow silence his laughter had left.

Cinhil's face froze and he looked down at his hands, not seeing them at all. He wondered what had possessed him to say so cruel a thing, realizing he had hurt her.

"If you marry me, you will be the mother either of kings or of traitors, if we all live that long, child. Are you truly willing to risk the latter, with a man who cannot love you as a husband should, who can never give you ought but woe?"

"Who cannot *love*, Your Highness?" the voice asked softly.

"I am a priest, child. Did they not tell you?"

Another long silence followed, and then: "They told me that you are the last Haldane, Your Highness; that they would make you king." The voice was low, almost husky with tears. "I said I would risk all, even unto my life, to bring back the Haldane line and end Imre's bloody rule; and so I shall." A short sob escaped her. "But if, in your heart, there is no room for love, I had liefer die a maid than be the unloved bride of God himself!"

As Cinhil froze in shock at the blasphemy of her words, he heard her footsteps running toward the door, whirled just in time to see a mane of wheaten hair disappearing from sight, a delicate hand pulling the door behind her, a slender ankle flashing beneath voluminous turquoise skirts. Then the door was reverberating from the force with which she slammed it, and he was standing there all alone, a hand unwittingly outstretched in the direction she had gone, his heart wrenched by her words.

He started to follow her, to apologize, to try to explain that he was not a king at all, that he was but a simple monk, that he had never wanted to be king or even prince—but then the old pathways took over and it was too late. Like an old man, he sank slowly to a bench beside the table, letting his hand fall loosely to his side.

And then he put his head down upon the table and wept long, bitter tears for his lost youth, his lost faith, for himself, for the girl—whose name he could not even recall—and for all of them who would be lost. They would find him there, unmoved, when they came a few hours later to prepare him for his wedding.

CHAPTER EIGHTEEN

The Lord said to my lord, "You are my son.
This day I have begotten you!"
—Psalms 2:7

It was on the Vigil of Christmas, the night of the Saviour's birth, that Archbishop Anscom of Trevas left his Evensong devotions in the Lady Chapel of All Saints' Cathedral in Valoret and made his way back to his apartments, there to watch and pray until it should be time to celebrate the first Mass of Christmas. As was his custom on Christmas Eve, he was preparing to meditate alone upon the successes and failures of the fleeing year. He was not expecting the gray-hooded shadow which stepped from a recess in the corridor just before he reached the refuge of his chambers.

"Will you hear my confession, Father?" asked a strangely familiar voice.

Anscom held his candle a little higher and tried to pierce the gloom and darkness surrounding the man's face. Then he realized that it was more than mere shadow which shrouded the speaker's visage. The man in the cowled gray robe was a Deryni, his head veiled in an arcane haze which obscured his features and also muffled his voice. And yet there was no hint of menace in the voice or the presence, no threat of danger. The mysterious visitor was benign, though still unrecognizable.

More curious and anticipatory than alarmed, Ans-

233

com bowed his head in acquiescence and held the door open for the man to enter, then closed it behind them. No words were spoken as Anscom crossed to his oratory and lit another candle, took a purple stole from the *prie-dieu* there, touched it to his lips, and draped it around his neck. But when he turned to face the man again, the visitor reached to his hood and pushed it back to reveal a head of gilded silver hair, a countenance long familiar and loved.

"Camber!" the archbishop breathed, then embraced the other man warmly.

"Praise God, I wondered where you'd been," Anscom whispered, as the two parted and he held his friend at arm's length to look at him. "When I learned that 'Brother Kyriell'— But, what are you doing here? Surely you know that the king has out a warrant for your arrest."

"Would you betray me?" Camber said with a smile which clearly indicated the preposterousness of the question.

Anscom fingered the end of his stole with a wry smile. "Even if I wanted to, you bound me by this. I am under the seal of the confessional. Whatever you tell me, I am bound to keep silence."

"I require more than your silence, Anscom," Camber said. "I require your help."

"You know you have but to ask," Anscom replied. "Tell me what you need, and if I can help you, I will."

"I am wanted for treason," Camber said tentatively.

"Are you a traitor?"

"By Imre's reckoning, I am. The facts speak a little differently. If you will agree to come with me now, I would rather show you what I'm talking about."

"Come with you? Where?"

Camber glanced at the floor. "I may not tell you that. I *can* tell you that we will reach it through your own Transfer Portal, that you will be perfectly safe, that I will not hold you to your promise to help if you decide otherwise once you know the facts." He looked up at his friend. "But you are going to have to trust me with the location. I may not reveal that, even to you, even under the seal of the confessional."

"Are the others there, too?"

"Evaine, Joram, Rhys, a few others—yes."

"Rhys? But he—"

"I would prefer not to discuss it here, if you don't mind. Will you come with me?"

Anscom hesitated for just an instant, torn by his curiosity to question Camber further, then inclined his head. "As you wish. How long will we be gone?"

"Several hours, at least. Can you make arrangements for someone else to cover your duties?"

The archbishop raised an eyebrow at that. "On Christmas Eve? You know that I'm expected to be the celebrant at Midnight Mass."

"We would be greatly honored if you would perform that office for us, Anscom," Camber said quietly. "When you see, you'll understand why."

Anscom studied his friend's face for a long moment, reading the importance there of the request, then gestured for him to step into the oratory and draw the curtain. When Camber had done so, the archbishop moved to the wall and pulled a velvet cord. A few minutes later, a black-cassocked priest knocked and entered. He found the archbishop sitting on his bed, looking quite unwell.

"Your Grace, is anything wrong?"

"I'm feeling rather ill," the archbishop said weakly. "Would you please ask Bishop Roland to take my place at Mass tonight?"

"The Midnight Mass? Why, certainly, Your Grace, but—is there anything I can do for you? May I send for the apothecary or a Healer to attend you?"

"No, that won't be necessary," Anscom murmured, lying back on the bed and giving a pained sigh. "Something I ate, I have no doubt. I shall meditate, and try to sleep. It will pass by morning."

"Very well, Your Grace," the priest said doubtfully. "If you're sure—"

"I'm sure, Father. Please go now, and on no account am I to be disturbed. Is that clear?"

"Yes, Your Grace."

No sooner had the door closed behind the priest than Anscom was leaping out of bed to draw back the curtains of the oratory doorway.

Camber chuckled at the look on the Archbishop's face. "Does this remind you of the pranks two young subdeacons played at Grecotha? Though, I'll warrant, neither you nor I ever handled a subterfuge with better wit or finesse in those days."

"Humph! I would hope that we had improved since then," Anscom rumbled. "What next?"

"Your nearest Transfer Portal."

"You're standing in front of it," Anscom replied, pushing Camber back a few steps farther into the oratory and taking his place beside him. "What do you want me to do?"

"Just open your mind to me and let me take you through. I promise to give you the background information as soon as we're there."

"And also ensure that I can't figure out where we've gone." Anscom snorted with a slight smile, folding his arms across his chest. "Go ahead. I understand why you have to do it that way. I just want you to remember," he said, closing his eyes, "that I see right through you, Camber MacRorie."

"And so you always did, my friend." Camber grinned and laid his hands on either side of Anscom's head from behind. "Open to me now . . ."

And they were gone.

And standing in another Portal, in another place.

Anscom opened his eyes, stunned, and turned to stare at Camber incredulously.

"You can't be serious," he whispered. "A Haldane heir *here?* It was the Haldane that was stolen out of Saint Foillan's? Camber, you're mad! It can't possibly succeed!"

"There are a great many who don't agree," Camber said quietly. "Even our Haldane himself is beginning to believe that it's possible and desirable. Unfortunately, his moral scruples are interfering a bit with his dynastic duties. Your sanction of his cause would be the seal of approval which he needs."

"You want me to give him my blessing?"

"I want you to acknowledge the legitimacy of his descent, to declare him a lawful Prince of Gwynedd, to release him from his vows, and to marry him to my ward—tonight. Will you do that for me?"

"What you're asking—"

"I know what I'm asking. If you cannot find it in your conscience to do it, then I'll release you, as I promised. We'll just have to make do with Father Cullen."

"Alister Cullen, the Vicar General of the Michaelines? He's here?"

Camber nodded. "And has been with us almost from the beginning, though it was Rhys who discovered the first clue to the prince. Cullen can do what I've asked you to do, but it won't carry the same weight."

Anscom drew himself to his full height and looked across at Camber indignantly, his craggy face a mask of resentment. "I forbid Alister Cullen to do those things. If they're to be done, *I* will do them."

"And will they be done?" Camber asked, controlling a smile and suspecting that he was about to net his quarry securely in the snare of sacerdotal jealousy.

"It is the prerogative of the Archbishop of Valoret," Anscom intoned, "to acknowledge the royal succession, to perform royal marriages, and to crown the kings of Gwynedd. While it is impossible to do the last tonight, I shall certainly perform the first two!"

"Good," Camber said simply. He turned away so that Anscom could not see the grin of triumph on his face. "If you'll come with me, I'll introduce you to our reluctant bridegroom and prince."

And the intended bridegroom was, at that moment, still reluctant.

"Father Joram, I beseech you, do not let them do this. I cannot go through with the marriage. I will be forsworn."

Joram, partially vested for his role as deacon later on, folded his hands and prayed for patience.

"Your Highness, believe me, I understand your hesitation—"

"My hesitation?" Cinhil shook his head and began

pacing again, the silver tissue-cloth of his wedding garments rustling with his agitation. "Nay, my refusal. It is all well and good for you to promise that Father Cullen will release me from my vows. But I did not make my vows to him, or even to his order. I made them to the Vicar General of the *Ordo Verbi Dei,* and to God. The archbishop himself could not—"

"Suppose we allow the archbishop to speak for himself, Your Highness," Camber said, entering the room with a man whom Cinhil had never seen. "May I present His Grace, the Archbishop of Valoret, Anscom of Trevas. Your Grace, His Royal Highness, Prince Cinhil Donal Ifor Haldane."

Cinhil had whirled, alarmed, at Camber's first words, and now stared with blank amazement at the gaunt, purple-cassocked man at Camber's elbow. The man introduced as Archbishop Anscom gazed sympathetically at the startled prince and made a slight bow before extending the ring of his office. Cinhil's resolve crumbled at that, and stifling a sob he seized Anscom's hand and dropped to both knees, pressing the ringed hand first to his lips and then to his bowed head as he collapsed at the feet of his superior.

"Help me, I beg you, Your Grace!" he choked. "I cannot do it! They say I must forsake my vows and return to the world. I am afraid, Father. I do not know the world!"

In compassion, Anscom laid his free hand on Cinhil's head, signed with his eyes for the others to leave them alone.

"I understand your fear, my son," he murmured, when they had gone. "I grieve with you that such a cup must be placed before you. But these are grievous times in which we live, and all of us must make sacrifices."

Cinhil looked up at that, his wide eyes abrim with tears. "Are—are you telling me that I must obey them? That I must forsake my vows, as they ask, and take up this crown that they would thrust upon me?"

"It is not always an easy thing to walk the path which has been chosen for us, Cinhil," Anscom said gently. "But we who strive to serve the true path, to listen to the will of God, must realize that we cannot hope to comprehend all which the Creator has laid out for us. You can do a great service for Our Lord, and for all His people, if you will take up this cross and bear it faithfully for Him."

"But I have given Him my life already! I have served Him these twenty years and more, and would gladly have given the rest of it for—"

"I know, my son," Anscom nodded. "You have served Him, and well. But now He demands a different kind of sacrifice. All of us have things which we alone can do best; now He asks for that unique service which only you can give. It cannot be by accident that the Lord allowed one Haldane to survive until this troubled time, waiting in safety and love until His will might be fulfilled."

There was a spark of defiance in Cinhil's eyes as he searched Anscom's gaunt face. "You're telling me, then, that I have no choice in the matter? That my fate is bound to Camber's futile cause?"

Anscom shook his head. "Not Camber's cause only, my son. And 'futile' only if you choose it to be so. Nor are you bound by other than your knowledge of God's will. He has called, and clearly; and the power to disregard His call is in your hands. But if you make that decision, the lives of many thousands of His people will be upon your head. The choice is yours; but you must also bear the consequences."

"Your Grace, how can you do this to me?" Cinhil whispered. "You are no better than they, playing on my emotions like a master lutenist, knowing exactly which strings will tug most insistently at my heart and mind. It isn't fair . . ."

"In your eyes, no," Anscom agreed. "But we are only mortal, Cinhil. We can only listen to that silent voice within, and remember that we shall have to live with the consequences of whatever we do, at least for the remainder of our allotted time here on earth. My conscience is clear, my son. Is yours?"

Cinhil could make no answer to that. Sinking back on his heels, he buried his face in his hands and wept silent, bitter tears for the road which now unrolled before him, and which he knew he could not choose to refuse.

The archbishop, a shrewd judge of men, finally knelt down beside the prince and laid gentle hands on his shoulders, holding the sobbing man close and letting him weep.

After a while, they prayed.

Half an hour before midnight, two women sitting in the listening gallery above the haven's chapel peered repeatedly through the viewing slits as they waited for the hour to arrive. Below, most of the inhabitants of the haven had gathered in the chapel—MacRories and priests and Michaeline knights—and the chapel itself shimmered with the light of many candles. Racks of holly-twined candelabra had been set along the faceted walls, throwing gay shadow-shapes among the ribs and columns of the shallow vaulting, glinting gold and amber on the altar plate. A rectangle of precious Kheldish carpet had been laid at the foot of the altar steps, where the ceremonies of recognition and marriage would take place.

In anticipation of the first Mass of Christmas (and, all hoped, the promised royal wedding), the altar had been dressed with evergreen boughs and the best altar linens which the haven could provide. There was an air of uncertainty, a hushed anticipation, as all waited for midnight and the coming of their king. The bride, at least, was present, though nerves were wearing more than a little thin.

Megan de Cameron, ward of the Earl of Culdi and soon to be Princess of Gwynedd, had borne up bravely following her lone encounter with her intended, but now fatigue and tension were beginning to take their toll. She was flushed with excitement and had not been able to eat since her arrival that afternoon. Evaine had tried to assure her that all would be well, but such attempts fell on deaf ears. She suspected that Megan would probably be just as nervous, even were the situation not charged with so much uncertainty.

All things considered, Evaine wondered how Megan

and Cinhil would suit if the marriage did take place
—and right now, there appeared to be no guarantee
that it would. Rhys had told her of Cinhil's mood
when he and Joram went to prepare him for the
ceremonies, and of Archbishop Anscom's unexpected
arrival. She wondered whether Anscom had been successful. According to Megan, the prince had not even
looked at her when she tried to speak with him.

That was bothering Megan most, Evaine knew.
And from as objective a point of view as she could
manage under the circumstances, that was Cinhil's
loss: Megan was beautiful. Of medium height, willow
slender, with wide turquoise eyes spiced by a spray of
freckles across the slightly tip-tilted nose, Megan even
moved with an unaffected grace—an unspoiled girl-
woman with, perhaps, just the right combination of
guile and innocence to appeal to the shy and
conscience-stricken Cinhil. She was gowned in silver
tissue, as befitted a princess, her wheaten hair caught
up in shining coils beneath the crown of holly and
rosemary. Truly a vision to turn a prince's fancy—
at least an ordinary prince. The question was, could
she turn the head of a prince who wanted to be a
priest?

The vision glanced at Evaine and twisted a fold of
silver tissue between shaking fingers.

"Oh, what's the use?" she whispered. "He does not
need me. He—he does not even wish to marry at all,
and I—I fear I do not please him."

"Give him time, Megan," Evaine said, laying a reassuring hand on the younger girl's arm. "He is as
afraid as you are—more afraid, for he had never
thought to marry, and you"—she touched the girl's
nose impishly—"you have been the object of men's
devotion almost from birth, beginning with your father, God rest his soul, and not ending with mine. For
you, it was never a question of whether you would
marry, but when, and to whom."

"But, he said—he said that the marriage was only
for dynastic purposes, and that I should be nought but
a royal b—broodmare," she stammered, her eyes reflecting her hurt.

"He said *what?*"

Evaine tried to keep the shock and anger from her voice, unsuccessfully, and wished she could take Cinhil by the shoulders and give him a good shaking, prince or not.

"Oh, I don't think he meant to hurt me," Megan added quickly. "He was lashing out at all his own hurt of the past few weeks. It can't have been easy for him."

"No, it has not."

"And I know what it will cost him to take me to wife," Megan continued softly. "For his own sake, I wish I might spare him, but for all our sakes, I dare not. If it were not to me, then it would be to some other maid he must be wed. Even I understand that."

She sighed resignedly, and Evaine studied her carefully for several seconds.

"I think you love him already," she finally said, not moving as Megan's head snapped up to stare at her. "You do, don't you?"

Megan nodded miserably, and Evaine returned a gentle smile.

"I know. It's difficult, isn't it, to love and not be loved in return? God grant his love will grow."

"Easy enough for you to say, who have Lord Rhys who loves you dearly," Megan whispered. "I shall have only a crown, and perhaps not even that, if we fail."

"And so, he needs you even more, don't you see?" Evaine answered. "He needs a gentle, loving wife— more than just a bedmate—who can comfort him when he is afraid and encourage him when he grows faint of heart. He is so much younger than you, Megan, in so many important ways, and he has such a heavy burden to bear. Do not make him bear it alone."

"But, I'm afraid . . ." Megan began.

"So am I. Constantly," Evaine replied gently. "But if we do not support our men in their good works, what hope is there for any of us? Think what has been risked already, even to bring us this far. You said that I am fortunate to have Rhys. Oh, how right you are! But he has been in grave danger for these many months now, and every day there was the chance

that I might lose him. Still, I would not have held him
back from doing what he had to do—nor will I.
Just as I would not expect him to keep me from my
part, simply because I might be harmed. Do you understand what I'm trying to say?"

"A little, I think." Megan sniffed, wiping at her
eyes, and finally managed a smile. After a minute,
she asked, "Evaine, will you promise me something?"

"If I can."

"Promise that you will not leave me when I am
queen. I shall be very lonely, otherwise."

"Oh, Megan!"

Evaine hugged the younger girl close, tears welling
in her own eyes, but suddenly there was the sound of
movement in the chapel below, and both of them
moved breathlessly to the viewing slits.

It was midnight; it was Christmas Day. And as the
door was thrown open and the processional cross appeared in the doorway, they knew that this day
brought the coming of more than just the Christmas
King.

*"Dominus dixit ad me: Filius meus es tu, ego hodie
genui te,"* the Michaeline knights and monks sang
. . . The Lord said to my Lord, "You are my Son.
This day I have begotten you."

And as the strains of the ancient introit swelled in
the chapel, reverberating from vaulting to the gallery,
Anscom led Joram and Cullen as escort to a pale but
stately Cinhil. Cathan's young sons followed the
princely procession, each bearing a silver circlet upon
a velvet cushion. The boys stood beside their grandfather, eyes wide with wonder, as Archbishop Anscom
ascended the altar. Cinhil, with Joram and Cullen
bowing to either side, knelt before the lowest step and
inclined his head, his face still and emotionless in the
candlelight.

When the prayers had been concluded, Anscom
turned and descended the three low steps, cope and
miter glittering in the candlelit chamber. Joram and
Cullen moved from Cinhil's sides to Anscom's, waited
for the archbishop to speak.

"Who art thou," the archbishop demanded, "who makest bold to approach the altar of the Lord?"

Blanching, Cinhil stood up and managed a nervous bow, all self-possession dissolving as the time came to speak the fateful words. "May—may it please Your Grace, I am"—he swallowed hard—"Cinhil Donal Ifor Haldane, son of Alroy, grandson of Aidan, great-grandson of King Ifor Haldane of Gwynedd, and the last of my line." He paused to draw shaky breath. "I come to claim the birthright of my name and family."

"And what proof bringest thou, Cinhil Haldane, that thou art, indeed, the true-born heir of Gwynedd and, therefore, Prince in this realm?"

The green-cloaked Rhys stepped forward and presented a sheaf of parchment. "Your Grace, I present the baptismal records of Prince Cinhil and his father, Alroy. Though the records were kept in the mundane names which the Haldanes were forced to use while in hiding these past eighty years, I vow and affirm that Daniel Draper, Prince Cinhil's grandsire of record, was, in reality, Prince Aidan, true-born son of Ifor Haldane, last of the Haldane kings before the present dynasty."

Joram brought forth the Gospel, and Rhys laid his hand upon it. "This I swear by my gifts of Sight and Healing, and may God rip them from me and destroy me if I speak ought but the truth."

At this Rhys bowed, Anscom bowed, and Rhys returned to his former place to be replaced by young Davin MacRorie, bearing his silver circlet on its cushion of velvet. As Joram extended the book once more, Anscom took the circlet in his gloved hands and laid it on the open pages.

"Kneel, Cinhil Haldane," he said in a firm voice.

Cinhil obeyed.

"Cinhil Donal Ifor Haldane," the archbishop intoned, holding his hands above the prince's bowed head, "I acknowledge thee Heir of Haldane and Prince of Gwynedd in exile." The hands came to rest upon the silvered head. "Though it is not within my power to restore thee to thy rightful place at this time, I give thee this circlet as a token of thy royalty." He took the circlet and held it above Cinhil's head. "It is my fervent prayer that one day soon I may replace it with a crown of gold, in regal, public splendor, as is thy due. Until then, wear this as a reminder of the weight of responsibility which thou assumest for thy people."

With that, he put the circlet of silver on Cinhil's head, then raised him up and bowed.

Cinhil acknowledged the bow awkwardly, then glanced at Camber and Rhys and, removing the circlet, knelt once more. "Your Grace, I accept this circlet in the spirit it was given, but I bear the burden of prior vows which prevent my full assumption of the duties that accompany it."

"Dost thou, then, wish release from those vows, my son?"

"Not for myself, but for the sake of my people, Your Grace," Cinhil murmured, barely audible. "I am the last of my royal line. If I shrink from my responsibilities, my people will suffer longer under the tyrant's heel. Though I love my former life, I am told that I may better serve God's purpose, for now, by taking up my birthright and my crown, to free my people from the bondage of the conquerors and restore just rule."

"We thank thee for thy former service and do release thee from thy vows. *Ego te absolvo . . .*"

As the archbishop recited the words of the release, Evaine stirred in the gallery chamber, to lead a frightened but determined young girl down the narrow steps to the chapel door. A moment later, the door was opening again, this time to admit a silver-clad princess who kept her eyes averted as she came to meet her bridegroom. All eyes turned toward her as she glided to the altar and made her obeisance—all save Cinhil's. The prince, standing to her right, kept his attention fixed mostly on the crucifix on the archbiship's breast, not daring to glance aside.

His vows released, it was this part of the ceremony which frightened Cinhil most; and he had difficulty concentrating on what was being said. He let himself be led through the ceremony, responding when he was told, until he suddenly realized that he had said the vows of marriage, and that a low, quavering contralto voice was now repeating similar vows at his side.

"I, Megan de Cameron, only begotten daughter of the Lord and Lady of Farnham and ward of my Lord Camber MacRorie, Earl of Culdi, wittingly and of deliberate mind, having fifteen years completed in the month of January last past, contract matrimony with the right excellent and noble Prince Cinhil Donal Ifor Haldane, Heir of Gwynedd, and take the said Prince Cinhil of Gwynedd for my husband and spouse, all others for him forsake, during his and my lives natural, and thereto I plight and give him my faith and troth."

Then there was a slender band of gold in Cinhil's hand, and he was slipping it on the finger of this strange young girl. *"In nomine Patris, et Filii, et Spiritus Sancti, Amen."* After that, he vaguely remembered joining hands with her while the archbishop laid the ends of his stole across their hands and pronounced a blessing—and then Mass.

He thought he remembered receiving Communion, but for the first time in his life he could not be sure. Because after that they bade him take the crown of holly and rosemary from Megan's head and remove the pins which held her coiled hair in place. It came tumbling down in a cloud of wheaten glory, sweet-smelling, soft as gossamer, reaching nearly to her waist—and he nearly dropped the silver circlet they bade him place upon her head.

Only when he was safely in his chamber, and she in another, was he able to think clearly again—and then, his thoughts did little to ease his anxiety. After a few minutes, Joram came in to help him undress, then left him standing numbly before the fire in a fur-lined dressing gown.

He did not know how long it would be before they came for him, and though he knelt dutifully at the *prie-dieu* in the corner of the room and tried to say his evening prayers, the words came stiff and meaningless, holding little comfort. He trembled as he knelt there.

All too soon, a knock at the door called him from his tangled thoughts, and then a torchlit procession escorted him to the door of the nuptial chamber. As the door opened, he could see the archbishop sprinkling the bed with holy water. A pale, shy face peered out above the top of the sleeping furs; it was surrounded by all-too-familiar wheaten hair.

He entered, hesitantly, and the archbishop bowed to the occupant of the bed and then bowed to Cinhil and blessed him with holy water as well. A reassuring touch on the shoulder as he passed, and then archbishop and attendants and ladies and everyone except the two of them were departing, the door closing; and they were alone.

Cinhil swallowed heavily and studied the floor with great interest. Finally, he chanced a cautious glance at the girl in the bed. To his surprise, she looked at least as frightened as he felt. He wondered whether he looked the same to her. He looked away quickly.

"My—my lady," he whispered, his voice cracking and betraying him as he tried to speak. "I—thou knowest what manner of man I am, that—that I know not the ways of women . . ."

His voice trailed off, and he dared to raise his eyes to hers. They were deep pools of sea-blue, eyes a man might drown in—and he could not have looked away now if he had wanted to.

"Then, we are even, my lord," she murmured, not quite so frightened as before, "for I know not the ways of men. But thou art my husband"—she extended her hand tentatively—"and I am thy wife. Wilt thou come and let us learn together the ways of men and women?"

The bed was wide, and she lay toward the middle. To take her hand, as he knew he must—and as he suddenly wanted to do—he had to cross the several feet separating them and sit on the bed. He did. And after a moment, when they had gazed into one another's eyes as best they could in the dim light, she brought his hand to her cheek and rubbed it gently. He was astonished to find her cheek damp with tears, incredibly soft lips brushing the back of his hand.

Alarmed that he might have frightened her, he shifted to peer at her more closely, and soon found his other hand stroking her hair, wiping her tears away. Then she was reaching up to touch his face, his beard, to run her fingers lightly along the edge of his mustache, to brush her fingertips across his lips; and he was responding, kissing her palm.

Camber, when he looked in on them in the early dawn hours, found them peacefully entwined in one another's arms, the bedclothes in disarray, Cinhil's fur-lined robe discarded across the foot of the bed. As he eased his way back out of the room, a smile on his lips, he breathed a silent prayer of thanksgiving to whatever saint watched over nuptial beds. Whoever it was, that saint had apparently done his or her work well.

CHAPTER NINETEEN

*And they put him in ward, that the mind
of the Lord might be shewed them.*
—Leviticus 24:12

The days stretched into weeks, and the weeks into months, until it was spring—spring, with its promise of new beginnings. Deep in the rockbound fastness of the haven, the exiles could not see the usual signs of spring: the flowering trees and the leaping forth of all the new grasses and blossoms of the meadows. But there was a greater flowering in the womb of her who was, perhaps, to be their future queen. Archbishop Anscom himself returned to the haven long enough to celebrate the Mass of Thanksgiving. And with the expectation of the royal birth in the fall, they at last had a timetable toward which to work; they had not dared risk Cinhil in a coup until the royal succession was assured. The next season's snow would bring with it the winter of Imre's reign.

For Cinhil, however, this spring was not a time of rejoicing. Frightened and conscience-stricken at what he had done, he betook himself more and more to his academic studies after that, shunning his young bride's bed and keeping himself apart as much as possible. Though Rhys assured him that he had fathered a son, and had only to wait until October to see the living proof, Cinhil pushed the knowledge out of his mind and raised his defenses even more. They might force him to become a prince, and even a king, but he did not have to like it. Never again did he come as

close to letting down his shields as he had in the chapel
that day at his last celebrated Mass, or on the afternoon of his wedding when he spoke of his vocation as
a priest. He refused even to address the possibility of
assuming Deryni-like powers on his own.

One rather curious gain had been made, however.
Though Cinhil still would not speak to Camber or
Joram or any of the other men in the compound about
other than what was required, he did talk with Evaine
sometimes. And, oddly enough, it was not until after
her marriage to Rhys on Twelfth Night that the break-
through began. Joram had blessed the union, with
Camber and the entire population of the haven standing proudly by. But though Cinhil had attended, with
Megan, and wished the couple well, he had retired to
his own quarters soon after the ceremony, oddly pale
and quieter than even he was wont to be. He had not
felt like celebrating, he told Evaine later.

But if Evaine's marriage shook Cinhil almost like
his own, at least it placed Evaine in another, safer relationship to him. He was not aware, and she would
never have dreamed of telling him and jeopardizing
the fragile trust which was building between them, but
there had been a potential there—at least on Cinhil's
part—for quite a different relationship than he would
have approved or been comfortable with. Whatever
the potential, however, that facet was closed to him
forever when she made her marriage vows to Rhys.
What Cinhil did not realize was that the way had
been opened for an even *more* intimate association:
he had no reference point for the union of minds.

It became their practice to meet each afternoon to
talk, occasionally with Rhys or Joram in attendance,
but more often just the two of them, sitting comfortably before the fireplace in his outer chamber. He
told her of his childhood, of his father and grandfather, and sometimes they even talked about his life in
the monastery—a thing he had never discussed with
anyone before, and certainly not with a woman.

And her reaction surprised him. He wondered at
the insight she displayed when he described the communion he felt with the Deity—not so much because

she was a woman, for that had not even occurred to
him (he knew of the great female mystics of past
centuries)—but he found it difficult to comprehend
that any layman could approach the spiritual ecstasies
which he had experienced in his own religious life. He
had thought such experiences a prerogative of those
totally committed to God—in a word, to those with a
religious vocation. And Evaine, married to Rhys
Thuryn, had clearly had no call to a traditional religious life.

For a while, he marked it down to her association
with her priest-brother, with whom she was very close.
But then he began to realize that she shared it with
her father and her husband as well, and he wondered
whether it was a trait coincidentally common to all
four individuals in question, or whether it was somehow related to their Deryniness—that otherness which
sometimes set them all so far apart. He examined
his own feelings in the matter, and he found that this
quality of otherness was really not so alien at all.
That, too, surprised him; but again, he kept pushing
the growing recognition out of his mind.

The true turning point in their relationship came
one day late in March. He had come upon her praying in the chapel, and had found such a look of peace
upon her, such tranquil oneness with the Universe as
she knelt there, that he had almost himself knelt in
awe of it. Shortly, she became aware of his presence
—or perhaps she had known it all along—and she
opened her eyes and turned to look at him. When she
did, there was a glow of such pure radiance, such
sanctity, about her, that he had not dared to speak
until they had left the chapel. Even then, he responded
to her few comments mostly in monosyllables until
they were safely in his study room and he had closed
the door. He felt that he must ask her of what he had
seen—felt he *could* ask. But he was having trouble
finding just the right words.

As she seated herself before the fireplace, he noticed
a small, golden stone in her hand. She toyed with it
unconsciously, her fingertips caressing its smoothness

with an abstract contentment. Suddenly, Cinhil had to find out what it was.

"What have you there, my lady?"

"This?" Evaine glanced casually at the stone. "It's called *shiral*. It comes from the mountains of Kierney, near my father's seat of Cor Culdi. He gave it to me last year, after I asked an almost identical question of him."

She handed it to him with a smile, and he turned it over in his hand, watching its surface catch the light in liquid ripples.

"Is it only a trinket, a toy?" he asked, after a long pause. "It occurs to me that I have seen you carry it before, though I never paid it much mind. It must mean something very special to you."

Evaine lowered her eyes, speculating on just how much Cinhil had seen; then she decided to venture an experiment.

"Aye, it is special, Your Highness. Partly because my father gave it to me, of course, but also for other reasons. Would you like me to show you what my father did with it, when I asked your question?"

His eyes flicked to the crystal, his features tensing as his fingers clenched on it spasmodically. Then he shook the emotion and looked back at her again.

"Your words are innocent enough, my lady. And yet, I feel a certain foreboding. Should I?"

She held out her hand, a gentle smile on her lips and in her eyes as she tried to put him at his ease once more. She knew, as he put the crystal into her hand, that he had felt something from it—even if he was not aware of what it was.

"You must not fear it, Your Highness—no more than one should fear to approach the Sacraments when one is in a state of grace," she breathed, couching her words in terms she thought he might understand. "The crystal itself contains neither good nor evil, though it does have power. But one must approach it with respect and awareness of what one is doing. It can be a link—perhaps with the Deity?"

She moved her shoulders in a shrug, the crystal

winking in the palm of her hand. Cinhil leaned forward to look into her eyes intently.

"Does it have something to do with the look I saw on your face in the chapel a little while ago?"

"It did not cause it, though it may, perhaps, enhance it," she replied softly. "That is but one of its uses."

Cinhil let out a long breath, never taking his eyes from hers.

"Show me," he whispered.

With a slight inclination of her head, Evaine sat back and rested her elbows on the arms of her chair, holding the stone lightly between the tips of her fingers, as she had seen her father hold it so long before. Staring into its depths, she took a deep breath and exhaled softly, willing her senses to extend around the crystal. At first, only the reflection of the firelight flared in its depths; but then it began to glow of itself.

Still in light trance, Evaine shifted her eyes to Cinhil's, the crystal pulsating coldly between them.

"It is a focus, and a finding," she whispered, her face expressionless. "This is but the beginning. From here, I could go—"

She broke off and shook her head, passing a hand before her eyes, and the light in the crystal died. Cinhil sat forward in alarm, not comprehending what he had just seen.

"Is anything wrong?" he asked, reaching out to touch her arm in concern.

Noting the touch, but not daring to react to it, Evaine shook her head and smiled, glancing at the crystal and then back at him.

"Nothing wrong," she assured him. "It's a trifle difficult to speak while maintaining the light, though," she lied. "I can better answer your questions in my normal state."

"Then, what you were doing was not—normal?"

"Well, it was normal for Deryni—or rather, let us say that it was not abnormal," she smiled. "The *shiral* crystal is an aid to concentration. Anything can be used as a focal point, but the *shiral* is better than most, because it shows you, by glowing, when you've reached the minimum level of concentration. Anything bright will do: a ring, a fleck of sunlight on glass. For that matter, you don't really need anything physical, though it does help, especially in the beginning."

"You use it as a focus of concentration," Cinhil repeated. "And that is what you were doing in the chapel?"

"Well, yes, I happened to be using it, but—" She glanced at him shrewdly, knowing that he was about to ask the question she had been leading him to for the past five minutes. "Your Highness, you surely aren't thinking to try the *shiral* crystal yourself? I don't think it will work for humans."

"At least let me try," Cinhil pleaded, taking the bait and swallowing, without even realizing the hook was set.

Wordlessly, Evaine laid the crystal in his hands and watched him settle back in his chair with a triumphant glint to his eyes. Holding the crystal as he had seen her do, he stared at it intently, tense with the effort of willing it to glow.

Nothing happened.

After a little while, he clasped the crystal in his hand and looked up at her, his swallow audible in the stilled room. It was obvious by the very line of his body that he had not given up.

"Show me how."

His harsh whisper was a command, and with a nod Evaine moved her chair a little closer so she could observe him from slightly to one side.

"Now, you must follow my instructions exactly," she warned, touching his empty hand lightly and gathering his full attention upon her. "I have never allowed a human to try this, and I would not see you harmed. I have told you, the crystal has power."

"I will do only what you tell me to do," Cinhil said. His eyes were bright and intent upon her as she turned slightly toward him.

"I want you to look at the crystal," she said, noting that the firelight caught and flared in the stone even as he steadied it before his eyes. "Stare at the crystal and let all else in this room recede from your mind.

Let my voice guide and guard you; for to enter the peace of the crystal, you must let all else slip away and recede for a time. Concentrate all of your consciousness upon the crystal, and let my voice be your guide. Imagine all the light of your essence pouring through your fingertips to gather in the matrix of the crystal. You see nothing but the fire of the crystal, hear only my voice guiding you, and now your universe is the crystal, and you are entering its domain . . ."

As she spoke, her voice low, almost a chant, his attention did focus on the stone, his breathing deepened and slowed, the taut lines of his face relaxed. Cautiously, then, lest she disturb the delicate balance which was forming, she extended her own senses around him and felt the resistance melt away, felt his consciousness receding. He was on the verge of a trance; he was in a trance. She closed her eyes and let her senses guide her around the interstices of his outer consciousness, felt them part before her as his shields crumbled and dissolved.

Insidiously, then, she entered and made certain adjustments, left certain instructions, forged certain bonds of will which would be undetected when she withdrew. She found his outer mind a place of order and beauty, as she had long suspected; but she dared not go deeper this time, for his trance was light and she must not tax his trust in her. Still, the seeds had been sown, and she knew that next time she could return him to this state—and deeper—at will.

Evaine withdrew then, erasing all signs of her passage as she went, and opened her eyes slowly. She glanced at him, his eyes unseeing, his face calm and untroubled—then felt her gaze drawn unbelievingly to the crystal between his fingertips.

It glowed! Faintly and haltingly. But *it did glow!*

Controlling the impulse to make some sudden motion, to let some word of wonder escape her lips, she softly began to speak again and lead him back to consciousness.

As his eyelids fluttered and his hands twitched a little in the coming back, the light in the crystal died

—but not before she was certain he had seen it, and had realized that this had been his work. He blinked several times and breathed a sigh of wonder, then carefully put the crystal on the chair arm between them, not yet willing to meet her eyes.

"Did I—did I really see what I just thought I did?" he finally asked, when he had stared at the crystal again for several heartbeats.

"Yes, Your Highness, you did."

He looked up at her then, a beseeching look on his face. "I know I should not ask, but I would like to keep the crystal, at least for a time. I—should like to examine this feeling more closely."

"What did you feel?" she said, not really needing to ask, but knowing he would expect such a question.

"I—don't know. A strange peacefulness, a—suspension of time." He turned his gray Haldane eyes upon her and his lips parted again. "May I keep it? Please?"

"Very well. But there is a condition: you must not try to use the crystal unless I am with you."

"That is understood."

"Your royal word on it?" she insisted. "And more, your priestly word?"

He picked up the crystal again and looked at it, then nodded and gave a sigh of relief; he stood and slipped the crystal into a small box over the fireplace. He caught himself on the edge of the mantel and rubbed his eyes, then half turned toward her with an ill-disguised yawn.

"I'm sorry. I don't know why, but I'm suddenly very tired. I think I ought to rest now."

"Work with the crystal can be very taxing," she said, rising and taking his arm. "Come. Let me help you to your bed."

Half an hour later, Evaine was telling Camber and Rhys and Joram of the afternoon's developments, sharing the experience with them arcanely. Camber's face beamed with pride as she told her tale. When she had finished, Joram let out a raucous whoop of de-

light and Rhys kissed her soundly. Camber sat back
in his chair and poured mulled wine for all of them.

"Let us drink to Evaine," he said, handing cups
around and lifting his in toast, "for doing what no one
else could do, for breaking through our prince's shields
without a hint of battle. The way is clear now. We can
go in and assess him, and he will never know, until
it's time to do what must be done. To Evaine!"

"To Evaine!" Rhys and Joram echoed, and drank
her salute in joy.

They talked more, then, long into the night, evaluating and assessing what she had learned in the very
shallow sampling she had made that afternoon, making plans, venturing theories. . . .

The following afternoon, after Cinhil had finished
his studies for the day and taken his noon meal, she
sought him out again. He had been waiting for her;
and as soon as she was seated, he wasted no time in
procuring the crystal and taking his place beside her.

"I have not touched it since yesterday," he told her,
putting it in her hand. "When I awoke this morning,
I was initially angry at what you made me promise;
but then I realized that it was too powerful a thing to
tamper with on my own, and that it were best to go
slowly. I had not thought to be so tired yesterday."

"That is a common reaction when learning to use
new abilities, even among Deryni," she smiled. "But,
you awoke refreshed this morning, didn't you?"

"Yes, and in my bed, my clothes removed. I"—he
lowered his eyes—"I don't even remember falling
asleep."

"You were very tired when I left, Your Highness.
I had Father Nathan come in and make you comfortable for the night, since I suspected that you might
not awaken before morning. I hope you are not angry
at the presumption."

"No, of course not." He folded his hands and
studied them for a few seconds, obviously much relieved by her explanation, then looked up at her again.

"May—may we try it again?" he asked.

"Sit back and relax." She smiled, moving the crystal

before his eyes. "And as I now place the crystal in your hand, you will sleep."

His eyes closed and his breathing changed, and he was deep asleep. With a sigh, she reached out and touched his forehead, taking him ever deeper, securing control. Then she rose and glided to the door to admit Camber, and resumed her place beside the sleeping prince. She could feel her father's reassuring presence as she extended her senses and entered Cinhil's mind.

She roamed its recesses for perhaps a quarter-hour, Camber watching through her mind, never touching Cinhil's directly. Finally, she withdrew, shaking her head lightly to clear away the last vestiges of her own trance, for she had been very deep. Cinhil slept on, oblivious to what had happened, oblivious to their presence. Camber smiled and brushed his daughter's forehead lightly with his lips, then quietly withdrew. After a moment, Evaine brought Cinhil back to the easy, gentle trance he had achieved on his own the day before. As before, the stone glowed faintly. She drew a sobering breath to steady herself.

"Cinhil, hear my voice only," she said, "and listen to what I say. Though you are in this state of otherness, you can still hear my voice and you can do what I tell you. Do you wish to see the crystal glow? You may answer."

The royal lips parted and breathed a scarcely audible "Aye."

"Then, when I touch your hand, I want you to open your eyes. You will remain in this state of otherness, you will still be in contact with the matrix of the crystal, but you will be able to see it and react. It is real, and you have achieved this task. Do you understand?"

He nodded his head slightly.

"Very well, then." She touched his hand. "Open your eyes and tell me what you see."

He obeyed, the long lashes rising slowly, his eyes like pools of quicksilver, tracking dreamily to the crystal. For a moment there was no reaction, but then the ghost of a smile tugged at the corners of his mouth and she knew that he saw.

"It glows," he murmured, his voice flat in the trance, but tinged with a little wonder. "And I have done this?"

"Yes." She touched his hand again. "But now it's time to return, remembering what you've seen. Wake now, refreshed and relaxed. You've been successful."

As his eyelids fluttered and he emerged from his trance, the light in the crystal died. But this time, though he sighed at the return to the real world, a smile was on his lips, and he closed the crystal in his hand instead of putting it down immediately. He stared into the fire for just a moment, savoring what he had seen, then looked at Evaine again and smiled, a genuine, relaxed smile such as she had not seen upon his face in all the time he had been in the haven.

"You remember, don't you?" she said.

He nodded. "It was beautiful. And *I* did it, didn't I?"

"You did it," she smiled. "This still doesn't mean that you should try it without my presence yet, but you're learning. I think you can see, from the way you feel, that it wasn't nearly as difficult this time. Oh, Cinhil, if you will only let us help you, we can make you such a king as the world has never seen!"

He looked away at that, as she had known he would, his face returning to its old, taut lines. But though the shields were back, they were not nearly so high or so fast as before.

She left him to ponder what he had seen; and though he stared long at the crystal after she had gone, he did not try to enter it again that day. He had, after all, given his word.

They worked with the crystal almost daily after that, until he learned to slip in and out of his Deryni-like concentration unaided. After a time, she allowed him to use it in his meditation; she did not tell him he no longer needed it. After that, he seemed not quite so bitter at his lost priesthood.

He still was not eager to be king. And he still avoided intimate contact with the forlorn Megan whenever he could, for he did not like to be reminded of this part of his dynastic duty. But his education progressed smoothly, and in ways which he himself did not dream. His work with the crystal, especially, was establishing paths of discipline which would be invaluable once Camber discovered how to unlock the potential that they now knew him to carry.

It was May before they were ready—the culmination of six long weeks of research and partial trial and agonized planning. They argued over how much he should be told; over whether he should be told ahead of time; over what form the unleashing of his powers should take—for there were options available, and they must choose the ones which would be least threatening to Cinhil and his rigid theological orientation.

They chose Rudemas for the day of conferring power: Rudemas, called Beltane by the old reckoning. Early that evening, before the prince's evening meal had been brought, Camber went with Evaine and Rhys to Cinhil's quarters.

He had been sitting in his chair by the fire, his slippered feet propped on a footstool, the *shiral* crystal in his hand, though he had not been using the stone. He had been thinking about it, but it was more a thing to occupy his hands than a focus for his mind just now. His stomach was telling him it was time for the evening meal, and he wondered why they had not brought it yet.

The knock at the door was not unexpected, then, though he was a little surprised to see the three of them instead of Father Nathan. With a slight nod, he bade them come inside, motioning them to the chairs before the fireplace.

"I thought you might be bringing my dinner," he said casually as he took his own chair. "Father Nathan is usually quite prompt."

They had waited until he was seated before sitting themselves. Evaine was in her accustomed place to his left, Rhys on the arm of her chair away from Cinhil, Camber to Evaine's left.

When they did not speak, Cinhil cocked his head quizzically and shifted uneasily in his chair.

"Is anything wrong?"

"No, all is as it should be, Your Highness," Camber replied. "It's time we had a serious talk, though. Of necessity, it will be brief."

"Why brief? The evening is just begun, and I have no place to go."

"But you do," Camber said quietly. "That's what we came to talk to you about."

"I'm afraid I don't understand." Cinhil sat a little straighter and placed his hands deliberately, formally, on the arms of his chair. He was not sure he liked the tone of this conversation.

He glanced at Evaine, hoping for some clue, some hint of what was to come. Instead, he saw her hand coming toward his forehead, knew suddenly that if he let her touch him he would be lost. He shrank away from her, trying to avoid the hand, but it was too late.

"Sleep," was all she said.

He felt the swooping, slightly heady sensation he had felt before when he used the *shiral* crystal—it was still in his hand, he realized dully—but this time he seemed to have no control over it. He felt his eyes close and he sagged a little in his chair. He could not seem to help himself, could not fight it.

"Now, listen to me," he heard her voice say—and her voice was the only thing in his universe. "You will not resist us physically. You can open your eyes, but you will obey me. Look at me, Cinhil."

His eyes opened and he did look at her, but there was a sluggishness about his response which he could not seem to shake. He swallowed and glanced at the others; he saw Camber rising to walk around in front of him, to lean both hands on the arms of his chair and stare into his eyes. He could not disengage from that gaze.

"Open to me, Cinhil," the Deryni Master said. And Cinhil knew what they intended for him.

He continued to fight them, mentally, all the way to the chapel, but it was futile. They walked him down

the rockbound corridors, and he could not run or cry
out or make one move to thwart them.

The chapel door was guarded by a stern Michaeline
knight—Cullen, Cinhil recognized with a start—a
naked greatsword resting with its quillons between his
mailed fists. At their approach, he touched a strangely
glowing doorlatch, then bowed his head in homage as
they passed. The door closed behind them with a thud
of finality which made him long to wrench his head
around for one last look at his now-closed escape.

But he did not. For they had not told him he might.
Instead, he went where he was bidden, stood compliant and unresisting in the exact center of the faceted
chamber, his feet on the jewel-toned carpet where they
had crowned him prince. By the light of the Presence
lamp and two tall altar candles, he watched with
fogged detachment as Joram came into view periph-
erally and mounted the three low steps to the altar.

The priest genuflected and stood awhile in meditation, hair and surplice and brocaded stole glowing in
the sparse candlelight. Presently, a taper flared as
Joram turned to regard him; and then the priest was
giving the taper to his sister, turning back to the altar
to spoon incense into a smoking thurible. Cinhil could
not see Camber or Rhys, though he knew they must
be somewhere behind him.

New beeswax candles in free-standing brass holders
had been placed at the foot of the altar and a few
paces to either side of Cinhil, and it was to the first of
these that Evaine now went. Cinhil seemed to recall
that they had passed a fourth one as they entered, in
which case he was standing at the center of a circle
defined by the four new candles. He could not turn to
verify that recollection—but that was not the issue,
anyway. What mattered was that the very concept of
the circle numbed him to cold panic. He told himself
that there was a rational reason for his alarm—tried
to dredge that reason from his memory—but his
mind was not functioning properly.

Evaine lit the candle on the floor at the foot of the
altar before him, then moved slowly toward the one
to his right, shielding the flame with her hand as she

walked. The otherness of the Deryni was like a sixth presence in the chamber, an icy finger prodding at the base of his brain. He had the impression that the cold he felt was not altogether the fault of the rock walls and floor.

Joram set what appeared to be a covered chalice on the floor at the base of the first candlestick, then gave Camber something wrapped in white silk. The object was small and delicate, from the way the Deryni lord was handling it, and Cinhil found his attention drawn to it almost irresistibly. It was as though time hung suspended, as though he watched through someone else's eyes.

Evaine lit the candle to his right and began to move around behind him.

"Would you please kneel?"

The voice at his side was Rhys's, and without hesitation Cinhil obeyed, unable to resist. He could see now that what Camber held was a large, cabochon ruby the size of a man's little fingertip, set in the claws of a red-gold mounting and terminating in a slender gold wire.

"The gem is called the Eye of Rom," Rhys's calm voice informed him, as the Healer's hands did something cold and wet to his right earlobe. "Legends say that it fell from the stars on the night of Our Saviour's birth, and was brought by the Magi as a gift to the Child. Whether or not that is true, it has been in the MacRorie family for twelve generations. We have endowed it with—ah—certain characteristics which will be useful to you a little later tonight."

Rhys handed a bright sliver of metal to Camber in exchange for the gem, brought the crimson fire toward the royal head. Again, Cinhil felt the Healer's gentle touch and realized that Rhys must have pierced his ear. He wondered foggily how he would look in an earring.

"There. That's done," Rhys said. He leaned back to inspect his work, then touched the prince lightly on the shoulder. "You can stand up now."

Cinhil could and did, and lost himself for the next few seconds in trying to fathom the significance of what had just happened. The faint, musical jingle of metal rattling against the thurible brought him back, and he saw that Evaine had finished her circuit of the chamber and extinguished her taper, and was now being censed by her brother.

She made a slight bow when he had finished, whether toward Joram or the altar or the first candlestick, Cinhil could not be sure, then remained with her back to Cinhil, her head slightly bowed. Joram, thurible swinging before him in a cloud of sweet incense, began retracing the circle which Evaine had just trod. Cinhil recognized the Latin Joram chanted: it was the Twenty-Third Psalm. He also, if he squinted his eyes just so, was getting the distinct impression that the circle glowed.

He must have drifted a bit, for the next thing he knew, Joram was censing those within the circle. Camber stood to Cinhil's left, Rhys to his right; and Evaine waited at the edge of the circle with the cup in her hands, uncovered. He heard the faint clink as Joram laid the thurible on the floor behind them, felt Joram's passage as he returned to Evaine and took the cup from her with a bow. He tensed as brother and sister moved to stand before him, fearing he knew not what.

The cup, he noticed, was half filled with wine. Odd, but he could not remember having seen this particular cup before, though he had thought he was familiar with all of the altar furnishings in use in the haven's chapel.

"I suspect that you've noticed this is not the chalice we customarily use in this chapel," Joram said, apparently reading his curiosity. "There are reasons for that, which will become apparent to you in a little while. The wine is sacramental wine, but it has not yet been consecrated. I tell you this to reassure you that there is no desecration involved in what we do or ask you to do tonight. If that were our intent, we would not be here, in this place. You may ask questions now, if you wish."

The words freed Cinhil's tongue, and he swallowed apprehensively, a dozen questions boiling in his mind. After consideration, he settled on a cautious approach, suspecting that he already knew the sorts of answers he was going to get.

"What were you doing earlier?"

"Warding. It is something you will learn, in time. It is a protection from outside influences, from forces which might otherwise interfere in what we do tonight. All within the confines of the wards are now sealed from harm."

"Then there is danger in what you do?"

"There is always danger," Camber said in a low voice. "We seek to minimize that danger by following certain carefully ordered procedures. Believe me, we would not risk you here if we did not believe it was safe for you."

"But what are you going to do to me?" Cinhil asked in a plaintive voice.

Joram's eyes met his, unblinking, deadly serious. "We are going to give you the means to stand against Imre."

"But—"

"Enough, Cinhil." Camber touched his hand and he fell silent. "Joram, tell him what will be expected of him."

Joram nodded slightly.

"The cup contains wine, though it will soon be more than that. Not physically different, though it will be bitter. But it will be changed in other ways which I cannot explain just now. It is not unlike what occurs during the Mass, though it is not the consecration with which you are familiar. It—" He looked to his father for guidance, bowing gratefully at Camber's nod.

"Those details are not important for your part," Camber continued calmly. "In a little while, Joram will ask you to repeat certain words after him. It doesn't matter whether you believe the words or not, though I think you'll find that they're very familiar to you. In the right setting, following the proper sequence of actions, they will accomplish our purpose. There should be no difficulties."

"And, after I speak these words?" Cinhil whispered, knowing that he would obey, whatever their answer.

"Then you will drink the wine," Camber said. "And what will be, will be."

At that, Camber moved a little more to Cinhil's left, Joram taking a similar position to his right. He felt Evaine move to stand behind him, the edge of her skirt brushing his ankles in passage. Rhys, with a smile which Cinhil knew was intended to be reassuring, turned to face the altar.

Cinhil was terrified, notwithstanding Rhys's gesture, for he knew that *it*—whatever *it* might be—was about to begin, and that he had no way to avoid it. Taking a deep breath, he tried to calm himself, tried to let the tension wash out of him a little—and was surprised to find that it worked. There was a moment of hush, and then Evaine's voice behind him, weaving a crystal stillness around them all.

"We stand outside time, in a place not of earth. As our ancestors before us bade, we join together and are One."

He watched as Rhys bowed his head, saw that Camber and Joram had done the same, inclined his own a little in response.

"By Thy Blessed Apostles, Matthew, Mark, Luke, and John; by all Thy Holy Angels; by all Powers of Light and Shadow, we call Thee to guard and defend us from all perils, O Most High," she continued. "Thus it is and has ever been, thus it will be for all times to come. *Per omnia saecula saeculorum.*"

"Amen," came the joined response; and Cinhil found that he had answered the same.

They made the sign of the cross together then, and stood a while in silence.

Finally, Rhys turned to face him again, his golden eyes hooded, sun on dark waters. As Joram passed him the cup with a bow, Rhys raised it to eye level between them, his right hand spread flat above the rim, not touching.

"I call the mighty Archangel Raphael, the Healer, Guardian of Wind and Tempest. As the Holy Spirit didst brood upon the waters, so instill thou life into this cup, that he who drinks thereof may justly bid the forces of the Air. *Fiat, fiat, fiat voluntas mea.*"

As he passed his hand above the cup and exhaled upon it softly, a swirling mist gathered above the wine and settled on its surface. The cup grew cold and frosted even as Cinhil watched, bright beads of condensation sparkling as they ran down Rhys's hand. Rhys bowed over the cup, then passed it to Joram. The priest lifted the cup as Rhys had done, spread his right hand over it.

"I call the mighty Archangel Michael, the Defender, Keeper of the Gates of Eden. As thy fiery sword guards the Lord of Heaven, so lend thy protection to this cup. That he who drinks thereof may justly forge the might of Fire. *Fiat, fiat, fiat voluntas mea.*"

A pass of his hand above the cup, a murmured phrase, and cold fire burned blue around the rim and on the surface of the wine. Cinhil closed his eyes and took another deep breath to still his terror. Movement behind told him that Evaine now held the cup.

"I call the mighty Archangel Gabriel, the Herald, who didst bring glad tidings to Our Blessed Lady. Send thou thy wisdom into this cup, that he who drinks thereof may justly guide the knowledge of the Water. *Fiat, fiat, fiat voluntas mea.*"

Then the cup was in Camber's hands, the great lord grim and somber as the night. For the fourth time, a hand was extended over the cup, Deryni forces brought into play.

"I call the mighty Archangel Uriel, Angel of Death, who bringest all souls at last to the Nether shore. Herewith I charge this cup, that he who drinks thereof may justly bind the forces of the Earth. *Fiat, fiat, fiat voluntas mea.*"

Another pass, a dustlike rain of some white powder upon the surface of the wine, and then Camber held it out to Cinhil.

The metal ran with moisture, glistening, cold; and about the rim played ghostly blue frost-fire. Mist brooded on the surface of the wine—wine which was darker now, more opaque. Cinhil felt an icy dread surge through his body, feared the words he knew would come next.

"Take the cup, Cinhil," Joram's voice commanded

from his right. "Hold the cup before you and repeat the words I say."

Trembling, Cinhil watched his hands reach out, felt the cup cold and wet and sleek within his grasp. Almost without thinking, he found his hands lifting it as they had lifted countless other cups, though not recently; he realized that what he had seen, what he was about to do, was no whit less sanctified than any priestly act he had ever performed.

That thought sobered him as all his reason had not been able to do. Precise and clear, he echoed the familiar words which Joram bade.

"Libera nos, quaesumus, Domine, ab omnibus malis, praeteritis, praesentibus, et futuris. . . ." Deliver us, we beseech Thee, O Lord, from every evil, past, present, and to come. . . . *"Per eumdem Dominum nostrum Jesum Christum Filium tuum, qui tecum vivit et regnat in unitate Spiritus Sancti Deus. Per omnia saecula saeculorum."*

"Amen," the four responded.

Then his hands were bringing the cup toward his lips, and he knew that he would drink.

Power was in the cup now; he could feel it tingling in his hands and surging down his arms even as he held it. The wine was cold and bitter, and he felt it hit his stomach in an icy, leaden mass, felt fire course through his veins, a flash of brilliance sear behind his eyes, as he drained the cup.

A rushing wind surged through his mind, rending, tearing, driving a wall of glass-green water before it; lightning flashing; chasms opening up in the fabric of his being. And pain—an agony so intense he could not even scream.

He felt the cup slipping from his fingers, faintly heard it ring against the muffling carpet beneath his feet. But then he was blind, and he was deaf; and he was falling into the abyss, his mind gripped in a soundless scream of terror.

And the darkness prevailed.

Chapter Twenty

Hear us, my lord; thou art a prince of
God among us.
—Genesis 23:6

He lay as one dead for a day and a night after that, his condition watched closely by Rhys, the others hovering anxiously nearby. When on the second morning he opened his eyes again for the first time, they were there, peering down at him eagerly, a dozen unspoken questions on their lips.

But he did not remember what had happened—or said he did not. And no, he did not seem to have any new abilities or powers—why should he? They could not even go into his mind again to see, having relinquished all control over him with the conferring of their spells. If Cinhil had gained power, he was not telling them—perhaps never would, if he was terribly angry at the way they had gone about their task. Or perhaps their attempt had failed, and nothing had happened, other than to throw their future king into a coma for a time. Until he decided to talk about what, exactly, had happened, there was no way for them to know.

They settled in to await the birth of Cinhil's heir, and to hope.

Summer passed. Outside the haven, Imre's reprisals against the Michaelines ground to a halt after his men sacked and burned a village adjoining one of the condemned monasteries. If Imre had not stopped it, he might have faced rebellion.

But if the Michaeline furor had died down by the end of the summer, the activities of the Willimites had not. Seizing on the by-now widespread rumors of a living Haldane heir, small bands of Willimite executioners worked their deadly morthwork by night, slaying a full score and more of Deryni folk whose crimes had gone unpunished by the law. At last a Deryni princeling toppled—Termod of Rhorau, cousin of the king himself—and Imre could ignore the Willimites no longer. Outside of Gwynedd, the madness spread even as far north as Kheldour, where human lords still held tenuous rule. Enraged, Imre determined to find the murderers and make an end to the Willimites once and for all.

Royalist troops, under the leadership of Earl Santare, were more successful at rounding up peasants than they had been at running the Michaelines to ground. (Less than a dozen Michaelines were eventually executed, in the seven months of intensive search for members of the ill-starred order.) By the beginning of autumn, more than eighty Willimites, among them the key leaders of the Willimite movement, had been captured, tortured, and horribly executed as an example. Imre, reassured by the dwindling numbers of the enemy he could see, began to worry less and less about one whom he could not see and whose existence, in fact, he had begun to doubt. From not one of the Michaelines or Willimites captured had he been able to get a shred of evidence of a Haldane pretender.

As Michaelmas came and went, still without that evidence, Imre relaxed even more. With Yuletide approaching, it became far easier to become caught up in the gaiety of the season than to worry about a disaster which would probably never come. Besides, it had been nearly a year since the MacRories had disappeared into oblivion.

And in hiding, the promised saviour of his people continued in his solitude. Though he had, by now, fully recovered from his ordeal of May—at least physically—the anticipated manifestation of power did not occur. Cinhil continued to read and study as required, seemingly resigned to the fate which had been chosen for him; and after a few strained weeks, he resumed the afternoon visits with Evaine; but there was never again the intimacy of their previous discussions. The Michaelines continued to prepare, and life continued in the haven; but Camber worried about the future—about what would happen when the child was born and they must begin their plans in earnest for the coup. Nor were there any ready answers.

Cinhil's son was born on the Feast of Saint Luke, as they had known he would be; and with his first lusty cry, his father's spirits and mental attitude began to change. Cinhil still had not displayed any evidence of arcane powers, nor volunteered any suggestions as to why he could not use them. (Camber suspected that he *would* not use them. They had gone over every step of the ritual, and there was no chance for error, in light of the reactions Cinhil had made at the time.) But the prince did smile more after the child's birth. And one night, over dinner with Rhys and Evaine, he actually made a joke.

The event of his son's birth became a milestone of sorts. Though Cinhil tried hard not to show it, it was soon apparent to everyone that the prince was more than a little proud of his new heir. Quite without prompting, he suggested that it might be appropriate if all of the residents of the haven were invited to the baby's christening. He even expressed an interest in planning the details with Joram.

Camber conveyed the royal invitation with relief and set the date. It would be November 6, the Feast of Saint Illtyd. Sext, the Sixth Hour, was set for the christening ceremony.

Few had seen the royal infant or mother in the past month, for the Princess Megan had had a difficult birthing, despite Rhys's best healing efforts. She walked with Cinhil's support at her elbow as they entered the chapel, radiant if a little unsteady still from her recent confinement. Evaine carried the infant prince to the baptismal font, Rhys at her left side. The look in Cinhil's eyes was one of dumbstruck awe, and he seemed not even to notice the heads which bent and bowed as he passed into the chamber with his princess, so intent was he upon the bundle of silk kicking lustily in Evaine's arms. His gaze never left his son as Archbishop Anscom began the form of baptism.

"In nomine Patris, et Filii, et Spiritus Sancti."

"Amen."

Rhys and Evaine, the baby's chosen godparents, stood before the baptismal font opposite Anscom and Joram and another Michaeline whom Anscom had brought with him from Valoret. The archbishop's gravelly voice reached to every corner of the faceted chapel chamber.

"Exorcizo te, creatura salis, in nomine Dei . . ."

As Anscom blessed the salt which the priest at his left held forth, Cinhil craned his neck to get a better view; in annoyance, he took Megan's arm and eased her to a vantage point at Rhys's left, where they could gaze at their son.

"Aidanus Alroi, accipe sal sapiente . . ." Anscom intoned. Receive the salt of wisdom . . .

The baby gurgled and fussed a little as the salt was placed on his tongue, but Evaine cooed and bounced him a bit and he settled down. Anscom, well used to the protestations of salt-tongued infants, went blithely on with the ceremony, laying the end of his stole across the baby's body.

"Aidanus Alroi, ingredere in templum Dei . . ." Enter into the temple of God . . .

When the archbishop had anointed the baby with oil on the breast and between the shoulder blades, he turned his attention on Rhys.

"Aidanus Alroi, credis in Deum, Patrem omnipotentum, Creatorem caeli et terra?"

"Credo," replied Rhys, answering for his godson. I believe.

"Credis in Jesum Christum Filium ejus unicum, Dominum nostrum?"

"Credo."

"Credis in Spiritum Sanctum et sanctam Ecclesiam?"

"Credo."

"Aidanus Alroi, vis baptizari?"

"Volo." I do.

Smiling slightly, Anscom picked up the silver ewer containing the water for baptism. He could scarcely contain his delight as he turned and offered the ewer to the prince.

"Would Your Highness care to perform this office for his son?"

Cinhil's jaw dropped and his eyes went round. *"I, Your Grace?"*

"Even a layman may baptize in necessity, Cinhil," Anscom said, his smile broadening as he watched the beginning of Cinhil's comprehension. "I believe you more than qualify."

Cinhil stared at the archbishop as though unable to believe his ears, joy transfiguring his face as it had not for many, many months.

"Can this be true?" he whispered. "I am to be permitted this?"

Anscom nodded gently and put the ewer into the prince's hands.

"Fiat, Frater," he murmured.

Bowing his head in humility, Cinhil took the ewer to his chest and bowed thanks, then turned back to where his son awaited him. The infant had quieted in Evaine's arms, and as Cinhil motioned her to move closer, the baby yawned and appeared to doze. Evaine shifted so that she could hold the baby over the font, and Rhys laid his right hand on the child's shoulder.

"Aidanus Alroi Camberus," Cinhil whispered, beginning to pour the water over the crown of the baby's head the requisite three times.

Camber's eyes flashed to Cinhil in surprise as the prince continued, for he had not known that his name was to be given to the royal child.

"Ego te baptizo in nomine Patris, et Filii, et Spiritus Sancti. Amen."

But as Cinhil returned the ewer to its place and reached for the towel which Joram held, Rhys froze, then laid both hands on the baby's head. The infant whimpered once, coughed and gave a little sigh; then it was still. As Rhys's jaw dropped in shock, Cinhil's eyes darted to the child.

"Sweet Jesus, what's wrong with him? Why isn't he moving? *He's not breathing!*"

Rhys stared numbly, not daring to speak the icy horror which lay beneath his hands, and Evaine raised stunned eyes to the prince.

"He—he's dead, Cinhil," she said in a small voice.

There was no sound in the chapel for perhaps five heartbeats, and then Princess Megan gave a little cry and fainted. Guaire of Arliss caught her as she crumpled, his stricken "My Lady!" breaking the still tableau; but even as Cinhil turned shocked eyes toward her, he clutched at his chest in pain and started to collapse.

He caught himself on the edge of the baptismal font, clung to it unsteadily, drunkenly, clamped his eyes shut and shook his head as though to break free of some binding force which would crush him. White-knuckled, he bent over the rim of the font, a long, almost animal cry escaping his lips as he stared into the water. Then he jerked upright to look wildly about him, a terrible expression lighting his eyes.

"They have killed my son!" he cried, his glance striking each of them as though with physical blows. "They have killed my son, and now they seek to destroy me!"

"Who is trying to destroy you, Cinhil?" Camber retorted. "Name your attackers! Tell us what you feel!" His eyes sought some clue around the room, yet were drawn back to fasten on Cinhil in dread fascination. He could detect no attack, no hostile threat at all. If Cinhil was under attack, his assailant was very skilled.

"No, not they—*he!*" Cinhil gasped. *"He* is in this room! He is one whom we trusted. *Do not touch me!"* he added, as Rhys moved as though to restrain him.

Whirling about abruptly, he snatched the body of the dead baby from Evaine and clutched it protectively as he backed against the altar.

"We will find him, my Aidan," he whispered savagely. "I will avenge you!"

"Cinhil!" Camber's voice cut through the rising horror as though he had shouted, though he had scarcely raised his voice. "Cinhil, there is nothing you can do. Let Rhys take the baby. Perhaps he can—"

"No. He is dead." The voice was flat, leaden. "I know it, Camber, with the sure certainty which you yourself tried to teach me." He swept his hard gaze around the room again. "One of you has betrayed me!"

"Has he gone mad?" Joram whispered to Rhys.

Rhys shook his head. "No. The baby was poisoned —in the salt, I think. I—"

The prince had been scanning everyone in the room, and now he whirled and strode to the center of the chapel, there to glare in outrage at a man in the habit of a Michaeline priest—the same priest who had been assisting Anscom with the baptism. The man's eyes were calm, unreadable, until Cinhil took a single step closer and whispered, *"You!"*

As all eyes locked on the priest, and those closest shrank away, a change came upon the man. His eyes came alive, the body stood straighter—and then the arms were upraised in the beginnings of a spell, fingers moving in a certain pattern of attack and defense.

Instinctively, Cinhil threw up one arm in a warding-off gesture, a faint corona of pinkish fire partially veiling his face. He gaped at the man unabashedly as everyone else crowded against the walls.

"You, a priest, would dare raise hand against brother?" Cinhil murmured, unaware of what he had just done.

The Michaeline said nothing; only stood and stared across at the Haldane heir, his eyes smoldering.

Power was building in the center of the room. But if Cinhil's attacker was a trained Deryni, Cinhil himself was at least untested, and neither had yet paused to cast a protective circle around the battle area. Camber, fearing for the humans among them, signed for his kin to shield the noncombatants. It was just in time, for Cinhil's next words shook the very air, the ancient, awesome phrases echoing from arch and joist and mosaicked panels.

Cinhil's words brought crimson fire to encircle him —a dancing, living flame which was not so much seen as felt and experienced, by those on the outside. It was a fire which was sensed, if at all, out of the corner of the eye—which disappeared when sought head-on, but which was no less deadly should it come within reach of the unprotected. Cinhil stood straight and terrible, his dead son clasped close against his breast.

The Michaeline moved toward him in a haze of gold, until only a few meters of sparkling air separated them.

The air glittered with power, visible lightning arcing across from one man to the other, only to be dashed ineffectually against the other's shields. The air was sharp and acrid, like the charged, moist stillness before a thunderstorm. The candles guttered wildly in the growing flux of energy. Energy howled and echoed in the rockbound chamber, coruscating around the heads of the two combatants like mad, misshapen haloes. A greater surge now blew out all the candles, and for a moment the wind moaned on in near-darkness.

Then the roaring of the wind increased in pitch, until the watchers could discern two voices—wordless, mighty, contending darkly in the abyss which had been opened by the forces locked in mortal combat. The pressure grew, and the watchers tried to cover their ears, their eyes, their minds, against the not-sounds, not-sights, not-thoughts which barraged the senses from every angle.

Finally, the Michaeline staggered and let out a low, desperate cry, his eyes at last clearing from their trancelike stare as he reached out in desperate supplication and fell. Abruptly, all sound ceased, and the room was plunged into blackness.

Silence. Velvet darkness, save for the fading aura, felt rather than seen, of the victorious Cinhil, wrapped in the living light of his now-realized powers, living arms still locked protectively around the dead form of his infant son.

It was Camber who finally had the presence of mind to break the tension, by stepping from his place against the wall to flare the candles back to light. Anscom was not far behind, walking slowly to the side of the motionless Michaeline priest, kneeling to cradle the man's head wordlessly in his lap. Rhys came and laid a hand on the man's forehead, but the priest was dead. Together with Anscom, then, Rhys entered the dead man's mind, clearing the way for Anscom to read what little still remained.

When Anscom raised his head, it was to turn shocked eyes upon Cinhil. He did not rise, but bowed his head in shame.

"Forgive me, My Prince. I fear that I am partially to blame for all of this. I should not have brought him here. He told me, before, that Imre's men had tried to capture him last spring—that was one reason I took him in. But he could not tell me that, in fact, they had succeeded. He—is not responsible. Please forgive him."

"The king had done this?" Cinhil asked, his voice low, dangerous.

"Yes, My Prince," Anscom whispered.

"And he can warp a man's mind to do such a thing against his own will?"

Anscom nodded, not daring to speak, and Cinhil turned his terrible gaze on Camber, then on the rest of them gathered still around the edges of the chapel, sweeping with his glance but not really seeing any of them. Then he moved purposefully to where Anscom and Rhys knelt by the fallen priest and stooped to lay his hand gingerly on the dead man's shoulder.

"For that you were vanquished by another stronger than yourself, and yourself wished me no harm, nor harm to my son"—his voice started to break, but he controlled it—"I forgive you."

He rose quickly to his feet, his face terrible in the candlelight.

"But for him who has done this thing to you and me and mine, there can be no forgiveness in this world or the next. Woe be unto thee, Imre of Festil, and to all thy base and cowardly line, who would strike down helpless infants and break good men to the yoke of evil. I will avenge them and all whom thou hast made to suffer by thy might. This I swear—I, Cinhil Donal Ifor Haldane—by my faith, by the Crown of Gwynedd, which my forefathers wore and which I shall surely wear again, if only to destroy thee, and by the body of my murdered son. There shall be an end!"

And as the Prince of Gwynedd stood straight and tall beneath the eyes of God and men, the raw power dying around his head as he became only slightly more than mortal once more, every knee bent in fealty, and every head bowed in homage. Camber, kneeling with the others, tried to push his own apprehensions to the back of his mind.

CHAPTER TWENTY-ONE

For out of prison he comes to reign; whereas
also he that is born in his kingdom becomes
poor.

—Ecclesiastes 4:14

They buried the infant Prince Aidan in a tiny tomb
beneath the floor of the chapel where he had died,
on the Feast of the Four Crowned Ones, who had also
been martyrs to royal tyranny centuries before. Cinhil,
terrible in his grief, would not permit anyone else to
touch the body at first, keeping watch alone in the
cold little chapel for a night and a day and a night,
taking no food and sleeping not at all. Only on the
morning of the second day did he permit them to
enter and seal the baby in its tiny casket and consign
it to the grave. He would not speak of the incident
after the burial.

The slain priest, too, was buried in the chapel a day
later, though it was only the Michaelines and Camber
who came to mourn him. Alister Cullen performed the
simple rites. Later, much later, there would be a
carved stone set into the wall where he lay, but the
words would be brief, as they had always been for
every Michaeline who died in the Faith: *Here lieth*
Humphrey of Gallareaux, a priest of Saint Michael.
Only that and the dates. Beyond that, they could do
nothing for him.

Cinhil was much changed after this. If he had been
withdrawn and subdued before, now he was cold,
ruthless, machine-like in his dealings even with his

allies. No longer the quiet, guilt-ridden priest-*cum*-prince who had wrestled with his conscience to reconcile his new calling, now Cinhil was coldly interested in every facet of the planning which was being carried out at fever pitch—for all that his interest was darkly colored by vengeance and shrouded by aloofness. He must know their military strength, and from where each group of men would attack when the order came, and who would command, and what provisions had been made for each detail of the infiltration plan. Most of all, he would know *when*. Delay now made him restless.

The information was his for the asking, though Camber continued to harbor some concern about his motives. The Michaeline knights, he was told, were gathering even now, the original fifty in the vicinity of the haven, and another century and a half at Dhassa. The Culdi levies were also preparing, secretly raised by Camber on one of his infrequent trips outside the haven, five hundred of them prepared to stand the city of Valoret to siege if the Michaeline assault should fail.

They planned their move for the first of December, the night of the opening of Imre's Yule Court, when everyone of any importance in the kingdom would be within Valoret's walls and, more importantly, within the confines of Imre's castle. Judging from past Yule Courts, it would be a night of drunkenness and debauchery—in all, a perfect night for invaders to infiltrate, overpower less-than-wary guards, and topple a dynasty.

They learned more, too, of the man who had been responsible for Prince Aidan's death. There had been no deliberate betrayal; and Imre's actions regarding Humphrey had resulted in a mere fluke. When captured, Humphrey had not even known for certain of the Haldane's existence, and had no idea of the location of the haven; even Imre had recognized this as soon as Humphrey's will was broken. But just in case Humphrey should happen upon word of such a man, the king had taken pains to plant the seeds of treachery and destruction. Humphrey was released with the

memory that he had not been captured at all, though
he had come close. Naturally, he had flown to Archbishop Anscom for refuge; and Anscom, unwittingly,
had taken Humphrey in. When Anscom returned to
the haven to baptize Cinhil's heir, it was the most
natural thing in the world for Humphrey to accompany
him. After all, were not the Michaelines his brethren?

This information was dutifully passed on to Cinhil,
along with all of the other intelligence they were
gathering; and it did soften his heart a little toward
the man whose physical body had been responsible for
his son's death.

But though Cinhil continued to show an astounding
grasp of the military tactics and planning with which
he was being bombarded, an aloofness continued to
surround him, couching an ever-deeper resentment for
the Deryni despite the circumstances of Humphrey's
betrayal. Camber became increasingly aware of it, as
his earlier fears were reinforced by Cinhil's actions;
and he discussed this with the others more than once.
But there was really nothing that anyone could do,
other than to be aware of the potential problem—
and to hope and pray that they would not have to deal
with it in any major way.

Cinhil's princess probably suffered most directly in
the weeks that followed. Though she was soon with
child again, Cinhil having been impressed with the
necessity of another heir as soon as possible, she was
a wraith-like shadow of the spirited, sensitive girl
who had come less than a year before to be the
bride of Haldane. A little genuine attention from her
lord husband could have eased her heartsickness considerably, but Cinhil was too busy, too preoccupied,
to notice her need. He was gently courteous to her in
public, as was fitting the mother of his future heirs,
and it could not be said that he abused her or even
ignored her, but there was a cool superficiality to their
relationship, as though living the role of prince and
future saviour of Gwynedd had sapped him of all ability to love or be loved. Though he now seemed to
have accepted his role as prince, he had an increasing
otherworldliness about him—not purely of religious

fervor, though that continued to be an integral part of
his personality, but more a clinical detachment, an
emotional divorce from the feeling of what had happened, and what must happen in the future, if all of
them were to survive.

Camber observed all of this in sadness—doubly
so, because he loved Megan like a father, and saw
how she was grieving and alone when she most needed
the love and support of her husband. Camber understood what it was to lose a child. He had paid the
price of a son, and knew that he would pay the price
of other children, and his own life, if need be, if there
were no other way to save their cause.

But to lose a child in battle with the enemy was one
thing; to have one pine away for lack of loving was
quiet another. He and Evaine and Rhys made special
efforts to try to comfort Megan, but it was poor substitute for what Megan really needed. He could only
hope that Cinhil would realize, after a time, what he
was doing to her.

The evening of the first of December found their
preparations complete, the first steps set irreversibly
into motion. Late in the afternoon, the fifty Michaeline
knights who would be leading the assault through a
Portal in the castle itself had attended a Mass of special intention for the prince's cause, reconsecrating
their swords to the holy fight in which some of them
were certain to perish. The other century and a half
of Michaelines, under command of Lord Jebediah of
Alcara and Jamie Drummond, was already at the
Portal in Dhassa, awaiting Transfer to the archbishop's apartments in Valoret. They would secure
the city itself, overpowering the city garrison and making certain that none but Haldane supporters passed
the city gates.

The final blessings given, all that remained in the
chapel were the principals: Cinhil; Camber and his
kin; and the noncombatants, who would remain behind. The men wore mail and helms and bright swords
girded at their sides, surcoats and coronets proclaiming the ranking among them. Only Cinhil was not clad

as all the rest—and that, in itself, was a victory of a sort.

Cinhil had not wanted to go armed at all. He had wanted to wear only a long, belted robe of white, to show the purity of his intentions. He was not a warrior. He had not thought it appropriate that a priest-king should go forth armed with mere mortal steel to battle the archenemy. After all, it would not be steel which would defeat Imre of Festil.

But the women had maintained otherwise, and had taken steps to ensure that their prince should go forth as a king ought. Megan, Evaine, and Elinor had labored for weeks, not showing him what they wrought. When, on the afternoon before battle, he had gone to his chamber to meditate before appearing for Mass, he had found a king's attire awaiting him.

He never learned where they had gotten the gold-washed mail, though the stuff had a cold, unearthly glow about it which he somehow did not care to think about. This was to go over an undergarment of white silk, a doublet of softest leather cushioning the metal links from his skin. Greaves of gold-chased steel buckled over leather breeches and boots; matching vambraces guarded his forearms. Scarlet gauntlets, rich-embroidered with his Haldane crest on the cuff, were the gift of the slain Cathan's Elinor. Over all would go the knee-length surcoat of crimson silk, with the golden lion of Gwynedd blazoned bold on chest and back in gold-bullion thread. Cinhil was speechless.

He put on the undergarment, the padded doublet and breeches, the boots. He stood a long time looking into the mirror, studying the regal warrior's face which stared back at him with level gaze. Then he called for the women to attend him; he could do nothing else. Gravely, he received them and thanked each one. After, he asked them to help him arm. It was fitting, he said, that a man who had never borne steel should be armed for his maiden battle by the women who had made it possible for him to go at all.

They armed him then, though many a finger fumbled with straps and clasps as eyes blurred with joyful tears. When they had finished, Evaine buckled a plain, cross-hilted sword over his surcoat—the white belt for purity, she told him as she brushed his cheek with her lips. Then she was stepping back to make a low curtsey, and it was Megan's turn.

The princess had saved her gift for last, watching shyly in the background as her lord assumed more and more the appearance of a king. Scarcely breathing, with her nervousness, she produced a coronet from behind her skirts—not the simple, silver circlet with which he had been crowned Prince of Gwynedd on their wedding night, but a band of gold and silver intertwined, surmounted by four bold crosses.

Her hands began to tremble as she looked into his eyes. Cinhil, deeply moved, laid his fingertips on hers, so that the coronet was held between them. She swallowed and started to draw away, but he shook his head gently and closed his hands around hers.

"Please forgive me, my lady. I have ill-used you when I should instead have thanked you—for my son, for your support when I needed it." He glanced down at her body, then met her eyes again with a strained smile. "And for our sons who are to be. There will be two of them this time, you know. Twin boys."

Her eyes widened, for though Rhys had told her that she was with child, and that there would be a boy, there was as yet no sign of it upon her. And how could he know that there would be two?

"You—*know,* my lord?"

"I know," he smiled. "I *know.*"

She lowered her eyes and blushed prettily at that, and Cinhil thought that he had never seen her look so lovely. He could sense Evaine and Elinor watching in the background, and the thought crossed his mind that he was probably making them uncomfortable with this moment of apparent tenderness, but he didn't care. It had suddenly occurred to him that he might well die tonight, despite his powers; and if he did, he should never again see this lovely, unspoiled child who was his wife. Strange, but he found that the term came easily now, no longer carrying the mental qualms it once had borne. Abruptly, he regretted the weeks of neglect, spent in brooding on vengeance, and in a flash of inspiration realized what he could do to make at least a partial mending.

He raised the coronet slightly and took it from her hands.

"I shall wear this token of my lady's favor on one condition," he said, looking down into those incredibly turquoise eyes. "That my lady shall wear it first." He lowered it briefly to crown her wheaten hair. "Let this be a symbol of the sovereignty we share, and the regency I leave with her on behalf of my sons that are to be. If I should not survive this night, my lady, you are Queen of Gwynedd, as the mother of my sons."

Her eyes misted with tears as he removed the coronet and placed it firmly on his own head. Then he kissed her lightly on the lips and led her and the other women into the chapel for Mass.

It was well after midnight when the Great Lords of Gwynedd finally lit King Imre to bed in his tower chambers. It was nearly half an hour after that before Archbishop Anscom could slip away from the others and make his way to the castle's chapel.

The evening had been tense and interminable for Anscom, harboring, as he did, the knowledge of how the night must end. He had found it far more difficult than usual to be civil to the numerous toadying hangers-on at Court; he had been curt and snappish more than once during the course of the feast and revelling. The lord chamberlain had even asked whether he would rather not be excused, since he obviously was feeling so out of sorts. Anscom had assured him that it was but a momentary touch of indigestion, and that it would pass. The chamberlain had thoughtfully brought him a cup of goat's milk, for the archbishop's touchy stomach was well known at Court.

He had made a great effort at least to seem to be enjoying himself, after that. But it had been an odd Court, full of strains and undercurrents not usually present at one of Imre's gatherings—and especially not at the opening of the Yule Court, one of the most festive occasions of the year. Anscom wondered whether Imre suspected that something was brewing, or whether his frenetic gaiety was only symptomatic of the general malaise which had been growing at Court for the last year. He also noted that Imre had decreed a green court this year—not the disastrous white of the previous Christmas Court. Perhaps that, and the memories of that last Yule, accounted for Imre's nervousness. Anscom could not say he blamed the king.

Princess Ariella was not in attendance, either—though no one had really expected her to be. She was seldom seen in public of late, and rumor had it that she had been quite ill for several months. More vicious castle gossip insisted that Ariella's "illness" was nothing which would not be alleviated by the loss of a nine-month's accumulation of weight, but such theories were never discussed where they might reach the king's ears.

Anscom himself had no opinion on the matter, though if Ariella were with child, it might be the result of an incestuous relationship with her brother. If true, the child could become a serious threat to the throne, should it live; but that was a problem to be dealt with when the time came. It was entirely possible that Ariella was quite innocent—though Anscom doubted it.

And so the Yule Court fared as Yule Courts will, when one is forced to be present at an affair where one has no wish to be. The meal was passable, if somewhat tasteless to Anscom's nerve-dulled palate; and the entertainment was of an enforced gaiety which only occasionally bordered on the genuinely amusing.

Still, when the Great Lords finally took up torches and conveyed the more than slightly tipsy king to his chambers—to the tune of drunken songs and lewd jokes—it was all Anscom could do to curb his impatience and pronounce the final blessing. When he finally reached the refuge of the chapel and slipped inside, he leaned his forehead against the cool bronze doors for several heart-pounding minutes until he could collect his wits.

Then he made his way to the sacristy door and fitted his key to the lock, stepping into total darkness as he closed the door behind him. A candle flared to light in the center of the room, and there stood Camber, Joram, Evaine, Rhys, and a few others, waiting for him, flanking the crowned Prince Cinhil.

"Stand not on ceremony, Archbishop," Cinhil admonished, when Anscom started to kneel. "How stands the situation without? Is the tyrant abed?"

Raising an eyebrow at the new title which Cinhil had apparently bestowed upon his rival, Anscom straightened his cassock and nodded. "I accompanied the Great Lords to his chambers but half an hour past, Your Highness. With the quantity of wine which he consumed, he will be stuporous by now. The guard is in little better shape. It is as we had hoped."

"Excellent," Cinhil nodded. "The outside strike force has already begun infiltrating the key defense points throughout the city. We but await your word to bring our smaller force of knights here."

Anscom sighed and nodded his head. "Then, begin, Your Highness. There is much work for us here tonight."

Two hours later, the castle was essentially Cinhil's, though sporadic fighting still continued in the corridors and in the castle yard. Guaire and a handful of Michaelines had slipped around and barricaded the doors to the guardroom and barracks where the main castle garrison slept, so that the rest of their force had only to contend with the guards actually on duty. Joram and Cullen led half a dozen knights and the royal party in a sweep up the main corridor to the foot of Imre's own tower, where they fought a quick but bloody battle to gain the spiral stair. Though four of their Michaeline brethren fell to enemy swords, it was a matter of only minutes before the rebels were making their way up the stairs to Imre's own door.

There was no guard outside, and no sound came from within. Joram wondered whether Imre had merely slept through the sounds of battle, or whether he waited, even now, to unleash a full arcane defense as soon as they should breach the door.

Lowering his sword, Joram wiped a blood-stained gauntlet across his brow and silenced a sigh as he reached the top of the stairs. Behind him, Cullen and Rhys and the two remaining Michaelines waited with their weapons still drawn, Camber sheathing his and standing escort beside a dark-visaged Cinhil, shielding Evaine.

Joram caught Camber's slightly nodded signal and turned back to the door, then raised the hilt of his sword to pound heavily on the polished oak, one, two, three, four times. The sound echoed down the spiral staircase which they had just ascended at such cost.

"What is it?" a sleepy and slightly wine-blurred voice grunted, nearly inaudible.

Cinhil tensed at the sound and turned to glance at Camber. As his lips mouthed the single word, *Imre?*, Camber nodded and Joram knocked again.

"Who's there?" the voice said again, louder this time. "I told you, I didn't want to be disturbed. Go away."

"Officer of the guard, Sire," Joram said, disguising his voice slightly. "I have a message for Your Highness."

"Can't it wait until morning, man?" the voice whined irritably. "I just got to bed. You know that."

"The gate warder said it was important, Sire," Joram replied. "Perhaps Your Highness should take a look at it."

"Perhaps My Highness should have you whipped for your impertinence," the voice snapped. "Oh, very well. Slip it under the door and I'll look at it later."

Joram glanced at the others in annoyance, then let a slender smile flick across his lips.

"I'm afraid it won't fit, Sire. It's a sealed scroll," he said, keeping the edge of smugness out of his voice, if not his expression.

They heard an exasperated sigh and a shuffle of movement from far behind the door, and then the nearly silent slap of bare feet approaching, the royal voice muttering incomprehensibly. As the bolt was shot, Joram and Cullen hit the door together. There was a *whoof* of surprise as the door struck the person on the other side.

They surged into the room, sweeping an astonished and indignant Imre before them, and Rhys slammed the door and shot the bolt all in one motion. Imre had been taken totally by surprise, and he paled to find himself confronted by the glint of steel.

"Treason!" he gasped. "Steel in my presence! Guards! Where are my guards? Who?—Camber!" His eyes went wide as he recognized the man with the earl's coronet. "How dare you?! What treachery is this?"

Camber said nothing; he turned instead and, with a slight nod of deference, bade Cinhil step forward. Imre blanched as the probable identity of the other man registered, and he backed slowly away from them until his bare legs collided with a bench. Nervous fingers plucked at the neckline of his nightshirt as he whispered, "The Haldane! He *does* exist!"

"The Tyrant of Festil," Cinhil countered, his voice low and deadly. "He, too, exists—at least for the moment."

Imre, drink-fogged though he was, shook his head as though he had not heard aright, starting as he caught the movement of the two Michaeline knights circling to cut him off from the sleeping chamber. In panic, he made a dash for freedom, screaming in terror as the knights tackled him and flung him to the floor.

"Ari!" he shrieked, as he struggled to escape them. "Ari, run!"

"Stop her!" Camber shouted, as the others scrambled past Imre and crowded through the doorway. "Don't let her get away! She carries his child!"

They almost caught her. But even as they poured into the room, the curtained bed seemed to explode in a flurry of pillows and sleeping furs and flashing white limbs. Ariella, a night-maned wraith with murder in her eyes, streaked toward the fireplace to disappear through an opening which had not been there an in-

stant earlier. Joram and Cullen were only a few paces
behind her, but it was far enough for them to rebound
painfully from solid rock where, a few seconds before, a doorway had stood.

They battered at the rock, trying to find the opening,
but by the time they could locate and force the trig-
gering mechanism there was no sign of the fleeing
princess. Cullen, with a resigned glance at Camber,
disappeared through the opening to search, anyway,
Joram following at his back.

Imre, standing now in the firm grasp of the two
Michaeline knights, glanced uneasily around him, sobering fast. Escape at this time was not likely. Even
if the two Michaelines had not held his arms, it was
doubtful whether he could get past his other four captors. Rhys and Evaine blocked the doorway leading
to the inner chamber, and Camber himself barred ac-
cess to the passageway which Ariella had used. Cinhil
stood near Camber, his eyes never leaving the face of
his enemy.

Not that the so-called Haldane really represented
a threat himself, Imre reasoned. For that matter, now
that he was thinking more clearly, there were remedies
even to the hold the two knights kept on him. A
lightning thought, and his personal shields flared silver-
bright, flinging his two captors' hands from his person.
Of course, the knights were Deryni, too; and Michaeline shields surged in response, to ring the captive in a
less visible but more constricting net—but that, too,
was to be expected. At least he was fighting on his
own ground now.

Disdainfully, Imre drew himself to his full height—
still almost a head shorter than his Michaeline guard-
ians—and gathered the shreds of his kingly dignity.

"You are ill-advised to lay hands upon an anointed
king," he said, addressing Cinhil. "And the traitor Earl
of Culdi breaks his sworn oath of fealty to aid you."
He glanced haughtily at Camber, then back at Cinhil,
annoyed that the Deryni earl's gaze did not waver.
"A real man would not fear to face me on his own,
Haldane! But, then, they tell me that you are really
an apostate priest named Nicholas Draper, so I sup-

pose that I cannot expect either manly or honorable behavior from you."

"I am not afraid to meet you on your own terms, tyrant," Cinhil said carefully, signalling the Michaeline knights to withdraw and guard the two balcony doors. "I am prepared to meet any challenge which you care to name—including the duel arcane."

"Oh?" said Imre. "You're bluffing, of course. You are human, if you're who you say you are. And without your Deryni traitors, your armed men, you and all your steel are nothing."

"I shall slay you without raising steel against you," Cinhil said, unbuckling his sword and letting it fall to the floor. "In truth, I should slay you with salt, if that were possible. It were a fitting end for the fiend who slew my son."

"Your son? I? Come, now, Haldane. And even if it were true, what magistrate in the land would hold me to answer for the slaying of a priest's bastard?"

"I have been released from my priestly vows," Cinhil said evenly, though Camber could tell he was only just controlling his temper, "and my lady wife is of gentle birth. But I will not grace your crude remarks with further answer. You are responsible for my son's death, whether or not it was your hand which did the deed."

"How so?"

"Do you deny that you captured a Michaeline priest, one Humphrey of Gallareaux, and tortured him until you warped him to your intentions? He learned his poison well, tyrant. My first-born died of the sacred salt placed upon his tongue at his baptism. It was your minion who did the bloody deed!"

Imre, astonished at the tale Cinhil had woven, clapped his hands in glee. "Humphrey did *that?* Oh, splendid! What subtle irony! I set him to slay the last Haldane heir. And that was your son, not you. So it wasn't a futile exercise after all. And now, you plan to slay *me* in retribution?"

"Yes."

"I see." Imre's face went coldly serious. "Tell me,

do you intend to have your traitorous cohorts cut me into collops? Or am I to be permitted the dignity of fair combat with my accuser?"

"Fair?" Cinhil mocked. "What is fair about poisoning baptismal salt? What is fair about executing fifty peasants for a murder in which they had no part? What is fair about striking down a friend in cold blood, on suspicion only, without even ascertaining the facts? Do not speak to me of 'fair,' tyrant! At this moment, I hold you in the deepest contempt!"

He stood there, glaring at Imre across the few meters which separated them, and for a moment the room seemed frozen in time and space, no movement or sound disturbing the tension which bound them there.

Then Imre shrugged, a maddening, insolent lifting of his shoulders, his hands, and one proud Deryni eyebrow.

The gesture was too much—the final insult which Cinhil could not endure. Raising his arms, he cast not only a crimson shield around himself, but a bolt of scarlet fire which Imre only barely managed to deflect in time.

Imre, recovering from his initial surprise, moved his fingers automatically in the counter-spell, throwing up his own shields and instinctively marking off a protective circle for battle. His manner was thoughtful, curious, as he moved a little to the right to give himself more working room. It was obvious from his very movements that he had not expected this, and was casting frantically for an alternative to the battle which now had become not quite so sure a victory.

"They said you were human," he said tentatively. "I see they were mistaken. If so, then you are no true Haldane—but you *are* Deryni, aren't you?" His teeth flashed white in the semi-darkness. "But, come. Deryni need have no quarrel with Deryni. Give this up, and I will reward you with a place in my kingdom, with riches beyond your wildest imaginings."

"Can you give me back my son?" Cinhil whispered, his voice hollow within the shields. "Can you restore to Earl Camber his son, revive the Willimite martyrs who, but for your want of enforcing the just laws of this land, would never have dreamed of rising against their anointed king? Can you resurrect the peasants of Earl Camber's village whom you slew?—victims of an injustice so great I cannot bear to speak of it. Is there anything which could make you care for those people whose welfare was placed in your hands? I did not want your crown, Imre of Festil. But I am bound to take it from you now. I have no choice."

"That man betrayed me!" Imre shouted, stabbing a finger at Camber. "That is why I slew his son. You do not know what Cathan's death cost me. I loved him!"

Camber bowed his head, compassion welling in his heart for this weak, misguided king.

"But Camber's complicity in *this* treason is proof that I was right," Imre continued, hysteria edging his voice despite his best efforts. "Coel knew. I was a fool not to listen to him sooner. I should have destroyed the whole MacRorie brood while there was yet time!"

With that, he lashed out, silver flame lancing molten and searing against the crimson nimbus surrounding Cinhil. The prince's defenses held, and for a moment he merely let the ravening tide of Imre's anger spill and course around him harmlessly. The fire flared and spat and crackled between them for a timeless while, neither man touching or touched, until Imre, in rage, abruptly changed his tactics.

Dread and hideous shapes began to condense and solidify out of the mists, then—grotesque creatures of night and unfathomed dark sea-slime, with gaping jaws and tentacles, and claws and teeth and mottled leather wings. The stench of rotten carrion and brimstone filled the air even beyond the shields; the screams of grisly slithering things pierced the air and hinted at forms guessed only in blackest nightmare.

Poisoned fangs clashed on prey which was no longer there; twisted talons grated on slate fouled with sodden, slime-sogged fur, touched shudderingly on barely shielded mind. Each one Cinhil managed to reflect back upon its creator, terror held in abeyance so that vengeance might prevail. At length Imre stood, sweat-drenched and breathless, to face Cinhil across only the flicker of their shields.

The king raised a shaking hand in interruption, nodded truce as Cinhil cocked his head to peer in question.

"I do not understand," Imre whispered, all swagger gone from his voice now. "I am nearly spent, and you —you stand still, hardly touched, strong, though only God knows how!"

He breathed deeply, hugging his arms close to his body as the chill of the room settled around him. Cinhil stood regarding him, unruffled, composed, scarcely a hair out of place on the darkly silvered head, the pale hands relaxed at his sides.

"Do you concede?" Cinhil asked quietly.

"Concede? You know I cannot." Imre shook his head. "I will not accept defeat from you. I have yet one escape. Not the way I would have chosen, but never mind." A wry smile contorted his face as he staggered against a table, his breath catching in his throat. "I am master still of mine own body," he gasped, "and that I shall never concede. *I* choose where and when I die. And I choose here and now, and by mine own—mind!"

With that, he collapsed against the table and slowly sagged to the floor, his face going ashen as his eyes closed and his shields melted away. Cinhil instantly dropped his own defenses and darted toward him, a look of shocked amazement on his face.

Camber started to raise a hand in warning, for it could be a trick. But then he saw that Cinhil was very much aware and on guard, despite his swift approach; he watched as Cinhil bent to touch the side of Imre's neck for a pulse.

The prince's disgust was apparent as he turned away from the cooling body. "He's dead," he said, thin-lipped with anger. "He willed his own death rather than bear defeat at my hand."

"He was Deryni, Sire," Camber said quietly. "You will learn, in time, that he truly had no other option.

Remember, I knew his father, and his grandfather before that."

Cinhil did not answer, but stood for some seconds looking steadily across at Camber. Outside, there was an uproar in the courtyard, the sound of fighting men, and Cinhil flicked his gaze toward the balcony doors in mild annoyance. Gesturing for Rhys and the knights to look outside, Camber, reached the paling Cinhil's side just in time to catch him as he crumpled to his knees and swayed in aftershock.

It was some time before Cinhil could raise his head. For several minutes, he simply shook in Camber's arms and fought the churning in his stomach, as the realization of the past hour's work stabilized in his mind. Finally, he raised his head and passed a shaking hand across his forehead, looked into the eyes of his mentor with a strange and distant gaze.

"I—am King of Gwynedd now, am I not?"

"You are, My Prince."

Cinhil bowed his head and took a deep, sobering breath, then glanced to where Imre's body had lain but a few minutes before—startled to see that it was gone. But in that same instant, he saw that the two Michaeline knights had taken the body, had lifted it under the arms as though it lived, and dragged it through the balcony doors. As the body became visible to the soldiers battling in the yard below, the sounds of conflict ceased, the voices died down.

Cinhil started to call out to the two knights, to ask what they were about; but Camber stayed his arm and shook his head. Numbly, Cinhil watched as the knights brought the body to the edge of the balcony railing and held it poised there, as though standing on its own.

For a still, heart-stopped instant, the body seemed to stand of its own accord before the silent soldiers. Then it toppled slowly, gently, over the edge. An instant more of silence, until it hit the unyielding cobblestones of the yard below, and then an ear-splitting roar of approbation from a hundred throats, and the growing chant of, *"Cin-hil! Cin-hil! Cin-hil!"*

With the chant assailing his ears even within the

chamber, Camber helped the new king to his feet and gestured toward the open doors.

"Your knights are victorious and call for their king, Sire. Will you show yourself to them?"

Wordlessly, Cinhil let himself be led to the balcony, and at his approach the others drew back to make him way. His appearance brought renewed cheering from the men below—a deep, joyful shouting punctuated by the clash of swords on shields and the rattle of spears on helms. As Cinhil rested trembling hands on the stone balustrade, he noticed that only a few dozen of the cheering soldiers wore the surcoats and mantles of the Michaeline Order. The rest were of the castle garrison, who had fought his men minutes before and now flung down their weapons and acclaimed him with one voice.

The cheering broke off abruptly, and as he turned to glance behind him for Camber, he knew the reason why. In the Deryni earl's hands lay the State Crown of Gwynedd, brought from within by a gently smiling Evaine. Rhys was at her side, his face oddly solemn beneath the familiar shock of reddish hair. Joram and Cullen had returned sometime in the last few minutes, grim warrior eyes telling Cinhil all he needed to know about their attempt to capture Ariella.

He swallowed nervously as the two Michaeline knights removed their helmets and knelt, swords resting with cross-hilts uppermost as they gazed up confidently at him. He knew what Camber was about to say, and had no way to stop him.

"Sire," said Camber, "will you exchange your princely coronet for the Crown of Gwynedd?"

There was a tightness in Cinhil's chest as he gazed at the crown, and for just a moment he swayed in an infinity of indecision.

It was still not too late, was it? Though he had toppled the tyrant, Imre, he could yet refuse the Crown. No man was *really* indispensable, despite their indoctrination to the contrary. Perhaps they would permit him to retire to his monastery now, his part in the struggle completed. Surely they could find another man to rule Gwynedd.

But he realized, even as he thought it, that the notion was absurd. He could no more walk away now than he could blaspheme the Name of God, or tread the sacred Host beneath his heel. With or without his consent, he had been bound to this people, to this throne which he had never sought; led thence by the might of men who called themselves by the name Deryni, the same as the fallen tyrant—and he shared power with them now, was practically the same as they.

The thought crossed his mind that the Deryni who had broken one king could easily bring down another, if he did not suit their fancy—but he immediately forced himself to dismiss it as unworthy. These Deryni were honorable men and women, dedicated to the same high purposes which he, himself, had so long espoused in theory; they had paid their own high prices to ensure that the tyrant, Imre, should not harm the people anymore. He must not—he would not—permit his own loss, his thwarted ambitions, to color his dealings with an entire people.

And yet, despite his awesome powers, he was human still, and must recall the evil done his own people during the interregnum of the Deryni. Now was the time for renewal and appraisal, for righting the injustices of the old masters. And if there were those, even among his apparent Deryni allies, who tried to thwart him— Well, they, themselves, had taught him ruthlessness. Balance would not be an easy thing, but it must be maintained.

Shuddering, then, in the cold, pre-dawn air, he gazed down at the hands which had called forth such slaying power but a short time ago. He glanced at the men standing expectantly in the courtyard below, at Camber and his children ranged beside him, at the Michaeline knights kneeling before him, their cross-hilted blades upheld to sanctify this moment.

Then he reached up and slowly removed his coronet, gave it over to Evaine with a slight inclination of his head. As he did, the men in the courtyard knelt and Camber raised the crown so that it caught the torchlight from the yard below.

Cinhil clasped his hands and glanced up at the brightening sky. His destiny approached; he could not but accept it.

"Cinhil Donal Ifor Haldane, thine ancient line is restored, to the great joy of thy people," Camber said, gazing at Cinhil with the eyes of a father and loyal servant, both. "Be crowned with strength and wisdom for all thy days." The crown was placed upon his head. "And may the Almighty grant thee a long and prosperous reign, in justice and honor for all thy people of Gwynedd."

"Fiat voluntas tua," Cinhil whispered, so that only Camber could hear. Let it be done according to *thy* will. . . .

APPENDIX I

INDEX OF CHARACTERS

AIDAN, Prince—only child of King Ifor Haldane to survive the coup of 822; royal name of Daniel Draper, grandfather of Prince Cinhil.

AIDAN Alroy Camber Haldane, Prince—infant son of Prince Cinhil and Princess Megan; killed by poisoned salt at his baptism, aged one month.

ALROY, Prince—royal name of Royston Draper, father of Prince Cinhil; son of Prince Aidan (Daniel Draper).

ANDREW, son of James—the second "Benedict"; at Saint Piran's Priory.

ANSCOM of Trevas, Archbishop—Deryni Primate of Gwynedd; Archbishop of Valoret.

ANSEL MacRorie, Lord—younger son of Cathan MacRorie; age three.

ARIELLA of Festil, Princess—elder sister of Imre; age twenty-eight.

ARMAGH, Master—arms master to Imre.

BEARAND, King and Saint—great-great grandfather of Cinhil.

BLAINE, King—fourth Festillic king of Gwynedd, reigned 885-900; father of Imre.

APPENDIX II

INDEX TO PLACE NAMES

PARTIAL LINEAGE OF THE HALDANE KINGS

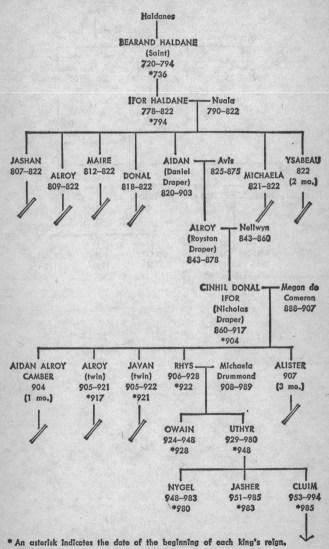

Haldanes

BEARAND HALDANE
(Saint)
720–794
*736

IFOR HALDANE — Nuala
778–822   790–822
*794

JASHAN
807–822

ALROY
809–822

MAIRE
812–822

DONAL
818–822

AIDAN
(Daniel
Draper)
820–903 — Avis
825–875

MICHAELA
821–822

YSABEAU
822
(2 mo.)

ALROY
(Royston
Draper)
843–878 — Nellwyn
843–860

**CINHIL DONAL
IFOR**
(Nicholas
Draper)
860–917
*904 — Megan de
Cameron
888–907

**AIDAN ALROY
CAMBER**
904
(1 mo.)

ALROY
(twin)
905–921
*917

JAVAN
(twin)
905–922
*921

RHYS
906–928
*922 — Michaela
Drummond
908–989

ALISTER
907
(3 mo.)

OWAIN
924–948
*928

UTHYR
929–980
*948

NYGEL
948–983
*980

JASHER
951–985
*983

CLUIM
953–994
*985

* An asterisk indicates the date of the beginning of each king's reign.

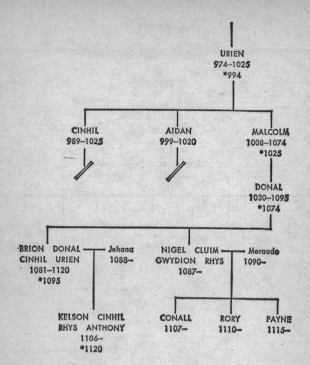

URIEN
974–1025
*994

CINHIL
989–1025

AIDAN
999–1020

MALCOLM
1008–1074
*1025

DONAL
1030–1095
*1074

BRION DONAL
CINHIL URIEN ——— Jehana
1081–1120 1088–
*1095

NIGEL CLUIM
GWYDION RHYS ——— Meraude
1087– 1090–

KELSON CINHIL
RHYS ANTHONY
1106–
*1120

CONALL
1107–

RORY
1110–

PAYNE
1115–

THE FESTILLIC KINGS OF GWYNEDD
AND THEIR DESCENDANTS

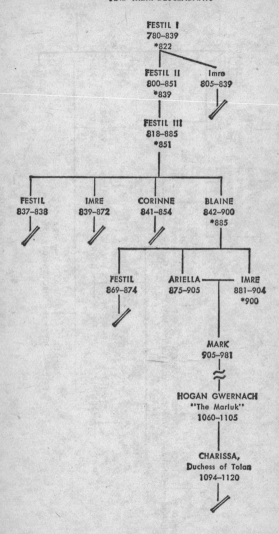

FESTIL I
780–839
*822

FESTIL II   Imre
800–851   805–839
*839

FESTIL III
818–885
*851

FESTIL   IMRE   CORINNE   BLAINE
837–838   839–872   841–854   842–900
                                                *885

FESTIL   ARIELLA———   IMRE
869–874   875–905   881–904
                                  *900

MARK
905–981

HOGAN GWERNACH
"The Marluk"
1060–1105

CHARISSA,
Duchess of Tolan
1094–1120

* An asterisk indicates the date of the beginning of each king's reign.

Appendix V

PARTIAL LINEAGE OF THE MacRORIES

MacRORIES

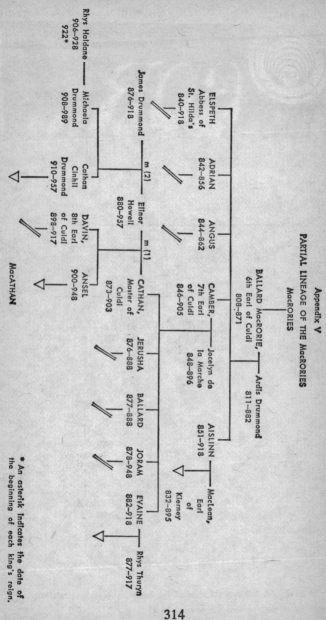

* An asterisk indicates the date of the beginning of each king's reign.

314

GOR...

a counter-Earth, a planet as strangely beautiful as any in the universe—and Tarl Cabot was chosen for a special mission.

by JOHN NORMAN

H. P. LOVECRAFT

THE GREAT
HORROR-FANTASY WRITER
WHO RANKS WITH POE

☐ AT THE MOUNTAINS OF MADNESS AND OTHER TALES OF TERROR	24301	1.50
☐ TALES OF THE CTHULHU MYTHOS, Vol. I	24687	1.50
☐ TALES OF THE CTHULHU MYTHOS, Vol. II	24688	1.50
☐ THE LURKING FEAR AND OTHER STORIES	24690	1.50
☐ THE TOMB AND OTHER TALES	24689	1.50
☐ THE SHUTTERED ROOM AND OTHER TALES OF HORROR (with August Derleth)	24302	1.50
☐ THE MASK OF CTHULHU	25095	1.50
☐ DREAM QUEST OF UNKNOWN KADATH	25299	1.50
☐ THE CASE OF CHARLES DEXTER WARD	25118	1.50
☐ THE TRAIL OF THE CTHULHU	25017	1.50
☐ LURKER AT THE THRESHOLD	25077	1.50
and . . .		
☐ LOVECRAFT: A BIOGRAPHY by L. Sprague de Camp	25115	1.95

Available at your bookstore or use this coupon.

L-15-76